# NAMANGA

## *"The Place Where Dreams Died"*

By
Alvin T. Guthertz

PublishAmerica

Baltimore

First printing

ISBN: 1-59286-188-1
PUBLISHED BY PUBLISHAMERICA BOOK PUBLISHERS
www.publishamerica.com
Baltimore

Printed in the United States of America

Other books by Alvin Guthertz:
*The Last Great Roller Coaster Ride*
*Low Fog in Eden*

# DEDICATIONS

*To Kenya where it first started all of us.*

*To the strangers who met while out on Safari
and who became close friends.*

*To those who dream, those who love and those who understand.*

*And above all to my family whose love and unity is
the bond of strength and support for all, and who stand as one
making me so very proud every day of my life.*

# ACKNOWLEDGMENTS

*While this is a work of fiction, it is based on the happenings and the people the author encountered and met during his trips to Africa. The author wishes to thank all those who gave this book its life and creation.*

*To Vicki who rose proudly, like the phoenix, to soaring new heights filled with ever greater love and wonders.*

*To Elisa for her constant, unstinting time and assistance.*

# FOREWORD

Three million years ago, during the Pilocene period, an Apeman who walked upright first appeared on this earth.

He had ape-like features combined with human characteristics such as teeth, legs, hip bones.

Above all he had stubby fingers replacing forefeet which enabled him and his female counterpart to make crudely fashioned stone tools that represented a level of development that no ape had ever before achieved.

The tools enabled the Apeman to hunt and gather in a more advance stage then any other creature found on earth at that time.

With that the Apeman was able to gain several important milestones: he moved from living in forests and trees to the open country and the great plains; then he developed hunting techniques thus changing his diet.

All of this eventually increased his physical and intellectual ability.

In the line of human evolution, this Apeman, named "Australo-pithecus" was more like modern man then was with apes.

He had passions, sexual appetites, was able to shed tears, show emotions, have feelings–and he was found in what was to be called East Africa in a land to be called Kenya.

# BOOK ONE

*"We carry within us the wonders we seek without,
There is all Africa and her prodigies in us."*
Sir Thomas Browning
1605-1682

*"Whither is fled the visionary gleam,
Where is it now, the glory and the dream?"*
William Wordsworth
1770-1850

# NAMANGA

Africa startles you at first with its colors and scents and sounds. And the sky of Africa, that magnificent endless sky which comes down and hugs the ground and sprawls out, surrounding you with its haunting beauty. The white puffy clouds are etched against colors so vivid you've never really seen them before. Sharp blues. Deep reds. Soft yellows. Gold. Pink. It extends like a vast ocean to the distant horizon, the clouds weaving about in the warm evening breeze. The sky really lets you know who you are, only a small microcosm in the overall scheme of things. The sky, with its endless beauty, calls to you and beckons you forward.

It started in Africa in a hot, blistering town called Namanga up near the Kenya-Tanzania border.

I had paused for a moment in the late afternoon simply to look at the sky and gulp in the magical air. Suddenly I stood surrounded by Masai, all of whom were milling about me, talking in Swahili, laughing, pointing their fingers, making strange gestures in my direction.

I felt a tap on my shoulder and turned to find myself looking directly into the dark sunken eyes of one Masai who was smiling and nodding his head at me.

"Welcome," he said in a guttural mumbling kind of English. The Masai was carrying a spear as tall as himself.

It was only when I turned that I noticed all the other Masai were also carrying similar spears. They had circled me and kept inching closer, grinning, saying words that I could not understand.

As they came near, too near, I quickly realized all their bodies were carved with a variety of tribal scars and their hair caked with dust-red clay. Their long, dangling earlobes were deliberately misshapen and filled with everything imaginable from colorful beads to thick, wooden spools of thread.

The first Masai reached out and touched my shirt feeling the material.

"Soft," he said in a harsh sounding voice. He stared directly at me for a long moment. Everything became strangely silent. Suddenly he turned and moved slowly away.

I felt an odd yet exhilarating combination of both relief and awe as I watched him and the other Masai walk with a kind of quiet dignity making their way casually down Namanga's narrow back road.

I looked at the surroundings and the Masai near me and asked myself what

11

was I, Michael Abrams, whose hair was starting to turn the color of early snow and with lines beginning to curl and creak around the face, what was I doing alone in this steamy, sullen little town, 150 miles from the equator where the searing heat makes clothes stick to the skin.

"Halla. Halla. Halla."

I looked up at the unexpected chanting which was growing louder as another group of Masai came running past. All were carrying spears and their bracelets making a jingling sound as they quickly darted along the narrow road kicking up small puffs of dust in the early morning heat.

All the Masai wore small gourds decorated with colorful beads which they carried strapped around their bodies.

"They use that for drinking both milk and blood," Allen, the concerned guide who had brought me to this remote place, explained, "They still consider blood, which they call 'Osarge,' as one of their main forms of nourishment."

"Back in the states we drink Bloody Mary's," I tried to joke back, "Guess that means we are all the same."

Allen paused to study me, sizing me up, not sure how I might react to his next statement.

"They get the blood by placing a small hole in their animals jugular vein and then drinking it warm as it slowly seeps out spilling into those pretty little gourds."

He was giving me some sort of test and when I did not gulp or flinch or gasp in astonishment Allen smiled. I had obviously passed his small exam.

I studied Allen carefully knowing he would be a link between two worlds, two civilizations and, like most who play a pivotal role, he appeared at first simply like any other ordinary person.

The Masai were colorful in their red cloth robes which they draped casually like cloaks around their bodies. All were decorated with brightly colored necklaces and bracelets.

"They still try to resist civilization as best they can," Allen said.

What an odd and strange sight all of this was to me, far removed from the teeming towns and cities I had known all my life with such smug confidence.

"Pic-tur?" another Masai asked as others again started slowly circling me. Filled with curiosity, some touched my body filled with curiosity. Their fingers, poking towards me, were long and boney.

"Trade shoes?" one Masai said, pointing to my feet.

"No thank you," I politely smiled my answer.

I noticed several Masai who appeared older were clustered together, sitting quietly in the nearby shade.

The equatorial heat hovered in the nineties but the thorn and acacia trees, those that are left, not yet destroyed by the elephants, offered some slight shade. There was a sweet odor in the air, like perfume, probably from the honey pots dangling from the nearby trees.

Namanga is a border town at the very end of civilization. Places like that have always fascinated me, located miles from anywhere, in the white blazing heat without any frills or false pretentiousness. Border towns are similar to an ocean backwash, where the debris of life flows in, backs up, swirls around, drifts aimlessly all about and almost always ends up with no place to go. They are empty little places designed just to exist and nothing more.

The town isn't much more then a block long, filled with broken-wooden shantys and meandering dirt paths. The narrow trails were busy with Masai going about their daily tasks, a routine that mostly included taking care of their cattle and children, both of which they accomplish with equal skill and love.

I was in Africa because I had grown up watching too many Tarzan films and reading Hemingway. I had heard that Africa is where it all really started and that everything began here. I had come because fifty years earlier guys like me ran off and joined the French Foreign Legion. The reason I was here? I called it the Twin Pains. Two women; two loves. Loves that were as destructive to them as to me. Loves that I vowed to bury and forget. Only somehow I could not forget.

There was one other reason why I stood this day in the dusty paths of Namanga. The shroud keeper had been but three days from claiming my body and had already started a dance of greeting on my chest. I still trembled with fear remembering that which I didn't want to remember.

I had come close to death that terrible year but, oddly enough, it was coming so close that I finally found out what life is really all about.

There comes a moment when you suddenly realize that destiny is like a picture puzzle with thousands of little pieces having to fit into their proper place. The problem, however, was at my age everything suddenly becomes a race against time.

All that was in the past, I reminded myself. Sing no sad songs for me. Tomorrow is another day and this is tomorrow and now I have that rare opportunity that everyone dreams about–to start life anew.

"Brac-lut," a Masai women suddenly asked me, her thin wrinkled face making it difficult to determine her age. Her hair was shaved like a man and she looked directly into my eyes with a half-smile revealing her missing teeth.

"Brac-lut," she repeated, offering a variety of colorful hand-woven trinkets.

"If you stop walking, even for a moment, you'll be surrounded," a voice behind me cautioned and I turned to see Gabriella, "They are quite inquisitive.

I noticed Gabriella when I first arrived in Namanga. She walked filled with self assurance and her slight accent fascinated me, adding to her charm.

"Thanks for the tip," I smiled. Our eyes held together for a long moment.

Gabriella was standing in the midst of the Masai women and nonchalantly ran her fingers lightly through her own blonde hair which she wore in a pony tail.

The Masai women were comparing her hair with their own, laughing among themselves. They wore bracelets and arm-bands made of brass and iron wire and the color added to their haunting, almost mystic beauty.

Gabriella's pony tail and smile combined to give her a youthful appearance yet her eyes betrayed a certain earthy sophistication which was especially noticeable even in this remote area.

The contrast between Gabriella and the Masai women served as my first reminder of the different cultures. Gabriella's pony tail made her hair almost as short as that of the Masai yet she wore soft lipstick and had the gentle fragrance of fresh perfume; the others had bodies tough like leather and filled with scars carved into their flesh. Each proved beautiful in their own way.

They continued milling around our small group, as interested in us as we were with them.

Allen had warned us earlier not to take photos, that it was strictly forbidden, unless the Masai themselves gave their approval.

"They think the camera can capture their soul and steal their power," he had warned, "On the other hand, some have come to realize that photos can mean money."

"Look, may I take your picture?" I asked Gabriella, quickly adding, "Well, not really take your picture. I want to shoot in your direction, make it look like I'm taking your picture but I'll really be shooting the Masai that are standing behind you."

"Yeah, sure," she answered, a thin wisp of a smile giving her a slightly mischievous look which slowly crossed her face. "Not a bad idea."

As I aimed my camera, I noticed Gabriella in the viewfinder. At the last second before I pushed the shutter, she was winking knowingly towards me, crinkling her nose, delighted that she was silently sharing this small secret.

I snapped the photo pausing for a moment to study Gabriella who obviously enjoyed this small bit of intrigue. Her eyes caught my attention for I had never seen blue eyes as crystal clear as hers. They were like a picture perfect day after the rain has passed and you feel you can see forever. They reminded me, oddly enough, of an old blue agate marble that was my favorite when I was a child.

Gabriella was obviously filled with confidence and appeared to be one of those fortunate individuals who can quickly adapt to any situation. She combined a sense of humor with casual worldliness.

I finished taking the picture, put the camera down and thanked her.

"You have quite a sense of humor," I said, "Do I detect a bit of a German accent?"

"I'm NOT German," and her eyes flashed in momentary anger, "I'm Swiss."

"Excuse my diplomatic blunder," I shrugged with a smile, thinking to myself that this was a fine way to start a friendship with someone you were going to be with for the next few weeks.

The Masai continued to circle around us, trying to sell their wares which included jewelry made from leather, plant fibers, elephant hair, bits of copperwires, even the entangled coil of an old telephone cord.

"Aren't these the most beautiful people?" a tall, distinguished American said, "I'm Herbert Hughes and this is my wife, Margaret."

"Their features are so elegant and handsome," Margaret Hughes added.

We shook hands already starting to feel a certain friendship with one another, knowing we were about to begin our small adventure together, all strangers in a strange land.

Bells signaled as a herd of Masai cattle made its way slowly down the street followed by a youthful Masai boy, about thirteen, already carrying his spear. He looked at us and nodded his head.

"Time to get moving," Allen called and we all quickly walked to a small hotel were Allen had planned a briefing.

I studied Gabriella as she followed Allen. She stood out that day in Namanga, smiling, sophisticated, radiating her own warmth in the tropical heat. Perhaps it was because I was alone in this distant country, seemingly at the very end of the earth, but I wanted to reach out as when you see an old familiar friend. I wanted to hug and to hold her. It happens sometimes when you first meet a stranger with whom you feel immediately at ease, as if you've known them all your life.

Africa does strange things, you've heard all that before, but on this day, alone in this town, meeting this woman, there was a lace-thin promise of more, of new meaning to this battered old life. Maybe it was the equatorial heat. Maybe it was the spell of Africa. Maybe it was simple loneliness. I looked at her and knew only one thing. I wanted to be with her, to talk to and to laugh and to share our thoughts. I wanted to be with her just for a moment, for an hour.

I cautioned myself that Gabriella was but the momentary fantasy of a man alone in a distant country, a man still recoiling from an agony that constantly throbbed from deep within.

I saw her warm smile and heard her soft voice and I knew, at that very moment, how much I wanted her, yet fully aware that I would never be able to truly have her. I realized it would never happen because I would not let it happen. I had erected that wall to keep feelings and emotions far away from me, trying to purge myself of all the memories.

I sighed softly to myself. This was all out of character for me, being alone in this place, longing for this woman. I thought of the past and I looked around and then I laughed again. I hadn't laughed like that since that terrible morning six months earlier.

I watched as Gabriella slowly walked away bathed in the soft colors of the sunset. It was as though the shadows and the fiery sky reflected the moods and the passions of Africa. I wished for that which I knew was impossible. Gabriella: The unknown woman; the familiar woman.

The sky slowly turned from its glowing pink into the jade blue of a silent twilight.

The last time I even noticed the sky, or tried to see it, it was dark and gloomy and death, my death, hung in the air.

# MEETING IN NAMANGA

"Are there any vegetarians here?

Everything in Africa was proving a surprise especially the very first question I heard in Namanga.

"Are there any vegetarians here?" Allen repeated, carefully looking at everyone, waiting patiently for an answer.

That was the least question I had considered, especially from the safari guide, and it gave me a smile as it did to the others gathered around the small, broken table which had been placed outside a weathered old bar in Namanga. Each time one of us sat down, the table made a creaking noise as if in welcome.

The bar was called the "Hoteli Ya Kingi Georgi" and we strangers looked at one another offering polite smiles. The bar was adjacent to a small, non-descript safari hotel located near Namanga. The plan was that we would have an opportunity to meet, rest and drive into Nairobi the next day for supplies before starting out on safari.

The table had been placed under a huge thorn tree which offered some shade and helped ease our way into the equatorial heat. It rested on some twisted wooden planks which made it wobble each time someone else sat down.

The air was hot and still but there was a sweet smell all around us, like that of Spring when out in the open country.

This was the beginning of our African safari and we strangers were meeting for the first time for a briefing and an introduction to one another.

"Namanga is the last town before we go out on safari," Allen said, "The guides will prepare the food and purchase the supplies in advance and we wanted to know if anything special might be required."

Allen, that was the only name he used, was to be the leader of the Safari. His soft-spoken voice had just a trace of a British accent, a small heritage he and most of his countrymen had inherited from the days of British colonial rule.

The eight people seated around the table glanced politely at one another but, as for Allen's opening question, no one seemed bothered about vegetarian diets.

I stared about the table, looking carefully at each person, eagerly trying to make some sort of quick, early judgement, knowing we would soon be all alone out in the bush with only each other to rely on.

I was trying to determine something about each one, searching for some key to their personality. Three weeks with strangers, out in nowhere, would either prove exhilarating or have everyone at each other's throats within days, sort of like two forest rangers stuck alone at some remote mountain outpost with nothing but each other for company.

The others must have felt the same way for I sensed an air of quiet electricity crackling around the table. It could easily be read on all of our faces, that feeling of apprehension, of fear of the unknown, concern about each of us who will be holding the other's destiny for the next several weeks as we trek out there alone in places none of knew anything about, none of us knowing what to expect or to anticipate.

A monkey suddenly leaped on the table, glanced at all of us, put its paw over its mouth and started to laugh. We in turn laughed back at the sudden and unexpected interruption and that managed to break the tension for a moment. It was as if the wind had suddenly blown in and swept out the stagnent air.

"That monkey is just a local friend," Allen explained, "Kind of a preview of coming things like they show in the movies." He had a magnetic personality and when he smiled his entire face came alive. He had a wide grin and a charming twinkle in his eye.

Only the smile quickly disappeared and Allen became silent for a moment. He studied our small group and I wondered if his thoughts were the same as mine.

At quick glance, those seated around that old battered table were a non-descript group, as it usually appears during any such first gathering. As with all such early meetings, I realized that eventually everyone's personalities, for better or for worse, would gradually emerge.

I was aware that once we got to know each other the politeness of this first formal meeting, with its stilted conversation, would eventually rip open. It always happens that way on any journey as strangers slowly get to know and become familiar with one another. The layers of politeness would gradually strip away and everyone's ideas, dreams, private thoughts would soon begin to emerge.

We made quiet conversation waiting for the meeting to start.

"Where are you from?"

"Did you have a pleasant trip coming over?

Why don't you all identify yourselves," Allen finally suggested, "As a way to get acquainted."

As the introductions were being made I noticed discreet stares throughout the room as each of us politely studied the other.

Gabriella, she used only one name, appeared confident, casual, wearing a blue blouse unbuttoned at the neck, which hung loose covering her trim body. She had on cut-off jeans, her feet were bare and she wore wrap around dark glasses perched on top of her blonde hair. Gabriella sat back quietly observing the others around the table exactly as I had been doing.

Gabriella's classic high cheek bones were the kind that any chic Parisian model would have desired. They blended perfectly with the freckles that were already blossoming from the Kenya sun and which were scattered across her face. She thus had a youthful look yet if studied her closely, one could easily determine a certain earthiness about her, something quietly smoldering just under the surface, much like the heat of Africa.

There was also the distinguished-appearing older American couple who had already introduced themselves. He was tall and stately, chin a bit weak but with an eager smile. Herbert and Margaret Hughes. Hughes sat erect, cool even in the African heat, his fingers tapping on the table. Margaret was a heavy-set women with just the first hints of grey hair and a warm smile, the kind that made you recall your mother.

The two sat throughout the meeting holding hands. It appeared that their love, at least, had made it and I thought "good for them." I noted with small amusement that whenever Hughes talked he had a way of raising his eyebrows to emphasize his every statement. He was wearing a straw hat, the kind you might see at a Midwest farm auction.

Alejandro was a young Spanish kid, good looking, who only mumbled his name when called upon, otherwise he never spoke throughout the entire meeting. I wondered if something might be wrong, thinking perhaps his vocal chords had been tangled. He had a small but distinctive jagged scar on his forehead that was shaped like a lightning bolt and his face was tan and weathered from too many days in the sun.

He was wearing a green sweater casually draped around his shoulder, like a college kid, only his face was older. Alejandro had the look of someone who lived years with great disappointment.

Mrs. Lewis, that was how she introduced herself, had thick glasses and her hair was held back in a tight bun. She wore a safari jacket, tightly buttoned even in the early morning heat. My first impression was that she might be just like her hair, uptight.

Only when she went over to get some tomato juice she walked with a limp and I immediately felt bad thinking that of her. As she walked, I could see how each step must have been one of great difficulty, making her small body weave off balance and in pain, but the kind of pain that she had become resigned to throughout the years. I thought of the courage it must have taken for her to come here alone.

"We are the Melkonian family," the next man proudly said. He had a huge grin on his face, the kind of personality you like immediately, and he put his arms around the women next to him saying, "I am Yuri and this is my wonderful wife, Sophie." Sophie had black hair and, while quiet, also appeared to be the determined one in the family.

"You should always call me Yuri for it is easier to pronounce," Yuri suggested. His eyes were tiny, like small electric lightbulbs, sparkling with charm.

The two looked at each other in the way that only married people can look, eyes briefly meeting, heads nodding, passing some silent message to one another.

"My name is Walter Corcoran," a puffy looking man with a sad, round face, small glasses resting on the tip of his nose, said as he rose, slowly glanced at everyone and nodded courtly to the entire group. He wore an old cardigan and khaki pants which looked as if he had worn them both for many years and his shoes were like him, scruffy and old. Corcoran's voice was deep, like what a stale cigar might have sounded, but there was a slight mischievous gleam in his eyes. His face was pale like someone who spent long days away from the sun.

Flora Zimmer, with a voice filled with spunk and drive, worried me at first. She was tiny and fragile and quite old looking. She wore a large floppy hat and white linen jacket. I wondered if she would be able to keep up with the pace that a safari promised.

"I'm Michael Abrahams and I'm from San Francisco," I said, always hating this sort of introduction, wanting to remain in the shadows observing, as any writer is supposed to do.

There was more to be said but I figured I'd save it all for another day, another time. These were strangers and no one really wanted to hear someone else's long story.

As a writer the many and varied possibilities of these individuals, camping closely together, living in tents for such a long time, went through my mind. They seemed congenial enough but one could only hope and pray how they might get along once they were alone out in the bush.

"We'll go to Nairobi first for supplies and then out to Amboseli," Allen continued, "And we suggest you take only what you'll really require. There isn't much room for luggage in the vans."

I remained fascinated with those gathered at the table wondering what had brought them here, to this remote corner of the earth. They all had to have put a hold on their lives for a few weeks in order to go out into the bush, live in small tents in virtually unknown surroundings for the simple pleasure of gazing at animals that could easiiy be observed in their hometown zoos.

For myself it was as far as I could possibly travel to get away from the wounds and the embers of a lost love as well as from the haunting noise and sounds of nightly anguish. Africa, the classic, ultimate escape.

"What about poachers?" the tall American asked, bringing me back to the present.

"They have been a rather serious problem, indeed,"Allen answered, "but the government has stopped them. There are but scattered reports. I wouldn't anticipate any problems."

"Our State Department, in America, issued a travel advisory," Mrs. Lewis said.

"Yes, I am familiar with that," Allen answered, "That is all very true."

We all looked at him. Mrs. Hughes pulled her chair closer to the table.

"It is a dangerous country," Allen continued, "Any country is dangerous. And yes, some poachers are out there but they are scattered over thousands of miles. The animals can be dangerous if you don't respect them. But it is the simple things that are the most dangerous. On my last trip one man stepped on his eyeglasses and, of course, there are no repair shops out in the bush."

There was some nervous laughter.

I had given little thought or worry about the poachers. They belonged somewhere else, in newspaper headlines, far removed from me. Only now, when Allen talked about the poachers, a small alarm within me suddenly went off. He had put too fast and to casual a spin on the subject, as if he was holding something back, afraid to say anything more.

"Look, I don't mean not to sound serious," Allen added, as if reading my thoughts, "The poachers are very, very dangerous. They sneak about at night. They destroy. They are violent men."

"Will we be safe?" Yuri asked.

"The game wardens all know where we are, "Allen answered, "And I am in contact with them by radio. Poachers haven't been seen where we are going for a long time."

A bird squaled in the approaching dusk and Flora Zimmer trembled at the unexpected sound.

"I suggest we all rest now," Allen said, as if eager to change the subject, "For we have a long day tomorrow. Ashari. Allow me to introduce you to your first word in Swahili. Ashari. It means friend. We will all become ashari before we return."

We all smiled but the question of the poachers bothered me. It only helped make me aware that I was now half way around the world far removed from anything I had ever known before.

There was no longer any past to worry or complain about. Yesterday was gone and all the songs had been sung. I glanced about the room and realized those seated around the small table all shared only one thing and that was the future.

On the way to Namanga we had heard the unfamiliar sounds of the bush, of birds and animals, the flutter of the wind in a tree branch. All served to remind us we were alone in this country whose legends and traditions have intrigued man since the dawn of time.

Africa had already opened itself to our small group. We had already seen its beauty and some of its eternal mystery and now it aroused unexpected passions in all of us. We heard Africa in its rhythm, a rhythm that was directing all of us towards a new life, urging us to travel towards a new destination.

Who were these people who would be with me out in the bush? Where did they come from? what are their hopes, their dreams? Like it or not, for better, for worse, I knew we all would soon find the answers.

What I wanted for my future was really quite simple: to breath fresh air, come alive, get a second chance at life, to be able to find feelings once again. But the only thing I knew with any certainty was that my most immediate future would be tomorrow out there in the bush, the unknown, where everything I ever knew about life, anything I had ever learned would simply come to an end and where life, my life, would start anew.

My eyes felt weary, not with sleep but with fear, fear of the future and what it might bring, fear of being alone, not wanting to get hurt ever again.

# SCRAPBOOKS IN TIME
## ROBERTA

Following the meeting I tried to relax but my mind kept clicking off every possibility of what I might need for the safari. I made a detailed list reminding myself exactly what I should take and going over the notes endlessly: Camera. Film. Passport. Binoculars. A few Kenya Shillings. Not a lot of clothes but just enough.

I finished going over my list for about the tenth time and figured that was all that I could do. Not wanting to disturb the others, I made my way down to the open bar for a glass of what quickly became half-warm tomato juice.

The heat rose from the ground and there was only silence in the far off bush. The sun still felt intense like a magnifying glass, burning down, seemingly ready to ignite everything in its path.

And just like a magnifying glass, the sun seemed to enlarge everything, especially that which I never wanted enlarged, like distant memories, the bad ones that were supposed to have been buried long ago. Only now they were being brought back into sharp focus.

I didn't realize it at the time but the journey to Namanga had probably started a thousand light years away, when Roberta and I stood proudly before a sea of happy, smiling faces.


"Mazeltov."

The Rabbi grinned at Roberta as he held our hands tightly together. He had a pleased smile when he nodded towards the wine glass wrapped in a blanket at our feet. Like a Hollywood director, the Rabbi looked at me and gave a silent cue for the next scene.

I stomped on that wine glass with all the force of a young man in love, confident in the secure knowledge that life was truly starting. The crunching sound brought delighted cheers of "mazeltov" from everyone standing nearby.

The Rabbi raised his hand high above his head holding a small piece of parchment paper.

"This is the marriage contract, the bonds of marriage," he said loudly enough for all to hear, "I now pronounce Roberta and Michael as husband and wife."

Everyone started to clap and circle the two of us. They were dancing the hora and someone lifted Roberta and I above their heads, spinning us about in a joyous circle.

Twenty-five years later, sitting alone in that Namanga bar at twilight, it had all returned, like sound bites in the evening news, a virtual newsreel of my life, a flashback like in a movie, taking me back to another time, another place.

Memories tumbled around me like old calendar pages being discarded on New Year's eve, tossed out the windows to swirl about an uncaring world, yet each page was once filled with special meaning. Like a scrapbook of my life with bits and pieces of memory all stuck together.

A bird fluttered from far off and the woman behind the bar slowly looked up and sighed. She was too young to be bored but she looked straight ahead with unseeing eyes, already resigned to the life that surrounded her. She kept making elaborate circles wiping imaginary spots off the counter top that served as a bar.

There was something about her look, dull and sullen, that reminded me of Roberta but only after the drinking had started and the marriage crumbled.

I wanted to forget but all I could do was remember.

Only now the only words that I recalled, with remarkable clarity, was that of the Rabbi.

"The bonds of marriage."

"Bonds."

"The heat getting you already?" Allen had quietly walked over and sat next to me. That wonderful smile danced across his face as he gently slapped me on the back in friendly greeting.

"Not really. I expected it."

"Keep your hat on. The heat can do things if you're not use to it."

"Makes you see things?"

Allen paused wondering about my unexpected question.

"Yes, it can do that, too. Then he smiled once again. "Are you seeing things already?"

"Only this beautiful country of yours."

He became quiet and studied me for a brief moment.

"Your eyes tell me you are seeing more. I've seen that look before. One becomes a good judge of all kinds of animals out here."

"What look?"

"There is the look of a kind of sadness." He paused for a moment, then added, "But just a small such look about you."

"Not to worry," I quickly answered. I didn't want him to think he had a problem on his hands. "I was just remembering. This is a big jump for me."

"Big jump?"

"An American term. Means a big deal. My going out alone in the bush."

"Well, I'm glad you're not sad," Allen said, "There is much to be happy about in my country."

"I wasn't sad. I was just remembering."

"Remembering. That can be good. Sometimes. And sad sometimes."

"I was thinking of someone from long ago."

"Africa does that to visitors," Allen said, "Only don't be sad out here. There is little time for sadness and you will soon find that the animals are beautiful. They will bring you happiness."

He offered a friendly grin but his eyes stayed on mine, as if searching for answers.

"Don't be sad," he repeated, "Not here. You are on safari and there is much to see. You should only be happy here. Remember not to stay out in the sun too long. Keep you hat on. We'll soon have much traveling to do."

Allen slowly walked back towards the hoteli.

I remained seated but my thoughts had already drifted back to another time.

"...Cheer, cheer for old Notre Dame,

Run down the field calling her name..."

I loved to sing college fight songs because they made me happy, filled my life with the wild enthusiasm of youth.

"Stop singing those dumb songs," she would say. "Your voice is awful."

It was a brief isolated moment but looking back it was the one that set the foundation for all the pain that was to follow.

It was on that day that I realized she would forever be Roberta, never Bobbi.

Even something as pure as first love can be turned into that which is grotesque, twisted out of its beauty, becoming hideously deformed, like a full moon that once glowed silver with love but which can turn slowly until nothing remains and the dark side emerges.

A marriage can decay, like dry rot, slowly eating away at the underpinnings of what had once been something happy and vibrant. Drinking destroyed it all. It silently and slowly infiltrated Roberta every night, first taking away the laughter and then draining the youth and the feelings and finally destroying that which was gentle and, with that gone, came the yelling, the frustrations, the endless screaming.

It began slowly, devious in its silent way, eroding the best that was in her, leaving only the pain, gradually making her distance herself from those she loved, letting her find only the sorrow and the tragic in life.

The marriage died the day she met the bottle. Everything changed. It was insidious, how it happened slowly each night, somewhere between the second and the sixth glass of sherry. It was then the nightly anger swelled out and became the endless shattering barrage of screaming and abuse. Sex became something only found in the bottle along with whatever other memories may have also been waiting there.

We had grown apart from each other, any trace of romance long ago vanished. She had become a drunk and I had become withdrawn, filled with bitterness and resentment. Nothing much remained but the empty shell casings of two broken lives. Two human spirits equally crushed. Our marriage had become destructive to both of us.

"The bonds of marriage."

That had set the pattern for all these years.

The joyful sounds of the wedding gradually faded into the twisted labyrinith of Roberta's mind. I had somehow become her enemy. She would erupt in sudden anger at the slightest imagined provocation, her eyes narrowing, screaming hateful accusations, things real and imagined, cursing, always cursing, yelling with rage and contempt and no longer ever aware of what she was doing. I had become a punching bag for her nightly tirades.

We had reached a stage that no matter what either one said it was already hurtful to the other. We no longer spoke unless it was to argue. Our conversation had deteriorated to grunt sounds that cavemen might have made, two people no longer able to even communicate. Years of relentless screaming echoed and rattled through both our bodies until we had become numb with pain. There was simply nothing left for either of us to give the other. We had become two embittered people leading broken lives.

"Deep in thought?" Herbert Hughes stood near the door wearing that old straw hat and glanced in my direction.

"Just planning what I'll need to take with me when we go out on safari."

"Good idea," he answered, "Always plan ahead. Can't get cut short that way."

"This isn't the place to be cut short," I answered.

"Yes," Hughes said, his eyes seem to be quietly studying me, "No phones once we're out in the bush."

He fanned himself with his straw hat even as his eyes remained on me.

Margaret waved to him and Hughes turned and went back into the hoteli.

Hughes and Margaret seemed happy enough living in a world far removed from mine.

I often wanted to leave but Roberta's fragility always held me back. The drinking, the relentless depression, even the occasional veiled suicide threats. It was like living with the mad Ophelia.

She tried desperately when she was sober, meant well, but she couldn't overcome the lure of the bottle. There were still brief flashes, the way she used to be, when the time was good, but they became more and more seldom and remote.

How bitter it had all become. Wanting to help; unable to help. The pressure never ending night after night.

That had set the pattern for all the years. Two people trapped in a world they both hated.

The endless battles burned deep into my very being like another nail hammered into the coffin of our marriage.

In one of those ironic twists of a bitter fate, I am the author of a successful series of romantic novels. That thought always make me laugh, for it is better then crying, when I think that the author of romantic novels can't even find love in his own home.

Somehow the year's tumbled by. I kept busy writing novels because they offered escape into a happier, freer time and place. Like Peter Pan soaring off to a private world. A moment away from the bitterness.

I started spending long hours alone, often walking aimlessly, wishing I had someone to talk to during my empty times. That someone suddenly appeared in my life carrying, of all things, a torn shopping bag.

# SCRAPBOOK IN TIME
## LAUREN

I had gone to the Western Book Sellers convention in San Francisco spending my time chatting with publishers and other writers when a woman, slowly making her way up the crowded aisles and deeply engrossed in the numerous exhibits, suddenly brushed passed me.

She had the smile of self assurance on her thin, long-lipped mouth, a youthful vitality about her and she walked holding her body rigid, head up, back straight like a West Point cadet on parade. There was something special about the way her mouth went and how it neatly combined with the curve of her high cheek bones.

The woman was wearing a bright yellow dress and a red blazer but what first caught my eye was the shopping bag she carried, stuffed with books and literature that the exhibitors were giving away.

As if a sign sent by the good Gods, at the precise moment we passed each other her shopping bag suddenly ripped open and her books tumbled all over the aisle. She looked around embarrassed for a moment and then quickly knelt down to collect her scattered belongings.

"Let me help," I said, already down on my knees and trying to retrieve a book that had rolled under a nearby desk.

We were both still on our knees when she looked up, grimaced in mild frustration, held out her hand with an easy assurance and simply said, "thank you."

That was how I met Lauren, Lauren Milken, with the dark brown eyes and the long brown hair that cascaded down to her shoulders like a thundering waterfall. Lauren Milken with long legs and a proud walk, who talked with her eyes and had a sleek, tailored look that went well with her.

"You've been doing a lot of collecting," I said, glancing at her books.

"I read a lot," she answered with a magestic smile that brought out dimples on each cheek giving her face a special warmth much like the sun coming out after the rain. The smile added to her delicate long-lipped mouth.

"If you've been collecting so much, perhaps its time to rest your feet," I said, "Might I buy you a book convention collector's drink?"

She looked at me and said nothing.

"This isn't going to be a pickup on main street," I said, aware of what she was probably thinking, "this convention is crowded and noisy but they have a neat little bar tucked away upstairs and it is a wonderful spot for book collectors to pause for a few minutes and catch their breath. Even rest their feet."

"I really should be going," but then she hesitated for just a single moment.

"Look, I'll even carry your shopping bag," I answered, "we'll only go for a quick drink and who knows, at the least two new friends will have briefly met each other."

She smiled, nodding her head in agreement. I reached over and took her shopping bag thinking how heavy it was and wondering how many books she had stuffed into it.

It was as simple as that. Nothing planned. Just a torn shopping bag but filled with what Lauren and I both loved, books. Lauren even collected first editions and I thought of my small library at home crammed with similar books. She was a book editor for a publishing firm and also wrote and illustrated children's books. Thus we shared even more in common.

The many aspects of Lauren were condensed into those few slender opening moments with this scintilating stranger.

That first brief drink was later followed by a lunch, then another lunch, then a dinner. Without plans or trying we drifted into the most casual of affairs.

Roberta and I hadn't made love for years, our ultimate rejection for one another, love making buried among all the rest of the animosity; with Lauren, when love came, it burst out as a gentle, sweet-lovely explosion, a true returning to ourselves, both our past and our future, became locked together with only our tomorrows to dream about.

Lauren gave me back the wonderous side of life that had been lost, a world far removed from the blistering sorrow that always waited at home. She gave me the greatest gifts of all, returning my feeling of youth, my laughter and my joy.

I was truly happy only in the moments we were together, simply being with her, quietly exploring that which was deep within us.

I sent her flowers, surprising her in the afternoon where she worked.

Sometimes she was like a mischievous child.

"I just called to say "hello," Lauren would whisper into my answering machine, "Hello." Then she would quickly hang up.

Lauren would call at unexpected times during the day for brief snatches of conversation and each time I heard her voice I would soar like a high school kid.

I was eager to see Lauren, to talk and to hold her, just be with her, to find my small escape. She was vibrant, alive and after a time offered the very love that had been diminished in my marriage.

Lauren would take me into her home, build a small fire, offer brandy, the two of us quietly talking, saying soft words that allowed the anguish to wash away. We would sit in the dark with the flickering light and talk quietly, holding hands like kids and the touch of her fingertips was always new and sweet and gave me warm chills. We shared everything. We laughed together. Sometimes we cried together. We shared our thoughts and our dreams.

Two Masai slowly walked down the road in front of the hoteli and glanced in my direction.

"Jambo," one called out.

"Jambo," I answered, raising what was left of my tomato juice in salute.

It was a warm evening and I sat alone at that old wobbling table.

I noticed Mrs. Lewis standing nearby. She was holding binoculars and looking off towards the bush.

"Good evening," I called to her.

"Good evening," she answered, putting her binoculars down.

She didn't move and I thought she was hesitant because of her limp.

"It's a fine evening," I said, "Everything's so clear."

"Lovely."

Mrs. Lewis held her ground. Perhaps she was shy because her body language was definitely polite but distant. Maybe she was concerned because the two of us were both alone on this trip and perhaps she thought I was already trying to become too friendly.

But on this early evening, my interest was also distant, lost a long time ago in some never-never land.

There came a day with Lauren, one of those days that later is recognized as a turning point, the kind that happens in everyone's life. I remember it clearly, every detail, all of it sharp and in focus even though it was a rainy San Francisco day. Not just a rainy day. The kind of grey, heavy endless rain that blankets out everything else, driving down in hard sheets, splattering against the pavement, making those walking move slowly, hunched over, trying to keep out the wetness and cold. It was the day after Thanksgiving and the City was quiet.

I was waiting for Lauren at Beppino's, a small Italian restaurant on Market Street where we often met for lunch. Lauren entered precisely at noon, much like Cinderella, always on time. Just seeing her arrive sent a shiver of anticipation through me as it did every time I saw her.

Lauren stood in the restaurant's doorway for a second, shaking the rain out of her long brown hair, scanning the tables looking for me. When our eyes met, she smiled and made her way through the restaurant, walking with that graceful self-assurance. Those seated at nearby tables watched her every movement, her beauty stood out as she weaved her way past the tables towards me.

She had a loose kind of walk, both arms swinging casually as she slowly moved forward filled with confidence, like a sprinter hurling towards a finish line. To the casual observer she appeared both elusive and earthy yet a smile betrayed that she was really soft and gentle.

"Hi," she grinned, leaning over and giving me a small kiss as she seated herself at the table.

It was the rain, I later decided, that really did me in. If it hadn't rained as hard, then perhaps we wouldn't have stayed sheltered in the restaurant for as long, drinking too much wine. Wine in the afternoon on a rainy day with someone like Lauren can prove to be too much, like an explosion rattling your very conscious.

Lauren was excited, telling me that her newest children's book was about to be published.

"It's called, are you ready for this, "Swish, Splash and Splatter" and its about three little waves that go all over the world and whatever beach they arrive on they find the people the same."

I sat there and grinned, glad of her accomplishments and proud of her. On the other hand, I was always proud of her. Proud to simply be with her.

At one point she reached over, held my hand and lightly kissed my fingers. That was too much for me.

"I love you, funny face," I suddenly blurted out, not planning to have said that, yet knowing even as the words tumbled out that it was the most profound thing I ever said in my entire life.

"I love you," and once it was said the words became easy to repeat. "I love you."

"I love you too," Lauren quickly answered. Too quickly.

"No, no, you don't understand," and I shook my head," I love you. From the heart. From the toenails. With everything I have. Love is a very sacred word to me. It's not a throw-away line like "love that new hat" or "love those pretty trees."

"I fell in like with you," she tried to joke.

"I love you," I repeated.

"The difference is when you say "in love," Lauren answered.

"I'm in love."

"You shouldn't say that," Lauren looked away, paused, then added, "How do you know?"

"I've known every kind of love. Puppy love. Teen crush. Roberta, before the tragedy came. Love for my kid. All kinds of love, new love, old love. But none of those loves had feelings like this, not what I have for you. Not ever. It's all different than what I've known before. My body cries its love for you."

Lauren paused and I knew she was thinking of me. And of Roberta.

"I fight being in love with you," she answered, "It isn't right. You're a married man. It just isn't right."

I couldn't answer for I knew she was correct. We sat quietly for long moments, just looking at each other. I don't know how much time lapsed but we finally left the restaurant and walked back out into the rain. I held Lauren tight, neither of us speaking, the rain lashing harder, the wetness running down both our face as we stopped on Market street and hugged and kissed, the rain hiding the grief that must have been reflected in my face.

That same grief disappeared hours later when the phone rang at home around midnight.

"If anyone says anything, tell them this is a wrong number," I heard Lauren's whispered voice, "But Michael, damn you, I am in love. In love."

At that precise moment, as if there had been a crack of lightning, I felt the entire world suddenly explode open, everything flowing together within me, as if destiny was pulling me forward, everything spinning out of control and filling me with new dreams, new desires, new promises.

That was the beginning of a new kind of love, deeper than any love I had ever known or thought possible, an all consuming love that enveloped both of us, together, we became one, loving and caring and living only for the other.

We quickly discovered a new life together, a world removed from anything I had ever known, a world without time or space or anything but only the longing for each other.

Allen was right, Africa does help you to remember. Just like the vivid color and the scents of Africa, all the memories vividly manage to tumble back. Even as I planned ahead for the safari, my thoughts kept racing backwards.

Yuri and Sophie came out of the hoteli and smiled pleasantly.

"Your Michael?" Sophie asked.

I nodded yes.

"I have such trouble with names."

"But she is good at remembering faces," Yuri quickly came to the proud defense of his wife.

"We thought we would take a little stroll before evening comes, care to join us?"

"Thanks but no thanks. I have to go and check my gear for the safari."

"Allen said will go to Nairboi first to get supplies," Yuri continued, "And after that our adventure begins."

Off in the distance I saw Gabriella talking to Corcoran, the two deep in conversation. Her trim figure contrasted sharply with his large girth. Corcoran was quite serious about something she had just said. Their soft sounds drifted and it sounded as if I heard them mention "poachers" several times. Both nodded their heads.

Yuri took Sophie's hand and the two walked off. They were happy together, a happiness that reminded me of a single day lost long ago.

One soft Spring afternoon we visited the zoo, walking carefree, hand-in-hand, Lauren in a red dress, my shirt opened, sleeves rolled up, two silly adventurers off together sharing a few moments alone.

As we strolled past an open park area I paused for a moment and glanced at Lauren.

"Gobble, gobble, gobble," I suddenly called, a harsh, gutteral sound like a wild turkey would make. Lauren jumped when she first heard it.

"That would scare anyone," she said, "What the heck is that supposed to be?"

"That, funny face, is the sound I use to make each Thanksgiving for my kid."

Lauren laughed and tried to repeat the sound.

It became a day for casual laughter. One filled with the pleasant scents of pop corn and roasted peanuts and a gentle breeze that quietly meandered through the zoo's tall trees.

We watched the antics on Monkey island laughing as one rascal quickly grabbed some peanuts from another and a Mack Sennett style chase took place up and down the hills; Lauren and I became absorbed by the near-human behavior of the gorillas who swung unconcerned from an old tire hung in the Primate Center; we stood in awe seeing the lions pace back and forth, their deep roars echoing, vibrating throughout the entire Lion House knowing it was near feeding time.

The elephants proudly roamed through their enclosure, frustrated with their small surroundings, seemingly distainful of several children who stood at the foot of the area busy waving arms, trying to attract attention. There was a sadness seeing them captive in their small compound.

"Confession time. I've always wanted to go to Africa," Lauren said, glancing at the children, "One of my life long ambitions since I was a little girl."

"I've always wanted to go to Africa ever since my first jungle movie."

"You want to run in your bare feet and give out a Tarzan yell and swing from tree to tree?" Lauren asked, nibbling on a handful of peanuts that was supposed to have been for the elephants.

"Something like that," I answered, "Me Tarzan. You Jane."

"What's really nuts is that I can actually see you doing that," Lauren said, "Running nude, wild, primitive. Happy."

She hesitated for a second, looking at me when she said "happy."

"Maybe we can go there together someday," I answered.

Lauren said nothing but squeezed my hand, holding it very tight. Somewhere, far off, the zoo's organ was playing a zestful tune and children were laughing and the world felt warm and wonderful.

We rode the children's train which weaved its way past the various animals enclosures. Lauren laughed and shouted and pointed at each animal like a delighted child. The engineer, enjoying her excitement, loaned her his blue-stripped cap which she wore jauntingly pulled down over her forehead.

"You know what the best part of this day is?" Lauren asked.

"What? The elephants?"

"Being with you because we are friends," she pushed the engineer's cap to the back of her head, "and friends are forever. You make my heart happy."

There, with the merry-go-round music and the children playing and all the animals that were nearby, and the soft smell of Spring in the air, it was there where I ran my fingers along the side of her face and I felt warm and good and at ease with the world.

On the way out I stopped a school teacher who was taking a group of children through the zoo and asked if she would take a picture of the two of us.

The woman nodded yes and I thanked her. I handed her my camera, adding for no particular reason other then wishful thinking, "We're on our second honeymoon."

She looked quizzically at us. I could see her mind working, thinking we were older then most newlyweds. Suddenly she beamed, proud to be sharing this small part of our lives.

"Congratulations to you both," she smiled, handing the camera back to me.

"Michael, you're awful," Lauren whispered as the woman left.

I made her day," I answered, "She thinks she did a wonderful thing for two newlyweds."

We both laughed, a kind of conspiratorial laugh, then we clung together that warm spring afternoon in the zoo. Far off we could hear the sound of the animals.

"...SCREEEEECH......"

The unexpected shattering sound seemed like something from the depths of hell, starling me, jarring my thoughts and sending me leaping to my feet.

A small bird had suddenly flown over the open bar. I half stood, looked around, tried to smile, feeling sheepish over my first African adventure.

The woman behind the bar grinned when she saw me jump. It was the only expression she had shown the entire time I had been sitting there.

Some children saw the bird and started to chase it.

"Go away," the lady called, talking to both the children and the bird at the same time, "Go fly off."

The children ran off down the dusty street laughing.

The bird paused, alerted to the sudden noise and flew off towards the waiting bush.

"The bird startled you, my friend," Corcoran walked over to my table and smiled.

"I guess I'm just a big city boy."

"Save you're being startled for when we are out in the bush," he said with quiet authortiy, "You'll find more to jump about when we are out there alone."

"You know the bush?"

"Not really," Corcoran answered, "But my work gets me around."

He paused and slowly sucked in his breath. He was wearing a shirt, soaked with sweat and filled with stains that could no longer be removed.

"I saw you sitting here," he continued, "And you looked as ease here as if you were seated at an outdoor table in Paris."

I felt Corcoran wanted to change the subject so I went along with his conversation.

"I was just watching the passing parade."

"Not much of a parade to watch in this God forsaken place," he paused and blotted an already dirty handkerchief at his forehead, "The parade will start out there in the bush."

All of our small group seemed to be milling about, getting to know one another, anxious for our safari to begin.

Allen was over by the van checking the tires.

Flora Zimmer sat in the nearby shade quietly reading a pocket book, her face covered by a large floppy hat.

"This is a bulletin I spotted at the hoteli, "Corcoran said, "Small piece about poachers."

"Allen said we shouldn't worry."

"I suppose not," his eyes looked around, "But I've been trained to worry about everything."

Corcoran went back to the hoteli. I knew it was time for me to return, to be sociable and to make small talk with the others but the screeching sound remained with me for a long while as I recalled similar sounds heard on other distant days. Sound that I hated and which changed my life forever.


I remembered everything ever said between Lauren and myself. What she wore each time we met. The delicate moments and the wild laughter. And sometimes the things I never wanted to hear.

There was a winter afternoon and we were lying quietly together when Lauren suddenly let out a long sad kind of sigh.

"Was that the sigh of love?" I asked.

Lauren said nothing. Then she turned away.

"You have to lie to be here," she finally answered.

There was nothing to answer; nothing to say. It was always on both our minds yet something we kept unspoken. Now her one sentence screamed out for all eternity to hear.

Nothing else was said. We both let it pass but we knew the pain of the truth of that single sentence.

Even though the love I felt was deeper then anything I had ever known before, with it came a strange kind of sadness, a premonition that worried me.

It started one day when we were having lunch at Ghiradelli Square, site of an old chocolate factory that had been converted into one of those charming San Francisco shopping places near the bay with its sweeping view of the Golden Gate and, just beyond, the gentle, rolling hills of Marin.

I had gone there in my childhood when it was still a real chocolate factory and I remembered staring transfixed watching the huge vats of boiling, thick chocolate being made.

Now, all these years later, I sat staring into Lauren's face as we waited for lunch to be served. At first she smiled, then turned away, became self-conscious and finally asked me to stop.

Only I couldn't.

"You're eyes light up like a little boy when you describe the old chocolate factory," she said, trying to make polite conversation.

I didn't answer at first but continued to stare into her face.

"It's really a well put together face," I said, "Everything seems to fit into its proper place."

"Knock it off." She turned and looked out towards the bay.

"No, please, don't turn away. That face is what it is all about."

"You're being nutzy and dramatic again."

"I want to see that face on the pillow when I wake each morning. Like a blooming flower opening fresh each day."

Lauren was silent. She watched a freighter slowly sail under the bridge.

"What is love, really?" she finally asked, "We keep talking about it. Only what is it?"

"Looking into the face of the woman you love and seeing all eternity."

She kicked me under the table.

"Love is the simple joy of being with another," I added.

"And you only want to be with one person?"

Lauren reached over and touched my hand.

"Then I really love you. So much," she said.

"In love?"

"You know that. In love. In love. In love."

Yet even as she spoke, I continued to stare into her face, feeling that odd kind of premonition, as if I had to cram every second of looking into Lauren's face for fear that someday it wouldn't be there and I would never see her again.

Lauren brought back a new vigor to my life, returned interest that had become lost, letting me finally forget the nightly tragedy always waiting at home. Yet not really ever forgetting. Not deep down inside. By its very nature an affair is doomed from the start. We both knew our love was built on quicksand and that everything would one day be dragged down.

We were together for months, then it became a year, then we lost track of our time together. Sometimes, but not often, we talked of the future knowing there could never be any future for constantly hanging just above us was the frustration born of deceit.

That deceit became clear and visible on a very sad day during the happiest time of the year.

Roberta and I had gone Christmas shopping and she was in a particularly happy mood, taking delight in the downtown crowds and the glittering store windows.

We had taken a short cut through Union Square, passing a group of Christmas carolers, when I saw Lauren walking directly toward us. She was carrying a shopping bag stuffed with gifts but all I really saw was the stunned look already crossing her face.

"Hi," I said trying to sound casual but thinking my voice must have sounded like a hoarse whisper.

"Happy holiday," Lauren answered, a frozen smile on her face, as she looked only at Roberta.

"This is my wife, Roberta," I said, "and this is Lauren Milken, an old publishing friend."

The two ladies shook hands as they offered friendly greetings.

We chatted aimlessly for a few moments, as people do when they happen upon a chance meeting, and then went off our separate ways. It was cold outside but I felt warm and my legs seemed like they would crumble from under me.

The call I knew would come happened the moment I walked into my office the next morning.

"Where were her horns?" Lauren was saying with surprising calm, "I thought she was supposed to be the world's top bitch and number one alcoholic and a screaming nut."

"We were Christmas shopping," I answered feebly.

"She is beautiful," Lauren continued, not listening to me, "She is a decent human being."

I was silent for a moment, trying to collect my thoughts.

"You gave me this 'wife doesn't understand me' bullshit," Lauren's voice was growing louder, the anger crackling over the phone,"It made me feel like shit seeing her. You and me, that's one thing. But now she's not just someone you talk about. She is real. I've seen her. And the whole thing is pathetic. It stinks. Makes me feel contaminated."

Lauren paused to catch her breath.

"How could you have done this?" she raved on, "It's cheap. You're a nice guy. She's sweet. I'm decent. It's cheap."

There was nothing to answer. She had never seen the true Roberta. No one who has not seen that could ever understand the nightmare world that drinking and hate can cause. Roberta remained fragile, like a crystal about to shatter. Pity had long ago replaced love.

Lauren understood all this. Our love helped guide us past that bitter chance Christmas meeting. We continued seeing each other but things were never quite the same between us. I loved Lauren. I was sure, certain she loved me in return. Only now everything was different.

Those clandestine meetings continued to bother both of us for there always remained the specter of Roberta and the lies and the deceit were something neither of us could never overcome.

Thus it wasn't a complete surprise when there came a day when all of our love suddenly vanished. Just like the snap of a finger the magic was gone, had been taken away.

Lauren had gotten tired of waiting, of meeting secretly, watching me slowly wither away at home.

"There's no future in it with us," she said one evening as we sat by the fire, "It isn't fun for me to come home to an empty house. I want to be with someone. I want to share my life but not in secret. Damn it, I want the simple things like darning socks and baking cookies and being able to come home at night with some guy just waiting for me. We can carry the groceries in together. Meeting in the shadows isn't for me. It's cheap and it makes me cringe."

She was right and I could say nothing in return. All I could do was try to reach out and hold her, hug her, touch her, knowing this moment, now, sitting by the red-gold firelight, might be our last minutes together.

For the first time Lauren pulled away, turned her head from me, pushed me away.

"You're hurting," I managed to say, my words lost in confusion, "That's not you. You could never hurt anything."

"I don't hurt people," she snapped in defense, "People hurt themselves."

There is that thin line between love and hate when emotions and frustrations rip apart and drain away all other feelings.

"That makes me a rejected lover?" I asked, feeling in a blurred daze.

"You're not a rejected anything," she half-screamed.

I tried to reach out and hold her hand but again she pulled away. "Hate the sin but love the sinner?" I whispered.

"That's a lot of shit and it's mean," she snapped.

She was on the defensive and deliberately finding things to quarrel about.

"Take whatever dreams you have and stick them up your ass," she screamed.

I drew back stung, wanting to shake her, to force out this venom that had suddenly erupted within her, somehow try to make her hear and understand what she was saying.

"What's wrong?" I asked in frustration, knowing the answer even before I asked, "What ever happened to your famous 'Friends are forever' bullshit?"

"Please, don't touch me," she said with brutal anger,"This isn't right. Go. Please go. Before I lose my respect for you."

"I'll go, sure, but someday remember a guy who once-upon-a-time loved you very, very much," I answered, adding, "And that you dumped on him."

Lauren stared at me but said nothing. For a brief second she started to extend her hands but suddenly stopped, slowly turning them into tight fists.

"Five minutes before you die remember who dumped who."

"Two people, with this kind of love, it happens only once in a lifetime," I continued, "Some people never find that their entire life."

"It could have been wonderful," she answered.

"It should have been."

Lauren paused and looked at me. She wanted to say something but then slowly turned away, offering only silence.

I started to reach out to her but I pulled back and shrugged, knowing it would all be useless.

"This can't be happening. Not to us," I whispered.

"It can't be. But it has."

Lauren looked at me for a long moment, then moved away.

I felt we both wanted to say more.

But there was only silence.

Those were the last words we said to each other, devastating and destroying words. My entire world had collapsed. I stood in shock wanting to hold her, knowing I could never touch her again. I turned away and stumbled as I made my way blindly out. No friendship was ever destroyed without some flesh being torn open.

That was the start of what I called the Twin Pains, the thought of both women cutting deeply and never leaving my mind. One woman was filled with agony; the other brought the promise of new love, a new life, renewed hope. Both had laid waste to me like Sherman's march through Georgia, with nothing left, not even a tree standing, and only dried bits of bark to nibble on.

It was then that I started to build a vast emotional wall, cutting off feeling and love, knowing I could never give of myself or open up to any person ever again.

It broke my heart. Really broke my heart. Little did I know how soon my waltz with death was coming.

The sweet smell of Africa surrounded me and brought me back to the Hoteli Ya Kingi Georgi.

I heard someone nearby cough and a dog was barking off in the distance.

This had been a moment to reach out and hold onto the past, to cling to that which was familiar. One does that when they are frightened and alone, especially in an unknown and strange land. It is particularaly good to remember at times like that. It can also be bad.

Roberta. Lauren. I blew each of them a kiss filled with love and hope and respect.

It was time to get back to my small group of new friends to complete plans for tomorrow and our journey deep out into the lonely bush.

I paused for a moment to look around, surrounded by the sweet honey smell that is Africa. There was a cackling off in the distance, probably a bird making the sound of the night, for now it was now the last of twilight and darkness was rapidly descending.

# NAIROBI

Women in colorful dresses walking with baskets balanced on their heads and babies strapped to their backs. Traffic zooming pass to the rhythm of wildy beeping horns. The streets hectic and busy. Crowded buses filled with passengers leaning out of windows, seated on the roofs, some clinging to the outside. Flat bed trucks, filled with African men standing, jammed together. Snappy looking policemen who looked like British soldiers, complete with swagger sticks tucked under their arms. All the sights and sounds of downtown Nairobi were at first overwhelming.

Africa is everything National Geographic had ever promised.

Nairobi suddenly burst upon you as a vast montage of blasting horns, crowded streets, blurs of color seen in quick movement, all simultaneously exploding in every possible direction as if engulfing you.

Our small group had a few hours alone when the guides went off to purchase the necessary supplies. We walked casually about exploring Nairobi's downtown area trying to get a feeling for the people and the country.

"Hey, Simba, welcome to Africa."

My first feeling of Africa came from the men who patiently hung around the tourist hotel waiting for visitors to emerge. They would instantly gather around, eager to sell a variety of trinkets from elephant-hair bracelets to hand carved walking sticks.

"Just keep moving, just keep moving," Walter Corcoran whispered, his mouth half-closed.

Flora Zimmer paused to look at an elephant hair bracelet that one man was showing.

"Best to keep moving," Corcoran again cautioned, snapping his fingers.

She glanced at him, then looked away. Her eyes narrowed as if to say, "Mind your own business."

Downtown Nairobi offered a never ending parade of colorful individuals rushing quickly through the crowded streets. A Muslim women in black chador and veil stood quietly chatting with a man wearing a fez who kept nodding his head as she talked. An East Indian woman in a colorful blue and gold silk sari moved down the street stopping only to calm a child that was crying. Two Englishmen walked past, one dressed in impeccable business suit and the other clad in safari jacket and bush pants. I noticed men holding hands and quickly learned that was considered a particular sign of friendship among African men.

Many of the low buildings had white-column arcades offering shade and giving the feeling of another era, almost like walking down an old western street. I passed the Parliament building and the Kenyatta Conference Center as I made my way down Mama Ngina Street.

"SPECIAL DEAL! SPECIAL DEAL!"

The merchants in the crowded City Market took great delight in beckoning and offering a "special deal" just for our group. The market was crowded with shoppers carefully studying the merchandise displayed in an endless variety of stalls filled with cabbages, coconuts, mangoes, all piled high. There was everything available from foods to hand carved African statues.

The flora of Nairobi is spectacular. Rhododendrons, wine-colored bougainvillaea, lilac Jacarandas, flame trees and Hibiscus, all of it blending together in colors of soft purple, rust, gold, yellow, pink, the city coming alive with a rainbow of quiet beauty.

"Nakusontelon," one merchant summed it all up when he noticed my looking at the flowers, "Nairobi is the place of all beauty."

I smiled and nodded in agreement.

"I wonder if I can find some Pepto-bismol in one of those shops," Herbert Hughes said, taking his wife and heading off to one of the small stalls.

I wanted to be alone so I left the others and continued my walk through the city.

"Hey, Mistuh, got a moment?" a young man nodding at me, suddenly emerged from a nearby doorway, his hands motioning me to stop as if in some sort of desperation.

He was dressed alright but there was something I didn't like about him. His eyes were cold and intense and there was a feeling of meanness about him. He looked at me without blinking.

"What's up?" I asked, remembering Corcoran's rule of being polite but to keep moving.

"What's up? That's a good expression," he half-grinned, "I'm a student and I want to go to the United States. What is the best college?"

He was wearing a shabby brown suit and a battered black felt hat with a large red feather stuck in the band.

Bullshit he is a student, I thought. Perhaps a pimp? Or drugs?

"Write to the University of California at Berkeley," I answered, not liking the way he kept pushing himself towards me.

"I've heard of that place, Berkeley," he said, "In California?"

"Good," I answered.

I was walking past the Thorn Tree, a popular outdoor restaurant, and used that as an opportunity to leave the stranger.

"Hey, mistuh," he called after me, not wanting to walk inside.

"Good luck," I grinned back, "It's a good campus."

"Fuck you, man," he muttered under his breath and his eyes narrowed.

There was something violent about him. He was too tense, his mouth set in a contemptuous scowl and his jaw too stiff, a mean flare in his eyes, like an animal about to strike. The eyes were dead, they looked without showing any emotion. There was evil all about him.

"Asente," the hotel doorman greeted me, quickly turning to assist some arriving guests from a cab that had just pulled into the entrance.

The restaurant has long been famous because of a huge thorn tree that dominates the center of the outdoor patio. The wide tree trunk is always filled with cards and messages, a tradition that dates back to the days of the great hunters who would arrive in town after a safari and used this same tree trunk to contact their friends.

"Big traffic," the doorman said walking over to me, "Just imagine eighty years ago Nairobi wasn't even on the map of Africa."

"We call that progress where I come from," I answered, then I thought of that stranger and added, "Who was that student who was following me?"

"I was watching you and you were smart," the doorman answered, "He is what we call a confidence man. Did he ask for money?"

"I didn't give him a chance," I said.

"Most people here are good," the doorman grinned, "We are all the same and all try to get along."

I had a sandwich and then continued my walking tour of Nairobi.

"Enjoy my country as you visit," the doorman called as he saw me leaving, carefully adding, "keep your eyes well peeled."

I wasn't sure if that was merely a friendly answer or some sort of cryptic warning. It was as though he was trying to tell me something more.

I visited the Kenya National Museum and the very first display I saw startled me. The skull of the original ape-man was resting in a glass case as the centerpiece for the museum's "ORIGINS OF MAN" exhibit. This pre-historic creature had been found not far from Nairobi. Near the skull were the fossilized remains of his first tools, stone hand axes and cleavers.

The exhibit made me feel as if I was standing near the very spot where time began and I suddenly felt very insignificant, my life not even the flickering of an eyelid in the history of time.

KENYA FREEDOM FIGHTERS was the exhibit located on another floor of the museum. One entire wall was filled with photos and posters showing what was titled the "brave fighters," a graphic display of the Mau Mau.

British media of the nineteen-fifties had reported that the Mau Mau were simply considered ruthless terrorists. The exhibit offered a completely different viewpoint displaying vivid photos of the British detention camps.

On one side was a photo of the proud British Lancaster Fusileers, all young boys, the first troops which had been sent to Kenya, to quell the "disturbance."

On another wall were displays showing Mau Mau being rounded up and led away, to be held without trial. Photos showed prisoners who had been beaten while simply being "detained."

Either way it was a "disturbance" that would cost 10,000 lives. All in the straining of a nation being born and propaganda being bent.

There were great portraits of Jomo Kenyatta, the man who led the uprising, and whose name means "burning spear." He had been put in jail, only to eventually return and proudly lead his country into "Uhuru," freedom, independence. In nineteen sixty-three, this remarkable man, considered a terrorist in his time, would become President and eventually rank as one of the world's great statesmen.

As with any war, it always comes down to whose propaganda you finally believe, which side of the stadium you sit on and for who you do your rooting.

I left the museum and walked back into the Nairobi sun recalling a line that someone had once written long ago: "The first casualty of war is always the truth."

Back outside I continued my wandering. The sight of beggars on the hot and cluttered sidewalks startled me at first. Their legs shrunk, bodies thin, twisted, crawling on the streets, only their heads and torsos seemingly normal, the more fortunate ones were transported about on wooden carts to be rolled about like a sack of deformed potatoes, only their heads moving, their eyes burning into you.

An old man passed me on the street. He was leading a blind child with a string tied between both their arms allowing the old man to walk quickly, guiding the youngster through the downtown traffic.

"I love you," a woman with a torn blue sweater and a face that looked like a dried potato-head shouted to me, "I love you. Do you want to fuck me?"

"I love you too," I answered as I kept moving, "but I'm fine."

"Come on, fuck with me," she persisted, rubbing her scraggly hand along my sleeve, forcing me to pull away, "Maybe you're too old and can't get it up anymore."

I pulled back thinking of what had been in my life and wondering if perhaps this street whore was saying something I had refused to admit even to myself.

"You can't get it up anymore." Her words were haunting, making me feel cold and frightened.

I thought of the pain that always remained and of the death dance and I wondered if this old whore had some special mystic power because I worried if my ability to love would ever return.

A man in a red shirt approached and the woman quickly left. I later learned those who wear red shirts are called "police informers" and work for the city police.

A bus roared down the crowded street jammed with passengers, many seated on top and several clinging to the front and the back.

"Wula la la," one person shouted who was leaning outside the open back door, "Always room for one more."

As I strolled past the downtown soccer stadium, a group of tough-looking men were clustered together in a tight circle. I became tense, alerted for possible trouble.

They were talking in whispers, their eyes constantly darting about, always on guard for something unknown. All were apprehensive and nervous.

One kept aimlessly tossing a knife onto the ground, letting it fall as close to his feet as possible. Then I suddenly froze and stood motionless in what seemed like an eternity.

The man tossing the knife was the same one who had stopped me near the Thorn Tree. I recognized the battered, black felt hat with the red feather stuck in the band. He looked up, saw me and grinned, extending his middle finger towards me.

"Blessings, blessings," he said with a smile and a voice that was filled with contempt.

The cold chill that suddenly surged through my body only underscored my feeling of danger. There was something brutal about all of them. I became rigid, everything within me suddenly alerted.

I was street wise enough to know the look and smell of evil when I saw it. All my inner alarms were blasting out warning signals.

One man let out a chilling, crazed kind of laugh, a twisted sound that I would never forget. The laughter reminded me of a jackal and it frightened me even there in the daylight of a Nairobi afternoon.

"Hey, man," the one in the battered felt hat called, "You be careful in my country."

His eyes stared at me with deep hatred.

"There are poachers out there in the bush," he continued to shout, "You want a good guide?"

He darted towards me but the others held him back.

He started to laugh and nod to his friends.

I moved passed, looking straight ahead, still hearing the echos of that dreadful sound.


Downtown Nairobi was still filled with traffic in the late afternoon as I made my way back to the hotel.

The sun's rays had already slipped behind the downtown buildings and an early darkness was starting to settle in. As in any major city when the day's work has ended, people were rushing about, hurrying home, going to meet friends, making evening plans, finding conversations and, perhaps, seeking love.

That thought only added to my feeling of loneliness, especially in this remote place.

It was my last night before going out in the bush so I decided to treat myself to one final elegant dinner. I was the only American in the entire restaurant and it reminded me of an old Humphrey Bogart movie. From another room I heard a group laughing and singing as you might in any hotel only this group was laughing and singing in Swahili.

Alone here, with a bottle of wine taking its advantage, thinking of what tomorrow might bring and what had happened in the past I allowed my writer's mind to soar on its own. Funny, in those old movies you'd think of a lost love and then your memory would be shaken when you thought you saw her face reflected in a mirror or a store window.

For me it was the Cobb salad during dinner that once again dredged up those old memories. Lauren had loved Cobb salads, often reaching over and taking bits of bacon from mine, a gesture that always made us both laugh. The only difference was that in this African version of a Cobb salad instead of bacon there was Oxen tongue.

"Here's looking at you kid," I sighed to myself, recalling Bogart's line in "Casablanca" and feeling the eternal romantic lost without anyone to love.

It was odd how I often felt that Lauren was with me, next to me, and now, at this very moment, I could sense her presence. But only for a moment. Then the feeling quickly disappeared and Lauren was once again gone.

"You're a walking time bomb." I also heard that other voice from the past, that haunting, horrible sentence that was to change my life forever.

It was like hearing the wind sobbing around the little cracks that once had been my heart.

Forget Lauren, I cautioned myself, place her far off, deep back in the recesses of the mind, back in the shadows. Forget her. Only I knew I couldn't. I missed her especially here far from anything I had ever known before and being alone with only strangers. My heart, at least what was left of it, cried out for her.

Lauren. Somehow she had become my salvation. And my destruction.

Every day I told myself that I survived another day without her, like a smoker trying to kick the habit, taking it one day at a time, only even as I thought that I knew it was all false for I really hadn't survived anything. The wine brought her before me, so vivid I could almost touch her. She appeared and smiled and I felt that magical chill which she always gave me.

As I thought of her, I wondered if perhaps she was thinking the same, remembering as I did, and that made me happy. Only I knew, no matter how numb the wine had made me, that it was all a lost dream and that she really no longer ever thought of me. Not now, not ever. She was happy in her new life.

Where had it all gone? Like they say, all too fast. One day a young, dumb kid tossing a ball with his Dad in an open field and the next getting bruised, groping his way alone into the September years. Looking into the mirror and seeing an old face that you no longer recognized. Suddenly my life was in the past tense. It all swirled by too quickly. As the wine became an ally I could see it all clearly. The memories circled fully around, that wild and witty circle which was what life is all about, one big merry-go-round and, when it ended here, on this lonely night, it jolted me back to reality.

There was a piano in the corner of the room. I wanted to go over and play "As Time Goes By" but I hadn't touched a piano since "Chopsticks" days so I sat quietly, sipping my wine and gulping down some succulent prawns that had come directly from the Indian ocean.

I sat at the table forcing myself to think only of Africa and the adventures waiting out in the bush.

It was a heady time for me, feeling as if I could now live forever, lucky to be alive, with nothing to worry about except what tomorrow might offer. In some ways it was the same sensation one might experience when leaping off into a great abyss and plunging into the unknown. I sat there secretly hoping all those legendary mysteries of Africa might somehow unfurl just for me.

I had learned the rites of passage taught by western civilization and now it was time to see what lessons the bush might offer.

Thus my quiet night in Narobi came to an end and my journey into the unknown was about to start.

# NAIROBI POLICE REPORT
## 13 JANUARY

We drove through the crowded streets of Nairobi, picked up a divided highway, went passed the airport, continued driving until the highway became two lanes and then country roads.

It was then that we began to see a series of police roadblocks.

"Quite common place," Allen assured us.

To stop vehicles in Kenya the police cross the entire road with metal spikes. The officers, mean and determined looking, stand nearby tightly holding machine guns.

"No one complains here about stopping," Corcoran said.

Allen continued on the road driving passed small farms. We passed a herd of cattle and a young Masai boy waved.

We were now deep in the country driving passed small thatched huts. Not one of us, except perhaps Allen, gave any thought to what life was like for those living inside the huts.

A Nairobi police report which I later saw helped give me a feeling of what that life was like. It helped reconstruct the background of those who were to later become still another part of my life.

Peter Osuna is a short, stubby man whose day usually started at four in the morning, getting up in a windowless shanty where he lived with his wife and seven children, plus one mangy dog who fought for the same scraps of food that Osuna's children battled over.

The family was always hungry and Mama Osuna cooked the same every day of their life, bending over an old cooking pot centered in the middle of the windowless, airless mud hut. Each day she would add whatever she could into the always simmering pot. Most of the time she was able to make a millet porridge, often there was maize and, on the better days, even cowpeas.

She would frequently stir the always bubbling mixture with an old jagged stick that one of the children had found. Sometimes the children also brought home small remains of discarded vegetables and Mama Osuna would make certain these were quickly placed into the cooking pot.

Osuna rose early every day, silently slipping on his soiled undershirt and torn shorts and would then walk several miles to the nearest road and wait in the morning cold for the truck to pick him up. It would already be crammed with other men all forced to stand crowded together in the open rear platform as they drove endless miles off into the country. The men then spent long days in the scorching sun working on the roadways, constantly smelling the tar and the sulphur, coughing as they gulped the boiling, wet tar deep into their lungs, bending and aching and seldom stopping until long after the sun would finally set and bring the merciful evening cool.

It would be the same the next day and the next unless, on what Osuna considered the "good days," he was lucky and found work out in the fields, pulling fresh fruit, the fields stinking of animal dung, his back stooped and constantly aching but at least the tar in the lungs was gone for a few days.

Osuna thought of the tourists that he saw passing each day on the road to Amboseli in their big vans and their nice clothes, always busy snapping pictures, wearing their cute little hats to protect them from the sun. He saw their smiling faces and the thought made him want to spit.

He also thought of forty dollars.

Forty dollars.

A fortune for Osuna and it would all be so simple. John Aduo and a few of his friend also wanted the same thing. The elephant and its ivory. Or maybe the rhino with its ugly hair-matted horn.

It would all be simple.

"You a good man," his wife said to Osuna, her lips hardly moving, "Don't listen to Aduo. We are decent people."

"I'm a tired man," Osuna answered, his eyes glancing about the cluttered room. Three of the children were curled together in their restless sleep, all on the same soiled mat, which was their only thin protection against the dirt floor.

"You'll get hurt," his wife persisted, "or go to jail."

"It will be out in the bush. No one around."

"Better you sell your soul."

"I see the visitors every day. Then I see us. Here. I want to piss on them."

Osuna thought of their youngest, her leg already starting to shrivel and curl with the disease, knowing it was already too late to save the child from being crippled and forced to beg on the streets of Nairobi.

Forty dollars.

It would all be so easy.

Aduo was very different. No family. Few friends. He lived alone, on the street, his hatred for the foreigners always burning.

His father had been a colonel in the Mau Mau in 1954, during the time of the uprising, when ten thousand had been killed as a country fought for its freedom from British colonial rule. Today the Mau Mau are regarded as Kenya Freedom Fighters and national heroes but to the British in those early years they were classified as pure terrorists.

His father had been caught and interned by the British, beaten until his balls bloated and his head was nothing but a smashed broken lump. That was how Aduo viewed his father the day he had to go into the prison to bring the body home.

Kenya had long ago grown to its eventual freedom, a country which proudly proclaimed that everyone consider each other as brothers and sisters, all living in harmony, but Aduo's hatred never changed. He would choke with rage.

He had started at six, silently walking behind the white tourist, too small to be noticed until in one quick movement he would reach out and grab the visitor's camera. Before they could react, Aduo would already disappear into the crowded Nairobi streets.

Ten years later he had developed his own particular style of casually approaching tourists and telling them he was a student. A woeful look on his face long perfected by standing before a small hand-held mirror, was planned for added sympathy. He had become part of a gang that walked the streets of Nairobi looking for strangers as easy prey.

"I'm a student," he would stop the visitors, "and am seeking to get into veterinary college in your country," he would implore, "what do you suggest? Which is the better?"

Often the tourist would stop, taking special delight in being considered an expert as well as thinking they were helping a young student.

The moment they stopped, Aduo knew he had them. He would speak softly, quickly continuing to gain the stranger's confidence as he casually started to guide them off the main street, into the shadows of a side street, always continuing to talk, smiling, moving the tourist towards a doorway and then, quickly, silently, an unexpected knee to the groin, a closed fist slicing into the stranger's neck. Within a moment it was over.

Aduo would quickly go through the stranger's pocket, the hands of an expert searching for hidden money belts and then, another second or two, he would walk off, happy, feeling the new money now in his own pocket. The only thing he ever regretted was that the violence ended too soon. His anger grew more intense against the foreigner with each attack.

The ivory had become the biggest prize of all and now Aduo met with Osuna, outside the soccer stadium in downtown Nairobi. Neither man could afford tickets but stood with the others in the milling crowd standing out in the street, listening to the roar from within the stadium.

Aduo talked quietly, finally taking out a small map, hand-written on the back of a soiled napkin.

"This is where the animals are best," he told Osuna, "This is where we will go."

His fingers pointed to the map. It was Amboseli.

# THE BUSH

There was only silence.

The early morning fog hung low, clung to the ground, distorted what the vision could see, the twisted forms of the Thorn trees and the acacias offered only shadowy ghost-like shapes looming out of the grey mist, all adding to the strange feeling of the unknown.

Grey, that was the only color that engulfed us giving each a quiet moment to search our inner-selves, thinking this is exactly what it must have been like at the very dawn of time, when Cro-Magnon men roamed this very space, all of us aware that mankind was born not far from where we now stood.

An elephant trumpeted far off in the distance adding to the sense of wonder and astonishment that was proving our first morning in Africa, alone, out in the bush.

We heard a monkey screech from somewhere nearby.

One lone bird, chirped nearby in the grey mist, offered some sense of the familiar in these stark surroundings.

All of us looked out into this endless expanse, lost in the feeling of timeliness.

We had arrived in Amboseli late the previous afternoon and quickly set up camp, all eager to begin our trek out into the waiting bush.

Our small van had made its way towards Amboseli, one of several game parks in Kenya. The morning fog had begun to burn off and we could see long, open stretches ahead. The road, if you could call it that, was jagged and twisted, filled with holes and dust.

"Giraffe," Allen said nonchalantly, pointing to the right, "The world's tallest living animal."

There was tall brown grass, bending slightly in the morning breeze. Suddenly a giraffe's head stretched silently, haughty, high above the tall grass.

Far off in the distance we saw just the top of other heads, six of them, all busy nibbling at a tall tree. Everyone gasped almost in unison, suddenly aware that for the first time no zoos protective fence stood between us and the animals. The giraffes were only a few feet away as they moved towards our van with a slow and elegant grace.

They moved like a slow motion film, gradually making their way towards us, completely unconcerned with our presence.

That was when we all truly became aware, for the first time, that we were really deep out in the bush.

It quickly became apparent that our group was but a small dot set against the endless African landscape.

We drove deeper into Amboseli, none of us daring to take our eyes from the window.

The sun became white and my shirt already clung to my back. Hughes fanned himself with his straw hat.

"Tropical Africa," Hughes said, glancing at my shirt with distain, "The equator is only three miles away."

I nodded politely but I wanted to tell him to mind his own business.

"Zebra," Allen called, his eyes sharp to every movement in the bush. Allen had the ability to spot animals long before any of us saw anything more then what appeared to be only small black dots out on the sweeping horizon.

The herd of Zebra passed about fifty yards from us, moving slowly, some pausing to eat the bush. Cameras throughout the van simultaneously clicked together. Suddenly the zebras dashed off in full gallop, all that black and white quickly blending together like a movie projector that had gone out of focus.

Lauren loved animals and I clearly saw the grin of excitement she would have had as she greeted each one with childish enthusiasm and delight.

Allen drove further then suddenly stopped the van a few minute's later.

"Look over there," Allen became excited, pointing his hand towards the bush.

Off in the distance we could see two lions seemingly resting in the sun. Both were moving about in the shade of a Thorn tree, busy in their own activity.

"Look how contented they are," Mrs. Lewis whispered as Allen drove the van closer to the lions.

As we neared, we saw why they appeared so contended. It was our first shock of Africa.

The lions were silently sprawled over a dead gazelle which they had just killed, chomping on the bloodied carcass they had ripped open, pulling off great chunks of meat and bone, chewing on the dead flesh. We only heard the sound of crunching in the otherwise silent bush.

One lion slowly looked distainfully at us, bored, he turned and went back to his eating.

"The lion bites the spinal cord," Allen explained, "and it is over very quickly. It has so much strength it can pull twice its own weight."

When they were finished, the largest lion slowly drew its head regally high, its yellow-brown mane gently fluttering in a small breeze. The other sank down and curled in a semi-circle as if in deep sleep.

"Survival of the fittest," Hughes whispered, "The very law of the jungle."

"Life tested to its utmost," Yuri said. It seemed he was thinking of another time and another place.

Flora Zimmer looked away and said nothing.

Allen quickly backed up the van and moved away from the lions.

"Let's try to find the monkeys," he said, "They are usually good for a laugh."

Two Masai strolled passed us, deep in their own conversation, oblivious to our van of excited passengers.

Allen carefully explained to us what is described as the "Big Five" - lions, rhinos, buffalos, leopards, elephants - but he smiled knowing that we would soon be seeing much more. It all waited out in the bush, zebras, giraffes, monkeys, this land condensed almost as it was in neolithic times.

"My nation has a President but the animals are really the boss," Allen said.

This is their land," Corcoran said with a respectful sigh, "They allow us but the privilege to visit them."

We drove deeper across the great savanna finally out into the open plain.

Finally we arrived at our campsite and everyone began to put up their tents, a subject I know very little about. I had disliked the Boy Scouts with a passion and never went camping with my buddies. Suddenly I was confronted with a massive sheet of canvas and a few metal poles. All I could do was stand holding everything and feeling like a silent era movie director was about to film a slapstick scene with me in the middle of the bush.

"Can I help you?" Gabriella asked. Her tent was next to mine and it was obvious her Swiss mountain youth had been quite thorough, for her tent had been the first to go up.

"Once again I must thank you," I said, as she hammered in the stakes and inserted the metal poles.

"We all work together," Gabriella said, pulling on a rope as the tent went up.

When I saw the tent standing it proved to be quite a surprise, about six feet high, complete with flapped windows and even a zippered mosquito net at the front.

"Welcome to my home," I joked, starting to unload the supplies I had brought with me. The "supplies" consisted of my sleeping bag, a small air mat, one large bottled water, a tin of Pepto-Bismol, a plastic bag stuffed with clothes, flashlight, camera, film, binoculars, notepad and pen. I glanced at the list that I had made earlier to make sure my life-line to the civilized world was in proper order.

Gabriella paused for a moment before returning to her own tent and we shared a drink from the bottled water. Everyone had brought similar supplies for none of us really knew what to anticipate out in the bush.

By the time we completed our tasks it was too late to start out on safari. Allen suggested that we get a good night's sleep adding that we would leave around six the following morning.

It was already dark and the guides built a huge bonfire which illuminated our entire camp site. All our tents were arranged in a small circle with one large open tent set off to the side which was to be used for our lengthy dinner table.

We stood around that campfire, hearing the animals that were close to us in the dark bush.

A trumpeting sound came from out of the darkness.

"Isn't it thrilling knowing the animals are just out there," Sophie quietly said.

"Maybe only a few yards away," Yuri said.

"And nothing between us and them," I added.

The group started making small conversation, half out of nervousness, aware that the animals were near in the darkness and we were alone in the bush. We all spoke in hushed whispers as if to not wake any sleeping nearby animals.

"This is an opportunity for each of us to really begin to get to know one another," Hughes said.

We talked of our trip and of our plans but the conversation was just a bit formal, the way it usually is when strangers first meet.

We still had that reserved silence, still held back, hesitating to let ourselves really open up, all part of our Victorian legacy to remain proper. Once the ice is broken, however, watch out for often anything may be heard.

I glanced at the group and thought the fire's light revealed much about all of us.

Walter Corcoran moved next to Flora Zimmer but she quietly walked away.

Yuri held his wife's hand in the darkness, a pleasant smile on his face.

Mrs. Lewis stood quietly alone in the shadows. She was enjoying the conversation but I had the feeling that even as she smiled there was something she wanted to say but was holding back.

Alejandro silently stood alone, off to one side.

Corcoran finally squatted on the ground, his bulky weight looking uncomfortable. He sat quietly studying the stars which were hanging low.

I saw Gabriella's face in the soft orange glow and it was like the fire itself: warm and inviting.

"You think such nonsense," I cautioned myself, "Always the writer's mind at work."

Our group became quiet for a moment listening to the fire's crackle.

Herbert Hughes, whose thick eyebrows gave him a devilish look in the light of the dancing fire, took matters into his own hand, deciding to loosen the conversation by telling a perfectly terrible riddle.

"A man wearing a mask is waiting for someone at home," he said, "Who is he?"

After several minutes of incorrect but humorous answers, no one was able to determine the punch line and we gave up trying.

"The person is a baseball player," Hughes answered with great glee, "and the person waiting at home is the catcher."

We all offered mock groans knowing it was all silly but also a good enough start to bring us together as a group.

The night was remarkable. The moon was incredible, blood red, then yellow, full and closer than I had ever seen the moon before, rising just above our heads, giving us the feeling that we could reach out and touch it.

I stood stunned by it all feeling an immense sense of freedom.

Surrounding us were the sounds of the bush at night. Shrill calls. A sudden and unexpected wail from off in the distance. A growl. We heard trumpeting and snorting coming from somewhere nearby. There was suddenly the whoop of a distant hyena. Sounds that were haunting and beautiful.

For a brief moment I had the feeling that there was something else out there in the darkness watching us, stalking us. I felt eyes staring but quickly shrugged the thought away, attributing it to my writer's imagination.

I immediately pushed my strange thought out of my mind and joined the others sitting around the flickering campfire.

A log crackled and tumbled forward, scattering a few ashes.

Looking at their faces I thought that only a day earlier we had all been busy with our individual lives. Fate had drawn us all together and now we had spent our first day being bounced and jostled back and forth over rugged back roads out in the African bush, all heading towards adventures unknown.

We softly continued talking, sometimes laughing, all of us alone in the darkness. Then Allen walked over, sat down and quietly started to speak.

# ALLEN

"Friendship starts with conversation," Allen said that first evening after we had finished and the campfire had been started.

He explained how he noticed on other such safaris that once everyone got to know each other, felt at ease with one another, the safaris were always far more successful.

"People often like to talk around the campfire and tell about themselves and what brought them to Africa," Allen said, "You know, a way to say hello to everybody. First of all, nothing brought me to Africa. I was born here. Welcome to my country."

Allen had a wide, proud grin and Herbert Hughes applauded.

I overheard Yuri turn to his wife and whisper, "We have such a story to tell," but she quickly shut him off by putting a finger to her lips, nodding "no" and softly saying, "They are not ready for this yet."

"Most nights I'll be spending over with the guides and you folks can entertain yourselves. My only purpose on this safari is to see that each one of you has a wonderful time."

"You know so many animals," Mrs. Lewis said.

"Well, that is my job," Allen answered.

"The people we saw around Nairobi seemed always busy," Hughes added, "Constantly moving."

"Jua Kali, the "hot sun," Allen answered, "Many survive by creating new things from the old. Did you notice a donkey cart we passed when we left Nairobi? That was once an old Pontiac automobile. Old oil drums can become everything from frying pans to lamps. Nothing goes to waste in my country."

I mentioned my odd experience with the group of men I had seen standing in front of the soccer stadium

"Many keep busy but there are always the others. One must be aware to survive in Africa. Smile politely, be pleasant, treat everyone equal and keep on moving. Always keep on moving."

"Sounds just like home," Mrs. Lewis quietly said.

There was silence for a moment and then Allen glanced slowly at all of us.

"Perhaps I should take a moment and tell you my own little story."

Allen was the oldest of nine children and, when in his late teens, his father was killed in an auto accident.

"His body just fell off a crowded truck going to work and he lay in a field for a long time, "Allen said, "and then he was just gone without even a moment to say farewell or tell him the things I would have wanted to say."

Allen paused, wondering if he should continue.

"It hurt my mother and she became withdrawn. Quiet. Seldom spoke. She grew frail. Kind of dried up. Then, a couple of year's later," Allen paused, his voice became softer,"she had become so lonely and tiny and one day she just died in my arms."

Allen again stopped, suddenly aware that he had become far too serious. Then he smiled.

"It was a sad time but it became good. I was now the poppa of all those little children."

"Pass the ball," Mali, Allen's young wife, called, "I'm free. Over here."

The small boy heard his mother and tossed the ball in her directions.

Only Peter, at seven their oldest child, reached out and blocked the ball.

Allen smiled as he recalled how his entire family would play the game. Peter and Allen teamed against Mali and Hanitra, their daughter. Roger, their five year old, played on both teams.

Mali would get the ball and dribble slowly down the small, cluttered court.

"Watch her," Allen would call to Peter, "She is a tricky player."

Mali shot and the ball hit the rim, circled about, then bounced off.

"Mama," Roger called, "You missed."

Allen and Mali loved those moments in the early evening, after dinner, the good times with all the family, when Allen was home from his long safari trips.

Allen picked Roger up and carried him on his shoulders and the other children followed, clapping their hands.

"My hero," Mali called to them.

The family called themselves the Simbas all looked forward to playing each day after school. Allen had made a small basketball court near the tiny compound where they lived on the outskirts of Nairobi and it became a kind of community center for all the local children. He taught the youngsters how to shoot and dribble the ball, always shouting encouragement to them.

He recalled the echoing sound of the basketball as it bounced around the tiny courtyard already getting dark with the late afternoon shadows.

"I would move to the right then quickly, like a good dancer, spin my body left, turn it around and shoot towards the basket," he explained with a huge grin.

The basket was part of a rusted barrel-holder attached to the trunk of a tree.

"Missed a lot of good shots because of branches from that old tree. So much for me and the Harlem Globetrotters," Allen joked, "I wanted to be the first to start the K.B.A.," he quietly said.

"And what does that mean?" Mrs. Lewis asked.

"The Kenya Basketball Association," and Allen laughed at his own small joke. His laughter was contagious and made all of us laugh.

"I wanted to be a school teacher," he said as the smile left his face, "but with no folks, I didn't have time to waste. Got up way before the sun, walked five miles into Nairobi and worked as a porter at the Hilton Hotel. That's how I came to know all your strange customs."

He laughed again at his own joke, nodded his head, then continued.

"What I found was that I liked people. No. Loved people. I like to study them and learn from them," he continued, "and everyday in front of the hotel I would see all those safari people hawking their trips. That was when I got the idea to become a guide."

"You simply joined a safari group?" Yuri asked.

"Oh, no, it should be as easy," Allen answered, "In Kenya we have Utali College. Most difficult to get in."

He glanced at Gabriella and smiled.

"Your Swiss government helped to start the college shortly after our independence," he said, "We knew tourism was important and our government and the Swiss worked together on the college."

Allen explained that the college offered a varied program including hotel and restaurant management, food production, housekeeping and laundry, everything that is essential to the hotel industry.

"Only here there was much more, things you find nowhere else," Allen added, "we have a course in the "Social Aspects of Tourism" and we have to know English as well as our choice of French or German. Best course is learning about all the animals. They take you out in the bush and you just learn. Like basic training."

"You must have received straight A's," Margaret Hughes said.

Allen grinned.

"I was like the American Abraham Lincoln," he answered, "I walked those five miles to the hotel, then another three to the college after work and then eight to get home. Only I didn't have to walk through snow like he did. The only bad thing was that I was too tired at night to play anymore basketball."

Allen paused for a moment and looked around our group.

"It all works out," he added, "We are all like brothers and sisters here and everyone is happy in what they do."

Allen talked about Mali who worked in the travel office. He took out an old wallet held together by a rubber band and proudly showed us her photo hugging three children. She was smiling warmly at the children.

"See that locket on the little girl. I got that for her birthday," Allen said proudly.

"My wife, her name is Mali, not Molly," he shyly said, "and those are my three kids. Our kids. Mali is an accountant with the travel office. Someday we hope to have our own little travel business. We dream about that. Then I'll have plenty of time to play basketball."

Throughout the safari I would notice Allen spending his free time writing to Mali and his children as well as to all his brothers and sisters.

"Just want to keep that family all together," he quietly said, "There are too many distractions, is that the proper word, in today's world."

Allen was a quiet kind of man who usually kept to himself yet was always there when needed during the safari. If anyone had any questions, he was quick to assist and was eager to point out everything about his country.

"Best to get some good rest," Allen said, "Tomorrow we start to explore Amboseli."

When he finished talking, Allen nodded to everyone and then walked over to his tent, several feet away, and joined the other guides.

I watched Allen for a moment as he walked away and something caught my eye. It appeared the other guides had all been waiting for him and they quickly began what appeared to be a very serious conversation, pointing their hands, nodding their heads. Something was bothering them.

They were speaking Swahili but I thought heard the word "poacher" and "Amboseli" but I wasn't sure.

Even Allen seemed a bit jumpy and I wanted to ask him what the problem was wondering if he might be keeping something from us. I decided it was none of my business and I simply walked back to my own tent feeling a bit like an intruder. I felt uneasy thinking there was some sort of an undercurrent, something I couldn't quite understand, as though everything wasn't quite right.

Walking back to my tent I also noticed that there was a soft scent in the African night, like perfume. A cold moon floated above.

As I neared my tent, I stared up at the stars and felt stunned by the sheer beauty of it all. Everything that night felt warm and wonderful. The tranquility put me at ease and I quickly forgot my concern about Allen.

# SAFARI
# DAY TWO

Today the sun broke early, clean and sharp, no mist as in that first morning.

The campsite was already active, everyone ready for their first day out in the bush.

Alejandro, still would not talk to anyone although he always had an agreeable smile. He was already off alone, standing quietly several yards from the tents, whistling at the birds. Alajandro had a damn fine whistle and it seemed that the birds were actually trying to whistle back.

Gabriella came out of her tent and I noticed she had a Swiss army knife tucked in her belt.

"We match," I greeted her, showing my own Swiss army knife and hoping it might prove an opportunity to make up for my misunderstanding about her German-Swiss accent the other day.

Hughes noticed this and suddenly produced his knife and it was all quite humorous.

Hughes' knife was tiny, really just a handsome keychain; my knife was medium sized with all the parts carefully hidden away but then Gabriella showed her knife, a real Swiss Army knife, and we all laughed. It was over a half inch thick and had everything in it from a magnifying glass to a Phillips screw-driver.

"Be prepared," she said, "Isn't that what your Boy Scouts always say?"

"What's a nice girl like you doing with a knife like this?"

"I'm in the Swiss Army," she explained matter of factly.

That was also the reason she was able to put her tent up so quickly, I thought to myself.

"You folks train for peace," Hughes said, "We train for war. The Swiss Army has always intrigued me, especially for a neutral country."

"We may be neutral but politically every Swiss thinks for themselves," Gabriella answered,"The Army means independence from foreign agression but it is mostly important for our internal security strategy."

"I believe it all started with the Congress of Vienna in eighteen-fifteen," Hughes said.

Corcoran arched is eyebrows but said nothing.

Hughes and his notepad. I figured he must have a note for everything.

"Such a small country. Don't you ever feel trapped?" Sophie asked.

"One is only trapped in the graveyard," Gabriella said, turning away for a moment, not wanting to talk about herself.

"When do you get out of the army?" Mrs. Lewis asked.

"At thirty-two we call it the marching out age," Gabriella answered, softly adding, "but as you can see, one can volunteer longer if they wish."

Margaret nodded her head and smiled in understanding.

"That's how I got here to Africa," Gabriella continued, "I volunteered for a special job. I was in what equals the American Signal Corps, if you can believe that, and I offered to come here to help open a new telecommunication center at Gilgil. Most advanced, with very sophisticated components all designed to help the country's huge digital rural phone network."

Gilgil was a small town about fifty miles from Nairobi and that explained how Gabriella knew much about the Masai that first day when she helped me take that picture.

"We do much work in third world countries," Gabriella added, "and the new center was most important, even helping some of the neighboring countries. Besides the assignment gave me three weeks leave which is how I have been able to join you wonderful people."

"And that is our pleasure," Yuri grinned, making a polite bow.

Allen started the van and our small group of adventurers eagerly took off anticipating the day ahead.

Walter Corcoran walked to the back, glanced up and down, and then, with a small, wicked grin, stuck out his fingers and wrote "Follow me" on the back of the now dust caked van.

No one noticed for the dust and the thick red mud that clung to the wheels and under the van told everything.

"We can anticipate some tough driving," Hughes, always the leader, explained. He held a small piece of paper and fanned himself in the heat.

"We have to hunt for the animals and go off where they live."Allen said, "Often the trails you see just disappear and I drive by instinct, like a pilot flying blind."

Allen wasn't joking as he drove with both hands clutching the wheel, taking us over roads that were really not much more then trails filled with chuckholes, debris, fallen trees, water hazards. We encountered every imaginable obstacle as our small van bumped its way forward.

Sophie let out a soft sigh, tightly clutching the side of her seat steadying herself as the van bounced over the ever deepening rut holes.

The van was crowded with all our gear on the floor. I noticed Mrs. Lewis quietly rubbing her leg, hoping that no one would notice. Corcoran said quietly constantly wiping the perspiration from his glasses.

The land changed constantly. One moment we drove past low flat areas then, within a second, we would see bush standing as high as the van's windows. The earth was dry and parched in some areas while within a mile or two it would become wet, bubbling with underground wells.

"Look there, quick," Allen said, pointing outside the window.

A cheetah, slinking through the underbrush, must have been within a yard or two of my arm. I gasped, quickly pulling my arm inside the van while watching this proud animal as it soundlessly moved ahead, its stalking head bent close to the ground.

"This is the real thing, isn't it?" Margaret Hughes said half-aloud, wiping small beads of perspiration from her face, "We really are in Africa, aren't we?"

Yes, we really were in Africa. Within moments our van passed wildbeest busy grazing in the bush, not even looking up, totally ignoring us; gazelles, long and slender and handsome, delicate horns and thin legs, waltzing gracefully past us. We spotted hippopotamus, just able to see their brown tops, like stepping stones, as they lay snuggled in a muddy water hole. We heard the gruff of a nearby lion.

"Monkey at two o'clock," an excited Walter Corcoran shouted, pointing his hand towards the bush as if he were a pilot in a bad World War II film.

As we neared them, Several of the animals ran in seemingly crazed circles, unsure which direction they should head. I thought they acted strange.

"Are they frightened of us?" I asked Allen, sensing some sort of undercurrent in the air.

"No, Pappa, all is normal," he quickly responded.

I felt Allen answered just a bit too quickly but said nothing. Only I remembered my Grandmother telling me how early one morning she went outside to get some bottled milk that had been left at her front door. She had noticed all the dogs and cats in the nearby acting crazy, running all about, making odd sounds. Thirty minutes later San Francisco's 1906 earthquake happened.

"The bush looks stark," Yuri said, "Is it healthy for the animals?"

"Don't judge the land by how it looks," Allen answered, "Look at the animals. If they are healthy then the land is good."

We drove for several hours passing huge herds of zebras. Allen was always quick to point out the animals which frequently blended in with the bush camouflaged by nature.

"Very rare, very rare," Allen suddenly called, excitement in his voice.

Just ahead a hyena, stalking close to the ground, was carrying a baby in its teeth.

"Moving to a new nest," Allen reported as he rolled the van to a spot that appeared to be only a hole in the ground, "that's where the hyena just came from."

An excited troop of baboons made a sound as if mocking the hyena while off to the side a herd of zebras galloped past our van.

Not far off buffalos moved slowly in huge herds, making their way across an open plateau.

None of us spoke. We were all absorbed by the graceful beauty of the animals and our being alone with them, as we bounced our way across the open savanna in our small van.

We returned to our compound for lunch and time to relax before the afternoon's journey back into the bush.

As we sat around the table in quiet conversation I suddenly noticed Gabriella look behind me. She had become rigid and her mouth started to tighten. The light bulbs that Yuri had for eyes suddenly flashed wide open and his nostrils flared. The others had stopped talking and were looking behind me, all with startled glances.

I turned to see a Masai warrior walking alone into our campsite.

He was tall, wore the traditional red robes and carried a spear which he promptly threw into the ground much as he might have thrust it into an attacking lion.

The Masai slowly made his way towards us. Actually he came directly to me and I quickly wondered what Doctor Livingstone would have done in a similar situation. I noticed his face was lined with tribal body scars.

I long ago learned that all men, no matter where they live or what their heritage or understanding might be, all are really the same and that a pleasant smile can open any door.

I smiled.

"Jambo," I said and extended my hand to shake his as if I had just encountered a long lost friend.

"Jambo," he answered back, "Ashari."

"Ashari was the Swahili word for friend only his eyes never left my wristwatch.

"Tick tick," he said, pointing to the watch and to a small sword he was carrying.

"Nice watch," I answered trying to communicate through a combination of sign language and broken English.

"Tick tick" he continued, touching the watch, making gestures to let me know he wanted to trade his sword for the watch.

I glanced at the others on the safari, still seated around the lunch table, all with looks of grave concern as if they had suddenly been surrounded by a group of Apaches on the warpath.

"These are my friends," I said realizing he probably didn't understand the words but knew what I meant when he saw their smiling faces. I took him around the table where everyone stood, in awed silence, much as they might have been if royalty had suddenly visited us.

"Jambo," he said, shaking everyone's hand.

"Jambo," they all answered.

He paused for a moment to look at the scars that rolled up my chest, across my stomach, down my leg.

The Masai looked at each stitch with great admiration and called over to Allen asking if they were a form of tribal identification.

Then he returned to my watch. I saw his sword and the spear sticking out of the ground and thought it was now time for me to talk to Allen who had remained a distance away.

"Look, is it OK to trade him a tee-shirt for his sword?"

"Sure, try," Allen answered.

Which is how one of the great legends of our small safari was started. I went to my tent and dug out a San Francisco Forty-Niners football tee-shirt and took it over to the Masai.

It was my turn to talk trade. I pointed to his sword, being careful not to use the hand with the wristwatch he wanted, while simultaneously holding up the shirt in front of me. The Masai looked at the bright colors and scripted writing and nodded his head showing he understood. The trade was made, much to the delight of the others on the safari.

"Neat bit of slight of hand," Hughes whispered.

Alejandro applauded and whistled his delight.

The Masai walked over to Allen and put the shirt on over his red robes. It was only then that I really felt bad, seeing him in the Forty-Niners shirt which looked tacky compared to his proud red robes.

"Score another crummy credit for modern culture," I said to Gabriella and she nodded in agreement.

It was better a few moments later when he took off the shirt, nodded to our group, picked up his spear and walked silently back into the bush.

"He was probably what they called "Moran," Yuri said, "meaning a junior warrior. They have a period of circumcision about once every seven years when they first learn their social responsibilities."

"Kind of like a bar-mitzvah," I answered.

"He was more like twenty-two," Gabriella said, "handsome kid."

"He was what they call "Evnoto," Allen corrected, "he is young but already considered almost a tribal elder."

"Well, no matter what, I had my trusty Swiss knife at the ready," Hughes said, "Just in case."

"And what exactly would that have accomplished?" Corky answered.

"Can't let our guard down," Hughes continued, "Especially out here. Danger lurks all about."

"Lurks?" Isn't that a bit dramatic, "Yuri said.

"Hughes means we should all be street wise," I said, "Like back in Nairobi."

"Only there are no streets out here," Margaret Hughes said, "And danger is all around. The animals know that better then we do."

When the Masai left, Flora went to her tent to wash some clothes; Sophie busied herself writing a letter and Yuri sprawled inside his tent, quickly snoring deeply.

"He sounds like the mating call one of the animals," Margaret whispered.

Allen called me over with a sly smile lining his face.

"You barter good, Pappa," he said, "you're a kind of easy going person."

"I'm interested in everything," I answered.

"Then remember to use your mosquito net at night," he grinned, "It will protect you from the Ratel."

"Ratel?" I wondered outloud, "Is that a mosquito?"

Allen laughed as if he had told a special joke.

"A ratel is a small, tiny little, animal," and he became quite serious, "who likes to climb into the tent at night, crawl into the warmth of sleeping bags and feast on male private parts."

70

"Should I warn Hughes and Yuri?" I asked.

Allen looked at me and grinned.

"I'm just kidding," he proudly grinned, testing me and knowing I had passed another small exam, "Well, sort of kidding. It's just a rumor. Never been really proved."

At that moment I knew Allen and I would get along fine, both sharing the same sense of humor.

Finally it became time to begin our afternoon journey. The safari was planned with one trip early in the morning that lasted for about three hours, back to the compound for lunch and rest and then a second three hour ride late in the afternoon.

"The sun isn't as hot," Allen carefully explained, "and it is those times that are best to see the animals, when they are near the waterholes or out eating."

I learned early the benefits of my Australian outback hat which I wore constantly as my only fashion statement during the entire trip. It was ideal to ward off the sun, could hold water when necessary and was quickly resilient when crushed, as frequently happened during the excitement of the moment. Pith helmets are for Tarzan movies or for photos to send home to the relatives.

"...Over hill, over dale,

as we hit those dusty trails..."

We sang in dreadful voices which must have echoed through the silent valley as our van bounced its way through the bush.

"Merrily we roll along,

roll along..."

We would track for hours, bouncing in our van, caked with dust, criss-crossing our way through Amboseli. It's an area that is filled with springs and swamps, runoffs from Mt. Kilimanjaro and the nearby hills, all of which attracts animals for miles around.

At one point Allen slowed the van and we were immediately surrounded by chattering monkeys, like ham-actors, coming to stand in front of our van, showing off, acting silly, seemingly clapping their hands at us. One daredevil suddenly leaped up and swung over the top of the van chattering away, laughing at the funny tourist.

"Oh, my. Oh, my," Flora Zimmer said, holding her floppy hat.

"Careful my dear," Walter Corcoran said.

"I can take care of myself," Flora snapped back.

The monkeys crinkled their faces at us as if we were the ones in a zoo, herded inside the van, not allowed to go out while the animals had the right to roam at their will. It was an ironic twist and one that made us all smile.

"Zebras at three o'clock," Corcoran shouted again, making a donkey-like sound.

"Don't do that. You'll startle the animals," Mrs. Lewis snapped, "We are like guests in their house."

Corcoran said nothing. He had never been to Africa before yet it was strange how well he knew the terrain and the topography. He kept himself busy, even with the van's constant jostling, by constantly writing notes and drawing diagrams.

After about an hour Allen stopped the van and let us walk towards a small hill that at one time served as some sort of outpost. It offered a sweeping view of all Amboseli and one could look for miles at the eternal space and grandeur that is Kenya.

Hughes walked ahead, as if to safely mark the trail, always the brave scout.

Walter Corcoran was walking next to Flora Zimmer.

"You can call me Corky," he was saying.

"I'll call you Mr. Corcoran," Flora quickly answered.

"And you shall be Miss Zimmer."


"HELP, HELP," it was Mrs. Lewis, screaming in desperation, from the other side of the small slope.

We rushed over to find horror.

She was shaking, tears surging down her face as she pointed to a clump of brush.

A gazelle had been caught in a wire snare and had broken loose. Only its left leg remained stuck in the trap and the jagged wire had cut deep into the leg, tearing it all the way to the bone. The crippled animal had tossed hopelessly around on the ground, each time it moved the coiled wire cut deeper into its leg. It had been left to die like that. Vultures plucked its eyeball as it lay trapped, unable to escape.

All that remained of the gazelle were twisted ribs sticking through its thin sides. Much of its carcass had already been devoured by other scavengers. The air was filled with the smell of rotting flesh.

"The law of the jungle?" I asked with horror, feeling as if my stomach was about to explode.

"No, of man," Allen was shaking with anger," This is the work of poachers."

"They left this animal to die such an agonizing, slow death?" Hughes said.

"They also left it for other animals to destroy, "Allen snapped.

"I thought it was just the elephants that the poachers attacked," Sophie said.

"They attack anything," Allen answered, "They even take lions claws thinking it is a good luck charm. Over a thousand rhinos die each year just to make decorative daggers for men in the Arab countries."

Mrs. Lewis put her hands to her mouth and for a moment I thought she might vomit.

"The poachers, the bastards, put wire snares near the waterholes," Allen continued, "and this one must have been caught and managed to break loose."

"I thought your government is trying to crack down," Hughes said.

"Yes, yes, but there is much ground and few men," Allen bitterly answered, visibly shaken, "The police asked me to keep my eyes open on this trip. They had a rumor. But everyone said the poachers were not around where we are going. What good does keeping your eyes open when men like this sneak in by way of darkness?"

That was the reason Allen and the guides appeared agitated on the first night, I thought to myself.

"My own people betray me in front of visitors to my country," Allen continued.

"If they hear rumors, can't they be stopped?" Mrs. Lewis asked.

Allen looked up and quietly added, "The primary concern for many people here, unfortunately, is for their own food and shelter. Hungry people must take care of their own bodies first."

He became silent and started to walk away. Then he stopped.

"Look here,"Allen pointed towards a clump of grass where butchered meat lay drying in the sun.

"They must have been here within a few days," Allen said, "Besides the tusks, they butcher and dry the meat for their own use. Pick some remote location like this, usually far from roads. Then they have runners sneak what they steal out of the park. I'll radio the game wardens."

"See if they think its safe for us to be out here," Mrs. Lewis asked.

"And tell them their damn rumor was quite accurate," Hughes said.

Yuri kept looking toward the bush with his binoculars, searching for the unknown. Gabriella rubbed her fingers along the side of her knife. Everyone was jittery and became tense at any movement.

Allen looked at me, said nothing, but he spoke volumes with his eyes.

Perhaps it was because we were both alone on the safari but Allen and I had already developed a special kind of understanding.

His glance at me said much and it sent shock waves through my entire body.

Allen was sending me only one message: The poachers were far closer to us then he had ever anticipated.

The trip back was one of only silence and that night, around the campfire, there were no jokes.

Africa, with all its vibrant life, its blazing light and deep colors, is always set against the darkness of tragedy that is constantly waiting out in the open bush.

"The animals struggle for life and fight to survive," Allen half whispered, "This can sometimes be a violent land."

"Life is full of such struggles and contradictions," Hughes added.

"The damn animals are dying," Corcoran said, "And you talk of struggles and contradictions. A wonderful time to pontificate."

Hughes looked sharply at Corcoran but said nothing.

"It's mans inhumanity to man,"Yuri added, "And to beast."

"Sometimes man is full of shit," Corcoran answered, then, looking shyly at Flora quickly added, "Pardon me."

"Even with the horror there will always be beauty out here," Yuri, the eternal optimist, said,"Natural beauty. Just waiting for an artist to capture it."

"If we don't get captured first," Corcoran whispered.

"There isn't much beauty to be found on this day," Mrs. Lewis added.

"Maybe beauty is the key. Artists have always managed to change the world," Yuri answered, "Look how they have managed to change all the world's culture. The Greek, the Roman, the Elizabethan period. Such great things were accomplished."

"If it hasn't all been destroyed first," Gabriella said, thinking of the poachers.

Even the red glow of the setting sun seemed to cry out with pain and the clouds that moved slowly overhead appeared as if they were bleeding.

Our campfire became hushed again and no one spoke.

Then Hughes stood up, he was the man I would soon call Houdini, he looked at us, with that campfire light flickering, and quietly spoke of why he and his wife were in Africa, on their odd and unusual quest for world peace.

# HOUDINI

His was a dream for world peace, one that he hoped to forge into a reality, started by one man with simple, decent desires, communicating those thoughts to still another, hoping a chain would form linking each person, one telling another, then still another and all of this done by slight of hand.

We sat soundlessly around the fire that night. Hughes and his wife, Margaret, both with traces of grey hair and pleasant smiles, sat in the semi-circle, their eyes twinkling at one another as any couple deeply in love, even after, as they explained, thirty-seven years.

Hughes was tall and dignified appearing and exactly what one would expect of a member of the Board of Regents of the University of Michigan. He also served on the Board of several major corporations, was a hard-hitting attorney yet always remained soft-spoken, even when frequently called to debate the merits of various national issues. Twice he pleaded cases before the Supreme Court. With all that background, Hughes was most proud of but one thing: He was a damn fine magician.

Hughes hadn't always been such a leader. At twelve he was a quiet, shy blond-haired youngster who seldom spoke, always wanting to remain far behind the others, seeking to stay in the shadows.

One Christmas, under the family tree waited a box wrapped in gold foil which would change his life forever. It was a small magic set complete with wand, playing cards and magic sponge balls.

In the loneliness of his room, Hughes quickly learned how to make three red sponge balls disappear into a plastic cup. He repeated the small trick over and over for endless hours until he had it perfected.

When he showed his parents they marveled at his magical skill and ability and had him perform his small routine at the next family gathering.

With that encouragement, Hughes started showing his trick to the other children at school. One day his teacher noticed what he was doing and asked if Hughes would entertain at the next school assembly.

Hughes was frightened that day, could hardly talk, was even afraid that he might wet himself, but he forced himself to walk onto the stage, mustered all his courage and stood alone before the entire student-body with his magic red balls and those little plastic cups.

When he finished the trick all the children applauded and Hughes stood alone for a long time on that empty stage listening to that sound and loving every second of it.

Hughes entertained us as he told his story with a series of slight-of- hand tricks using small bits of rope, cards and some coins.

Margaret watched his illusions around the campfire with new delight, as though witnessing the trick for the first time. Her background proved as interesting as Houdini's. Margaret was a history professor at Michigan, had served as director of the Red Cross in her area but the highlight of her career, if one could read a smile and a special eye twinkle, was the time she served as a Pop Warner football coach.

"You can bet we had plenty of trick plays," she said, glancing at her husband,"but we missed the championship because of a field goal that went wide to the left in the last moments."

I felt there was more to Margaret. I could see it in the way she looked at Hughes, encouraged him as his parents had once done. She was the one who gave him his ambition and his strength.

Hughes stood tall and had a proud smile as he related another of his many stories, this one about Creighton B. Monroe whom TIME magazine called "the most feared leader of corporate take-overs in America."

"I cautiously stuck his well groomed head right into a small guillotine," Hughes grinned.

Monroe was annoyed at this seeming indignity but the judge had said it would be admissible if it proved a point.

"It was during a complicated corporate merger trial," Hughes explained with obvious delight, "The defense claimed thousands would be forced out of their jobs and Monroe clearly recognized just the opposite would happen and that additional thousands more would find employment."

Hughes had brought a guillotine which he used as part of his magic act to the trial.

"The defense attorney screamed and fussed all about," Hughes smiled, recalling this moment, "and Old Judge Bremmer kept warning me to get quickly to the point and to keep the theatrics down."

Hughes explained how he had Monroe stick his head into a small guillotine that was placed on a table in the courtroom.

"First I put a carrot in and the blade cleanly chopped it off," Hughes added, "and then when I asked Monroe to place his head in I thought the man would faint."

"You didn't chop his head off," Sophie asked, "But what happened?"

"Nothing. The blade went right past his head and every single strand of hair was left all in one piece," Hughes answered, "And I won my case. Proved my point that statistics can lie and things aren't always what they may seem."

"Forever the eternal magician, lawyer, professor," Margaret Hughes joked. "They're going to run out of wood for your office shingle."

"Always look for that one kernel of truth," Hughes answered, "I learned that from the campus community. Find that truth and you'll stay right on the proper course."

With all his trial and corporate commitments, Hughes explained how he liked the campus life best.

"I ride my bicycle around about the campus," he said, "Filling my lungs with fresh air and enjoying the exchange with all those young intelligent minds."

He loved the atmosphere of the peaceful campus, its tree-lined streets and everything in its precise order and proper place.

"I especially like the young folks," he repeated, "Always offering some kind of challenge, the give and take, everyone ready to debate, quick to respond."

Hughes enjoyed the campus life but he also knew, as the professor, he held the ultimate hand for he could never lose any discussion. No matter how skilled the youthful questioners might prove, no matter how argumentative students might become, no matter what knowledge a young scholar might thrust at him, no matter how precise or clearly defined any debate would become, Hughes was the professor and thus always held the ultimate, final word.

That was a position he relished. Like a judge who could raise his hand, pound his gavel and give out the final words of authority, knowing that those standing meek and quiet before him could only listen and never answer.

I had started calling Herbert Hughes "Houdini" during the safari as he frequently helped pass the time by entertaining us with various and delightful bits of slight-of-hand. We all carefully watched his every move but he was a master of deception.

I would sit in the quiet of the campfire and quietly applaud our attorney who, on this night, actually helped calm everyone after the incident of the poachers.

Houdini loved it, his eyes were alive, filled with a child's imagination and they glowed with a special delight as he enjoyed captivating even our small group of travelers.

"I've used magic from courts to the board room," he told us. "It's such a wonderful way to boldly illustrate that things are not what they may always appear at first glance. Won some heavy bargaining sessions with a simple flick of the wrist and finger."

As he spoke he cut a piece of rope in half and, within seconds, had already restored it to full length.

Corcoran nodded his head in approval and Flora Zimmer grinned to herself.

Alejandro, the one who never spoke, proved magic was universal by the grin on his face as he watched the slight of hand. He let out a soft whistle in admiration.

Houdini had written several books ranging from the law to magic but his most monumental undertaking was his quest for world peace.

"Only I want to see world peace through the eyes of children," he quietly explained. "Margaret and I have traveled everywhere from the South Pacific to Russia and it is the children who are always the same."

Magic was something for everyone and Houdini explained that no matter where he might be, he would always pick one child out of the crowd who would understand enough to tell the others.

"They seldom knew any English but all understood what they were seeing," he continued, "and their eyes would shine and their faces grin and then they would start to tell other children what they had just seen happen. If we can communicate through magic, there is no reason why we can't communicate in other ways."

"Everyone is the same," Margaret Hughes added, "The children. Parents. Grandparents. On a person to person basis, this is one damn fine planet."

I glanced at Yuri who was sitting and nodding his head in agreement.

Mrs. Lewis, who was rubbing her lame foot, smiled. It was as if she was always holding something back.

"Why not show them?" Margaret grinned at her husband and he nodded his head.

Hughes started to move his hands about, his fingers, long and slim like that of a fine pianist, moved rapidly opening and closing and before he finished he produced an orange. Remarkable. Here, in the bush, in this remote area, by the fire's glow, there was suddenly an orange.

Gabriella grinned and Alejandro burst into applause and I rose, went over and shook Hughes hand.

He smiled but it seemed set and well practiced, like that of a used-car salesman. I thought it was probably the same smile he used to charm the jury in a court room.

"There will come a day," he said, looking at us in a suddenly dramatic voice, the way I imagined Clarance Darrow might have sounded, "When all the world's children and all the world's doubters will draw together, blend as one, and create a magnificent new world for everyone."

"Sounds like he's doing some old fashioned preaching," I whispered to Corcoran.

"Only to himself," Corky answered, "He is full of the old muck, isn't he?"

I glanced at Corky and smiled.

The people on the safari amazed me as I realized they wouldn't have brought themselves to this remote place if they didn't all share a sense of adventure.

That night, in the loneliness of my tent, I thought of Houdini and I prayed to myself that maybe, despite his blustering attitude, just maybe, Hughes might really have the right idea for world peace.

It was hard to sleep thinking of Houdini, listening to the lonely sounds of the bush outside my tent and knowing that tomorrow we would be visiting the elephants, the most majestic of all animals.

# SAFARI
# TIME OF THE ELEPHANTS

"Elephant at two o'clock," the usual blase Corcoran could not contain his excitement.

When we looked to where he was pointing we all simultaneously gasped our astonishment.

It was breathtaking.

"Tembo,"Allen said, pointing in several directions at once, "The elephants!"

We were surrounded by vast herds, walking their endless domain with quiet, elegant dignity. The last of the earth's true nobility. The most magnificent of all God's creations, majestic in their every movement, slowly roaming the open bush in their own proud groups.

Allen stopped our small van in the middle of the herd. We sat quietly watching, listening, enchanted and feeling like intruders in another land.

The elephants would coil and uncoil their trunks, their big ears flopping open and close and we heard the snap of branches being broken as they moved their brown-grey bodies through the open bush.

"One of the world's greatest living wonders," Corcoran said with quiet admiration.

We sat in hushed awe at this spectacular sight as the elephants slowly lumbered their way around us.

The baby elephants, closely nestled together, cuddled near their mother, trying to keep pace with the entire herd. They would pause against the trees to rub their backs or find water holes for bathing. The youngsters spent their time splashing each other, wallowing in the mud, raising their tiny trunks to spout water.

Mrs. Lewis pointed to the side, put her finger over her lips and smiled.

Two elephants were rolling in the mud of a small water hole, flapping their ears in play.

"Only a mother could love that," Margaret Hughes grinned, busy taking pictures.

"They use their trunks for food, drinking, washing, smelling, to signal each other," Allen said, pausing and adding, "Even caressing."

They paraded before us, coming within a few feet of our van, flapping their large ears in greeting, proudly trumpeting their powerful sounds, their ivory tusks standing out to guide their way through the bush.

Kilamanjaro served as the perfect backdrop for all of this, towering high above the flat and open plain, far off in the distance, its snow-covered top lost in the surrounding clouds that ringed the mountain's peak.

"The white mountain," Hughes said in awe.

For a split second I looked up at Kilamanjaro and thought of sprinting the four miles to its top and, once there, high in the clouds, spreading my arms wide apart, tossing my head back and shouting for all the God's to hear, "Lauren. Lauren. FUCK YOU."

It would be a way to expunge her once and for all from my conscious.

Only instead of doing that, I quietly turned to Allen and said, "Look at the size of those tusks."

"They use those tusks like toothpicks," Allen explained, "To get the bark they want. Each tusk weighs about ninety pounds each."

One elephant brushed against the side of our van. We could hear the snap of the branches under his feet as he moved next to us.

"The elephants are the soul of all Africa," Yuri said.

Look at the trunk," Allen suggested. "when the trunk is up it means the elephant is mad. When it is down, they are only bluffing. Means they are friends."

A moment later two of the elephants paused and entwined their trunks together and then rubbed tusk against tusk to underline what Allen was telling us.

"They are the most gentle of all animals," Allen added, "Very sensitive."

"Tell me, Hughes asked, "Is there really such a thing as the elephant's graveyard.?"

"All nonsense," Allen answered, "Once their skin starts to sag and their teeth go, they begin to move too slowly and then one day they just fall. The bush takes care of its own. Scavengers. Decay. Decomposing. In a week's time there is nothing left. Then the bush grows quickly. The bush, yes, that is there only graveyard."

Corcoran started to say something but changed his mind.

"The herd moves on but what might be considered a graveyard is when they often return and find just a tusk,"Allen added, "They pick it up with their trunk, and smell it. It is an odd ritual for a dead friend."

I noticed Hughes busy making notes and I figured that was the kind of off-beat information he would later enjoy telling at his local Rotary Club weekly meeting back home.

"More elephants at three o'clock," Corcoran said, pointing off to the distance.

Older male elephants could be seen alone, remote from the herd. Allen explained that they were shunted off when they reach puberty to join other males.

"They only return when the female is in heat," Allen added.

Gabriella glanced up, said nothing and quickly looked out the window.

"How do they know that?" Mrs. Zimmer asked.

"They make much noise when they are like that. They scream and bark and snort, roar and growl," Allen grinned and added, "It is like the music of the bush."

"What happens when they want to make love?" Corcoran asked with his dry sense of humor.

Allen hesitated and looked away for a moment, stalling for time.

"It's OK to tell us," Hughes said.

"Just like anyone else. The male has special glands on both sides of is head and they swell up and his cheeks get stained looking. The skin around his private parts gets like a green color. They'll be like that for months."

Yuri held up his binoculars for a closer look.

"And she'll be pregnant for a long while," Allen grinned, "Twenty-two months."

Mrs. Lewis let out a deep sigh and we all smiled.

"The male stays about one half mile away,"Allen continued, "When they fight for the women you can hear the tusks clashing all over the bush."

One elephant must have sensed our nearness and raised its trunk to ward off possible danger. He kept trumpeting and the sound echoed throughout the open space. This was, after all, the elephant's territory and anything else was an intrusion, merely allowed the courtesy to simply pass through. It was like this was another time, another place.

"They are damn smart," Margaret whispered.

"They have good intelligence just like us," Allen said, "They get puberty around twelve, become young adults at twenty, are in their prime at thirty and maybe live till seventy or eighty."

"Sounds like me," I quietly said, knowing there was more truth then humor in my comment.

"It takes as long to teach an elephant as it takes me with my own children," Allen answered, "Only the elephants already stand when they are only five minutes old."

One elephant's trunk curled up and snapped off a top branch, then twisted it low, just off the ground, picking up some small debris.

At dusk, through some unknown signal, the small herds slowly started moving closer together, coming from every direction, surrounding our small van, hundreds of elephants, as far as the eye could see, much like some sort of giant conclave being called to order.

"This happens every evening," Allen said, and although he had witnessed it many times he sat transfixed by this incredible spectacle.

"The gathering of the clan," Corcocan said.

It reminded me of that day at the zoo with Lauren and the contrast bothered me seeing the elephants here freely roaming the bush. I realized I could never again visit another zoo or go to a circus where the elephants are made to wear funny hats and are called cute names like Tinkerbelle and Pennie. The thought of seeing them paraded all about, putting on a show for the paying customers, had now become repugnant to me.

I remembered the huge red ball they were given in the zoo to play with and how they were forced to roam within the strict confines of what was pompously called the Pachyderm House.

If Lauren had seen them now, in their own land, she would have been stunned at the way civilization had raped them of their dignity.

Here in Africa the elephants were majestic. They were powerful, proud and free. We sat back enchanted by this spectacle. It was now nearly dusk as we watched the elephants gather in their own place, feeling at ease with them and with ourselves.

Alejandro first noticed the horror. Though still not talking, he suddenly started to whistle wildly, excitedly jumping up and down, moving his arms, trying to attract our attention to a clump of bush near the side of the van.

A blood stained tusk from an infant elephant, about the size of a small statue, lay half concealed. The tusk had been hacked off with axes and saws and torn from its very roots. In their hurry the Poachers had also hacked off the faces of the elephants, the flesh left dangling where their tusks had once been.

The still damp blood, sticky and smelling oddly sweat, lay all about in great pools and some had squirted high into a nearby tree. Their once magnificent bodies were now swollen and bloated in the heat.

It was easy to see what had happened by the position of the dead elephants who lay close together, almost in one huge clump. They were near where the bush was thickest which was probably how the poachers were able to sneak so close to them.

Margaret pulled back, flinging her arms in front of her face, not wanting to see the horror.

Sophie started to gag and held her hands over her mouth.

A pack of whimpering hyenas were scrounging the elephant's carcass.

Allen leaped out of the van and bent over, putting his finger on a small bit of dung.

"It is still warm," he whispered, "This happened short time ago."

What he really was saying was that the poachers were closer then anyone had thought.

"The legacy of the damned," Corcoran cursed under his breath.

Allen returned to the van and said nothing for a long time.

"My country fights hard to stop this," he finally said with a hoarse whisper, "but they come at dark, when no one is around. Some of the old tribesmen think the night makes them invisible and they have no fear."

It was the second such attack and this one seemed to be getting closer. We all sat in shocked silence, worried, saying nothing.

"How do they get away with this?" Gabriella asked.

"All they need is a few square yards of bush to butcher the animals, far from the road, invisible from the air. But my government is trying. Our soldiers are trained about poachers, to shoot to kill.

"They're not trying hard enough," a shaken Mrs. Lewis said. Her face had turned chalk white and she seemed cold and vulnerable. She was rubbing her bad foot.

"This is an evil coincidence,"Allen sighed, "Twice in two days. This hasn't happened like this before. It must be one renegade group, operating close in this area. They are bandits."

The lines that circled Allen's face revealed how deeply betrayed he felt, especially now when he had been so proudly showing Kenya to our small group of visitors.

"At least the safari just to kill the animals has been stopped, "Allen flashed his anger, "Your own American President, Theodore Roosevelt, he came here once and brought back over five-hundred trophies. Five hundred! And he was proud of that accomplishment."

Allen, feeling he had talked too much, fell into silence, saying nothing else as he drove us in the early darkness back to the camp. You could feel his dejection at the second sighting of the poachers.

We passed a weathered road sign that had long ago been erected with humor. "Elephants have the right of way." Only no one laughed.

Everyone was silent, knowing that the elephant's destruction had already begun. It seemed the deeper we got into the bush, the more tense we all became.

Allen drove but his eyes kept constantly probing the bush for the unknown.

It made me feel that things were coming that no one can prevent, exactly as I felt that dreadful night month's earlier when I first leaned my own lesson about life and death.

Our conversation at dinner that night was hushed and stilted. We were all quite jittery and I noticed Hughes who kept staring out into the dark bush as if he expected to see something.

"Perhaps we should leave," Sophie said.

"Run off in fear?" Corcoran said.

"I know this kind," Yuri added, "They have done their little deed and by now are far off."

"Killing some other poor animals," Mrs. Lewis said, "I read that an elephant is killed in Africa every ten minutes. And for what? Someone's little trinket."

"A poacher gets a few dollars here," Corcoran said, "and then they make maybe a thousand dollars on the back streets of Japan and by the time they ivory is sold it cost the buyer thousands of dollars."

"Unfortunately there is even more to the tragedy. It also disrupts the elephant's breeding pattern, the entire ecosystem," Hughes added, "The old elephants are killed first and then the poachers start on the young."

I wanted to walk away from the sadness and started to stroll to the edge of the camp.

"You can't go any farther," a voice called to me in the darkness.

It was Gabriella. She had also wanted to walk but Allen had set the limits on our first day.

"Only to the edge," he explained. "Don't take a chance walking because you don't know what animals are nearby."

Gabriella and I stood silently at the most distant corner of the campsite, alone from the others, saying little. Far off in the darkness we could hear the elephants roaming about.

The African night, far removed from the city streets and glitter, is dark as a thousand inkwells. We stood alone looking at more stars then I had ever seen before. The air was warm and a soft wind whispered in the bush.

"You can almost touch them," I said, glancing at the stars, "Puts man and animal back on the same level as it was meant to be."

"I saw this once," Gabriella answered, "On a rare, crystal clear night when I was near the top of the Matterhorn."

"They say that for every new star a nova explodes and is destroyed. Like life itself. For every beautiful birth there is one lonely death."

"That is sad. It makes you sound so bitter."

"Today was bitter."

"It's horrible," she became quiet and looked away.

We stood again motionless. The tragedy we had seen earlier still clung to us and was something we could not easily forget.

"They'll fight the poachers," I said, "The world has become aware."

"I know, but to see it is so tragic."

"Funny, we can go to the moon but we can't change man's basic nature. It's the same as it was a million years ago."

We became quiet for a moment looking at the startling African sky.

"What brought you here, to Africa," I asked, trying to change the subject, wanting to add, but not saying, "alone."

"The Swiss army gives us leave and I like to travel," Gabriella answered. Her voice was low and smoky sounding.

"Do you have to serve in the army?" I asked, anxious to hold onto this moment, talking to her, here, under the stars.

I was also aware that I was walking a thin line between the softness of the moment and the hurt of the past.

"We all serve," Gabriella answered, "We take great pride in it. A million people can be mobilized within hours."

We chatted quietly, talking about the nice things we had seen on the safari, the antics of the monkeys, the grace of the zebra.

I felt we both spoke guardedly, wanting the conversation to continue but careful of what we said, keeping everything general, perhaps quietly thinking of far off possibilities.

"The people with us are wonderful," she said and I nodded in agreement.

"I call Herbert Hughes 'Houdini'," answered. "He is very clever. I did some magic as a little kid growing up in San Francisco."

"Was that your hobby?"

"Oh, like any kids. That and stamp collecting. What about you?"

"I had pen pals," she answered, "All over the world."

"I had that myself, some girl in Denmark."

"It brings the world closer," she said, "Not a bad thing."

In the time honored tradition of man and woman, we were really shadow-boxing with one another, like two fighters in the first round, looking for an opening, feinting, jabbing, feeling each other out, only now it was Gabriella and I, politely moving in and out, like those two fighters, learning of our interests, our strengths, even our weaknesses.

There was a slight mist and a sliver of a covered moon which reflected Gabriella's face making her look hauntingly beautiful in the darkness. I wanted to hold her but I held back knowing that was impossible.

"We are such stuff as dreams are made of."

"What?" she asked.

"Nothing, It was something I read somewhere and I just thought of it. It seemed appropriate for the moment."

"We are the stuff that dreams are made of," she repeated, "I like that."

For a split second it seemed that her eyes stayed level with mine, not moving away.

"This is why I came to Africa," I said, looking at the deep black sky, "To be able to just reach out and touch the stars."

Gabriella smiled in agreement.

"It's all coming down to the technical world versus the natural world," I added, "And the technical world seems to be winning."

"I think maybe this is why we all came," Gabriella answered, "To be alone with all this endless space."

"Far from the crowds and the constant noise. Traffic jams. Smog. Long lines. Which country do you think is really more civilized?"

I wanted to kick myself for saying that. Here I was alone in Africa, standing next to a beautiful woman, a moon overhead, starting off on the right track about the stars and what do I jabber about but traffic jams and smog. Some romantic conversation.

I was eager to talk but I suddenly felt as if I no longer even remembered how to make the most simple of conversations with a women.

"What do you Americans say, "Need your space?"

"Exactly. Here we can be ourselves, lost in this timeless land."

"Timeless land," Gabriella repeated. She had become sad, remembering something from her past, "Yet we all should live for our moment in the sunshine."

We paused and looked at each other, both now silent, simply enjoying the endless night that surrounded us. The mist had lifted and the evening had become humid and warm.

"The animals are so lovely, so proud," Gabriella said.

She had given me an opening and I hesitated but only for a quick second.

"We are all some kind of animal," I casually said. "What kind are you? Do you growl or do you purr?"

Gabriella looked at me, frowned but said nothing.

"What jungle are you from?" I persisted. It was one of those dumb things you sometimes say that doesn't come out just right and you immediately feel foolish.

"You talk like a bad movie," she chided me like a school teacher correcting an errant student.

"Yes, old bad movies," I answered, "That is my heritage."

It had been long I had even the most casual conversation like this and I felt awkward, like a high school kid on a first date, groping for the proper words.

Gabriella, also uncomfortable with the way the conversation was going, tried to change the subject.

"Doesn't the sky look as if all the old masters had gotten together to create one last special painting?" Gabriella said, "I see such soft colors, pastels, like Gauguin."

"How about a Reubens landscape," I added, playing the game.

"Yes, and over there, Van Gogh's ear," and Gabriella laughed out loud at her own joke.

For a moment I thought of Roberta and our empty marriage as if it had been created by some mocking artist who had once made something beautiful and then finally had it slashed and ripped to shreds.

"You have become silent," Gabriella said.

"Sorry, I was just thinking about something from before," and then, wanting to say more, I added, "The sky, the heat of Africa, it is like a warm embrace. Africa brings things out. I'm sorry."

Gabriella nodded knowingly. She looked at me with those deep eyes which seemed to call out to me. Then she turned away, once again wanting to say something but holding back.

It was getting late and we decided it was time to get back to the others. The campfire was starting to burn out as we neared the tents and most had already retired for the night.

I shook Gabriella's hand and we both stood looking at each other, our hands seem to cling together for a split second longer then necessary. Neither of us spoke but I knew there was much more we both wanted to say.

I returned to my tent and lay thinking of the elephants, but only the good part, smiling at their antics, applauding their wisdom.

Then I thought of Gabriella and wondered how some people seem to have a special magnetism that radiates all about them. Gabriella was drawing something out of me, something lost for a long time. The ability to share with another.

Once I looked out when I heard a slight sound and saw Allen with a light inside his tent. He seemed concerned about something and was looking over some maps and charts. I had that same strange feeling as on the first night when I noticed all the guides deep in alarmed conversation. Allen was very conscientious and I knew he was worrying about the poachers and the mark they had left on our safari.

It all bothered me but I thought again of Gabriella, then the elephants and finally all the sights we had already seen started dancing through my mind.

A cold moon floated above. I could hear the elephants moving slowly about in the bush, only fifteen yards away from my tent. In the distance I could also hear the birds making their soft, nightly lilting sounds.

"Everyone picks their own way to die," an old friend had once said.

That reminded me of something else I had once heard.

"Life threatening situation."

I'll never forget Dr. McMahon's words that awful day a few months earlier. I remembered he also had the same look of concern that I had just seen on Allen's face.

That had been my introduction to the dance of death.

A cold chill surged through my body as I forced those thoughts out of my mind. Then I stretched deep into my sleeping bag trying desperately to forget.

# NAIROBI POLICE REPORT
# 17 JANUARY

They gathered in the pre-dawn darkness moving silently about like shadowy ghosts of doom.

Osuna looked at his sleeping family in the hut filled with flies. He saw the crippled child wince once in pain even in her sleep and Osuna felt sadness; when he smelled the odor of urine which always hung about the hut he felt only anger.

"Hurry, man," Aduo called. He stood in the darkness with about ten other men waiting for Osuna.

The men carried an odd assortment of weapons: several had axes, one held a sickle over his shoulder; most had fashioned heavy wooden clubs; Another had World War I boltñaction repeating rifle.

One man carried a large coil of steel wire which he had earlier stolen from a telephone work crew in downtown Nairobi.

"It is cold out here," Aduo whispered, "let's get going. Before the dawn, eh?"

Osuna looked at his wife and knew she was awake but, in her anger, was pretending to sleep. He bent over and kissed her forehead. She turned away and Osuna shrugged his shoulder.

One of the men had borrowed an old truck from the farm where he worked. Its sides were dented and only one head light worked but it was enough for what they needed.

The men nodded when they saw Osuna and, except for the driver and Aduo, all climbed onto to the back of the truck, standing soundless in the morning cold.

It took the driver several twists of the starter and much cursing but, finally the old truck's motor made a weak sputtering noise and they were off, driving into the darkness, heading towards Amboseli.

No one spoke. They stood in the darkness letting the morning chill surge through their bones, all thinking of what lay just ahead. They thought of what they would do with the forty dollars they would earn. Women. Drink. Gambling. Osuna thought of his wife and children and the stench of the stale urine that never left his nostrils.

As they reached Amboseli one man poked at Osuna and motioned off in the darkness. An impala had suddenly darted out of the bush, made a wide sweeping graceful arch as it leaped over a fallen Thorn tree.

"Like it has wings," Osuna said, "Just to fly far away. That is truly freedom."

The men smiled in silence. They were almost at their destination.

"Remember, profit or die," Aduo whispered.

Almost at that same time in our campsite, we were sleeping our various sleeps, unaware of what was happening nearby. It was only much later that we were able to piece together what we had been doing at that precise moment.

Yuri was turning in his sleep. He was dreaming of a child lost long ago in a prison camp, a dream he had almost nightly. Sophie knowing what he still suffered, reached out in her sleep to automatically calm him.

Mrs. Lewis was in a deep sleep in her tent. On the other side of the compound, Alejandro slept, snoring, dreaming of the women of Spain.

Corcoran slept well in his tent as did Flora Zimmer who had fallen asleep while reading a detective story.

Gabriella, in her sleep, was recalling an almost mystical Adonis on a motorcycle from long ago and there was much sadness in her troubled dreams.

I rested in the darkness of my tent thinking of Gabriella and considering what had been and what promise the future might hold.

The only thing I knew with any certainty is that one cannot appreciate the future until the past is clearly understood and, for me, that past no longer existed.

Even as we lay secure in our tents, lost in our own dreams, the poachers finally arrived at their destination, one which they had carefully selected for its concealment from both the nearby roads as well as possible sightings from the air.

Elephants were everywhere in this bountiful area. They sleep standing up which makes them an easy target for the poachers.

The poachers first stopped to eat. They had brought two old rusted cooking pots and maize meal for their breakfast. They knew they would soon have enough elephant meat.

Finishing their hasty breakfast, Aduo and his men moved silently in the dark, first reaching a baby elephant that was startled by the sounds and started to cry, its small body shaking with fear, moving back and forth, seeking help.

One poacher, a Wakuria tribesman, had a bow with a poison-tipped arrow, something his tribe had used for years. It was a poison brewed from the bark of the Aeokanthera tree, an art had been handed down from his great-grandfather. The poacher thought with contempt of the great warriors his people had once been and now, for the most part, they were only content as field workers.

The poacher thought all of this as he calmly stalked through the bush, quietly getting close to the elephants, finally shooting his arrow in the darkness. Within seconds, the small elephant sank to its knees. The other poachers grinned at the sight of the elephant falling. The mother elephant, sensing danger, started trumpeting, awakening the others. The entire herd suddenly moved about in circles, their bodies all trembling, trunks held high and shaking with rage.

It took only brief moments to cut off the baby elephant's tiny tusk with a chainsaw, blood spattering in every direction and drenching the poacher using the saw who cursed out loud.

Then he leaned over and cut a strip of skin away from where the poison arrow had entered, knowing the rest of the meat would be fine for eating. The following morning there would be racks of dried meat around the poacher's camp.

"Maybe we might have some meat even to bring home," Osuna whispered.

"Silence," Aduo warned.

Aduo studied the bloodied tusk but wanted more. He was the one who was street wise and knew well the formula for success: more tusks, more money. He looked at the herd, now moving in crazed circles, crying out their shock and fear.

Aduo realized they could have easily shot any one of the elephants with their old rifles but was afraid the noise would roar throughout the soundless bush. He motioned to the poacher with the poisoned arrows and pointed towards another nearby baby elephant.

The poacher nodded and again made his way silently towards the elephant as it stood near its mother. He raised his bow and quickly shot the arrow, skillfully hitting the elephant almost between the eyes.

The small elephant let out one weak sound, then slowly fell to the ground. The arrow hadn't killed but left the elephant wounded and dazed as it rolled on the ground.

The poacher, who was already covered with blood, ran out and started hacking at the ivory tusks. Two other poachers held the elephant down. The hack saw was old and rusted, the blade dulled with time and thus the bloody work took longer than usual.

"Hurry," Aduo call, his eyes darting all about.

This time the poachers were not concerned with food but only getting still more tusks which were quickly cut away even as the elephant shook from side to side in pain.

It was over in a moment. Without its tusks, the baby would follow its mother, cuddle with her, walk with her until, unable to eat, it would finally drop dead of starvation.

The poachers gave no thought of the elephants left to rot as they eagerly sought more victims. With all the elephants now aroused they decided to move elsewhere. Even with the first glint of the morning sun, they were already busy setting up their wire snares to trap other animals which could easily be butchered for their meat. They carefully stalked their game planning to live from whatever might be found.

The poachers finally selected a quiet spot near one of the animal's favorite watering holes and then set about laying their traps.

The loops in the wire could easily catch the animals neck or leg. There would be a frenzied struggle as the animal tried to escape but the harder it would pull, the deeper the wire would cut, sinking ever deeper into the broken flesh. It was a slow, torturous death, the animal's legs would be mangled, leaving a twisted stump.

Some of the poachers would watch in quiet amusement; others would turn away in horror.

The trail they left was one only of blood.

Elephants, crying, would often stand over their dead, trying to rouse them in a desperate attempt to bring them back to life.

The poachers took what they wanted, leaving the rest to rot, letting it disintegrate into food for the maggots and, eventually, leaving only bones left to bleach in the sun.

The tusks which would be smuggled, were hidden away in old rags, beneath bits of brush, to be taken out when it was dark.

"YEEEEEEEEAHHH," and the sudden noise penetrated throughout the entire bush.

Far off animals screamed out at the unexpected cry of death.

"Shit," Osuna said, looking at one of the poachers.

The poacher had been caught in his own wire snare and the sharp coils already cut into the man's leg. Osuna called the others as he bent over trying to help the fallen man who, in his horror, kept screaming and turning over, thus allowing the wire to twist ever deeper into his ripped legs.

"Stay still," Osuna whispered.

"Fuck, man, fuck," the poacher screamed, tears filling his eyes, his body trembling in fear and in pain.

"Stand back," Aduo shouted as he ran over to the victim, "Stand back."

"Help me," the man's leg was already shattered and the smell of blood penetrated throughout the bush.

"We'll help," Aduo said, turning to Osuna and motioning him to head back to the truck.

"Help him," Osuna said.

"There is nothing that can be done for the stupid fool," Aduo answered, "The more he moves, the more he is being torn. You want to get a nice, polite doctor."

"Aggghhhhhhhh," the man screamed again.

"Shut up, Aduo said, his eyes narrowing, "Shut up."

"I can't stand the pain, help."

As he cried out the elephants turned, trumpeting, in a panic, bumping into each other, they started to stampede.

The poacher looked up, his eyes wet with fear, as he saw the herd coming directly toward him. He pulled harder on the wire, not feeling as it cut deeper into his flesh whch starteed to show a piece of bone.

Aduo looked up as the elephants raced towards the poachers.

"Move out," he shouted, leaping over some stones.

The poacher, trapped in the coil, tried to scream again but no sound came as he saw the elephants coming closer, moving directly toward him, his body, now full of his own blood, jerked again as he desperately tried to free himself.

The only sound was that of bone being crunched as the lead elephant's massive foot came stomping down on the poacher.

For a brief moment there was silence as the herd continued its stampede, moving further off into the bush.

No one spoke.

"Get in the truck," Aduo said, "Or else we are all going to be caught."

They drove away in silence, no one looking back at the fallen poacher.

Hyenas were already sniffing the blood of the poacher as they moved closer for this unexpected feast.

95

Soon the only sign of what had happened that entire morning would be the gnawed and broken bones of the poacher who had been left behind.

It appears the greatest and most bitter of all ironies is that the elephants bury their own dead. They also bury the dead bodies of humans they sometimes find out in the bush.

# YURI

The moon, that incredible full moon, slowly rose above us, now changing to blue-silver and casting a soft glow with the flickering camp fire.

We returned late to our compound feeling exhausted from the long day.

Flora and Corky stood off to one side in quiet conversation; Mrs. Lewis went directly to her tent to prepare for tomorrow's trip. Yuri helped the guides begin the nightly campfire.

I looked at our small group and realized one thing the poachers had accomplished. They had brought us closer together.

We were no longer a miscellaneous gathering of strangers but a single unit thinking, acting, even breathing as one, all of us concerned about the other.

As it happens sometimes with a well coached football team or a theatrical ensemble or even a precision marching band, we had become as one. More than mere friends. We were now far removed from the casual strangers who had met around that conference table in Nairobi only two days earlier.

Mrs. Lewis, now relaxed and at ease, placed her bad leg up on the bench, something she would never have done a few days earlier.

Hughes unbuttoned the top buttons of his shirt and Alejandro moved around the table slapping palms, giving us all high fives.

Our polite evening conversations had slowly altered and now, as the campfire's embers flickered into a warm glow, we had become at ease with one another. Slowly we started to open up and began to share stories and private thoughts as old friends often do.

Allen and Houdini had told there stories and now, on this night, it was Yuri's turn. He felt this comradeship as he stood around the campfire. It was only then that the Armenian, at least that is what he proudly called himself, and his wife, started to talk. First he looked at Sophie and she slowly nodded her head.

"I'm Yuri Melkonian," he gently said, "and this is my wife, Sophie. But you already know that. We want to thank you all for your warm and wonderful companionship on this trip."

Everyone smiled and nodded in agreement.

"Ah, the evening campfire," Corky whispered, "Must be time for show and tell."

I realized that sitting out in the bush, in this remote place, already having seen that unexpected horror, all of this produced a unique intimacy with one another, enabling us to tell each other stories and dreams that we otherwise might never have discussed.

"We feel like we have known you already for years," Yuri continued, almost underlining my own thoughts, "and for us that is already quite an adventure."

He offered a pleasant smile as he spoke, one that was both warm and filled with a kind of love, charming in its quiet dignity.

"Sophie here is the smart one in the family," he said.

"I let him do all the talking," she smiled.

"We were high school sweethearts. This is the one who taught me good English. Saved my bacon."

"When he first came here, he use to say "save my crackers." but he is a quick learner."

Their life together had been a free flow, back and forth, chiding each other, helping one another, all the things that true love is built upon.

"But if you want a real camp fire story," he continued, "we have one for you."

"Yuri, they are not interested," his wife said, "Don't be such a pest."

"This is the campfire time and it is the time for conversation," he looked at her with that wonderful smile. "We are getting to know each other quickly enough. Let us continue to break the ice."

With that he opened his wallet and removed a much battered birth certificate, its edges torn with age, and passed it around the campfire for all to see.

And we saw much. Yuri Arthur Melkonian. Born in 1943. Birthplace: Manchuria. Stamped across the center, in large red letters: AN ENEMY OF THE JAPANESE PEOPLE WAS BORN THIS DAY.

Yuri explained he had been born in a Japanese prison camp and had felt pain almost from his first moment on earth. His mother had been swollen with child when Japanese troops marched into their small province just outside of Manchuria.

"My parents had always known some kind of trouble," he said in a soft voice, reflecting back on an earlier time,"They were already refugees from Russia, White Russians they were called, when they first came to China and opened a small print shop. After all their problems the print shop was a success and, as people say today, they made big bucks."

We all sat intent, almost able to visualize the story Yuri was telling us.

"Everything hummed nicely until that day they heard the armored cars driving down the narrow streets, their sirens making a piercing sound that vibrated off the walls of nearby buildings.

"We are now in control," a shrill voice kept repeating on loudspeakers. "There are now new rules, regulations, strict regulations. We are now in control. Everything will now be under the rule of the Japanese occupation forces."

Yuri became quiet for a moment, remembering what his parents had told him, how the Japanese troops marched into the main street, led by a single drummer, another soldier carried the flag of the rising sun. The soldiers were all smiles, some even tossing candy to the children as they passed by. The Chinese and the others stood quietly, their faces swollen with tears.

Yuri's parents knew it had arrived once again, the Armenians tragic history, a history filled with blood and death since time immemorial. Roman legions thundering into their villages; the cruel time of Byzantium rule; the savage of the Tartars; the Turks; each bringing their own misery and death throughout the centuries. Now once again, even far from their own homeland, it was the Japanese.

"Persecution, torture, humiliation, that is our cultural heritage," Yuri said.

Mrs. Lewis sat silently, her eyes not moving from Yuri.

"Within two days my parents were simply taken, along with others, to a Japanese prison camp. My mother, ready to give birth, was forced to stand on the open rear of the truck, wedged in with fifty other people, children screaming, everyone crying, fear all about, not knowing where they would be going. "

"Stand back. Stand up," the Japanese soldiers shouted. All had bayonets pointed in our direction and they used their rifle butts to make us move quicker."

"As the truck drove down the main street, my parents could see their small sweet shop shuttered, wooden boards placed around the windows. It was gone. Just like that. There was nothing left."

Because his parents spoke many languages–Japanese, Chinese, English, Russian, Armenian–the Japanese immediately wanted them to serve as interpreters.

"When they refused, they took my father and beat him, smashing his head with a baseball bat." Yuri softly said, "But my mother, God bless my mother, she had that thing called guts. She organized the other prisoners who were about to riot if the Japanese didn't stop. And for some reason, maybe because she was pregnant, they did back off."

Herbert Hughes held Margaret's hand in the darkness.

The camp kept everyone on starvation diets. Yuri explained that the Japanese hadn't really anticipated capturing as many prisoners in such a short time and were not prepared. They were short on their own supplies.

"That's not a whitewash of our captors," he quickly added, "They were still very brutal, always shouting, always quick to hit. Everyone worked from sun up until late into the night at some sort of a job. In the fields. Building roads. Whatever. The only sound ever heard was that of screaming or of tears. Or of bodies falling at their workplace from disease or malnutrition."

One month after they had arrived Yuri was born. There was no physician available and other prisoners helped, men holding his mother down, women gently trying to assist with the birth. She lay on the floor, twisting her body from side to side, trying desperately not to cry, fighting the pain that was kicking from within. Finally they all heard the distant sound of a baby, new life, and they looked at each other and grinned with happiness and relief. There were hoarse whispers of congratulations.

"A baby sent from heaven," one prisoner said, "who arrived in hell."

Outside the small room they could hear the Japanese guard making his evening rounds, his footsteps echoing against the barren wooden floors.

"That was how my middle name came to be called Arthur," he said, that wonderful smile once again crossing his face, "a kind of secret between us and the Japanese. Yuri Arthur Melkonian. I was named for General McArthur."

Everyone around the campfire burst into cheers and applause.

"So where does that name Yuri comes from?" Hughes asked.

"My folks always wanted to get back to Europe," Yuri answered, "I guess it was a kind of reminder to them."

Corcoran, sitting off in the shadows, placed his arm around Flora Zimmer who gave him a sharp look and pulled away.

Four years later American paratroopers liberated the prisoners. As weak as they were, wearing only rags, his parents went immediately back to their village with plans to reopen the sweet shop.

"Everything was fine once again," Yuri added, "and then what do you think? The Chinese Communist troops marched in. They were on their Great March and they stormed through our village. Because we were like capitalists, because we owned our own business, our shop was one of the first to go, set afire."

"Whatever side we were on, it was always the wrong side," Yuri joked.

Along with the other homeless, he and his parents drifted into that lost, empty world of the Displaced Person, nowhere to go, nowhere to turn. Finally they arrived with only a small patched suitcase at a DP camp in the Philippines.

"It took a special act of the American Congress to help us get out," Yuri explained, "and finally, finally, we sailed to San Francisco. When we sailed under the Golden Gate bridge my father had only fifty cents left to his name and he tossed that into the bay as a kind of good luck gesture."

His parents worked for a large San Francisco insurance company but at night opened a small print shop in the financial district. Because of their charm, the ability to speak several languages, the many people they had met in their strange odyssey, the family quickly made friends and the print shop became quite a success.

"Let me tell you what my dad taught me," and Yuri's voice suddenly became dry sounding, "It's good for everyone to know about the human spirit. As long as you believe in a cause, any cause, whether it be this safari or life itself or whatever, nothing can ever stand in your way."

His wife held his hand tighter and he nodded his head.

"I know, I know, I'm about to sound like a philosopher," he continued, "but my dad had this belief. And because of that he could stand up to any conditions. The prison camp torture. No food. Being disgraced and humiliated. No matter how hard they tried to break his spirit, he withstood it all and because of that we all survived."

Yuri paused and looked around the campfire.

"It was only after we got to the United States and the fear was gone and the shop did OK, only then did it all catch up to him," Yuri continued, "His belief, his cause had been taken away. He saw that his family survived. With the survival, the cause gone, he self-destructed."

"What happened?" Mrs. Lewis asked in the darkness.

"One day he just turned and walked out the door. We never heard from him again. So that is the great American success story," he concluded, "And I have probably talked your ears off. But I wanted to explain why we are both happy just to be here, with all you wonderful people."

"The history of your people is so tragic," Flora Zimmer said.

"Unfortunately it isn't all history," Yuri said, "Azerbijan happened only recently. A thousand years ago, today, it is all the same. We just get pushed around."

Our small group became silent for a moment.

"That's quite an adventure you've had," Hughes finally said.

"My biggest adventure started before I was born," Yuri answered, "After we came to San Francisco I just wanted to become an American. Even had my mother bake apple pie on the fourth of July."

He paused and looked at Sophie.

"So what do they love to talk about in America?" Yuri added, "Marry their childhood sweethearts. And, as you already know, this is her, my Sophie."

Gabriella, who had been seated next to Yuri leaned over and hugged him.

Yuri, grinning that whimsical smile of his, stretched his arms out like a master of ceremonies introducing the next act.

There was quiet applause around the campfire.

Alejandro, who did not understand everything that was being said, joined in the applause.

Sophie started to stand, then she sat back down, a shy smile on her face.

"Yuri, just you wait," she cautioned, shaking her finger in his direction.

Sophie paused, collecting her thoughts, deciding exactly what to say.

"I'm supposed to tell my story? It's not much. I write advertising copy."

"Tell them,"Yuri whispered in the darkness.

"Meet the proud husband," Sophie said, pointing to Yuri, "My biggest claim to fame, maybe you heard it, is that commercial that ends with "Buy by.""

"I've heard that commercial," Mrs. Lewis said, then she cupped her hands and let out a playful "Boo."

"So that's my story," she said.

Sophie hesitated for a moment. She became silent and her smile slowly narrowed, finally disappearing among the lines in her reflective face. Sophie wanted to tell more but changed her mind and abruptly walked away, holding back. She had suddenly remembered something and it bothered her. Something she could not talk about.

Yuri watched Sophie and nodded his head knowingly.

We sat quietly in the darkness, thinking of Yuri's story. Then slowly we went back to our own tents to prepare for tomorrow's journey.

I wondered what had suddenly frightened Sophie and why she held back. It also made me wonder what stories the others had and what might suddenly be heard around the waiting campfire.

# SAFARI
# WHEN THE SKIES WERE PINK

The sky turned pink as thousands of flamingos suddenly rose as one, the only sound that of their wings as they splashed off from Lake Nakuru and circled about over our startled heads.

A line of birds skimmed along, just above the surface, like a child skipping stones across the water and watching as they bounced from place to place.

They made wide, sweeping arches, circling back and forth, in complete freedom, filling the sky with a soft pink cloud.

"A'ha, at last, a life long search has ended," Flora Zimmer said, pointing to an ostrich that was standing nearby, "They don't bury their head in the sand."

Even Walter Cocoran's usual dour face had a grin on it.

Flamingos, pelicans, storks. And comorants. The African hawk eagle. The buff-crested Egyptian goose. The hornbill that looked like a strict British school master. The silly looking Guinea fowl. Thousands of smaller birds, sitting perched like royalty atop trees, chirping their greeting, flapping their wings as if only for us.

More birds then anyone could imagine, all flying freely about, oblivious to the world around them. The bird watchers on our small safari kept poking each other as they spotted still another different bird.

"Look at that one," Margaret Hughes half shouted taking out a small book she carried that was filled with bird photos, carefully marking the one she had just seen, "by the time we are finished I'll have seen every bird in the book."

Hughes, in one of his rare moments of silence, stood quietly looking at the birds.

Alejandro held binoculars and whistled each time another bird flew passed, trying to make the same sound as the bird.

The birds image reflected on the still lake as it would in a huge mirror. Off to the side waterbucks, impalas and even some baboons were spotted dashing about in the bush, all adding to the wonderous charm of this moment.

"They all coexist here," Allen grinned.

"Don't tell the damn poachers," Mrs. Lewis said.

"How do the flamingos get that beautiful color?" Margaret asked.

"There is some kind of pigment in the algae around the lake that makes them pink," Allen answered, "and all those birds together eat about one-hundred and fifty tons of it every day."

The forest came almost to the shore of the tranquil lake and, not far away, Allen showed us Baboon Point, a small hill that served as an observation point. We strolled to the top, cameras and binoculars in hand.

"There are millions, as far as the eye can see," Sophie said in respectful amazement.

I looked at Gabriella and she grinned at me, that special, youthful grin that slowly moves across her entire face. We both nodded to one another.

"My God, there's Bambi," an excited Mrs. Lewis half shouted, pointing out the van's window.

"A dik-dik," Allen answered, "Very graceful. Like a ballet dancer."

This was the salve we needed after the two poacher sightings. We were far removed from that horror and the birds helped all of us feel at ease as we tried to forget the tragedy. There was once again time for laughter and amazement.

A day later we were at the Masai Mara, the northern extension of the plain of Serengeti, we spotted more lions and cubs resting lazily in the sun. One rolled on its back, stretching, twisting from side to side, looking at us with almost haughty contempt. He was curled silently under a bush, at ease in his own domain.

"Those are the lionesses with their cubs," Allen explained, "The males go out and only come back at mealtime."

We should all be so lucky," Yuri said and Sophie gave him an exaggerated slap on his wrist.

Another lion, alone, off to the side, was too busy chomping on a huge bone, pausing only to glance in our direction.

"Curiosity filled the cat," Corcoran joked.

"No fences between us," Gabriella said, "This is a tremendous thing."

"They give a feeling of raw power," Corky answered, "Almost sexual in its way."

"Like those who derive sexual feelings out of war?" Hughes asked.

"Something like that," Corky answered.

Flora Zimmer gave both men a glance, complete with raised eyebrows, but said nothing.

Allen guided us to Hippo Point where the giant animals, their thick skin making them appear like a relic from the dinosaurs, waddled slowly about, horns pointing high, as they searched for the nearby water to rest.

Cheetahs, leopards, wildebeests, gazelle, all roamed the grasslands where we traveled, each more beautiful then the other.

A small Thompson gazelle suddenly leaped across our path, seemingly coming from nowhere and Mrs. Lewis applauded.

Our safari had spent several days criss-crossing through other Kenya game preserves. With each new location the spectacle became a kaleidoscope of brilliant colors and sights, watching the Masai pass by, the animals constantly offering the unexpected and, always in the background, everything filled with the perfumed fragrance that was Africa.

One of the highlights on our journey was a low hill suddenly rising alone in the middle of the bush. Allen carefully checked the area and allowed that it would be alright for us to hike to the top where the view was overwhelming. We could see for miles around from the top of Kilamanjaro rising in the early morning mist to several nearby rhinos soundless, sleeping, half submerged in water. The entire vast panorama of Africa was virtually at our feet with the bush extending off into the far distance, like a still painting in the early morning silence.

"Would you like a peek?" Gabriella stood next to me and held out her Swiss army binoculars.

"Quite a view," I said.

"No traffic jams here," she smiled.

I looked at her and nodded my head, realizing she was having fun with my earlier conversation.

Gabriella handed me the binoculars pausing for a slight moment.

Once again there was that feeling of something more to be said but we both managed to hold back.

"No attachments," I warned myself, "No responsibilities."

It was my writer's constant imagination intensified because of the sultry African heat that lay heavy around all of us.

The heat that was everywhere. Mrs. Lewis had finally taken off her bush jacket while Sophie kept wiping perspiration from her forehead.

Those were good moments, up on the hill, our small group clustered together, finding time for laughter and relaxation. After only a couple of days on safari we were all starting to feel like seasoned African travelers, filled with confidence, aware of the bush and what it offered.

There was something else, not found in any guide book, but which proved a salvation of sorts for all of us: Allen and the other guides had erected a small square tent and slung a canvas bag, filled with water, over a tree branch that towered above the tent. By jerking two ropes, water would pour out, just enough for a proper shower.

The cold water would pour out but after the dust and the unrelenting heat and no shower ever felt as good as standing alone in that canvas tent, under a thorn tree.

Each of us tried the shower with reactions that varied from laughter to singing. Alejandro whistled in the shower. Flora Zimmer hummed tunes from Broadway shows.

At first it was the animals that had drawn us together, then the poachers and thus our friendships began to grow. We learned to trust each other, relied upon one another, all sharing much with each other.

"This is truly an amazing collection of people,"Yuri said, "All of us gathered here on this small adventure."

"We have made our own little island surrounded only by the bush," Mrs. Lewis added.

"Just us, what you see is what you get," Flora said, "No frills, no nonsense."

"No pretensions," Corocran added, looking at Hughes.

Every night at dinner, after the guides had prepared our meal, a couple of us would stand at one end of the table and help dish out the food. Following dinner, others would volunteer to clean and scrap the plates without anyone ever telling the other," It's your turn." We all just pitched in and did our small share to help, something that doesn't always happen even in the most civilized of places.

Without previous plans, Gabriella and I ended up seated next to each other at dinner each evening at one end of the long table.

We both joined the conversation with the others but also found moments for only ourselves.

"Who was the sexiest man in America?" she asked me one night, filled with that sudden, unexpected youthful exuberance.

"I don't usually think about sexy men," I answered thinking that I liked her opening comments far better then my silly one about smog and traffic jams.

"Your old President Kennedy," Gabriella answered her own question, "Baby face. Very intelligent. Good humor."

"Humor is important," I agreed.

"Women look for that first."

"What about sexy women?" I asked.

"Brigitte Bardot," she answered.

"Yes, when she was young. There are no more sexy women. Just weak imitations."

We became silent for a moment and I added, "Linda Darnell. She was special."

"Who is that?"

"An old movie actress. I was in love with her. No one knows her any longer."

"Except maybe old movie fans."

Gabriella looked at me with that face whose youthful freckles belied her worldly sensuality.

She was truly an original: cool and sultry, youthful and sophisticated. Knowledgable in the ways of the world. Gabriella was the classic definition of the total woman.

Only I held back each time I talked to her fearing of going to places where I had already been and never wanting to return.

On the other hand, I felt my body starting to rise and ache for her.


At night, alone in my tent, I would write notes holding a small flashlight between my teeth to guide my pen in the darkness.

I sat in the solitude of the tent and thought of the poachers, moving out there in the bush, bringing their slaughter with them. The sight of their butchering had cast a spell on our journey but the beauty that was Africa managed to overcome some of the horror.

In the silence of the deep night, in the most hidden recesses of my mind, I also thought of other things. Of Lauren and of Roberta. And now, of Gabriella.

I fell into a nasty half-sleep, tossing restlessly for the tragedy of what we had seen also brought out the tragedy within myself.

I had a cruel kind of nightmare, one that frequently recurred. Lauren was standing on one side of a wired fence, I on the other. A huge canyon separated both of us so that there was no way to reach one another. We both shouted to each other only no sound could ever be heard.

I woke in a shudder feeling afraid and lonely.

The nightmare and the tragedy made me think of Lauren and I lay in the darkness for a long time with the only sound being my heart pounding.

I always had another dream, a tiny feeling, kept it deeply hidden, that Lauren and I would one day meet again. Only now, in the darkness of my tent,

I realized that would never happen. Not in this lifetime.

"Lauren," I whispered to myself in the darkness.

When you are lonely and afraid it is good to hear a friends name said outloud.

Something about the bush and its vast horizons allows you see things in their true perspective. Eyes become sharp and focused noting every detail. It can sometimes be a matter of survival.

"Lauren."

Only now I knew and understood. She had turned her back and the gate had clanged shut; It was all over.

In the darkness of the night I cried for the yesterdays while fearing what all the tomorrows might bring.

# MICHAEL

"I am not an alarmist," Dr. Merv Cohn had said looking me squarely in the eye, "but you are a walking time bomb."

No one spoke that night around the campfire until Gabriella playfully said, "Come on, Michael, it is your turn."
We had all become familiar with death in recent days so I decided to tell my small story. It would be kind of like show and tell, the way we use to tell scary stories to the Boy Scouts each night at summer camp. I looked at Gabriella, the fire reflecting her face, and I decided to hold nothing back.
"My life really started just a few month's ago," I began.

I hadn't planned to visit anyone in New York let alone a physician. Roberta and I had made the journey as a kind of last prayer, a final attempt to try to salvage a marriage that had long ago started to crumble. Only a nasty tightness in my chest had suddenly began. It was like a savage heavyweight boxer sending smashing blows directly to my chest. making me straddle the side of a nearby building, thinking I might go down.
An hour later I met Dr. Cohn for the first time.

"It's a life threatening situation," Dr. Cohn had continued.
I looked out the venetian blinds and everything suddenly seemed like a bad Bette Davis movie. Across the street I could see Central Park, children playing, the Hansom cabs making their way along the tree-lined trails. None of it seemed real. It was like being in a war and thinking not me, never me, I'm invulnerable, hit the other guy.
"I suggest you take the first plane out of town and see your own physician in San Francisco,"Dr. Cohn said, shaking his head to emphasize the seriousness of it all, "Or I can put you in a hospital in New York. It's as simple as that."
"I'll call my Doctor tonight," I managed to slowly answer as Dr. Cohn wrote some prescriptions, "And I can be home by tomorrow."
"New York has been here for a long time. So has San Francisco. You can always come back," the physician said, putting his arms around me, "get these prescriptions filled immediately. Take it easy. Be careful. If you need help at all, please call me at any time."

Everything was a daze when I got back onto the street, my mind racing with every possibility knowing only that I had to get back, that suddenly, in the past two hours because of some odd unexpected pressure on my chest, I had become a "walking time bomb."

My life had somehow changed forever. The afternoon had turned warm but I felt only a chill surge through my body.

The smallest detail suddenly became vivid in my mind. I felt I could remember every face, every aspect of the strangers who now passed me on the street, as though any one of them might be the last sight I would ever see.

A child's blue balloon had broken loose and was slowly rising towards the heavens. Towards the heavens? Some sort of wretched symbolism? Please don't play jokes on me, not today, not now. Please.

"It will only take a moment," a pharmacist said soothingly, knowing immediately what the prescription for nitroglycerin tablets meant.

Only a moment. That final moment might come at any second with my heart ready to explode.

Like a master story teller, I paused to glance at those seated around the campfire. A bird squealed in the darkness. Gabriella's head jerked alert. No one spoke. All seemed interested in what I was saying but I held back for a moment remembering to myself what happened next.

Roberta was standing in front of the hotel glancing at her watch. She smiled with relief when she saw me and waved her gloved hands in my direction.

"What happened?" she asked anxiously, oblivious to the noise and the sounds of the street.

"Inside," I whispered, "Let's talk in the lobby."

I told Roberta what had happened and she immediately left to make plane reservations. When she returned neither of us spoke. We had long ago become accustomed to long silences between us.

"I like to remember that girl I first met," I said looking at Roberta.

She was wearing a silver pin shaped like a butterfly I had given her for our wedding anniversary.

"Don't get maudlin," she cautioned, "You'll be OK."

"The first time we dated each other was on the Marina Greens," I continued, trying to drift back to another time.

"The Golden Gate Bridge was in the background and you were nutty that night, singing to me like you were Sinatra."

"We were awfully young then."

Roberta and I forced ourselves to forget what was happening by sharing memories of long years that now swirled together far too quickly, memories when we were young and filled with life and our own little dreams, we thought of Stephen and watching him grow into manhood, of old friends, long ago moments.

We remembered the laughter before the stillness.

"Remember that time at the Little League championship?" I asked.

"When Stephen got hit on the head by the fly ball," she answered as quickly as I had asked.

We both paused, recalling our own memories.

"What about every Thanksgiving, just before I'd bring out the turkey," Roberta said, "and you made that dreadful noise."

"Gobble. Gobble. Gobble," I whispered.

"Thank God this time you did it quietly," Roberta said, glancing around the room, "You use to make Stephen laugh with that odd noise."

"He never knew which way to look," I smiled.

Families all have those small memories and we recalled summer afternoon picnics and gentle spring evenings. Pondering over what Holiday greeting cards to send out each year. How to help a child build a kite for a Cub Scout contest and carve a pumpkin for Halloween.

We recalled the tears of a teenager whose love was hurting and the pitiful look on a child's face the first time they bravely went off alone to summer camp. All our memories tumbled together as if they had happened in a single moment.

Every memory had to last a lifetime, I thought, then softly cursing to myself remembering the Doctor's warning, knowing that very lifetime might be just a second away.

"The marriage held such promise," she sighed, looking away.

Roberta and I sat silently, looking at each other.

"The dreams of youth," I said softly, realizing love had long gone but that the caring would always remain. I wondered how long it had been since we had last spoken so softly and decently to one another.

"Twenty-five years is supposed to be silver," Roberta bitterly tried to joke, "But for us everything has become tarnished."

I wanted to hold her hand but knew it was useless and that she would only pull away. I had given up simple hand-holding years earlier when the loved died.

We had a sandwich and then Roberta went back to the room. I held back in the lobby thinking there was one last thing I had to do.

I asked the hotel clerk for some stationery and then stood off to the side of the registration counter, a very frightened man, unsure of myself and angered that my body had betrayed me.

I wrote to Lauren.

It was a brief letter written with pure feelings because we had never talked since those last horrible moments. I just wanted to say "good bye."

It was also a kind of calculated chess move, hoping, praying she would respond and that I could hear her voice one more time.

*Dear Lauren:*

*I'm in New York and a doctor just told me my ticker was acting up and that I am a walking time bomb. He warned that I should get on the first plane to San Francisco.*

*Don't worry–I'm NOT going to let myself croak (only the good die young) but I wanted to tell you that everything I ever said was honest, my love remains true and sincere.*

*I wanted you to know our few moments together always meant everything to me.*

*I'm scared. That doctor was very serious when he warned me.*

*Damn it, I do love you, funny face. IF anything should happen, I just wanted you to know how much I value and treasure your friendship and I'm sorry about so much.*

*The last dreadful words we ever said to each other still bother me and I deeply regret what was said–by both of us. I know you too well and I'm sure you feel the same. I'm very sorry; someday, maybe a million light years from now, try to forgive me.*

*Anyway, who knows what the future holds. Perhaps if all this nitroglycerin stuff works then maybe, sometime, we can have that final dinner together.*

*Sorry about all this small melodrama but I just wanted to get it all off my chest (my chest is carrying too much pressure at this moment–bad joke.)*

*I'm writing this in a bit of a shock but IF anything happens, IF I were to know in advance, I'd want to have that last opportunity to say "goodbye"*

*because you meant so much as a pal and a friend and I simply wanted to say
"farewell" and "thanks."*

*I'll be around for another hundred years but just "IF," I wanted you to
know that once-upon-a-time there was another human being who loved you
very much.*

I signed it 1940/90, a kind of code that Lauren and I used and which
referred to a comment she had told me long ago when she said, "We are
nineteen-forty people living in a modern world."

By writing I was able to say words that could never be spoken. The letter
wasn't looking for sympathy but more as a thin hope that perhaps Lauren
might call and I would her hear voice one last time.

I was writing my heart out and that dark thought gave me a small smile. It
was all such a cynical twist of fate.

"What happened when you returned to your hotel room? Hughes asked.

I had grown silent for a few moments remembering and Hughes discreetly
returned me to the present. I looked into the safari fire and saw my yesterday.

I had remembered far more then I could tell strangers. Flora Zimmer
would have understood Roberta but she would never have wanted to hear
about Lauren for that would have made me seem like some sort of old
fashioned scoundrel in her eyes.

They all seemed interested but I felt I was talking too much. The casual
observer suddenly thrust directly into the spotlight and letting it all out.
Perhaps it was a kind of catharsis, whatever it was it was my time at bat and
I may as well make the most of it. Perhaps it might help me stomp out Roberta
and Lauren forever from my memory. One final hurrah for the past and then
goodbye.

Allen had felt betrayed at the poachers; I had felt betrayed by my own
body.

When I returned to the hotel room," I continued, "Roberta was already in
bed, reading a magazine, not wanting to think what the next few days might
bring. I looked at her and I felt sorry, sorry for both of us, sorry for what we
had done to each other.

That night I lay in the unfamiliar bed and I was more frightened then I had
ever been in my entire life.

"You are a walking time bomb," and I heard those deadly serious words and remembered the look on the Doctor's face. My entire life was coming to some sort of an end and it wasn't one I had ever planned.

Ten at night in New York; seven on the Pacific Coast. A Wednesday night. I thought of Lauren and wondered what she was doing right now at this precise moment. How I wanted to call out to her.

It was odd when I got into bed but I suddenly remembered that old prayer from my childhood and I quietly recited it to myself.

"Now I lay me down to sleep,
I pray the Lord my soul to keep,
If I should die before I wake,
I pray the Lord my soul to take."

I fell into an exhausted sleep, my last thoughts were of that prayer and I vaguely wondered if, in fact, would I make it until the next morning.

The sea of puffy white clouds, extending as far as the horizon, reminded me of heaven.

But I saw no angels with harps waving at me so I sat back in the plane and relaxed. Tried to relax.

As we took off from New York the pilot, in a soft, honeyed Tennessee voice, proudly announced the flight plan.

"We'll soon be over Johnson, New Jersey, then up near Madison, Wisconsin and over, in an almost straight line, to Des Moines, Iowa; Scott's Bluff, Nebraska; Malta, Idaho; Reno, Nevada and direct to San Francisco."

It all sounded like one last grand hurrah; a small composite of Americana; flying over the wheatfields and the cornfields and the highways and the bi-ways of this great country, the stuff they sing about like "My Country Tis Of Thee" and "God Bless America."

Well, folks, I thought, "Strike Up the Band." Maybe even the triumphal march from "Aida." Maybe.

"You're a time bomb," and those words flew with me every inch of every mile as we headed home.

What if my ticker gave out now, here, in the air? I'd inconvenience the other passengers. Fuck, I'd inconvenience myself.

This plane was rushing me to my destiny and I sat with perspiration starting to soak into me.

"Hey, Stephen, lad," I thought with black humor, "Start tying your own neckties. You'll be the man of the house, Tiny Tim. I may be checking out."

Roberta sat silently next to me meticulously folding the cord on her earphones over and over. She had a constant scowl on her face.

Across the aisle was a guy who looked self-important, complete with a blonde mustache, a small computer resting on his lap. A young girl was opposite, two black olives for eyes, she held a tennis racket and wore a crushed sailor's hat. An older women sat in a double-breasted blue blazer, just looking straight ahead, never talking nor moving.

"A time bomb, right here, folks, right next to you," I wanted to scream in desperation.

Then I started to think of those forties movies, songs, book titles. "Only Angels Have Wings," "Fly Me To The Moon," "God Is My Co-Pilot." I needed more than God as a co-pilot, I needed Him sitting on my lap, hugging me, kissing my forehead.

I saw a small town far below, who knows where.

"Hello folks, down there," I whispered to myself, "Goodbye, folks."

The drone of the plane's motors lulled me into a fitfull sleep.

Then I thought of an ugly little sentence and I couldn't get it out of my mind:

The biggest thing in life is death.


A twig crackled in the slowly dying camp fire.

Gabriella looked as if she wanted to say something but I didn't give her an opportunity even though my words were now directed really at her. Once I started telling my story I knew I had to continue. Get it all off my chest, at least what was left of my chest.


"You're dying," Dr. Harold McMahon told me, "You've got maybe three days to live."

He had been our family physician who had cared for my kids through measles and chicken-pox and everything in-between. He was a gentle and scholarly man who had seen my family through the good and the bad. On this day he leaned over my bed in the recovery room and spoke with an unexpected Sharpness in his voice, looking at me with unblinking eyes.

The moment I had returned to San Francisco they rushed me into "Cardiac Catheterization," inserting a long, narrow, flexible tube through my body, letting it wind its way along the blood vessels to my heart.

After the operation I was taken to the hospital's recovery room. It was then that Dr. McMahon rushed in, his face red and alarmed, looked my square in the eye and made his no nonsense statement. He had read the charts and there was only one conclusion.

"You're dying," he repeated, "you need immediate open-heart surgery."

I merely looked blankly at him, unable to truly comprehend what he was saying.

"The main artery going into your heart is blocked," he continued, "Maybe ninety per cent. Like a rusted pipe which won't let the water get through. Your blood isn't moving properly."

"What are my options?" I finally asked.

"Maybe three days. Possibly three weeks."

Dr. Jim Kilgore was to do the operation. A short, dark-haired man with a pleasant enough smile and a very concerned look on his face.

"What will be happening?" I asked anxious to learn every possible detail.

"There isn't much need to worry," Dr. Kilgore answered, "the operation has become quite common-place."

That was when I started to worry.

Dr. Kilgore placed a small model heart on his desk and used a pencil as a marker as he proceeded to tell me the graphic details of what I was to anticipate.

"We cut through the chest bones, stop the heart and put you on a life support machine, transfer blood, cut deep into the leg to remove the good veins which will then be put into your heart."

"You use a saw," I asked, "a big one?"

"You don't want to see it," he answered.

Dr. Kilgore offered slight encouragement when he said I caught this before actually having a heart attack and that my veins were solid and healthy. Because of that I would actually have a better and stronger heart when the operation was over.

"If I'm alive," I thought to myself, thinking of his description which was really saying they were about to slice me in half like a side of prime beef.

"You'll be out for hours," Dr. Kilgore added, "When you come around there will be several tubes down your throat but they'll be quickly removed. Not to worry but when they are taken out, for a couple of minutes, you'll sound a bit like Donald Duck. After that it is all uphill and you'll be on the well known road to recovery."

"The Road To Recovery," I thought again, "that was one Bob Hope and

Bing Crosby film they never made."

I tried to find some humor but all I could think about was the operation. And of Roberta and Lauren whom I loved but in different ways.

The last I heard of Lauren her publishing firm transferred her to their London office. I knew her well enough and realized she had deliberately gone away trying to forget everything in her own way.

Roberta. Lauren. Everyone lives; everyone dies. Everyone picks their own way to die. It is the loving that is the tough part.

Dr. Kilgore started to leave the room but I called him back.

"Tell me, Doc," I asked, "Is it possible to get a bum ticker from a broken heart?"

He paused and smiled.

"No one ever asked that before," Dr. Kilgore answered, "but psychologically maybe, sure it might be possible. Stress of a lost love, that type of thing."

The embers of the safari campfire were burning low. Hebert Hughes sat rigid, listening to my every word. Yuri was holding Sophie's hand. They were waiting patiently for me to continue. Corcoran had a look of concern on his face.

The nurse came in and had me shower, washing myself with some sort of yellow antiseptic soap to remove any germs. That was the moment when it all really hit me. This might well be my last possible night on this earth and I was spending it scrubbing myself with this yellowish soap.

I wondered if the odor of the soap was similar to the smell of death.

After the soap and the shower a shy Chinese woman entered the room and started to shave my hair, all my hair, quickly, professionally, like Delilah skinning Samson. Gone was the hair on my chest, on my legs, even the hair around my testicles which were left to dangle, flopped out, loose and barren, feeling cold without their old familiar fur covering. It was as if some sort of heritage from my very birth had suddenly been removed. Hairless.

All of that suddenly made me fully aware of where I was and what would soon be happening. My skin caked yellow made me think of pictures I had seen of African tribes. Perhaps that's what made me first think of Africa. If I survived this damnable operation. If... If...

Africa made me think of Lauren and that day at the zoo when she told me she had always wanted to go there. Perhaps that would give me some sort of goal to survive. If. If I made it, I would go to Africa. For her. Kind of like some holy pilgrimage. She would be with me every step of the way. I would kneel and kiss the Plain of Serengeti for her.

It was a kind of game, thinking of Lauren and Africa, something to get my mind out of this room which was now turning dark with the rapidly fading light. The shades were down and I lay alone and frightened, waiting for them to wheel me to the operating room.

There was only the silence of the empty hospital room filled with uncertainty, with only the occasional muffled sounds from the empty hallway where I could slightly hear nurses whispering at their stations, perhaps even talking about my life which was now hanging in the balance. The hushed, muffled sounds of a hospital corridor can be deafening.

I thought of death and the silence of the room rapidly became the sounds of terror not knowing what the next few hours might bring. They would soon put me to sleep and I knew it was a sleep from which I might never wake.

A nurse looked into the room and I gave her a thumb up sign. Only that reminded me of the Roman gladiators and I realized that a thumb's up can just as quickly become thumb's down.

I thought of Lauren, wanting to sit down and hold her hand one more time and tell her of my love, how deep it really was, how it curled around me and touched my very life, how it came from the heart, at least what was left of my heart. I wanted to reach out and tell her of that love and of those feelings.

Only the doors suddenly opened and they wheeled in a gurney and the show was about to begin.

I couldn't tell those listening around the campfire but I suddenly remembered much more. I became silent for a moment recalling those moments alone in the operating room.

Lauren was there enveloped in the mist of my memory, smiling at me, arriving exactly at noon for our lunch date, slowly making her way across the crowded restaurant, everyone glancing at her, the way she carried herself with confidence, self-assured, her long brown hair gently bouncing as she moved past the tables, her beauty, smiling at me, blowing me a kiss as she came closer, those two dimples once again blossoming out underlining the warmth of her greeting.

Everything was cloudy, like a soft haze.

It was New Year's eve and she was there, in a black silk suit, weaving through the crowded room, that smile, that special smile, just for me, coming towards me at the stroke of midnight, her arms open, outstretched, waiting for me to hug.

The vision would slowly come, then go, fade out into a grey distance.

Now we were alone having our first dinner together, clinking glasses, holding hands, she asking, "Are you nervous?"

"No, are you?" I answered with some assurance but knowing that we were both as nervous as kids on a first date.

All through that dinner my feelings glowed from deep within, my entire body was somehow radiating just being with her, alone with the woman I loved.

"Hello, funny face," I had started calling her "funny face" because her face was classically beautiful, the stunning combination of girl-woman: earthy and sophisticated one moment, enchanted with a child's delight the next. It was a face of sheer, haunting beauty.

Again she would fade out, I wanted to call her, "Come back, come back."

"Michael, you're doing fine, just fine."

I heard the voice way off, in a dream. It was Lauren and she was there and had come to the operating room. I was relaxed from the operation but still in the dark, only now starting to regain consciousness. I heard her voice and it made me feel warm and good.

"You're doing fine," she continued, "You can't talk yet because of the tubes but I have a pad if you want to write any notes."

Lauren's voice was soothing and I was happy she had come.

"YOU ARE TERRIFIC" I tried to write on the small pad.

"Thank you," the voice answered only this time it wasn't Lauren. It was an Oriental voice. I was beginning to regain consciousness and I tried to open my eyes. It was like great weights were on them, holding them down but I managed, finally, to open them.

Standing over my bed was a concerned nurse, watching my every movement, checking my pulse. I was hooked-up to a variety of plugs and cords all monitoring every pulse from my body. The nurse continued to offer her encouragement.

"You are doing just fine."

I rolled my head to the side knowing I had survived the operation with or without Lauren at my bedside.

# MOMENT OF TRUTH

It had taken three months for me to recover.

At first I could only hobble up and down the hallway, those few feet gradually became half a block, then a full block, finally I was able to even walk to the mailbox two blocks away. After two months I was able to drive for about a mile. Gradually my strength returned and each day became a new victory, like climbing to the top of Everest.

The time of healing was over. The novel was finished and suddenly there was time and space in my life.

I felt that I had opened up too much during my campfire talk so, when the fire finally dimmed, I said goodnight to the others and returned to my tent. Only my mind kept remembering.

Roberta's concern and the sweetness of New York had given way to the old anguish and imagined hatreds. Only now she was blaming me for my operation as though it was something I had deliberately done to her.

"I should have let you die," she screamed looking at me with those dulled eyes.

"Please, stop," I yelled, cupping my hands over my ears to drown the unrelenting sound of anguish, "find another punching bag."

"I'll never stop," she raged on, "I'll never let you forget what you've done to me. You took my youth away. All the broken dreams."

"I had dreams too," and I reached out to her, "Just hold my hand, touch me, hug me. Show some affection."

Roberta answered by rolling her eyes toward the ceiling, as if she had been trying to communicate with a fool for whom she only had contempt.

It was always devious, never knowing the precise moment when the alcohol would slowly seep through her body clicking something inside causing the anger to suddenly flare. Her drinking had made her unpredictable and that was no longer anyway to live.

Roberta had given her love to me, shared our love and our dreams and then destroyed it all with vast, endless rage.

I remembered one night glancing in silent resentment at the glass of wine Roberta held knowing it was but the first of many throughout the evening.

"That's where your problem is," I said with contempt,, "in that glass."

"What?" Roberta asked pretending not to understand.

"Look at yourself," I yelled in frustration, making her glance towards the mirror, "You smell like a winery. Your skin is starting to get a purple pulpish color. Look at your eyes in the mirror. They're glazed, dulled this time of night."

"There is nothing wrong with my eyes or my face," Roberta yelled, turning to leave.

The room was soundless for a few minutes then she suddenly returned. Roberta had put on fresh makeup, her lipstick bright red, eye shadow just right, there was the soft scent of perfume.

"See, it's not from drinking," Roberta continued shouting, "It's my makeup. I don't wear makeup this time of night."

She stood in the doorway with her arms folded daring me to respond. It was grotesque, almost surrealistic, a sight as distorted and twisted as it was pitiful. Roberta was so far gone, she no longer knew who she was or what she was saying. She was now grasping for a world that never existed except in the dark recesses of her own mind.

She took another sip and it always seemed as if Roberta had become transparent, as though you could see the alcohol surging through her body, flowing about in her blood stream, for that was when her speech pattern slowly changed, her eyes narrowed and only meanness would come from her lips.

"You're a nothing bastard," she said in a strange, hollow sounding voice.

It wasn't just the face or the eyes but the way she talked, the change in her voice, taking a split second longer to speak, being careful to prevent slurring her words; it was how she carried herself; doing everything just a little slower, careful of her own movements.

I wanted to cry seeing her like this, knowing nothing could be done any longer. I picked up Roberta's wine glass in frustration and held it out to her.

"Have a picnic," I whispered, hating myself for talking like that, aware that the drinking was dragging both of us down.

Neither of us spoke for a long time, both lost in our own frustrations.

"I can no longer fight this monster that invades your body every night," I finally said.

I had frequently offered to help. I had talked quietly to Roberta; I had shouted. Nothing worked. She simply denied her drinking and would not listen or accept it. Roberta would turn her back cursing me, thinking I had created some sort of evil plot against her.

I wasn't much better. There had been just as much shouting on my part born from the same sense of frustration and defeat. You try to build a bridge and then watch as it all crumbles around you.

I knew at that moment as she swayed belligerently in the doorway wearing all that stark makeup there was nothing left. Everything was gone forever between us. I could no longer watch as she continued to destroy herself and everyone around her. The marriage had finally taken its toll for both of us.

"You're a failure," Roberta would snicker trying to provoke a fight, taking some private delight in this endless torment.

I felt like a once proud bucking bronco, full of life, wild and free, filled with spirit, but now, after so many verbal beatings, finally broken, my zest for life fading. I no longer knew what to expect in my own home and her mood shifts kept me constantly off balance.

It had been a good marriage with much love until the drinking came and brought the anguish. Somehow the love and the pain got all mixed together and it became difficult to any longer know what was the truth.

"Drinking is a sickness," I anguished to myself, "how can you leave someone who is sick?"

I could visualize Roberta standing alone in front of group of nameless strangers, standing up and quietly saying, "I am an alcoholic." Only I knew it would never happen. She was now driven by the demons unleashed in the bottle.

Only she would never confront it, the classic denial of the alcoholic.

it slowly occurred to me that Roberta really didn't want to be helped. That she would remain like this forever.

I thought how close to death I had come, how many years I had waited, always thinking that perhaps tomorrow might bring a new day. Only tomorrow never came.

I had become crippled emotionally wanting only to keep any feelings locked deep within myself.

The years of verbal abuse had to come to an end. I had tried, I had hoped, I had prayed. Now it was over. The operation had taught me one thing, finally and forever: There is little time in this battered old world. And in that remaining time, I also had a life to lead.

That is nothing to be proud about. We both had failed. A lot of years down the drain. We both loved each other but our own faults had now become intolerable to the other.

"You've changed," she kept saying, blaming the operation. It wasn't that I had changed. It was that I considered myself lucky to be alive and how precious few moments anyone is allowed on this earth. I had learned how delicate life can really be.

The good and the bad, all of it just melted away until nothing remained. My leaving would be better for both of us. We decided it was time to end a long but tragic love.

As for Lauren, she was now but a memory of another time and another place. She never answered my letter from New York and that told me everything. Lauren had chosen another life and was gone forever.


All the memories had started to crumble. It was the time of the warm champagne and the big tears.

I silently packed as Roberta watched, not speaking. I'm sure we both had looks of fear that the unknown etched on our faces. It was a lot of years to simply kiss away. We had shared our own small tragedy and now it was the twilight of Roberta's life and mine.

I walked about the silent house and heard it echoing with memories. Of dinner parties. A child's laughter. Conversations with friends.

Roberta must have heard it too, in her own way.

"It's been a long time." she finally said.

"A lifetime," I answered. I could remember both of us once filled with the dreams of youth.

Funny, after all these years, we were both hesitant with each other, awkward, like two strangers, for there is never a proper way to leave someone who has been a part of your life.

Suddenly the bitterness was gone. And the anger. There was nothing either of us could say or do any longer. There was simply nothing left.

"Well, I guess this is goodbye," I said, taking my bags, glancing out the window one last time.

"You take care of yourself," Roberta answered, "I'll worry about you."

"Thank you," and we both stopped, not knowing if we should have one last farewell kiss or shake hands like old friends or simply turn and leave.

All I knew was that the door opened and I was gone.

It ended just like that.

Everything came down to three last words.

"Goodbye," we said simultaneously, and we laughed because we knew each other so well, "Be well."

And then we were both alone.

# WHISPER OF AFRICA

"What the hell do you want to go to Africa for?" Dr. McMahon asked with bewilderment, "Most guys after open-heart surgery want to prove they are macho."

Much had flashed silently through my mind while sitting around the campfire but now, alone in the silence of my tent, the memories continued to pour out, like some hugh flood gate that had suddenly been forced open.

"My going to Africa has nothing to do with macho," I tried to respond, returning to my earlier conversation with Dr. McMahon, "But something interesting happens when you come close to death and walk away from it."

"I know," Dr. McMahon said, "Your entire life flashes before you."

"No, not quite, it's just the opposite," I quickly answered, "It's your future that flashes before you. You learn how vulnerable you really are. How quickly it is all over. Poof, just like that. All of our days on this earth are measured only in time and my time damn near ran out."

"You're not Marco Polo," he answered, shaking his head.

"Is it better if I start to shop around for a rocking chair for my old age," I snapped, "or should I try to start a new life?"

Dr. McMahon stared at me but said nothing.

"There are two kinds of Africa," he finally said, "Club Med and Ethiopia. Which one are you planning to visit?"

"Neither. I don't want to swing on trees. I'm not Superman. Just an ordinary guy who wants to see the Africa of our heritage."

I held back adding, "An ordinary guy who is also in search of himself."

Only Dr. McMahon knew me to well for he added,"Africa of our heritage? That sounds like old fashioned hog wash."

"Take a look at a map, any map, and look at the outline of Africa," I tried to explain, "You of all people will appreciate it. Africa looks like a heart. Might even be the one you saved. Maybe the old broken heart. Maybe my new heart seeking its destiny."

That was when I really thought of those Tarzan movies and of Hemingway and Ava Gardner and Stewart Granger and all the tranquil beauty I had ever heard about Africa.

It was hard to believe that just a few months earlier my body had gotten this far in life without a scar or scratch and now, looking at myself in the mirror, I didn't know if I should laugh or cry.

There was one jagged scar that carved itself the entire length of my left leg, from ankle to groin. Another scar, this one a long, steady line, climbed up my entire body starting at my lower stomach, moving along the chest and finally ending just below the neck. There were even twin holes in the middle of my stomach from the insertions that had been made during the operation.

I looked at myself in the mirror and it reminded me of all those travel articles I had read showing the body scars of various African tribes. I thought how similar I must now appear.

I thought how stale my life had grown. How lonely and bitter I had become and I vowed to myself not to let this continue. It was like a poison slowly seeping into my system.

I also thought of Lauren and her life ambition about always visiting Africa.

I was suddenly aware that I had somehow entered a new kind of race and that I would now constantly compete against the clock, against my own death.

Thus I began thinking of Africa and that it might prove a kind of pilgrimage in memory of Lauren. I also considered that it could be some kind of escape for me, a way to finally find myself.

I could almost hear those drums calling me.

A few days later Doctor McMahon gave me a series of shots for all the things that no one wants to think about: typhoid, cholera, yellow fever, even meningitis.

Afterwards he quietly sat at his desk and wrote a variety of prescriptions filled with medications that covered any potential havoc from diarrhea to asthma.

"You won't find any neighborhood drug stores to run to out in the bush," Dr. McMahon said, simultaneously writing, shaking his head and glancing at me with the side of his eyes.

For this old arm chair traveler, who was perfectly content watching old movie travelouges, the most fascinating prescription was one whose label sternly warned: Take two weeks before arriving in malarial area and continue to take when returning home."

What did I know about malarial areas? This vial of tablets was real and I knew that the time had come. Looking at them made me finally feel like Dr. Livingstone.

I knew now there was no turning back.

And that is how a guy who had never strayed far from home before, set out on a small adventure, kind of like Tom Sawyer or Huck Finn. After thirty years I was alone, like Christopher Columbus sailing off into unchartered waters to learn about life anew and to travel alone half way around the world on a journey to Africa.

The only reminders of my surgery was my swollen leg and a constant feeling pressing against my chest as if I were wearing a Roman gladiator breast-plate. It served as a reminder letting me know my chest bones continued to knit together. It also left me aware of how lucky I had been and how close I had come.

For a middle aged guy with all the expected creaks and groans, I never really felt as good as those moments alone out on safari.

"Out on safari."

I hoped, no, I prayed, that this might be the journey where I would find my life once again.

# FINDING THE
# ORPHAN ELEPHANTS

As we criss-crossed the area, Allen wanted to return to Nairobi for supplies and to report to the game wardens about the recent poacher sightings. Gabriella and I elected to accompany him while the others remained at the campsite.

We sat close together in the van and the mid-day tropical heat played its tricks on the mind. I longed to know Gabriella better as I had during our first meeting in Namanga, yet I held back, not wanting to push anything. The emotional wall I had built continued to keep any new intruders far out of reach. I felt I would never again be capable of starting a relationship, or truly opening myself to anyone for fear of the hurt I had already known.

"I notice the different tribal scars," I said, trying to make small conversation as we drove through the crowded streets.

"Beauty through scarification," Allen routinely answered. I realized he must frequently hear that same question.

I glanced at Gabriella and thought she also seemed to carry scars, but the kind that can't always be seen.

Moments later we arrived at the game warden's office on the outskirts of Nairobi. A one story building covered with vines.

"His name is Tyke but his real name is Hector," Allen whispered to us grinning, "Only he thought Hector didn't sound like a proper game warden name."

"Good health," Tyke looked up from his cluttered desk and smiled in greeting.

"Good health," Allen answered.

Tyke, or Hector, was seated in a small office and listened carefully to Allen's report, typing everything on an old standard standup typewriter, the kind I had not seen for many years.

A torn lamp shade was tilted over the typewriter to give him added light. All of the papers on his desk were neatly stacked in a squared pile, almost with military precision. There was the smell of oily linoleum on the floor, whose edges had long ago been torn from years of wear. The paint on the walls was chipped and the floor boards splintered. Tyke was a grumpy-looking man, a bit of a sourpuss who sat smoking a pipe. His faced was dark, like old leather, made even darker from the endless suns he had known.

He frequently interrupted Allen to either ask him to repeat some bit of information or to relight the damn pipe that kept going out. Tyke's reactions were alerted to alarms that I had never known.

"Our country has done much to discourage poachers," Tyke said, glancing at us in a kind of apology, "But still they manage to sneak in on occasion. Right now, thanks to Allen, we've got them spotted just outside Amboseli."

He and Allen started to talk in Swahili, their conversation growing louder, until at one point they were almost shouting at each other. Allen finally shrugged his shoulders and turned, motioning for us to follow him out of the office.

"What was that all about?" I asked.

"The wardens are really wonderful," he answered, "but they are limited. Limited in their funds and in their man power. It is frustrating for them."

"What did he say that angered you?"

"He said nothing but he grumbled like an old mama," Allen answered, "he said he could only do what was possible with what he had to work with."

"But he looked directly at Gabriella and me."

Allen hesitated to answer and was silent. I noticed he often became quiet when he didn't want to say anything that might offend.

I did not push the point but as our van neared town center, Allen looked at both of us and sighed.

"He said what people spend on safari in one day is as much as he makes in an entire month," he paused, then added, "And that a poacher can make three years pay with those tusks."

No one spoke as we realized the game warden was correct and that was but another reason for the poachers to exist, leaving their path of destruction wherever they went.

When Allen went off for supplies, Gabriella and I took a cab and visited a baby orphan elephant farm about twenty minutes from downtown Nairobi.

Getting there is like a miniature safari. We made our way along a small, jagged path for a few hundred yards, walking passed a muddy stream and suddenly, in the bush, were six baby elephants that only reached up to our hips.

"Oh, God, look at them," Gabriella half shouted, as excited as a child at Christmas, suddenly standing in the middle of the babies.

The small elephants were cuddly, surrounded by attendants who kept talking quietly to them, giving them food, even showing them how to properly drink milk.

"Elephants are the most difficult and demanding of all animals to raise," one volunteer attendant, with a Dutch accent, told us, "The first year or so they are totally dependent on milk and without their mothers to show them, we become the teachers."

The small elephants clustered around her as she patted each one.

"The elephants can feel when someone loves them," the attendant continued, "Just as we all do."

"There are so many orphans?" Gabriella asked.

"Most are here because of the poachers," the attendant said with sudden bitterness, "Sometimes entire herds are killed. We get what's left."

"This is a place for survivors," Gabriella pulled back, whispering to me, remembering what we had just seen in the bush, "A sanctuary for murder victims."

"Good is being done here," I answered, my voice surprisingly hushed.

"We've already seen the bad that is being done out there," Gabriella answered, moving close to me, casually brushing against me.

"These elephants are the ones that made it," the attendant continued, "One arrived here unconscious and we thought she would never pull through but she did. She is very tough. That one over there missed her mother, killed by poachers, and refused to eat. Even developed stomach problems."

As she spoke the attendant kept gently brushing one of the elephants, much as any mother might do with a new born baby.

We saw the babies sitting regally in their own small waterhole, rubbing their ears against the nearby trees, gulping water in their tiny trunks and letting it splash about them as if in their own outdoor shower. Before we might have laughed, now we felt only sadness for them.

One baby elephant strolled over to Gabriella, stared at her, then lifted his trunk, allowing it to roll slowly along her breast.

"You be good," she scolded the elephant, shaking her hand in mock anger.

"Some wise elephant," I laughed, "Now he'll always remember you."

Gabriella looked at me but said nothing.

A line of small school children passed by and Gabriella nodded at them. Two nuns led the children who walked laughing, talking, holding hands with each other.

"Aren't they adorable," Gabriella whispered.

One young girl grinned as she imitated an elephant, walking bent over, her arms swaying from side to side pretending they were an elephant's trunk.

The other children laughed until one boy raised his hand and extended his small fingers making them into the shape of a pistol.

"Bang," he shouted.

"Never, never do that," one nun screamed grabbing the boy. The other children backed away from her sudden anger.

"But my poppa says there is good money with the tusks."

Gabriella turned and put her hand to her mouth as if to hold back from choking.

"Another generation already starting?" she whispered.

Gabriella and I moved away, both of us shaking and sat under a tree for a long time.

Finally it was time to rejoin Allen who had filled the van with supplies that would be needed for the next several days. We got back inside and Allen slowly started to drive through Nairobi's busy downtown streets making his way out into the country, past the rolling green hills of an African January day, the same hills that Hemingway had loved.

Along with the supplies Allen had gotten a Nairobi newspaper which he kept tucked deep in the grocery bag.

"What's happening on the outside world?" Gabriella asked when she saw the paper.

"Not much," Allen hesitated, then slowly handed the paper to Gabriella.

The stories reported local events except for a small box tucked at the bottom of the second page.

It was an article about the increase in poacher's in the various game areas.

Neither of us said anything knowing Allen was aware but did not wish to cause any concern without reason.

"Where do we go next?" Gabriella asked as we neared Namanga.

Allen looked at her and pointed to his small map.

"Back to Amboseli," he answered.

# NAIROBI POLICE REPORT
## 18 JANUARY

They had also discovered Namanga.

Osuna, Aduo and their friends sat around a hoteli, their shirts off in the warm African evening, drinking beer, nervously talking about their plans.

The room was plain, just an old wooden bar with a few tables. The only decoration in the barren room was a torn magazine photo, yellowing with age, of Jomo Kenyetta talking to President Carter. A leaky faucet made a constant tapping sound sending dirty water dripping into a plate whose bottom was already rusted out.

The hostess knew they were strangers in Namanga but was aware of their activities. She had long ago developed a sense about poachers, much as one would consider thieves who come in the night, and she remained well away from them, contemptuous of those who did this thing, only approaching when one raised his hand to signal for more beer. She chewed on a toothpick, her eyes never leaving these strangers.

"...appetizing young love for sale..."

A scratchy Ella Fitzgerald recording was playing in the background, the same song over and over.

"...who will buy my supply..."

Quarter, that was the only name he went by, was an old friend of Aduo's from the backstreets of Nairobi and had joined the group in Namanga.

"Quarter is my name," he would often boast. "Because I give no quarter."

He was a tall, lean man with tribal scars decorating his body. Quarter had a perpetual smile seemingly frozen on his face; one eye was permanently closed and slightly distorted as the result of long ago battles.

"...Who will pay the price for a trip to paradise..."

"That's what we need here," he said, glancing at the hostess, "A trip to paradise. We are men without women in the bush."

"You talk too much," Aduo said, sipping his beer.

Quarter started dancing by himself, slowly gliding around the room, holding his bottle of beer like it was a woman clinging close to him, a grotesque dance in the small, barren room.

"I love that Ella Fitzgerald woman," he sighed, speaking only to himself.

Osuna looked away, embarrassed by this man whom he had only met hours earlier. There was a meanness about him that Osuna felt and didn't like.

Fitzgerald started singing "Night and Day" and Quarter let out a small cry.

"Hear that part, like the beat-beat of the tom-toms," he became cynical, his voice mocking, "that means us. Out here in the bush. The beat of the tom-toms, jungle drums, we are primitive out here. Just helpless old natives."

Quarter stood near the hostess, his hands moving towards her breast, a thumb touching her nipples.

"Move," she said, starting to reach for a pan under the bar counter. Quarter said nothing, putting his arms high in the air in mock surrender, then quietly moved away.

"She should give some love for sale," Quarter said continuing his aimless swaying on the dance floor.

"Shut up, Quarter," Osuna said, "You are making a fool of yourself. You always turn away like a coward."

"Quarter is right, you know," Aduo answered, "The visitors come and go out on their fancy safari and they laugh at us."

He gulped more beer and his eyes, turning red, started to narrow.

"That group that is here now," he whispered, "Those bastards are the ones who reported us to the game warden. Fuck them."

Osuna turned away, thinking of his wife and children, wondering if they were now asleep in their small room. He had never liked Namanga, thinking that nothing good ever happened to him in this place.

"You know, we should have our own safari, man," Aduo suddenly said, standing up and slamming his fist on the table, "Maybe we should be the ones to go out and look at the pretty animals and the lovely view. It's our country isn't it?"

"You drink too much," Osuna said.

"And you worry too much, like an old woman," Aduo answered, "Those pricks reported us. Maybe we should have a safari. Our kind of safari. Show them what a real safari is all about."

Quarter kept dancing his grotesque, lonely dance, his eyes shut, lost in another world. Lost with his memories of Kgase, his Kgase and wondering who she was bedded with even now. Silently cursing her.

The hostess sat alone at the wooden bar wishing the strangers would simply leave.

There was suddenly silence in the bar as Aduo quietly sat down deep in thought.

"...like the beat-beat-beat of the tom-toms, when the jungle drums are near..."

Aduo sipped another beer. His face flashed anger as he thought of something.

Then started to laugh outloud.

# GABRIELLA

It was Gabriella, to my delight and amazement, who decided to talk that night around the campfire.

Hughes and Corcoran were discussing the difference between American baseball and British cricket.

Flora sat quietly near the fire knitting.

Sophie and Margaret sat next to a small lantern studying a map of Africa.

When the fire's embers start to dim and the last huge log had rolled over, the group became silent, starting to think of the next day.

"I hear everyone's wonderful stories," Gabriella slowly said, "Perhaps you might like to hear about life in Switzerland."

"And the Swiss Army," I said. Gabriella looked at me and nodded her head. I sensed more in the look and it made me feel good sitting there by the fire listening to her.

When she was nine she was fat and lonely, painfully shy with few friends to play with. Gabriella found companionship with her various pets, from one dog, that she described as more of a mutt, to a kitten who had long ago lost its tail. By the time she had turned sixteen she had become a young lady discovering the mystery of Swiss boys, learning to act with patience when they talked only of skiing and mountain climbing. When she was twenty-three, she blossomed into a beautiful, knowledgable women, engaged to a wonderful man.

"It is more then just those few facts," she continued, "I was very lonely as a little girl. Had my dolls and my pets but no one to turn to so I spent hours, such long hours, walking those tiny hills near my home. I could look out at the mountains and see the tiny streams twisting in the valley far below. That is where I sat with my books and read poetry."

For amusement she would stand at the edge of the small hill and recite her poems outloud, listening to the words as they echoed back from the nearby mountain tops.

"Helllloooo," I would shout, just like you read about, and then I would hear "hellllooooo" back again and that became my only friend as a child. I called the voice the giant of the mountain and I would have wonderful conversations with this great person."

She paused for a second, recalling this moment from her childhood.

"It was a lovely, hidden valley, near Lucerne, in the lake region, only high up, overlooking the green hills, and I had my wonderful hot chocolate and my secret friend, the echo giant of the mountains."

Gabriella stopped and started to smile.

"And yes, before any of you ask, our little village did indeed look like one of your chocolate candy wrappers," she added, "We was surrounded by all kinds of beautiful valleys and picturesque villages, like a series of color postcards."

Sitting around the campfire, we all smiled at the description, typical of Gabriella's sense of humor.

"The man I was engaged to was a courier for a Swiss bank and had a motorcycle," she softly said, "And every weekend we would go off into the country, I sitting perched on the back of his motorcycle, holding tightly to this young Adonis, the wind blowing and tossing my hair like crazy."

They rode over the mountain passes and people in the villages who frequently saw them would wave as they soared passed.

"His name was Dedi, such a silly little name," Gabriella's eyes turned away and I thought she blushed, but only for a second, "Friends called us "The Happy Ones."

The two spent long hours in Gabriella's lonely childhood place, only no longer as lonely, and they would read poetry and have lazy picnics, taking long walks through the gentle hills. When winter came, they returned to ski through the same trails where they had often hiked together.

"Dedi use to cut paper into the most delicate shapes,"Gabriella recalled, "His work was so beautiful. He would cut for hours and then scroll out the paper and it would be filled with such intricate designs and patterns."

Gabriella paused for a moment collecting her thoughts.

"He would sit quietly absorbed with the paper cuttings while a fire burned in the tiny chalet that overlooked the valley. And I would lay on the floor near the fire and dream those beautiful dreams that only the young have."

Gabriella would watch her finance slowly, painstakingly, cut the paper, an old Swiss craft which dates back over two hundred years.

"Dedi had a little scissors and his work was so graceful, just as he was," Gabriella paused for a moment, "He was so beautiful, so sensitive."

She again glanced away, paused and then continued.

"It was a wild flower that suddenly changed my entire life," she shrugged her shoulder and became almost secretive, turning away from us.

No one spoke, we sat around the campfire in silence.

"We had gone on a picnic, as we often did, and he went to pick me a wild flower and he fell backwards. Not a big fall. Just a tiny, small trip. Only Dedi hit his head. And Dedi died. Just like that. As simple as that."

I noticed Gabriella's accent always became more pronounced when she was excited. Her "w's" became "v's" and she said "da" for "the." It made her seem even more vulnerable and I wanted to reach out and hug her as one would do with an old friend but I held back.

"After he was gone I retreated from the world," she added, "I couldn't find myself. I went from a bookish loner to trying to learn about life. So I went out and got lost in the catcombs of Europe."

Gabriella became silent, deciding if she should continue. The only sound was the crackling of the campfire.

"You can learn of life quick. In Marseilles some wretched old man, a fisherman, wanted to find love and offered me two cigarettes for the privilege," a bitter looked crossed her face as she remembered, "I went out and bought him a carton and told him where he should smoke each one."

There was some uneasy laughter in the darkness.

"I know, I know, this sounds perhaps naughty but it is part of life," Gabriella added, "And I was lonely, bitter lonely. Only now I feel you are no longer strangers but friends. So maybe I talked a little bit too much."

"We understand," Sophie said quietly.

"I wanted to forget so guess what I did. I joined the Army," Gabriella grinned as she said that, "We have a volunteer Army and all Swiss are proud of that. I skied. I hiked. The Army was already familiar for me."

"What else do you do when anguish comes?" I thought to myself, feeling I was a self taught expert on the pain of love, "Join the army or go to Africa, go anywhere to escape when dreams die young."

"That must have been very difficult for you," Sophie said.

"Not too bad. I held up good. Except maybe for the Alpine Corp survival training when it would get so cold sometimes I thought my nose would even explode," Gabriella answered, "I even became a marksman and got a small medal."

"Markswoman," Flora Zimmer said. She was the oldest among us but thought like the youngest.

"It wasn't just the Army," Gabriella nodded, "I often found time to return to my little place on the hill and I would think of him. When I was alone I spent my time playing with some of the small animals that wandered by trying to forget."

Gabriella looked at me for only a brief second yet managed a lot of communication with just her eyes. Now I knew. I understood what gave her that occasional shrug of cynicism.

"I thought of him every night, every moment, every second. It took years, like my life had been taken away. I felt like I had started to become tough. What do you say, like a hard-boiled egg? I became lean and mean, at least that is what one of those American businessmen once told me in Zurich."

I frowned to myself feeling jealous of something that I had no right to even be jealous about.

"Now I'm OK. I learned about life, as you others also speak of it. The good and the bad," Gabriella added. "These days, here, they are good ones. I learn to take care of myself and to laugh like before. Once again I find the amusement that is in life. So don't feel sorry for me, there is much here. And the animals, like all of you, they are beautiful."

Margaret rose and put her arms around Gabriella and our entire group became silent.

I went to my tent that night and I felt lonely. I had felt hurt with Roberta and Lauren but Gabriella had known much worse. She and I shared similar sorrows.

Both of us had been brushed by life's defeats and now we were feeling a dangerous kind of loneliness, feeling it deep within each other.

Just like that first day, I wanted to call out to her, to reach out, to be with her. Only in the darkness of my tent there was nothing.

# WALK IN NAMANGA

Funny how the entire world can change, move a notch or two in a completely different direction, always at the most unexpected times and often by the most simple of happenings.

In this case it was the broken break pin on the van which started Houdini and his wife and Gabriella and myself, off on that small quest for peace that he had often discussed.

"The brake has something wrong," Allen told us as we started out one morning, noting that the only service station was back in Namanga. Most of those on the safari elected to stay around the campsite catching up on their washing or letter writing but the four of us saw it as an unexpected opportunity to revisit that small border town.

As we drove into the main area we could see the flags of both Kenya and Tanzania fluttering just up the street at the border station. The Masai sat as we had first seen them curled to the ground in the shadow of a nearby building, idly watching as we approached. An old African man in a dark blue uniform carried a heavy club, as he moved about the group. He had only one arm and kept the empty sleeve tucked into a pocket. The was obviously the local policeman and to show his authority he occasionally poked his club at some of the seat Masai.

The moment the van stopped at the service station we were immediately surrounded by the Masai who once again offered their hand-made gifts for a few shillings.

"Pen," one older man, with missing teeth and terrible breath, asked me. His eyes were deep-set and swollen and he never smiled, "pic-tur for a pen."

Sitting off to one side of the road in a colorful red and yellow robe was the most striking Masai woman I had ever seen. The women all shave their heads but this one looked beautiful with that close-cropped style. She sat quietly alone, breast-feeding her baby.

"Jambo," I said in greeting and she looked up and nodded her head.

"You visit here?" she softly said.

"You have a wonderful country," I answered and she again nodded, perhaps not quite sure of what I had meant.

"How many children?" I asked her, nodding towards the baby.

"Six," she said, continuing to hold the baby against her breasts, her eyes carefully studying me.

The morning heat was already starting to swell around us as I looked up the two lane road. Tanzania, on the border to nowhere, yet I had known women in San Francisco who would have craved to have had the same natural charm as this Masai mother.

Namanga was really not much more then just a cluster of shack dwellings spread out over a few dust covered streets. The hoteli where we had stayed that first night was located just on the outskirts.

When I asked her about that she nodded her head, "Hoteli means restaurant here."

I turned to meet another Masai, only he was dressed in brown slacks, a tee-shirt which read "BEACH BOY," and a baseball cap sitting jauntily at the back of his head that proclaimed YANKEES.

"Not bad for a one horse town, eh?" he said, speaking with a clipped British accent.

"You're a baseball fan?" I asked, startled by his poise and understanding.

"Been to your country once," he answered, "New York, San Francisco. Never made it to Hollywood with the movie stars," He smiled and his teeth were yellowed and broken, "Do you know Frank Sinatra?"

"No," I answered, "but San Francisco is my home and it is a long way from Namanga."

"This is my home base," he grinned, "I saw your American freeways. Here I see the elephants. You think I got it wrong?"

We both knew he was right and I shook his hand African style, as Allen had taught me, a shake, then a grab around the fingers and then another shake of the hands.

"You're a quick learner," he grinned, "Do you like my country?"

That was the same question I had heard at the post office in downtown Nairobi, asked by the clerk who was wearing a suit and tie. There was a pride in their country that I seemed to find with everyone.

"We are all like brothers and sisters here," he said politely.

He had been a long distance swimmer and visited America as part of a swim team years earlier and, between races, found much time to learn about the United States.

"I should do a story in, what is you call, the National Geographic magazine on your customs," he joked, "Instead of your always doing one on ours."

He stared at me for a moment and then added, "Be careful as you travel out there in the bush, my friend, there is tension in the air. I feel most apprehensive."

I studied the man for along moment. His eyes stayed on mine and he become quite serious.

"Why not?" I heard Gabriella's voice and it made me turn away. She was standing next to the van talking to Allen who was nodding his head, "no."

"I'm a big girl and I'll be perfectly safe."

Allen continued to nod his head from side to side.

Gabriella saw me and made a mock pout.

"I'm not like Little Red Riding Hood," she said standing her ground with Allen and being quite determined.

I already determined that Gabriella could take care of herself and that she could be soft or tough as necessary. I felt that just under the surface always remained a certain feeling of weary worldliness about her.

"What's the problem?" I asked.

"I thought I could simply walk down the road, straight ahead, and when the van was ready they could pick me up."

"I must account for all," Allen said. "We stay together. It is better."

I remembered Gabriella and I talking about our missed walks, thinking how I found myself strolling in circles around the campsite each evening trying to stretch my legs.

"Look, Allen, what if I go with her? Would it be OK?"

Allen hesitated for a moment. He ran the safari on a set schedule and both the broken break pin and now the unexpected discussion of a walk called for special consideration.

"Perhaps we can join them," Hughes and Margaret both said.

Allen understood safety in numbers for he said "OK" cautioning us to remain on the road at all times.

"Asente sani," Gabriella smiled and Allen grinned as the four of us started off on what would prove to be one of the world's most memorable walks.

Gabriella, filled with her usual enthusiasm, led our small group, camera and binoculars strapped around her neck, constantly on the look-out for her precious birds. She was wearing light-blue shorts and a yellow tee-shirt; perched on top of her head was an old sailor's cap, the brim flopped down for added shade.

"I think over there," she said pointing to a nearby tree and slowly raising the binoculars, "Is a Secretary bird." Her face lit up with enthusiasm.

Sitting perched atop a nearby tree was a large bird, its wings extended, feathers fluttering like a woman with flirting eyelashes.

"Lazy old bird, doesn't fly much," Gabriella said, "Uses those big wings mostly to balance itself on top of trees."

"What a wasted life," I said, perhaps thinking of my own life, "Just sitting around a tree top waiting for something to happen."

"It does its part," she answered, giving me a quizzical look, "Kills snakes for one thing."

A Masai clad in the traditional red toga, walked past, carrying his spear. He was followed by his wife and son.

"Jambo," I said and they all smiled.

We passed a rather elegant white stucco home, which seemed out of character in this dusty village, and I wondered what local dignitary must have lived there. Across the road were the small dung huts that we had seen all around our campsite. The Masai are nomads and follow their cattle.

"When they reach a suitable location, the wives build the huts out of dung and the husband sleeps inside, along with his goats and sheep," Margaret Hughes explained with a grin, "Not a bad idea."

The two continued down the road and I watched them, wondering if Hughes made love the same way he walked, stiff and reserved.

"Oh, my," Gabriella suddenly said, becoming serious and pointing to the ground.

A small earth mound was in front of one of the huts and we realized that the Masai bury their dead right where they live.

We continued our walk until Houdini suddenly stopped and held up his arm, signaling us to pay attention.

He had heard it first and what he heard made us all smile.

"Happy birthday to you,
"Happy birthday to you."

Off in the distance we clearly heard the sound of youngsters singing "happy birthday," at least we heard the tune only the words were being sung in Swahili.

"Must be a school nearby," Hughes said, pointing to the area where the singing was coming from.

"Let's do our thing," Margaret said.

"With your permission," Hughes said, turning to Gabriella and myself.

We looked at each other for a moment.

"I mentioned this thing I am doing, a study on world peace, that everyone is the same. Kind of like the same principle that the judge is the equal to the man he judges, that he has to put his trousers on one leg at a time."

"Get to the point," Margaret said, adding, "professors talk a lot."

"I'm using the magic, as I mentioned, to show that everyone is the same. I'd love to see how these children react way out here."

"What if the van passes without us on the highway?" I questioned.

"They couldn't have made the repairs this quickly," Margaret said, "and this experiment in world peace won't take but a few moments."

With that the four of us started to walk towards the school, over a trail that had now turned to a chalk-like red dust.

Hughes was eager and made quick strides as he led us moving swiftly over the jutted trail. He paused once only for a brief moment, taking off his old straw hat to wipe perspiration from his forehead.

The school was another shanty, the paint long ago blistered away by time, the front door broken and hanging by a rusty hinge. Carved on the outside was "SCH O L." One letter had long ago broken off with age.

We knocked and Hughes, now in his element much like Houdini, opened the door and asked, "May we enter?"

The teacher, standing next to a small blackboard, was startled by the visitors but quickly realized this might prove an unexpected and valued lesson for her class.

"Yes, yes, please do come in. Thank you very much."

She also proved unexpected to us, for here, in the middle of the Masai village, was this African woman in white silk blouse with a puffy bow, a crisp red skirt, her hair short and stylish. She was obviously a modern women, aware of all the world's changes, yet serving here, respecting the traditions of an earlier era, making herself a bridge between two cultures.

"Jambo," one of the students, seated near the front, said and the four of us smiled back.

The children, seated on long rows of wooden planks, must have been around six or seven. All stared at us with great curiosity. They wore tee-shirts and short pants. Only one or two had shoes. They stared and giggled at what may have been the first outside visitors to ever walk unannounced into their small school.

"This is the first grade," the teacher said proudly.

Houdini explained the reason for our visit adding that we had only a few moments. He then asked the teacher if he might offer the children a small magic trick.

"Thank you very much," she repeated.

Houdini walked to the head of the class looking every bit the magician, his eyes filled with that mischievous twinkle. His brushed back grey hair added to the appearance of a wise elder.

He said nothing but moved his arms about in the fashion of any magician until he gradually produced a small bit of rope which he silently cut in half.

I glanced at the children who were intently watching his every move. Houdini held up both ends of the cut rope for all the children to view and then closed his fist. He again circled his hand in the air. When he opened his hands the rope was entirely back in one piece.

"Simba," one boy called loudly.

A girl in the second row cupped her hands over her mouth and giggled.

One grinning boy, taller then the others, seated in the back, clapped his hands and then all the other children, along with the teacher, whispered their approval.

"Everyone understands," Hughes said, turning to Gabriella and myself, "Magic really is universal."

"And perhaps a path to world peace," Margaret Hughes added.

I noticed an old, scratched piano off in one corner of the room and I thought I might make my own small contribution to world peace. I'll never know what possessed me, I had thought about it for a second that night alone in Nairobi, but now, perhaps it was this unusual setting in the middle of nowhere, or maybe it was these wonderful children, or perhaps as simple as the heat of the day, but I walked over to that piano, dusted it off, sat down and started to play.

I hadn't played the piano since I was a child, not much older then these same children. I sat at that piano and I thought of those Masai women with their elongated earlobes, all their colorful necklaces, the many strands of beads and copper on their wrists and their fingers and then, without any warning, an old song my grandma had taught me years earlier suddenly boomed out in that ramshackle old one room class.

"...Sure she's got rings on her fingers and bells on her toes,
Elephants to ride up, my little Irish rose..."

The children clapped to the music, not understanding the words. I glanced at Gabriella standing alone against the wall. She was cupping one hand over her mouth laughing, just as the children were also doing.

I was on a roll, what the hell, I thought, and I continued to bang upon that old piano, certain the sound of my atrocious voice could be heard all the way back into the bush.

"...Sure she's got rings on her fingers, bells on her toes,
elephants to ride upon, my wild Irish rose,
Come to your nabob and on next Patrick's day,
Mombo, jombo, jitty bob jay. Oh, shay..."

I finished and the children cheered and clapped. One even let out a small whistle. Another stood at his desk shouting, "oh shay. Oh shay." It all gave me a kind of cold chill. I noticed the teacher was also applauding and I heard her say, "Thank you very much."

I glanced at Gabriella who seemed as enthusiastic about my awful singing as the children.

"Magic and music," Hughes said, "it cast its own spell every time."

"Always leave them wanting more," Margaret said, thinking of the van and nodding to us to leave.

At the door the children gathered around making us feel like a combination of knights mounted on white horses, the U.N. and even Santa Claus all combined in one.

"Thank you very much," the teacher nodded her head and waved her hands.

We went back on the road and there still wasn't any sign of the van so we continued our walk. A small herd of cows were passing with a young Masai boy, not much older then those in school, leading them.

"That was cute," Gabriella whispered to me, "I didn't know you were such a singer."

"Please don't rub it in," I answered. I hope I didn't make an ass of myself."

"It was perfect."

Houdini and his wife were walking about thirty yards ahead of us, stopped every once in a while to admire the colorful roadside flowers.

Gabriella and I walked slowly down the road, not talking, each thinking our own thoughts about this morning.

I noticed she wasn't watching for any birds but was looking straight ahead. Sometimes we glanced at each other, both contented, smiling pleasantly at one another.

We walked quietly together. Gabriella had the grace of a giraffe, moving quickly yet seemingly in slow motion.

After a few feet our hands brushed against each other. Neither spoke. It was simple as that. Without any plan, without any rhyme or reason, we started walking holding hands.

Our fingers intertwined, her touch was light and her hand soft but it sent a current through my arm and charged my entire body with a feeling of wanting, reminding me of my constant loneliness.

In the heat of the early morning, with those soft, rolling hills off in the distance, we stopped, neither speaking, and for a brief moment we clung together. It was there, in that remote and lonely place, in the glaring heat of the noon sun, it was there that I finally got the hug that I had longed for since the very first day.

The van came and Allen beeped at us, looking out the window and shouting, "How are the hikers?"

Gabriella and I got into the van and sat alone in the back, continuing to hold hands. Her eyes stayed with me, just as they had done once before, only this time I felt they were trying to send a private message, one meant just for me.

That night, back at the campsite, after the sun had sat, there were no stories around the fire. I was alone in my tent writing when there was a kind of scratching sound on the canvas.

I shined my flashlight and, standing there, alone, Gabriella was smiling at me. A thin orange glow from the campfire slipped into the tent as Gabriella opened the flap.

She unzipped the mosquito net that lined the tent flap and soundlessly entered, felt her way in the dark and sat down next to me on the sleeping bag. Slowly Gabriella pulled the red ribbon that held her pony tail back and shook her head, allowing her hair to slowly fall around her shoulders.

"I wear the hair up for the Army," she whispered in the darkness.

"There are no sergeants here," and I was surprised at how quiet my voice had become.

There was only silence.

I had forgot how to be with a woman yet somehow, without planning, we touched and my hand rested on her breast. She held it there and made no effort to remove it or to pull away.

Neither of us spoke but that night we clung together. Then we made the soft sounds and the gentle movements much like the animals that were not far removed from us out in the dark bush.

# BOOK TWO

*"The dream, alone, is of interest for
what is life, without a dream?"*
Edmond Rostand
1868-1908

# CHINEE CHARLIE

"Hi, I'm Chinee Charlie."

The man with the round face and a huge grin, with a mustache that curled around his lip like a tired serpent, held out his hand in friendly greeting.

Chinee. I wanted to correct him and say "Chinese" only I stopped because he was Chinese and could thus say whatever he wanted to about himself.

"I'm the only Chinese guy in all Kenya," he boasted, his grin growing even wider, "And besides that I'm a Jew."

Chinee? Jew? The man standing in front of his small, crowded grocery store intrigued me. He had a lengthy handlebar mustache, carefully waxed, the kind any villain of old would have been proud to twirl, a stark contrast to the Masai's shaven heads. I stared for a moment trying to size Charlee up.

"I'm Charlie Jue," he said proudly, laughing at his own small joke.

I fell for an old line that Charlie must have used with all his visitors and Allen, aware of it, joined in the laughter.

Gabriella put her hand over her mouth and grinned.

Then I started to laugh. That was when I figured this "Chinee Charlie" was my kind of guy.

Gabriella and I had gone with Allen to get some additional supplies for our group and I glanced at her when Chinee Charlie made his joke. We both smiled together.

This day had already become one of renewed promise for I realized Gabriella had chipped away a small part of the wall that had been built. Last night there had been warmth and affection and everything that had been missing for so long.

I had found a pal and I glanced at her again, hoping Allen would not notice. I wondered if people could somehow tell, if we gave off sparks, if the glance of an eye could betray feelings.

Gabriella and I were being discreet but I realized we were standing just a little too close together; Instead of holding hands, our knuckles brushed against each other.

Allen noticed. He noticed everything.

He seemed to smile and I wondered if Allen knew, for I learned early that Allen missed very little.

"I was educated in your country,"Chinee Charlie interrupted my thoughts, using a deliberately bad Asian accent as if from a low budget World War II movie, "At U.C. Davis."

"Hey, I'm from San Francisco," I answered.

"I figured you had that bay area look," Chinee Charlie answered, "Two long lost lanzsmen."

Gabriella was standing near my side and that made me feel good.

"Davis is one of the best college to study animals," I explained to Gabriella and Allen.

"Tell me about it," Chinee Charlie said, "I studied Animal Husbandry for two years. Wanted to be a vet. That was my dream in life. Only guess what?"

"What?" Allen took the bait that Chinee Charlie threw.

"I got bit by a dog in a lab," he answered, still grinning, "Bit by a dog. No fooling. And I learned one great lesson. I was afraid of animals."

"You've come to a good place for someone who is afraid of animals," Gabriella said.

"I must be mishuginar," Chinee Charlie said, "At home I was number two son and I guess I just wanted to prove myself. Overcome my fear of animals."

A young Masai girl, her hair already shaven thin, wearing bright yellow robes, walked in and Chinee Charlie gave her a dried piece of meat which looked kind of like beef jerky.

"Neat people around here," Chinee Charlie added, anxious to talk to someone from home, "They're all honest and open. Can't hide around a bush here like you can in the states."

"Charlie hasn't closed his doors since they first opened eight years ago," Allen said.

Gabriella's fingers casually brushed against mine and Allen noticed.

"See any poachers around here?" Allen asked, suddenly becoming serious.

"Those schmucks," Chinee Charlie answered, "There's been some talk. I think they could be nearby because I smell them."

He rubbed his stomach.

"Something here, in my tummy, something gets tight when poachers are around, like an invisible warning," Chinee Charlie added, "And then I can smell their stink."

I didn't want to think of poachers or even the safari, at least not for a few hours. I wanted to go off with Gabriella and just be alone with her.

I asked Allen if Gabriella and I could get some supplies and slip away for a brief picnic but I already knew the answer.

"Don't even think about it," Allen answered, "We're all for one and one for all. No one gets lost. You already had your Namanga walk."

He was like a stern father talking to one of his children, trying to be agreeable but leaving no doubt that Gabriella and I couldn't wander off alone, even for a few hours.

A man in a torn tee-shirt came in and stood near the rear of the crowded store, picking up cans and reading the labels. He was tall and gaunt looking with one eye that appeared permanently closed. A smile was frozen on his face and his body decorated with tribal scares. His long thin face, out of proportion to the rest of his body, looked as if it might have been squeezed together in a vise.

The man really wasn't reading anything and seemed to be stalling. I noticed his eyes constantly looking at all of us, trying to size everything up.

"You know that tummy warning I just talked about, "Chinee Charlie said, looking at the stranger, "It just went off."

Allen studied the man who remained quietly at the back of the store who continued to keep busy by picking up merchandise, then putting it quickly, nervously down.

"Maybe we should get back," Allen said, continuing to look at the man, "You OK, Chinee Charlie?"

"I'm scared of animals but not of trash," he answered, his voice suddenly dry and filled with contempt.

The man in the back overheard and looked up for a second.

"Anyway, Allen, looks like you got two African love birds on this safari," Chinee Charlie said, trying to change the subject. He looked directly at Gabriella and myself.

Everyone noticed. Maybe living out in the bush sharpens the eye for the casual gesture.

"The birds of Africa are fascinating," Gabriella answered combining a sight flush of anger with a small grin.

"I'm busy getting supplies," Allen quietly said, "If my back is turned, I couldn't stop you from slipping off for a beer."

We both nodded, perhaps too quickly, like kids about to go on holiday.

We were eager to be alone because neither of us really knew or understood what had happened the night before.

Had it been but a moment's gratification, two lonely, hurt people coming together only for a brief moment?

Or could it have been like the first brush of Spring, when life starts anew?

Gabriella and I looked at each other and smiled and, once outside the store, held hands as we eagerly walked along the narrow, dust-filled streets of Namanga.

"Fifteen minutes only," we heard Allen call, "And don't you dare stray off the path."

There was a small hoteli a few door's away and Gabriella and I went inside and ordered beer.

The Arab owner quietly brought our drinks then went back outside, finding a shady place to lean for protection from the afternoon sun.

We had both been anxious to get away and talk but then an odd thing happened.

Neither of us spoke.

"Was last night Marseillaise all over again "I finally asked, "The panderings of a dirty old man?"

"Did I offer you cigarettes?" Gabriella answered, defensively.

We were both silent.

"Maybe it was just part of the African life cycle," I quietly said.

"And what does that suppose to mean?"

"Africa and its eternal hunting," I answered, "Everything here hunts and is hunted. Live, die, survive. That is the order of life here."

Gabriella said nothing.

"Everything stalks each other," I continued.

"Like man and woman?" Gabriella answered.

She turned away and became silent.

"There is no need to talk," she finally said, "Why must you Americans always have to define everything. Everything must be so analytical."

"It meant much."

"Shhh, just enjoy," Gabriella cautioned, "I enjoyed."

She paused and idly brushed a bit of hair back that had curled over her forehead.

"No tricks up our sleeves?"

"It just happened and it was nice."

"It was good."

"It was a moment," Gabriella answered.

"A nice moment."

"We were too lonely people," Gabriella continued, "And yes, it was nice."

We both became silent.

152

Gabriella reached out and held my hand and I looked into her crystal blue eyes and it made me happy.

Allen was outside beeping the horn. Gabriella grinned at me as the two of us walked out to the waiting van.

Chinee Charlie told us later what happened moments after we had left to go back to the safari.

"I think you might have put a tin inside your pocket by accident." Chinee Charlie said to the man who continued to hover at the back of the grocery store. We later found his name was Quarter.

"I'm honest man, sir," Quarter answered with contempt. When he spoke a fowl odor came from his mouth. His teeth were yellowed and decayed and two were missing which gave him even more of a sinister appearance. His voice was high pitched.

"Are you from around here?"

"No, sir, I'm from over at Masai Mara," Quarter answered.

"I think maybe you're a schmuck," Chinee Charlie said with a disarming smile on his face.

"What?" the man answered, "Are you talking Chinese?"

"Never mind," Charlie continued, "I think maybe you took something. I thought we are all supposed to be like brothers here."

"I'm no brother to a Chink," Quarter said, taking the can from his pocket and throwing it at Charlie.

"Filthy poacher," Charlie screamed, "You're a lousy gonif."

"Fuck your mouth," Quarter answered, pushing Charlie hard, making him tumble against the counter.

The young Masai girl was standing near the door and watched as Quarter grabbed some tins of food and ran out. She rushed across the street yelling for the "white suit man," though she was afraid she would have to look into his face. The young girl knew she could never do that.

Charlie lay on the floor, a small gash starting to appear around his forehead.

"I'm OK," he shouted to the little girl when she returned, not wanting her to be frightened, "He was mishuginar but he's gone."

Dr. Herbert Lom, the "white suit man," ran into the store and immediately bent down to wipe the blood from Charlie's face. Some had already started to cake around his mustache.

The young girl turned away frightened when Dr. Lom entered, not wanting to look at him, afraid of what she knew she would see.

"You'll be fine my friend," he said, "Your Hebrew life has saved you once again."

"This is a weird place," Charlie answered, "It's the people who act like the animals."

"You're lucky they didn't feed you to the lions," Dr Lom snapped. He turned his head away from the young girl so she wouldn't have to look at him.

"We both better be careful," Charlie said, trying to smile, "You know that poacher alarm warning I've told you about inside my stomach?"

"Yes."

"Well, right now it is ringing like crazy."

# DR. LOM

The Masai stood silent, not making any sound, but what he was trying to say was universal.

He was holding a child whose tiny body was limp, the arms dangling down, head bent to the side, eyes closed.

We had just returned from the next morning's journey of animal watching when he quietly appeared, saying nothing, standing near the entrance of our small compound.

No one noticed him at first. Hughes was writing letters. Yuri and Sophie sat near their tent. Corky was singing Broadway show tunes in the shower, something I found mildly amusing because Flora Zimmer was the one who usually sang those tunes in the shower.

The Masai stood motionless, just looking at us. He was crying.

Allen was the first to notice and walked over to the stranger. The two exchanged words speaking Swahili. Then Allen looked away, scratched his head, and nodded, "no."

The Masai turned to leave when Allen reached out and held his arm.

"OK, OK," was all he said.

Allen glanced at us, explained that the Masai's child had fallen into some sort of coma and the father had asked for help.

"There is one doctor in Namanga," Allen said. "I'll drive the child there. We can always use more supplies anyway."

"It's a long ride, I'll go with you," I volunteered.

"You should stay and rest," Allen answered.

"You might need help."

"This won't be a pleasant trip," he answered, "The doctor's office isn't on any tourist map."

I didn't know what Allen meant but I looked at the youngster and thought of my own children. Dr. Cohn had always been there and I understood the concern of the Masai.

We got into the van. The Masai sat in the back, holding the youngster, mumbling something softly in Swahili.

In his rush, Allen misjudged a water hole on the dirt road and the wheels suddenly spun out of control.

I cracked my head and held the baby tighter as the van came to a jarring halt, stalling as water quickly rose above the tires.

Allen immediately leaped out of the van, aware that time was important. We stood hip-deep in mud, started to push and shake the van loose. When the Masai realized what we were doing, he quickly joined us.

The commotion, the shaking movement and suddenly being left alone made the baby cry, deep, gulping sobs, making him lose what little breath it had.

I picked the child up and the Masai reached out to stop me, his face alarmed not knowing what I was going to do.

Then I did something I hadn't done for twenty-five years, something I had last done when Stephen was a baby. I placed the child on my shoulder, patted it on the back and started singing college fight songs.

"...Cheer, cheer for old Notre Dame..."

The Masai stared with suspicion as I sang, his eyes starting to narrow, looking directly at me. He held his spear tighter and I noticed his knuckles had become white and tense.

The baby fit onto my shoulder just as Stephen once did. I held the child only for a few moments but it made me think of the young Roberta, proud and happy, sharing our love for the miracle we had created.

"...Fight on, for USC, fight on to victory..."

The baby paused in its crying.

"...Come join the band, and give a cheer for Stanford red..."

The baby let out a deep sigh and the crying stopped. The Masai smiled at me.

"The kid may be dying," I said to Allen, "We have to rush."

"You're a good man," Allen answered, starting the motor.

It took almost an hour to reach Namanga and none of us spoke. We drove down the familiar dusty street, and I was only a bit surprised when Allen finally stopped at a white stucco house. It was the same house I had noticed when Gabriella and I had taken our walk.

"I'm going to leave you here and get some supplies," Allen said, seemingly anxious to drive away. "You sure you want to go in?"

"I'll wait here." I said, getting out of the van.

"Yes, you and Dr. Lom," he answered, "Enjoy your visit."

Allen quickly drove off leaving us in front of the white house.

Dr. Lom had no face.

He wore a soiled white shirt and patched jeans. But he had no face. I could see two slits that served for his eyes. His nostrils were but small holes pressed deep into his skin. His mouth was not much more then still another circular hole. All of this was lost in red, twisted scars that made jagged streaks around what might have been his face.

I was startled and recoiled back, embarrassed by my reaction. I was careful not to move my eyes as if trying to glance away from what was before me.

Dr. Lom was amused.

"Not to worry," he said, reading my mind, "I've long been accustomed to that look of greeting."

He reached out and took the child, nodding to the Masai.

"You'll find my only concern is medicine," he said, briefly glancing at me, "I'm not some sort of freak."

I wanted to say something, my instincts telling me not to stare, to look away. I noticed the Masai had already seated himself on the floor, saying nothing, looking only at his child.

"Everyone greets me the same, please be at ease," he said, placing the child on a small table, "Look, I tell you this once. Then you know. Then we go on about our business."

Dr. Frederick Lom had always wanted to be a man of science, a physician, one of those rare individuals who know almost since childhood what he wanted to do with his life. As he carefully probed the child, not looking at me, Dr. Lom spoke of his youth in London, told me that when he was about the same age as this sleeping Masai child he conducted a scientific experiment. The experiment blew up in his face, around his neck, sending glass driving into his body, blowing away two fingers.

"Now I am Doctor Grotesque," he laughed, "You should have seen me at the London Academy of Medicine. Dr. Frankenstein they called me. Fuck them. "

He glanced at the baby for a second, then looked up.

"They say everyone should laugh, cry, think every day," he quietly said, "Well, look at my face, my friend, I am able to do that every day. Perhaps I am the lucky one."

I looked about the small office that was attached to his home. The room had only one chair, the work table and a small, cluttered desk. Torn shades pulled half-way down made the light poor. That was it. Nothing, not even the smallest decorations could be seen lining the bare walls.

"Don't worry, my friend," he continued, "It's dirty and cluttered but out here, in this small infirmary, it is like heaven. Not what you are used to in the States but like heaven for these poor people."

"They are lucky to have a physician here," I answered.

"Are you talking down to me, patronizing me?," he snapped, "all over Africa are the do-gooders. Dr. Livingston. Dr. Schweitzer. I'm Doctor Hideous. The faceless Doctor. I dedicated my life to medicine. I dedicated my face to science."

He became quiet as he leaned over and carefully listened to the child's heartbeat with his stethoscope.

"There are decent Doctor's out here, sure," he whispered, almost talking to himself, "But you should have been here before, use to be medicine men who knew the knife better then most of the alleged skilled surgeons in London. They would cut into the patient's head to calm headaches and take care of the deranged, like me. They did a damn fine job only now you know what they use that skill for?"

I nodded my head, "no."

"They carve soap-stone figurines for the tourists," and Dr. Lom shrugged his shoulders to underline what he had said.

"Ever see a female circumcision out here?" Dr. Lom suddenly asked, "No, of course not. All you see are the bright lights of Nairobi and the pretty animals. There are many aspects to this place, you know."

He rubbed his fingers gently along the baby's side, then again looked up and stared at me.

"They still do it in some places with a rusty razor. They hold the child down and slice off the clitoris and then they even slice the inner lips. They close the entire bloody thing up with a piece of tree branch. Then they stitch the mess leaving only a single small opening for urination and menstruation. It is mutilation of their own. And you know what?"

"What?" I half shouted, frightened of this strange, intense man.

"The families encourage this. They think it will hold back her sex drive. What it really does is gives her a heritage of painful intercourse, infertility and, if they are lucky enough to add to this overcrowded country, painful childbirth."

We were both silent for a moment.

"I am quite contended with my cigars, stale though they may be out here. I have my music. Part of the self-deceptions of civilization."

I had trouble looking in his direction and he sensed that.

"Look around and tell me what you see," he suddenly asked, then added, "No, tell me what you don't see."

I noticed nothing unusual and shrugged my shoulders, thinking Allen was right, perhaps I shouldn't have come.

"No mirrors," and he laughed again, "No reminders for me. You see, this is really the place for me and my face. I am accepted here. These poor creatures accept me. In London I was the best show in town."

He gently pushed open the child's eyelids and carefully looked into the pupils.

"These people don't know how well off they are," he continued, "Why, I even fight AIDS. I put AIDS signs up on all the tree trunks warning how dangerous it is. No one even notices. The signs get pulled off for firewood."

Dr. Lom became quiet for a moment and stared out the open window.

"You have medical research, I have tree stumps," he finally said, "God is on the side of the big battalion."

"Napoleon?"

"Voltare," he tried to smile his answer.

He turned to look at the baby.

"If you want to fuck, you fuck. It all does a shit load of no good," and then he laughed that wild laugh again, "you'll not find all of your precious Ten Commandments out here."

I was silent.

"So I put you off, I intimidate you," he said, "Well, you have to excuse me. I've lost the social graces. I jack-off a lot. I should have long ago said welcome to Namanga."

"You are doing good," I tried to answer.

"Never shit a shitter," he answered. "I'm here to escape only with this face there is never any escape. What brings you here? Come to solve the ancient riddle of the Nile? Looking for its source? Well, you're too late. It was all found. One hundred years ago."

Dr. Lom paused for a moment and then added, "Or are you part of the great herd of tourists to my adopted country?" He was obviously enjoying his own small pun.

"I always wanted to go on safari."

"Ah, the dream of every little boy. Safari. How magical that sounds. Well, my friend, look under the trees and see the real Africa. All the wonderful dreams die out here."

He held the child up and patted his back.

"See the real world," he continued, "the hunger. The poverty. You hear about the poachers. I like the fucking poachers."

I must have looked startled for he paused, then continued.

"When I first came here there were fifty-thousand elephants out there in the bush. Two years ago there were less then four-thousand. Who knows what happens in the next ten years. Fuck them too. They had their time on this planet and now they must go, like all God's creatures."

"I thought doctors are supposed to save life," I said, "All life."

"I can't carry the weight of the world on my back, my friend," he answered. "I am a doctor. I only fix the broken bones of humans."

He was again hushed as he looked directly at me.

"I see the hunger," he whispered, "One elephant steps on one farmer's crop, a crop that took a family an entire year to grow, and in that one single step that bountiful crop is gone. One five ton elephant steps on it and food that would have helped entire families is squashed. Fuck the elephants."

He turned his back and opened a drawer taking out a small bottle of medication.

"Don't save the elephants," he repeated, "But I tell you something. They will survive. There are always survivors. I have survived. But look at the bloated bodies of the children who starve. They are way off the tourist path. Little things with rickets and twisted bodies. Babies with soft bones and spines that are already starting to eat away. We all have to survive. We just don't have to dream."

Dr. Lom took out a bottle of medicine and a hypodermic needle and some liquid from a small brown bottle.

The Masai moved forward, putting his arm up as if to say, "No."

Dr. Lom shoved the Masai back with one hand while he tightened his grip on the younger's wrist.

"It is only a shot of Cortisone," Dr. Lom said to me, "And I become a hero. It adds to my legendary ability to cure."

No one spoke as Dr. Lom injected the child.

"This may be one of the lucky ones," he continued, "Two hundred thousand children get polio in Africa every year, even in this age of wisdom. They still die of measles and diarrhea. We just had some yellow fever cases. The winds of time move slowly here. Kenya has the highest birth rate in the world."

He slapped the child on the back. Then he repeated the movement. The youngster's head weaved to one side. A moment later one eye opened, then the other. The child started to cry.

"The children cried even more a few week's ago at Christmas when a troop of baboons leaped over the compound wall and stole the sweets that had been set aside for them. I felt even more sorry for the baboons who have become intruders in their own land."

Asente, the child's father, who had been sitting soundless in the corner of the room, stood and nodded his head when he heard the youngster start to cry.

"I cure the whole world. Everyone gets cured. Except me. You stumbled in here and can't wait to get out. What a story you'll have to tell over the bonfire tonight. The doctor with no face. A real witch doctor. Then you go back to wherever you came from, with your lovely photographs and stories, and I'll be here, fighting the endless fight."

The noon heat was swelling and I wiped the perspiration from my forehead.

"Don't wipe it, my friend," the doctor smiled, "Let the sweat pour out. Let the body get rid of its own poisons."

Before I could answer I heard Allen honking outside and knew it was time to leave.

"Go my friend," the doctor said, "Civilization awaits you. At least the thin veneer of what we call civilization."

He attempted to smile as he handed the child back to his father.

"Don't let the bush become part of you,"Dr. Lom turned to me and quietly warned.

He bowed in a most courtly manner, one that sent shivers through my entire body.

Late afternoon shadows had already started to spread across our camp when the Masai whom we helped earlier suddenly appeared.

When he saw me standing with the others he walked over and slapped me hard on the shoulder.

"Th-ank yo-u," he said in a frightened voice, trying hard to make each word sound perfect, then quickly shifting to his familiar, "Asente. Asente."

I shook the Masai's hand and his huge fist encircled my fingers. He smiled and nodded his head as the others who were watching broke into applause.

"You were quite a hero for that little baby," Gabriella said when the two of us later found time for a brief stroll, "The world needs heroes like that."

"I'm not a hero, far from it, just an ordinary guy trying to salvage an ordinary life."

"Baloney, you are one complicated guy."

"Baloney back to you," I answered, "Heroes are for dreamers. The guy that throws himself on a hand grenade to save the others is a fool."

"Double baloney," she said, "This world needs good people."

It was late and Gabriella paused in front of my tent, glancing about to see if the others had already gone to sleep.

The night was silent and honey scented.

"I need you too," she quietly said, slowly lifting the flap to my tent, "I need your warmth."

We lay in the darkness and neither spoke. We shared only the sense of touch. Finally, after a time, Gabriella whispered in the darkness.

"We both need each other."

# NAIROBI POLICE REPORT
# 20 JANUARY

"Which one of you is named Osuna?"

An old man, his back bent from too many years in the fields, jumped off a work bus and walked into the bar where he slowly, knowingly looked carefully at each face.

No one answered.

"I've been asking at every bar between here and Nairobi," the old man said,"If any of you know this Osuna, tell him his wife has a message for him."

"I am Osuna."

"Never volunteer anything," Aduo, standing against the bar, whispered.

"Sweet Jesus," Ohel mumbled under his breath.

"Your wife wanted me to see how you were doing," the old man continued, "And she said you should come home, your daughter, the one with the cramped leg, is in big pain."

Osuna's eyes narrowed for he knew immediately the old man was speaking the truth and that he would have to leave.

"Don't be a sucker, old one," Aduo said, trying told hold Osuna back, "We need you in the bush. Your kid will be OK without you."

"Fuck off," Osuna screamed, brushing Aduo away, "I must go. My wife wouldn't have sent such a message."

"Maybe it is but a trick of your wife to get you to come home," Ohel, standing next to Aduo, laughed that sound which was always like an evil giggle.

Quarter said nothing and looked away, unconcerned. He was thinking of Chinee Charlie and worried that he might have made a police report.

Osuna paid no attention to the taunting comments of the others. He immediately went out to a waiting work truck and asked the driver if he could get back to Nairobi, aware that once in Nairobi he could walk to his family.

"Sure, man, for twenty shillings the bus driver smiled his answer.

"I have only a few shillings."

"Good enough, get in, but keep your mouth shut," the driver cautioned.

Osuna climbed into the back of the open truck which was already crowded with others hoping to find work in Nairobi. Osuna had forgotten how awful the odor of everyone crowded together could be and he quietly shrugged to himself.

As the truck pulled away Osuna could see Aduo standing in the doorway silently looking at him. His eyes were filled with a look of hate and contempt.

Within five hours Osuna had made his way home, walking, mostly running the last several miles. Silently he opened the door of his small hut.

His wife looked up, scowled but said nothing.

"So you are back," she said with quiet contempt.

"How is the child?" Osuna asked.

"They have her at the Health Center," his wife answered, "Something was giving her big pain in the bad leg."

"I must go to her."

"Sure, go to her," his wife answered, "Then go back to your poacher friends. You only care for what you want."

Osuna wanted to answer but he was too tired and he knew he must get to the Health Center quickly.

"What I do is for you," he softly said.

"Go to her," his wife said, turning her back as Osuna left.

He borrowed the bicycle of a friend in an effort to get to the Health Center quicker.

It was a rickety, old bicycle and Osuna hadn't been on one since he was a child. He was only fifty-five but the years of working bent and twisted in the fields and on the roads had taken away his breath and his strength. Each pushing of the bicycle's pedal made him feel more like an old man.

Osuna was too tired to pump any harder and his legs felt as if great weights were strapped to them but he forced himself to forget the pain, only knowing the bike would get him quickly to his destination. The bicycle weaved in and out of the on coming traffic and several times Osuna heard horns and curses shouted at him.

At the Health Center he quickly flung the bicycle against the door and made his way down the long corridor asking where his daughter could be found.

"I am here, Poppa," he heard her small voice call, "My leg hurts so bad."

Osuna nodded at his daughter and then brushed her forehead unaware of the constant sounds of children crying and coughing in the nearby beds.

A nun in soiled white habit walked over and held Osuna's arm.

"The child will be fine," the nun said, "It will take a few days. The nerve on her leg flared up and has given her a great deal of pain but it will be fine

164

soon. We thought it was polio but it was only her bad leg giving her pain."

Osuna shook for a moment, then nodded his thanks at the nun.

"Try to sleep, sleep is good," Osuna whispered to his daughter as he kissed her forehead, "you are a brave warrior."

The little girl smiled and hugged her father as he started to leave.

Outside the night was still warm and Osuna looked up at the stars. He thought of Aduo and Ohel and knew his wife was right. It was better here. Far from the bush and the mischief that happens out there.

Osuna was glad he borrowed the bicycle because now he was anxious to get home to tell his wife he would stay, work even harder if necessary, tell her that somehow they would succeed.

Then he froze in horror.

The bicycle was gone.

Osuna ran all about the Health Center, at first thinking he had forgotten where he had left the bike, thinking perhaps it had fallen over and he couldn't see it in the darkness, then, finally, starting to panic as he realized the borrowed bicycle had been stolen.

Osuna screamed, a choked, gurgling scream that he kept stifled deep within his own body, making him feel as if he would retch, leaving him gasping for air.

The bike was gone.

He knew he could never repay his friend for it. Never. Unless, unless the poaching was good.

Only the poaching.

Osuna looked away, frightened, thinking of his daughter and his wife and of his family. He thought of Aduo and Ohel and that made him cringe.

He needed the money and now had nowhere else to turn. Money had been a plague to him. It had made him join the poachers to try to help his family. It had caused him pain seeing his wife bent over and the children always searching for a little added food. Now he had lost his friend's bicycle and Osuna felt trapped in a vast, dark hole with no place to run.

Osuna could not even say goodbye to his wife, he felt too ashamed, as he went out to the road and waited for another work bus to come by, to take him back to Namanga and out to the waiting bush.

"...Bless them all,
Bless them all,
The big and the little and the tall..."

For a moment the group of middle aged Kenya farmers from the Highlands forgot they had aged thirty-five years and thought they were still lads back in their early teens as they celebrated the anniversary when the British Lancaster Fusileers first arrived in British East Africa to fight the Mau Mau terrorist.

The small bar was filled with the raucous singing of men trying to recapture a moment in their lives as they shared an easy companionship between old friends.

"Here's to old General Erskine," one of the farmers, a bit plump and a bit drunk, raised his beer glass and shouted to his friends.

"My Dad knew something of the Royal Fusileers a man seated at the back of the bar said.

The plump farmer looked up, suddenly not quite as sure of himself, for it was the way the man at the back had talked, with a smile on his face and a certain amount of contempt in his voice.

Both men knew instinctively what was really being said. They both understood each other and silently had agreed to themselves to say nothing more on the subject. Black and white. My country, your country. Both men silently studied the other but neither dared to speak their feelings.

"Join me for a beer," the plump farmer said as some of the other old soldiers found an empty table and quietly moved away.

Aduo remembered as a child having to claim the body of his dead father with his he skull that had been crushed by British soldiers.

"It is no longer British East Africa," Aduo said, "We are our own people now."

"And so you are," the plump man said, again lifting his beer, "Here's to Kenya. We are all as one."

"Not all," Aduo snapped, "You dress nice and look like you eat good food. What were you singing about?"

"Just an old anniversary," the plump man answered, thinking it was not prudent to say more.

"You're far from the highlands," Aduo continued, "That land, our land, is fertile there."

"We've been out on safari," the man answered, trying to sound agreeable but remaining cautious. He wondered what Aduo meant by "our land." Did he mean land of the Blacks only or the land of all of us? The plump man felt his body getting tense.

Ohel and Quarter stood silently tense near Aduo.

"So you are on the way back," Aduo answered, already considering what might have happened had they met out in the bush.

"This dumb shit," the plump man thought to himself, though a thin smiled remained on his lips, "He must be a missing link to the past. Hasn't he heard this is a peaceful country now. Why must the world always have a few insane ones like this?"

The plump farmer recalled how crazy it had all been when his unit first arrived in Kenya back in the early fifties. He couldn't believe so many years had drifted past this quickly.

Young boys, mostly in their teens, smart ass kids, had been brought to Kenya from all over England. They came from Portsmouth and Dover and Liverpool and Bristol to do battle with something called the Mau Mau.

"You're still green under the arm pits," a battle-tough Sergeant-Major, his voice hoarse and tense, had called out.

All they had been briefed was that the Mau Mau was some sort of anti-white society terrorizing and killing the farmers. At first the young troops only noticed the weather change, from the chill cold of England to the warmth of Africa. When they were sent to the highlands to protect the white farmers, they observed the beauty of the area and the rich farm lands that lay throughout the valleys.

When they first arrived the units were greeted by pipes and snare drums but no one waved and on one cheered.

"Loyalty, men," one old man standing near the pier with a long white mustache, shouted, "Loyalty."

All the young boys knew was that bloody savages were on a rampage, killing whites in the highlands. All they heard about was the terror and thus they responded.

They heard that there were two-hundred thousand Kikuyu who were running crazy, killing "our own "white settlers. Most didn't even know what a Kikuyu was or even how to pronounce the name correctly.

Then the stories began. A lad in their unit whose arms and legs had been hacked away and his head stuck on a fence outside the barracks. Another, the boy who played the harmonica, had his testicles chopped off and stuffed down his throat until he died.

"Kill the fucking bloody colored bastards," the troops would tell each other, their hated and their fear growing with each new terror report. They heard of the atrocities and thus they responded.

"We will hit this people like they've never been hit before," General Erskine told the troops, smashing his fists together for added emphasize.

London had declared martial law and Whitehall gave the troops the power to detain suspects without a trial. One-hundred and thirty Mau Mau suspects were immediately arrested. That number quickly swelled to over two-thousand tribesmen.

A year later Jomo Kenyatta, the Mau Mau leader, was caught and had his trial. The courtroom was hot, the air stifling but R.S.Thacher, the British judge, sat cool and correct in his robes and looked at the man in front of him, the leader who had inspired such brutal savagery.

"Seven years at hard labor," Judge Thacher quietly said.

The Mau Mau responded with still another attack against the barbed wire enclosure of the Police camp, yelling, screaming, tossing stones, spears. The plump farmer, then that young boy, remembered wetting his pants that day.

The British soldiers continued to arrest anyone suspicious, smashing at those they captured as if that would be punishment for their dead friends, rifle butts cracking down, heavy boots smashed into weak bodies, never equating that their hatred equaled that of the Mau Mau.

"We gave the world the Magna Carta, Parliment, Shakespeare and Pitt and Churchill and Newton and Swift," one excited young soldier shouted in anguish, "we can never look up to people who sleep with goats."

"We are a superior kind of animal," another soldier added.

"We'll work out our problems," an officer said, trying to calm his men.

"They are our problems," another soldier answered.

In only four years over ten thousand Mau Mau had been killed.

That was when the plump man, still young and proud, realized how futile war had become. He only wanted it to all end. He wanted to settle in the highlands and start a small farm.

By the time Kenyatta was freed seven years later, the plump man already had his small farm. He had a wife and son and lived in harmony with all those around him.

"I shall work for equal rights for all races," Kenyatta said when he was elected the first Prime Minister of this new country, Kenya. The plump man was contented that the new President did, indeed, live up to his words and proved to be a just and good leader, true to his word, with all races, all people living together.

The plump soldier, who had turned to farming, cheered at Independence day, thinking that, finally, the world would be at peace.

He had long tried to be honest with those who worked on his small farm and offered a small hut for shelter, blankets, food rations and encouraged the workers to bring their families.

"I let the buggers off for tribal holiday ceremonies," he said.

Which is why he now looked with such dismay at Aduo, realizing there would always be one like this, no matter where in the world, the crazy one who lived only for violence.

Aduo sat silently in the back, deep in the shadows, and glared at the plumb British farmer. He quietly extended his index finger and slowly drew it across his throat, his eyes never leaving the farmer.

"It's time to turn the other cheek, lad," the plump man finally said to Aduo.

"What did you say?" and Aduo's eyes started to narrow with his endless hatred.

"You go to the holy church?" Ohel suddenly asked, moving in too close and making the farmers wish they had gone to another bar.

Quarter pulled Ohel back and glanced at the plump farmer. He knew he could kill this old soldier with one blow but his death would prove little.

A grey haired former sergeant, sitting in the back, slowly tightened his grip around the neck of a beer bottle.

"There'll be no fighting this night," a friend whispered, knowing all of their battle days were long over and that they all now lived only for a peaceful life.

"You heard what those devils did up in Kisil?" the grey haired former sergeant quietly said.

"You mean the witches?

"Stuck the suspects hands in a lot of boiling water and when they returned a few days later, if they showed any burn marks, they stoned them to death."

"Just like the good old days."

"Only it was last week. Up in Kisil. Makes you kind of shudder."

Over at the bar, Aduo continued to look at the plump farmer with quiet hatred and then turned and quickly walked out.

Aduo was content knowing there was far more important things waiting out in the bush.

Not that far away Osuna was making hs way back to Namanga knowing he would once again soon be out with the others in the bush.

Far off in the stark night he heard the trumpet call of an elephant.

As he got closer, his eyes filled with tears.

# LETTER FROM LONDON

The rain came down in hard, vast sheets, the first rain of the safari and it made a constant slapping sound against the tent's canvas.

Dark, steel-grey clouds had hung low over the endless African sky all day. It was bitterly ironic that the only time it rained during the entire safari was the one day Allen had gone to Namanaga to get the mail.

The envelope Allen handed me was postmarked London but I knew immediately who it was from, easily noting the familiar handwriting that slanted a bit to the left and the soft, light blue ink she always used.

I tossed it onto my sleeping bags, not wanting to even open it, fearing that if I did whatever might be inside would swirl out at me like a coiled cobra ready to strike.

I had kept my feelings hidden for so long that I felt they were ready to erupt and feared this unexpected letter might have been but part of a long fuse, twisting towards me looking for its detonator, ready for an incendary explosion.

I walked out into the rain and strolled into the grayness of the endless bush where the wetness was cool and made me feel fresh and good. The rain made the bush glisten much the way they spray water on vegetables in a grocery store to make them appear attractive.

When I got back to the tent, I finally picked up the envelope, then I tossed it back onto the sleeping bag. And then, still wanting to get far away from that envelope, I went out again into the rain, for I knew whatever message may have been inside, it would only manage to rip open the old sadness.

The rain lashed against my face as I walked but I was too deep in thought to notice Finally it was time to back to the tent.

The letter was from Lauren.

Just looking at the envelope, knowing it was from her, no matter what she might have written, just seeing her handwriting again, I already knew this would be one of the times of the bad hurts.

There was a wild swoosh sound as a sudden wind blew through the nearby trees. It reminded me of the London underground with the trains shooting quickly out of the dark tunnels that catacomb their way beneath the streets.

Then I opened the envelope.

*"I've defected to London,"* Lauren started with her usual cheery writing,

*"and now I'm one of those Great American Expatriates, circa this modern world of ours."*

Lauren wrote that she had gone to London working with the British office of her publishing firm and she was now living in a flat in Chelsea.

*"You would die over the bathtub,"* Lauren continued, *"the outside part is about four feet high and you almost have to be a pole vaulter to get your legs up and over to climb into the tub."*

I slowly read the note, curious as to what prompted this sudden correspondence.

*"I'm near the Kensington underground and manage to live in that transportation system. Cabs take far too much time driving through that London traffic. The other day I was rushing to a conference and got trapped near Buckingham Palace when the troops marched out to change the guard. They were cute with those big fur hats and bright uniforms but I was rushing and cursing and that was the end of the London cabs for me."*

I studied her old, familiar stationery with its blue L.M. embossed on the top. She had enclosed some old photos of the two of us in San Francisco strolling through the zoo. I wondered why she had bothered to send them and not just tossed them away.

*"I was cleaning my closet and came across these photos. That''s a good job on a rainy day and the weather here is maddening. It is always raining and windy and damp and cold. It gets dark so early and I miss my California Sun."*

Nothing moved outside in the bush as if everything had stopped just for this unexpected letter.

*"I've written a new character, 'Kandy the Kangaroo' and my publisher is talking about the possibility of a series of children's travel books."*

She wouldn't have written this letter just to be cute and chatty, and to talk about the weather, not to me, not after all this time.

*"You would love the women of Chelsea,"* she continued. *"Very chic. Very stylish. Not at all like the usual frumpy looking British women."*

The rain only seemed to underscore the sadness her letter brought to me. Damn her. I knew this would happen, the feelings again starting to break out like a Pandora's box.

I held the letter as if I were still holding Lauren's hand. My feelings had never changed. She was the one had who chosen a new life, a different place.

I put the letter down and looked out beyond the open flap of the tent and could almost see her out there, just beyond the mist, with that wondrous smile which lit up her entire face, that child-women look as she grinned at me, shaking her long brown hair to let the rain fall loose.

*"I read in Publisher's Weekly that you were off on a safari so I hope this letter reaches you, wherever you are,"* Lauren continued, *"I tried to track you down through the safari company. Speaking of letters, your note from New York only caught up to me recently because of my travels. You must be fine or you wouldn't be off alone stomping around Africa. That was always my place, remember? Is it better then fabulous?"*

She was sharp, old Lauren, never missed a beat, who else could have gotten a letter to me out in the middle of nowhere.

*"I met a columnist for the London Times, an American actually,"* Lauren wrote, *"You would like him. A damn fine writer, just like you. He writes a column about Americans working in England. That was how we met."*

She had written something else but crossed it out.

*"His name is Harrison. Harrison Giles. Neat name for a columnist, eh wot?"*

I had met him once at an award banquet. He was a good writer but very stuffy. I remember writing him off as an insignificant twit who had a mustache that made him appear like a walrus. To his credit, however, he had written one best seller which was made into a movie. Lauren would have liked that. Once she told me she wasn't "into material," that was her expression, "material," but she would have liked that glamorous life with all of its trimmings.

Lauren was stalling. I knew her well and could actually see her when she wrote this note, wanting to tell me something, yet not quite certain as to how to say it. The bombshell came in the next sentence.

*"We plan to marry in a month when Harrison finishes his next assignment,"* she wrote, *"And then we'll had a wee honeymoon at Stratford-Upon-Avon drinking in plenty of Shakespeare. I just wanted you to know because we always had such a special friendship. And our friendship will always endure. Friends are forever."*

Like hell, I thought. She knew how much she meant to me, she knew. That was the reason she wrote. Lauren always met things head-on and she didn't want me to hear it from anyone else.

Lauren proved that in the very next sentence when she concluded with a simple, *"I'm sorry,"* and then she ended her letter with our old code, "1940/90." She remembered that long ago comment she had made that we were "nineteen-forty people living in a modern world."

When I folded the envelope I found enclosed the photo we had taken that day at the San Francisco zoo. Lauren had scrawled a note saying she was cleaning her closet and found the photo. On the back she wrote: "Remember."

She remembered everything. That's what she really wrote to me, tucked in there somewhere between the lines, she was telling me she remembered it all.

I thought for a second that perhaps she was also trying to tell me something else. But then I was never much on secret codes or Chinese puzzles and I figured I was all wrong and that I just being that "dramatic person" Lauren often described.

"Well, I've tried like hell to get rid of you, Lauren. The future Mrs. Lauren Giles," I said aloud, then looked around wondering if anyone might have heard me, "Don't worry about me, kid. Your letter is but one more notch in the old agony."

I went out again into the rain and walked aimlessly. The grey wetness kicked in making me feel mellow and alone. Even the nearby animals were hushed and I wondered if they tried to find shelter in the rain or is it only love-sick humans who walk about getting drenched, crying to ourselves.

I held Lauren's letter and read it again. The rain made the ink run, letting all her words flow together as one.

Lauren Giles.

Well, they probably did have much in common. She wrote children's books and he wrote like a child.

We knew each other well and I wondered if through some sort of psycho-phenomenon she was in London right now knowing I had just received her letter. I felt certain she was thinking of me at that precise moment and a chill surged through my body.

The letter did open that Pandora's box and made me also think of Roberta. I glanced at my watch. It was midnight in the states and I thought of her probably half asleep, a TV set flickering in the darkness, lost in her own world, never wanting to change, happy only with the escape she found in her nightly drink.

Roberta had refused help, any help, until there was simply nothing left to give, everything was gone. During her last phone call Roberta said that she was dating and I only hoped that now she might find the happiness that always seemed to elude her.

As for Lauren, I remembered her small cottage at Stinson Beach and how the two of would spend long hours strolling the beach, letting the water softly slip in towards the sand and tickle our feet, making us laugh like children, walking arms around each other, sharing, sometimes not even talking, just happy together.

We strolled the beach down near the water, where the sand is damp and smooth and easy for walking. The fog came off the ocean in small puffs, clinging low, just above the shore. All was grey and the only sound was that of waves and, far off, foghorns. Even the water was dull-green, lost in the fog. Seagulls sat regally on the beach. One perched in front of the others like a teacher about to conduct a class, made Lauren laugh.

"I love the fog," She quietly said, "It's like walking into oblivion."

"As if we are the only two people in the world."

"It hides the real world and lets you imagine only the good things."

The fog hung low and swept quietly along the beach in great flowing mists. The waves cracked like soft thunder against the loneliness of the empty beach.

Then we walked silently listening to the nearby waves and, finally, found love in the salty afternoon air.

The raindrops trickled down my face as I walked about wondering if the memories would haunt me the rest of my life, the rain feeling like tears on my cheeks.

I forgot where I was for a few moments until I passed Gabriella's tent and she called to me.

"You look sad walking out there," she said.

"The rain makes me sad sometimes," I answered. My voice was hoarse and flat sounding.

She asked me to enter and I was always amused at how much neater her tent was compared to mine. It must have been that Swiss Army training.

Gabriella was curled up like a kitten on a rainy day. I sat next to her, stretching out on her sleeping bag, listening to the sounds of the rain.

It had become dark outside and the only noise was still that of the endless storm.

It was bitterly ironic that Lauren's letter arrived the first day it rained on the safari. It had also rained that day in San Francisco when I first told her of my love.

Laura Giles, I thought to myself.

For a split second I was no longer in the bush or Nairobi or even Africa but, like an out of body experience, for a single stunning moment, I was suddenly in the cold of London, with its traffic and noise. I was in Chelsa and Lauren was there, her long brown hair flowing and her smile bringing out those two dimples. She was there and her arms were wide open, waiting for me, waiting to hug and to hold and to cling close together.

As quickly as that thought came, it passed and I was back in the bush, with Gabriella returning me to reality.

When the rain eased up a little, Gabriella and I walked to the edge of the campsite. We found a Thorn tree the elephants had long ago knocked down and sat under its branches protected from the now soft mist.

From our snug resting place we could look out on a great open expanse, now quiet in the late afternoon dampness except, far off, we could see a herd of elephants slowly moving about.

The air was sharp, with everything clean and sparkling, all the views were fresh and alive and that sweet smell of Africa was all about.

"The eternal mystery of Africa," I said, looking at Gabriella, adding, "And the eternal mystery of women."

"Which is more mysterious?" she half teased.

"Women, always women."

"You sound like a corny writer," she answered, "Your letter left you bitter. Really sent you spinning."

"It was from an old friend, old friends have a way of doing that."

"She must have been more than an old friend."

"She was a special friend," I answered, "And I went down hard."

"Women can often emasculate a man," Gabriella said.

" I think of her often and what might have been."

"You and me," she softly said, "We are both lost souls of love."

"Love found. Love lost," I answered.

"It is supposed to be the other way around," Gabriella said.

We became silent listening to the sound of the elephants as they moved through the distant bush.

"Men can hurt to," Gabriella said, as if she read my thoughts, "I still frequently wake up crying, thinking of him."

"How long do you think the hurt will last?"

"It will always last," Gabriella said, turning away.

"The same with me," I answered, "I was wrong and I expected too much."

"Maybe you took too much," Gabriella added, "It's like here, in Africa, the best part is the hunt, stalking the prey."

"Like playing the game to catch one another?" I asked, "Making all the right moves."

"Yeah, sure, only the game is the biggest of all. Man and woman. Someone must set the trap."

"It's to late for traps for me. I haven't time any longer for game playing. Get old like me and see your youth drained away, just a bit at a time, each day, so slow you never even notice until it is too late," I quietly said, "And that is when all the dreams fade and die."

"You make yourself sound old," Gabriella said, "You're here, alone, on safari. You're not that decrepit, my friend."

Neither of us said anything for a long moment. A bird made a soft sound from far off.

"There is an expression in America. The days of wine and roses," I finally said, "For me it is more like wine that has turned and pedals that have fallen,"

"Sometimes it goes all wrong," Gabriella answered in agreement, "Like that scum in Marseilles. I still remember the stench of the green slime under that pier. The odor of dead fish all over. He smelled the same."

She paused, her eyes seeking, wanting to know if I understood.

"I was so young but I learned fast. I scratched his face," Gabriella looked away, then added, "The bastard made me tough on the outside but, inside, I am still cracking up, hurting, from that boy in Switzerland."

"It doesn't happen the way they told you when you were a kid," I answered, "Nothing works like you plan."

"Life doesn't always work out right," Gabriella said, "Sometimes the rules get bent."

"When you're young you fight for the woman you love," I answered, "When you get older, you become resigned to one more of life's tragedies."

She drew quiet in her private thoughts.

"True love will somehow always endure," Gabriella finally said.

"They say that in books but I don't believe it," I answered, "Perhaps one can simply love another too much."

We again became silent for a moment, each of us recalling loves from another time and another place.

"If you love somebody, set them free," Gabriella finally said, "I saw that once painted on the side of an old building. You and I, we still aren't free from the past."

"Those that remember the past too well are condemned to repeat it," I answered, "A guy named George Santanya, he was a philosopher, once said that."

"Things can always be worse," Gabriella shrugged her shoulders, "Like that American story of that man without shoes who complained until he met a man without a leg."

Both of us paused listening to the sound of the rain on the canvas tents.

"The worse part, you're too young to understand, but the worst part is that I see my life starting to evaporate like stagnant water. I still see parades from the past marching down empty streets that have become dull and grey in memory."

"That's nonsense," Gabriella answered,"You writer's make everything so dramatic."

"That's what she once said."

"The letter girl?"

I nodded yes.

"Did you ever hear "September Song?" I asked, "Well, I'm already in the October part of my life."

"Aren't you the one who said each day was new and fresh," Gabriella became quite animated, "Stop feeling sorry for yourself."

"You know what the true sad part is, "I answered, realizing the rain and the letter were really getting to me, "I can no longer relate properly to women."

"You related pretty good the other night."

"The last proud gasp of a lonely old man."

"You're full of bullshit."

"No, not really. You reach a certain age and realize this is "it." There is no turning back. No more youth. Either you grabbed the brass ring or you came up empty handed. The days of laughter and youth are suddenly gone. And all you have left is the future, whatever that may be."

"Michael, the bitter rain philosopher," Gabriella tried to joke.

"You know what the most important thing really is?"

"The rain makes you talk," she answered, "What is the most important thing?"

"Caring, simple caring," I answered, "Just like the baby elephants. The people on this safari, they all care."

"That letter knocked you for a loop," Gabriella said, taking my hand. The rain became hard again and we walked back to her tent.

I lay quietly next to Gabriella for a long while and neither of us spoke. We listened only to the gentle sound of the rain.

I kept thinking to myself that Gabriella was right and that everything was all only "bullshit."

Only then I glanced at her, this girl-women with freckles on her face, the smooth body curves like that of Kilamanjaro and I felt her understanding and her warmth.

Strangely, out of the bitterness comes new hope, a time to move on. Like when someone dies and we look for the good, we say, "It was a blessing because he died quickly," or, "he didn't suffer," or, "It was better going that way" but, no matter how you looked at it, the person was still gone forever.

That was when I also considered one chapter in my old life had finally come to an end but that another might, just might, be starting.

# NAIROBI POLICE REPORT
## 21 JANUARY

They all sat quietly around the campfire. A small strip of elephant meat was roasting on the nearby fire.

Aduo kept busy tossing his knife into the ground, always trying to aim it closer to the center of a small circle he had kicked in the dirt.

Osuna sat off to one side, alone, thinking of his family. He worried constantly about his daughter. He missed his wife, needing her love, his body aching to lay with her once again.

Othel sat shaking in the darkness, his mind unthinking, never clear, only aware of the fire as it glowed near him. He thought of placing his fingers into the flames to see how much pain he could stand then decided to do nothing.

Quarter was different than the others. He paced back and forth, restless, impatient, his mind ever alert, anxious for something to start.

In the darkness he worried about Chinee Charlie who he had pushed the other day and was afraid to tell Aduo. Several days had passed. What if the police had been called? What if those safari people had returned to the grocery store? Quarter liked to plan things for he never wanted surprises, not since that day long ago in his village.

The village made him think of Kgase, at least the Kgase of an earlier time, when she was beautiful. And his. Quarter wondered who she might be fucking right now, or if she even knew who she was fucking.

He smashed his fists together and the unexpected slapping sound startled the others in the otherwise silent bush.

The sound reminded Quarter of the horn, the horn of humiliation.

It was the sound of an auto's horn that frightened Quarter the day he and Kgase first arrived in Nairobi.

They had come from the hill country. Quarter carrying his few belongings in a rolled up sack and Kgase firmly holding onto an old cardboard suitcase because the clasps were broken and the sides were already starting to tear.

Both stood in the center of Kenyatta Avenue unable to move, overcome by the traffic and the noise and the sight of so many unconcerned people who quickly passed by.

The sound of the auto's horn made Quarter jump and Kgase laughed. Quarter's eyes narrowed with hatred for that unknown driver, already moving down the crowded street, who had made him feel humiliated in front of his woman.

For Quarter never felt humiliated. Back at the village he was the Simba, bravest of all. The others feared him for they knew his strength and, secretly, felt he was slightly mad.

He intimidated others because his face frightened people filled with scars, half closed eye and the mouth that remained always in a permanent smile.

All of that happened year's earlier, in one blinding second, over a fight for his chicken. Peter Morigi and Paul Kimotho had suddenly snatched him from behind, Morigi holding him while Kimotho grabbed the chicken and quickly ran away.

Quarter fought back, kicking out, trying to hurt the others, but Morigi was older and too tall. His weight forced Quarter down, even as he was still trying to lash back at his attackers.

Kimotho became panic-stricken at the screaming and the wild hitting fists. His small knife stopped the shouting and the kicking as it cut into Quarer's neck, back, even his legs. The first thin trickle of blood quickly began to meander like a slow moving river down Quarter's face and along his chest.

Quarter felt his eye being torn and the knife slicing along the side of his mouth. It took only a second but when it was over Quarter's face had been disfigured leaving him with a half closed eye and a seemingly permanent smile.

Kgase saw her young friend curled and twitching in pain, his body on the dusty road. Giving a startled yell, she bend over, trying to help and offered water.

Quarter turned away, the pain of humiliation cutting more deeply then the knife had. Only Kgase insisted on staying until Quarter could sit up and his shaking stopped.

The two had known each other since childhood yet on this day it was as if they had met for the first time.

Quarter always considered Kgase different. While he worked long days attending the goats and cows, she would spend time off alone, reading those torn and yellowed British magazines over and over.

Not many understood the words or even cared for the pictures, thus Quarter considered Kgase's reading odd in their poor village.

"Styles. Colors. Designs."

Kgase read and talked of those things, words that meant nothing to the others and Quarter would shrug his shoulders.

"That is the way of women," Quarter's uncle once told him,"They are the caretakers of the earth."

That was something Quarter clearly understood for he had seen as a child how men planted their seeds into the bodies of women. He watched and listened in the bed next to him, heard the movements in the dark, saw movement in the shadows.

He learned much as a child. Five of his friends died from the coughing disease. The one with the bad leg, filled with its puss, had the leg cut off and still died. One drowned. Another simply starved for there was no one to help. Two went off to Nairobi and never returned.

Sadness was a way of life in the village. Kgase knew the same and thus sought escape in the old magazines she would sometimes find after visitors had come to the village.

Both children had grown wise to the ways of the world, their childhood taken away, never to have existed.

"Want a sweet?" Kgase would ask Quarter, a term she used sometimes to give Quarter a piece of candy, other times to offer her body.

They found their freedom in the secrets of their own bodies, making love far out in the remote fields where the grass grew tall. Even there, as they found love, the village was always part of them. In the distance they could hear the cattle bells and, often, the sound of a baby crying.

"The magazines show the truth," Kgase would say, "There is great beauty in the city. Nice people. Nice clothes. We should go and see."

Quarter hated that kind of talk for he knew he could never leave his village.

Only there came a day when Kgase no longer offered her sweets and when Quarter complained, Kgase would only smile and once again talk of the city.

Quarter reached out to touch Kgase but she turned away.

"The city," was all she said.

The horn blared and Quarter jumped, Kgase laughed and nothing was ever the same again.

Kgase found work cleaning an office for her village skills had not prepared her for the city nor had the magazines ever talked about this part of city life.

Quarter found no work and the days became long, endless, as he aimlessly walked the streets, waiting for Kgase.

They shared a small room with two other families and Quarter hated each moment. The room felt as if it were choking his very life away. The openness and the freedom of his village had been taken away and he felt lost, as if everything crowded into him.

Quarter spent hours on the streets, glad for the small bit of fresh air he would feel after the odors of the crowded room. After a few weeks, as the patterns of the street became clear, he began to notice one man who had some sort of ability to stop complete strangers, talk to them for a few moments, then leave with his hands full of money.

Quarter studied the man from a distance and one day, when he finally gathered enough courage, approached the stranger.

His name was Aduo.

"It is the language of struggle."

Those were the first words Aduo said to Quarter when the two met.

Both instinctively knew the gestures of defense and attack and each stood tense, waiting for the other to make a move.

"I've seen you walking the streets," Quarter said.

"Yes, I also have eyes. I observed you, always watching me."

"I'm new," Quarter answered, "from the high country."

Quarter nodded realizing each of them was equally wise, one to the ways of the city, the other to the ways of the village.

Both men were about the same age and carefully studied the other. Aduo had been looking for an accomplice and thought this person, new in the city, might not be known to the police.

"I'm the enemy of the people," Aduo recalled words his father had once spoken years earlier.

Quarter proved a good student and listened intently as Aduo taught him ways to fleece a stranger. How to quickly obtain their interest, then their sympathy and, finally, their money.

"Look at their shoes, you can always tell by their shoes if they have money," Aduo said, "Then look at their clothes. Then look at them directly in the face."

Quarter listened to every word for he realized this might be the start of a new life for him in Nairobi.

"I am a poor student," Aduo continued, "Use that line and it works every time."

Before the day was over Quarter was already approaching strangers. The first was a British woman who gave him ten shillings.

Quarter rushed over to Aduo, excited to show him the money.

"The strongest survive," Aduo said, "That is the only way. The culture of violence."

"You and I, we are the young simbas," Quarter grinned, "The young lions."

"Yes, yes, we are the language of all Africa," Aduo grinned.


Kgase also learned the way of money when Samuel Dawson, the office accountant, offered her one hundred shilings to lay with him.

She had often noticed the way he stared at her but thought it was only her imagination. Dawson worked long hours, often staying late and once complained to Kgase that he had "an empty life."

Dawson was old and tired looking. He seldom smiled and wore neckties even in the heat of Nairobi.

"Do me a great kindness," he quietly asked Kgase one afternoon as she was sweeping near his desk.

When she understood what he wanted, Kgase's first reaction was to slap him, to run and tell the others but then Kgase thought of one hundred shillings and what it would buy.

She thought of those old magazines.

After that first time it was easy. Her body became like her own office, earning more money then she ever imagined.

Quarter knew almost immediately for his instincts of the village never left him.

"They give you a raise?" he asked.

"Yes," Kgase slowly answered.

"A raise for sweeping and cleaning the toilets?"

"Yes," Kgase repeated.

She was wearing a blue silk jacket she had purchased that afternoon and Quarter touced the soft material.

"You dress nice to clean floors."

Kgase said nothing.

"You're a whore," Quarter screamed, "The city, your city, has made you its whore."

He slapped Kgase and shoved her away.

"Fuck you," She screamed.

"How much you charge me?" Quarter shouted, raising his hand to hit her again, "You learned the language quick."

Kgase spun away, kicking at Quarter. The unexpected blow startled him.

Kgase ran out the door, already thinking there was nothing in this small room she would ever again want.

Quarter recalled all that in the bush and cursed to himself.

Then he thought again of Chinee Charlie and wanted to go back and carve him just as he had once been cut. Only he remembered Aduo's caution not to create any disturbance in the area, not to attract any attention.

"We have to be invisible," Aduo had told the others, "until it is time."

Quarter thought of Chinee Charley who had yelled at him and of the safari people who had been in the store.

Once again he heard the horn of humiliation.

# CEREMONY IN THE BUSH

We heard an odd, lilting kind of music, almost like a zither, in the still night air and it was as haunting as it was beautiful, slowly rising out of the bush, an unknown sound whose soft-sweetness penetrated deep into our souls.

How we had arrived at this unusual zither playing, and the stunning scene that followed, is quite another story. It began a few hours earlier when Allen stopped by my tent.

"Say, Ratel," Allen used that name to joke with me when no one else was around, "You've looked dejected since I brought the mail the other day."

"I'm fine," I tried to sound pleasant enough but the thought of the letter once again made my defense start to bristle.

"You are a cool kind of customer," Allen continued, "The manifest says you write. I think you like people, right?"

"You got it," I grinned.

"Suppose I take you some place when the others are napping," Allen said, "I'll show you something you will not believe."

"The others aren't invited?"

"No, no," he quickly answered, "You are cool. If they know or saw, it would not go well for me. They might report it. You are the cool one."

Allen's offer came as no surprise because of the special friendship and understanding we had developed.

He said we would leave when the others were busy with their afternoon chores and that I could bring a notepad but no camera.

"What about Gabriella?" I asked.

"No Gabriella, Pappa."

"She's cool," I said, using his own jargon.

Allen hesitated. He looked around, paused, thought for another moment then said, "OK. But she must promise to tell nobody."

An hour later Allen nodded in my direction and Gabriella and I casually walked towards the van. Two of the guides were also there and nodded when they saw us. Then they smiled at each other.

"Where you guys going?" Mrs. Lewis, who had been sitting quietly in the shade, surprised us.

"Just getting a few supplies," Allen quickly answered as we climbed into the van and got settled. He immediately turned on the motor and started to back out.

"We got some good Kenya beer for you." he said, "It will loosen both of you up just a bit. Get you in the mood for what you will soon see."

Then we drove off into the bush, over those rutted roads, with only Kilamanjaro in the distance giving us any sense of direction as to where Allen might be taking us.

At one point Allen slowed down, telling us both to be quiet. We then drove for several minutes in silence.

That was when we first heard what I thought was a zither, its soft sound rising from somewhere deep out in the bush. Drums made an accompanying, constant sound.

Allen stopped the van and motioned for us to start walking towards the sound. Gabriella looked at me but said nothing.

We heard muffled voices, a chanting noise, more like a harsh, guttural sound, and Gabriella grabbed my arm. The sound was repeated over and over.

A moment later we saw them in an open clearing, hundreds of Masai, jumping up and down, in some sort of wild dance, almost in a frenzy, their eye shut as they continued that hypnotic chanting.

What had sounded like a zither was actually a carved hollow piece of wood with wires strung to small pegs, which a Masai played with nimble fingers. Another Masai accompanied him with a long, twisted horn which took both of his hands to play. A constant clicking sound accompanied the music.

"That's a kumbra," Allen whispered, "An old instrument."

Other Masai were off to the side, kneeling on the ground, hitting drums in a constant rhythmic movement. Some of the drums were beautifully painted while others appeared to be empty gasoline drums.

"MORAN," one Masai yelled and most of the dancers moved back, leaving only the young men who immediately responded to this call, moving closer together, continuing to dance wildly in a small semi-circle.

"What is this all about?" Gabriella, was excited and her accent returned. She turned towards Allen, never taking her eye from the spectacle before us.

"The young ones are at an age to serve their community," Allen whispered, "Now they'll go off and learn old traditions, ways to hunt. They are showing their devotion to each other and that they are like the warriors of old."

We stared at the ceremony which was unfolding all around us.

"It is a way to rub culture back into us," Allen grinned. "Masai culture is older then Christianity."

Young Masai women circled the dancers and clapped their hands and Allen grinned. An ox was being roasted and great puffs of white smoke hung over the entire encampment.

"They also want to show off to their women and show off to visitors from other areas who are here paying their respects," he said, "Makes them want to dance higher, faster, better."

The Masai men all held long sticks, faces painted a reddish color, their hair caked with red clay, beads and colorful stones strung around their arms and ankles. Many of the women that encircled the dancers also wore colorful rings, actually huge bracelets, around their necks, arms and legs. Some of the men and women, swaying to the rhythm, were playfully hitting each other with the bent sticks.

"They smear their body with a paste made from blood and sheep's fat," Allen explained, "it protects them from the heat and insects."

Several of the Masai had their faces painted entirely white, giving them an almost evil look, like the masks of death.

"That's white lime," Allen said, "They are getting ready for circumcision."

Gabriella tapped my arm and pointed to one of the dancers, a fierce looking young man with his white painted body different then the others. A rust-colored painted snake curled along his entire body, from arms to legs, ugly and nasty looking yet almost a work of art that should have been on canvas.

He did not carry a spear like the others but, instead, held a long pole whose tip was carved like a phallus and Gabriella smiled.

"That one visits from the Sudan," Allen whispered.

It was an ancient ceremony, one illustrating the Masai's traditional hunting and war-like spirit. As they danced their movements became more rapid, gaining momentum, finally one warrior at a time would move into the center of the circle, dance about and then suddenly leap high into the air, both feet tight together, while the others would slowly move back, still jumping in place, watching, waiting their turn. Several seemed almost in a trance because of the constantly swaying rhythm and movement.

Every movement was accompanied by great physical emotion, eyes almost closed, bodies held rigid. Even the women surrounding the circle were bouncing together to the never ending sensuous arousing sounds.

I glanced at Gabriella and she was also swept up into the emotion of the dance, swaying in place, her eye narrowed, a devilish smile on her lips. An almost sensual, sultry look crossed her face. She was wearing those cut-off jeans and a yellow tee-shirt which clung to her in the African heat.

Click. Click. Click.

The rhythm of bones hitting together underscored the constant, hypnotic chanting, almost mystic like, all of which blended together giving movement and a blistering passion to this odd ritual.

One man danced about, a wild kind of dance, all the time making his own accompanying sounds by playing two bones he held in his right hand.

"Those aren't really bones," Allen explain, looking at me but turning away from Gabriella, "They are from the penis of an Oryx. Dried and hard and perfect for the sound."

Gabriella and I looked at each other but neither of us spoke. She continued to move her head slowly from side to side, her long blonde hair falling down over her eyes as she swayed to the rhythm. She moved with the beauty and the grace of the nearby gazelles.

Click. Click. Click.

Allen watched Gabriella dance and smiled.

"She's being playful," I said.

"Playful like a simba," Allen answered, "But be careful around here."

Allen knew we remained his responsibility and he was being cautious; at the same time he didn't want to hinder anyone's fun on the safari.

Gabriella had started the dance with humor enjoying the fun of the moment. She was giggling, feeling saucy, laughing but then she changed and quickly became serious. You could tell by her eyes, the way they narrowed, almost dreamy, staring directly at me. I felt as if I could smell the sweet scents of all Africa as she moved slowly closer, swaying, constantly swaying, always to that haunting beat, never removing her eyes from me. Her arms reaching out, beckoning me, as she moved closer. Closer.

Our hips locked together and I started to sway in rhythm with her, laughing at our strange dance.

Gabriella said nothing but gracefully slid her arms around me, her eyes looking only at mine. The smile, with its hint of something more, remained on her face. It was that combination of playful girl and sensual woman, as her mischievous sense of humor flared once again.

"You need good laughter after your letter," she whispered.

Gabriella moved closer to me, pressing tighter, her hips nearly touching mine. My own body movements starting to betray my emotions.

"They had a good harvest, fine cattle," Allen said, getting mildly nervous at Gabriella's dance, "And they are happy. This is a rare sight."

One of the warriors raised his arms and walked over to us.

"Unatoka wapi?" he asked. He stood close and we could smell something like garlic on his breath. His eyes were red and his teeth stained. A lionskin headdress, with its yellowish mane, towered above his head.

"Means where do you come from?" Allen whispered.

"San Francisco," I answered, "San Fran-cis-ko."

The warrior nodded.

"I know, I know," he said in an unexpected high pitched voice. He was grinning and shaking his head.

"Yes, yes," I was eager to answer, "You've heard of the Golden Gate bridge?"

The warrior again nodded, not really understanding but slowly turning towards the other dancers, wanting to make sure they all heard and knew of his conversation regarding worldly matters.

"Unaenda wapi?" The warrior asked.

"Means "where are you going," Allen interrupted.

"Safari," Gabriella added, now intrigued by this unexpected conversation.

"Yes, yes, safari," the warrior answered, then turned, raised his arms and the hypnotic music continued.

"Ngonja kitoko," he called.

"Wait a minute, he wants to say something else," Allen said.

The warrior walked back and pointed a long finger directly at Gabriella, his eyes looking at her breast.

"No," Allen shouted and moved in front of Gabriella. It was easy to understand what was on the warrior's mind for his gestures and his eyes spoke an international language.

"We got a problem?" I asked.

"E Cuma Matanta," Allen answered, never taking his eyes from the warrior, continuing to nod his head, "No problem. Just a small incident."

I looked at Allen and he seemed to relax but I thought of my old Boy Scout troop, the one I hated so much as a child, only I remembered the one thing that I had learned: Be prepared.

The warrior finally shook his hand and slowly walked away, back into the circle of the swaying dancers.

Allen waited until he was several yards away and only then did he grin.

"You're lucky, Gabriella," he said, "That guy wanted you to be his wife. Said you were white and soft like a cloud."

"Proves he has good taste," I quickly said.

"He was excited about the ceremony. He said you were young, like the animal just dropped from its mother," Allen added, "He was just joking, but only by half."

Gabriella stopped dancing and squeezed my hand, still being mischievous like a mocking Lorelei who lured men rocky deaths. Only her sense of humor had been to realistic and the Masai had no way to understand.

Suddenly the Masai turned around and walked back, mumbling something in Swahili. He walked directly to Gabriella and reached out, grabbing her around the wrist.

"Take your fucking hands off me," she shouted.

I first thought the Masai was simply being frisky, like kids anywhere showing off to their own but suddenly everything changed.

He started to slowly stroke his hand along his extended penis, still smiling but his eyes narrowed looking at Gabriella.

Her military training enabled Gabriella to react instinctively. I saw her body become rigid and her hands set ready to strike.

I grabbed Gabriella and pulled her back trying to avoid an incident in a crowd where we were outnumbered.

"Bastard," she yelled at the Masai.

I stood between Gabriella and the Masai just as Allen ran over, shouting in Swahili. I started to feel like Stewart Granger in a bad Hollywood film.

There must have been nearly fifty Masai and they all began milling around us, looking ferocious with the paint on their faces, the dyed red hair and those damn spears which they all carried.

"Look, but don't touch," Gabriella shouted, "Or there will be one Masai with banged balls."

She always said she could take care of herself.

Every other sound had stopped. The dancing had halted. The Masai were all standing in place, no one moving nor talking.

"You," the Masai said in that high pitched voice.

"Fuck off," Gabriella answered, her eyes remaining level with his.

I stood between both of them thinking what part of the Masai could I hit first. I also tried to estimate the distance between us and the van.

Allen also moved in, putting both his hands up to hold the Masai back. He yelled something in Swahili.

"You're a God damned magnet," I shouted to Gabriella as everyone started pushing and shoving back and forth.

At that moment another Masai walked over. He was one of the fierce looking dancers whose face was painted with the white clay. The Masai walked ram-rod straight and carried a spear which he tossed with one quick movement into the ground.

"Let's start backing out of here," I shouted to Allen.

The Masai with the white face shouted something in Swahili and the Masai holding Gabriella loosened his grip and slowly moved back.

I was breathing hard but felt the pressure was off, at least for a few seconds.

The Masai with the white face looked at me and grinned, patting his hand on my shoulder.

"Tick, tick," he said with a small laugh.

Underneath all the layers of white paint I recognized the Masai with whom I had traded the 49er tee-shirt. He was hugging me, greeting me as an old friend whom he hadn't seen in years.

The Masai grinned, giving me a huge bear hug while talking to Allen in Swahili.

"He wants to apologize for his friend," Allen interpreted, "The friend just got carried away by the ceremony."

"The friend almost lost his balls," Gabriella answered, brushing herself off.

She had held her own all this time, now she turned and held me.

"Perhaps we should return," Allen suggested.

Gabriella put her arms around me, leaned her head on my shoulder and whispered something.

I couldn't hear Gabriella because the background sounds and chanting became louder and I asked her to repeat what she had said.

She looked at me and smiled.

"He was the wrong warrior," Gabriella answered, taking my hand as we walked back to the van.

The coming of age ritual for the young Masai was also proving quite similar for myself.

For the first time I started to think that the wall I had carefully erected might actually one day shatter and that I might still discover I was capable of giving and finding affection.

Gabriella and I walked back holding hands, both of us anxious to return to the camp.

It was nearly dark as we drove through the bush. I had my arm around Gabriella who was resting her head on my shoulder, starting to fall asleep.

Suddenly the van's radio crackled and we heard an excited voice yelling in Swahili.

Allen listened for a moment but said nothing. He looked at us, shrugged his shoulder, then quickly looked away.

"What's he saying?" Gabriella said, immediately alert and responding to the unknown message.

Allen did not answer for a moment.

"Poachers. Spotted over near Tsavo."

"Is that near us?" I asked.

"Another park. Quite a distance away."

I looked at Gabriella.

"The game wardens know we are here," Allen added, as if to reassure us, "They have us plotted on their charts. There should be little problems."

The voice on the radio had stopped and there was only the sound of static crackling its deafening noise.

"It is far away," Allen repeated.

Later, when the camp was quiet, Gabriella came into my tent. Her hair was down and she had that same playfull smile I had seen in Namanga. Only now Gabriella said nothing but started to make a soft clicking noise, similar to the sound we had heard that afternoon. Slowly she made her way towards me, arms outstretched beckoning me, silent, like a dream, doing a lusty satire of the dance we had seen earlier.

She grinned putting her arms around me, hugging tightly, in a near perfect imitation of the young warriors.

"Click. Click. Click." Gabriella made that hypnotic sound.

"Who is more primitive now?" she whispered, still swaying in slow motion, running her hands along the side of my body.

"You're wild, lady," I answered, playfully slapping the side of her leg. I felt a carefree kind of abandon, filled suddenly with the lost strength of youth, the adrenaline flowing throughout my entire body.

"Did Allen tell you the song they were singing?" Gabriella asked.

"What?"

Gabriella became silent and smiled.

"They were singing in Swahili," her voice had a slightly mischievous sound.

"So what were the words?"

For a moment Gabriella hesitated, the way a comedian does before delivering the big punch line.

"Make love to me if you want to or not," she grinned.

Then we both became silent as we reached out, touching one another.

"We are doing like Africa," she softly said.

"What?"

"Exploring each other."

I slowly ran my fingers through her hair, then they found their way down her neck, along her waiting body.

Gabriella responded in the same way, coming closer, gently touching me in places, hidden places, special places.

There was the eternal smoothness of two bodies moving together, in rhythm, slow, faster, soft, hard, Gabriella's legs locked rigid around me, both of us touching, caressing, my fingers gently sliding along her breast whose nipples were soft yet firm, feeling her fingers as they slowly, gently curled and stroked along the length of my own blazing spear.

Even in that moment, it was odd, but I still distinctly heard that click sound from far in my memory.

Click. Click. Click.

Only now the sensual rhythm matched the thundering movements of Gabriella and I, alone, together, as our bodies shook, trembling from deep within, our love-feeling surging out, until we both exploded as one.

Our bodies finally spent, we lay silently together. I let out a soft moan in the darkness of the tent.

"Don't wake the others," Gabriella said as we both slid down onto the sleeping bag, "Be quiet, my young warrior."

Gabriella later left for her own tent once again concerned about the others, thinking it would have appeared awkward had she been seen with me when the dawn broke.

"Mrs. Lewis would never understand," she said.

"No one would," I answered, thinking of Hughes and Yuri.

It was only in the damn pale blue light of the early morning hours when I lay awake that the old memories would once again flare and the hurt start to return.

I felt a kind of sadness aware that you can never go back and yet I was also frightened not knowing what the future might hold for any of us.

# ALEJANDRO

"Redeep, redeep," I kept repeating, "Redeep."

Still Alejandro sat around the camp fire with a blank, bewildered look on his face.

I crossed my hands together and extended my fingers out as if they were flapping.

Alejandro merely nodded his head to say "no."

Hughes came over and drew a picture of a frog on the back of a torn piece of notepaper and kept saying, "Frog, frog."

Alejandro smiled but only shrugged his shoulders.

We were all trying to explain the word frog but Alejandro merely grinned and shook his head. It wasn't that he was unable to speak, as I had first thought, but that he spoke only Spanish and none of us knew any Spanish. Which is the reason Alejandro usually kept to himself and never spoke. He was in his own form of isolation and it had proven a mild frustration.

All of us tried to communicate in one way or another using everything including sign language, broken English, pig-latin, even bits of Swahili but nothing worked.

As with the others, he wanted to tell his story around the fire that night but he spoke in soft Spanish and used a good deal of sign language and exagerated gestures. Oddly enough, it was beginning to work.

"Froagh," he slowly repeated and then he knelt down on all fours and hopped around the fire to show that he understood.

Everyone cheered his efforts. Margaret patted him on the back and Gabriella gave him a huge hug. Corcoran smiled and raised his fist as if a touchdown had just been scored. Flora Zimmer blew him a kiss.

Alejandro stood opening his mouth and tossing his arms about and it was Mrs. Lewis who picked up that message.

"You're a singer," she said, humming a few bars.

He smiled that she understood but shook his head "no," pulling out his pockets and turning them inside out.

We all looked quizically trying to determine what he was trying to tell us. It had become a unique pantomime game that we were all playing out in the bush.

"Too poor," Hughes half shouted, "I understand that. No lessons. Too poor."

"Por, Si," Alejandro placed his fingers in his mouth and let out a long whistle. Then he pulled pockets inside out to illustrate the traditional sign of empty.

Excited at the break through in communications, he grinned nodding his head to say "yes."

"So what do you do?" Yuri said slowly, repeating even slower, "what do you do?"

Alejandro made a gesture with his hands together, flinging forward over his shoulder.

'YOU'RE A FISHERMAN," Mrs. Lewis shouted, delighted as though she had just broken a foreign code.

He was from Barcelona, had saved his money from fishing for this trip, was proud that he had finally overcome the language barrier.

"Your country," he said, pointing to the tee-shirt he was wearing and which read: OREGON STATE BEAVERS.

Alejandro had one of those enchanting personalities, a smile that would charm anyone. He was always among the first to pitch in and help serve the meals or assist others setting up their tents. His only bad habit was that of biting his fingernails and, when finished biting all the nails, he would start on his finger tips. They had become raw and were always peeling. Alejnadro would shrug his shoulder knowing it was a terrible habit but one that he could not control.

"You're too nice a man," Mrs. Lewis cautioned, "Don't do that."

Alejandro only shrugged his shoulders again, not understanding, but smiling that wonderous grin of his. He nodded his head and started to whistle a rousing version of "Lady Of Spain." We all joined in singing the familiar words, clapping to the tune, a raucous sounding group if there ever was one sitting out there alone in the silence of the dark bush.

He was a bullfight aficionado, Alejandro gradually explained, beginning when he was only twelve and living on a small ranch.

"Tienta," he said, a term meaning the testing of the young calves to determine their strength, bravery and endurance.

It was also a test for a twelve year old who only dreamed of wearing the Traje de Luces, the bullfighter's suit of light. A twelve year old's bravery can also be foolish as the day Alejandro pretending he was already a brave torrero, filled with youthful enthusiasm, leaped into the small ring and faced a young calf who charged towards him. As Alejandro backed to one side, the calf suddenly hooked to the left knocking the youngster down, the fall breaking a leg which left him weak, never to have the strength that a torrero would need in his legs.

That was when Alejandro knew he would never be able to wear the suit of lights he had dreamt of and, instead, turned to the life of a fisherman.

He stood tall before the fire's light and, in the darkness, showed us the passes he might have made in the bullring, proudly holding an imagined moleta, the bullfighter's red cloth. Alejandro made a series of sweeping veronicas, a graceful pass, shouting "ole" and whistling at the imagined bull. He stomped his feet in the bush as he would in the ring to attract the bull's attention.

"Huh, toro," he called, his eyes alive, looking out into the shadows.

He thrust his right foot forward and continued to make a series of sweeping passes, rapidly moving in an imaginary dance of the bull ring. It was easy to visualize him standing alone in the middle of the ring, the trumpets sounding in the late afternoon.

"Ole," shouted Hughes.

"Bravo," Mrs. Lewis clapped her hands.

Alejandro held his cape rigid and with great dignity. It was easy to see that if he had been a bull fighter he would have shown great courage.

"Toro, toro,"Alejandro called into the darkness, "ole."

"It is the battle within the man, to see how close they can come to the bull,"Yuri explained to Sophie, "a test of courage. Like my father had."

At the mention of the word "father" I noticed Sophie look up, bristle, then slightly move away from Yuri. She wanted to say something as before but again held back.

Alejandro's movements were graceful, flowing like moving art and we all recognized the bullfighter he might have become.

Instead he would never know the roar of the crowd. He lost his parents at an early age, became a fisherman in his teens, only found the ways of love when he matured on the backstreets of Barcelona.

Alejandro shyly explained all of this to us and then he started to applaud and gestured with his hand for one more moment.

He walked over to his tent and when he returned held a graceful African hunter which he had carved. It was something he had carefully whittled out of the bark of an Acacia tree and had worked on it since the safari began.

Alejandro walked over to Mrs. Lewis and held it out to her.

"For you, Please."

It was difficult for him to say the words but he handed the carving to Mrs.

Lewis who smiled and understood.

"It's beautiful. Thank you."

"Thank you," Alejandro repeated and he smiled and was pleased.

I had glanced about the campfire and saw all our faces reflected in the soft yellowish light, everyone listening intently as Alejandro related his story, and again realized how we had all become as one these recent days, knowing each other, feeling for one another.

I put my finger on Gabriella's lips in the shadow of the fire and she kissed it back.

"Nakusentelon," I whispered recalling that Swahili word which meant, "Place of great beauty."

Gabriella only smiled at me.

The fire had died down and the camp had become silent.

I looked at Gabriella but said nothing.

I knew, within moments, Gabriella and I would be together, and we would both find that place of such beauty.

# MISTER FUNADA

Jimmie Funada, dressed in an impeccable grey silk suit, sat quietly in his mahogany walled office located on a Tokyo side street. His thin eyes always with a cold-steel stare and his mouth permanently set in a deep frown.

He sat stroking his maltese, "biscut," imagining that he was running his fingers through deep fur, hardly noticing the young women sitting soundlessly across the desk from him, elegantly dressed in an Italian designer yellow silk robe. Her soft skin showed years of delicate pampering, her face shone like one of Jimmie Funada's own art works. She sat placid pouring tea from a hand-carved silver teapot.

Jimmie Funada watched her and smiled to himself. She was like a delicate ivory carving and that thought always pleased him. He glanced at the carved oriental characters that sat on his desk, knowing the twin set of ivory carvings was worth over $100,000 and he felt pleased.

Jimmie never liked his own name. It did not seem appropriate for someone in his late sixties and that is why this long-time Japanese civic leader and businessman always demanded that his business associates refer to him as Mister Funada.

He had no concern for the African runner who at that very moment, was darting his way through the Kenya night, his lungs gulping air, feeling as if they were ready to burst, knowing he must not stop even though he had already run for miles, carefully carrying his heavy, bloody sacks. He paused only long enough to scrap dried blood off the trunks he carried.

Mister Funada was but one of the many destinations that those sacks, filled with tusks of dead elephants, would be delivered. Offices from Tokyo to Hong Kong eagerly awaited such deliveries.

While Hong Kong remains one of the world's major dealers in ivory it is Japan that has become the world's largest consumer of ivory goods.

Prestige for many Japanese is to have a simple ink pad carved out of ivory for signing their names.

Mister Funada knew well the human lust for ivory which dates back almost to the dawn of time. Five thousand years ago, the soft-white cream carvings gracefully decorated the tombs of Egyptian Pharohs as they started their voyage towards heaven.

Toothpicks. Chopsticks. Cowboy pistol handles. Rings, necklaces and bracelets designed to adorn the body of expensive women. All made from the tusks of the African elephant.

"You western folks did pretty good," Allen had told us one day while driving through Amboseli, still feeling remorse at the recent poacher sightings, "In the twenties we had over sixty thousand elephants legally killed just to make billiard balls and piano keys."

The poachers trail is well known starting in the bush, then smuggling the tusks out usually at night to boats waiting near Mombasa or to planes at small hidden airfields, all of it eventually heading to ports in Arabia or South Africa, often with bribes readied for corrupt officials. The trail usually included Dubai, then Singapore, frequently ending in the shops of Hong Kong and Tokyo.

That is why throughout our safari we would frequently see police roadblocks on Kenya highways. They used steel-spikes stretched across the roadway forcing all vehicles to stop for quick searches of everything from gas tanks to luggage.

The forty dollars that a poacher would receive in the bush for a tusk would become one thousand dollars in Japan and, when the ivory was cut and carved into graceful art objects, would be sold for three times that amount.

Downstairs from Mister Funada's office was the cluttered work room where eighty year old Akuro Ito spent long days, delicately carving each piece of ivory. slowly turning the tusks into objects of beauty. The room was narrow and always filled with ivory dust. Ito would often curse to himself when his knife hit a bullet still lodged in the tusk.

Mister Funada recently spent nearly four million dollars in the purchase of three thousand tusks, about twenty-six tons, all illegally taken from the elephants that he cared little about. He gave no thought to the elephants that had been left dead or crazed, having to roam the bush, unable to eat, finally dying that slow, painful death.

This never bothered Mister Funada for the only elephants he had ever seen was when he took his small grandson to the Tokyo zoo. The two would laugh together at the elephants silly antics and Mister Funada always purchased a bag of peanuts for his grandson to feed the "funny elephants."

Mister Funada's main concern, at the moment, was that the size of the tusks seemed to have started to shrink from eighteen and twenty feet long down to around nine or ten feet in length. Many of the older elephants had already been killed and the poachers were now shipping the tusks of baby elephants.

This made Mister Funada furious as he sat in that mahogany office thinking of ways to get back at the poachers, knowing it was useless, for he was aware how much he needed them to supply the merchandise.

He turned to the serene woman seated near him, sighed and then, without a word, the two went into a room adjacent to Mister Funada's office. He walked slowly, in command of his every step, feeling secure in his own power. Each move was careful, deliberate, exactly as when he made his business deals.

The two entered a spacious completely outfitted gymnasium and spa. There was a massage table at one corner. A variety of silk robes and fluffy towels hung from nearby brackets. Soft lights came from small lamps, resting in ivory carved bases, that lined the walls.

Silently they took off their clothes and got into the warm, bubbling water which quickly covered them sending powerful jet waves that massaged their tense bodies. Both found brief relaxation as the curling water engulfed them. Neither smiled or showed signs of any pleasure.

Under the surface the woman's body, in the lapping water, felt soft. Mr. Funada's hands went out to her breast and he started to gently stroke her nipples.

Usually Mister Funada would relax at this moment but today his thoughts remained on those small tusks. He felt betrayed by the poachers and their recent shipment of baby ivory.

# SCRAPBOOK IN TIME
## LAUREN

The bush was still in the early evening breeze. Most of our group were in their tents resting and the guides were busy preparing dinner.

I looked out of my tent towards the bush, passed the Thorn trees. I Looked way off into the distance where the bush is flat and open and I saw Lauren.

It was as if she were out there walking quietly, slowly through the thin wisp of fog that just touched the top of the bush. Her letter still bothered me. Knowing her so well and being familiar with this Harrison Giles, because of all that I lay quietly in my tent and was able visualize much of their time together in London.

I once again heard the laughter in her voice and I could see her smile and those wonderful eyes that glowed with life.

She had explained in her letter that she moved to London and I figured it was probably for the same reason I had gone to Africa: to forget.

I remember what she had long ago told me about being tired of coming home alone to an empty house, her wanting to share with someone, to have somebody to talk to in the evening.

"I want to bake cookies for someone," she once said.

We both knew about loneliness. How cruel it can be and how it can grow and become a part of you and how it can destroy from within.

I imagined Lauren alone, an American lady in the regal realm that is London, at first busy with her new job and charmed by the sights offered in that fairy tale city.

I envisioned her window shopping in Chelsea and being amused at the high fashions; viewing the crown jewels at the Tower of London; exploring the massive food halls of Harrods.

Lauren had a heavy double-breasted polo coat she used to wear in the fog of San Francisco and it would have been perfect for London. I could see her walking through Hyde Park and Kensington gardens, her coat collar turned up, hands thrust deep into the pockets.

Harrison Giles, on the other hand, was a shrewd reporter, trained to observe and he would have immediately spotted her loneliness and understood.

"Hello, California lady," would have been the kind of thing he probably said when they first met. He would have used some sort of attention getting dialogue.

"How do you know I'm from California?" Lauren might have answered, flashing that stunning smile of hers.

"You're the only lady in all of London town with a such a healthy tan," Giles would answer in his charming way.

A lonely lady.

A sophisticated reporter.

Two Americans alone surrounded by the enchantment of London. It was a combustible combination.

He would take her to Covington Gardens; for tea at Claridge's; even to Fordham and Mason to show her the clerks in their frock coats.

"The Royals are from an other world order and there is place for them in our modern society."

I visualized Giles taking Lauren to Speaker's Corner on a Sunday morning to listen to the street orators.

"They stand on a soap box," he would explain, "Because then they are not touching on British soil and can say whatever they want."

"Giles, smart ass, street wise," I jealousy thought to myself, "Playing the world-weary reporter."

He would take her to small, quaint pubs and to the British museum to show off his intellectual side and then he would take her to Petticoat Lane.

"They say you can lose your wallet at the start and buy it back at the end," Giles would explain.

Lauren would listen, and laugh and forget her loneliness. It would feel good to be with someone, especially in this most magical of all cities, and she would listen to Giles and be charmed and give much of herself in return.

Maybe sometimes, but just sometimes, she might remember Old Michael. Like when she saw the British soldiers march passed or observe her first London Bobby for she knew how I admired these heros of my youth.

Regency Park would also give her a moment to remember. That's where the London Zoo is and she would surely visit there because of her love for animals. That is when she would have recalled our visit to the San Francisco zoo.

It was like the day she cleaned her closet and found that old photo we had taken together at the zoo. She had included it with her letter from London.

The drizzle, that fine, light drizzle which frequently falls in London would have helped Giles for it would added to Lauren's feeling of melancholy. I pictured him opening his umbrella and dancing about in a smug imitation of Gene Kelley in "Singing In the Rain" and Lauren would have thought that cute, and laugh and she would begin to give serious thought to this new-found friend.

She would imagine that she was falling in love, only it would not be love, not "in love." I knew this, with all certainty, above all else, it would never be "in love."

At least that is what I kept telling myself. Lauren and I had shared too much, knew each other too well and I felt certain I could not be that wrong about her.

"I'm lonely, you're lonely, let's not be lonely together," Giles was sharp and would have easily put a neat little spin on both of their feelings.

It would have been easy for Giles to create some sort of emotional bond between them. That may have been when she first thought of tracking me down and sending her letter. Not to hurt me, that wasn't like her, but just to let me know.

Only what she really wanted was something I couldn't understand. My blessings? My opinion? I felt there was more in that letter, that there was a piece missing. Why write now, after all this time, about being engaged? Something just didn't fit into place. Because I knew her so well, I felt certain she was holding something back. Only what?

I clung to her memory as one would grasp at a piece of driftwood, hanging on by the fingertips, knowing it offered some last desperate bit of hope, never wanting to let go, aware that a wave could wash it all away at any moment and that all would be gone.

It was all merely small puffs of a dream, still loving Lauren, always aware that it was all impossible. The truth was that we would probably never meet again in this lifetime but knowing, within myself, that a love can still grow and endure through all eternity.

I lay in my silent tent, my body throbbing.

Then I heard the sound of the soft breeze in the twilight and wondered why, what was the piece in her letter that was missing?

# SAFARI NIGHT

"…roll out the barrel,
we'll have a barrel of fun…"

Far removed from Mister Funada, alone out in the bush, we continued our daily travels, never knowing what sights might be encountered at the very next turn of the road.

"Hey, Herbert," Mrs. Lewis called, "spot any Forest Hogs today?"

"Only the one who swiped my pillow last night," Hughes answered, smiling at Margaret.

We were all feeling lose and carefree and rapidly becoming familiar with what Africa had to offer.

"I don't care how you bring 'em, just bring 'em back alive," I said to Allen one morning as the van made its way through the bush, "That was the saying of an old time movie hero. Frank Buck, an African explorer."

"He sold lots of candy bars at Saturday matinees," Flora Zimmer added.

Allen answered with only a polite grin not sure of what we meant.

Each day were spectacular new sights to behold. A herd of zebras stood quietly in the bush, clustered together. Nearby a group of comedic acting monkeys would suddenly bounce upon us from nearby trees, their wild antics as seemingly sent to us merely as comedy relief.

"Damn you," Yuri suddenly shouted, shaking his hands in the air.

He had rested his wallet on top of the van as he filmed the monkeys when one swooped down, picked it up and was scattering its contents from the tree top.

"Good timing for your song," Corcoran said, "a barrel full of monkeys."

We all helped Yuri collect his belongings as the monkeys stood nearby surely laughing at us.

There was a more sophisticated style of humor which happened later that night. Gabriella and I continued to be discreet, feeling secure with our little secret only sometime in the middle of the night the entire camp suddenly heard:

EEEEEGGGHHHHHHHH.

Everyone in each tent must have leaped up simultaneously at the unexpected sound which was an eerie combination of growl, groan, Indian war-whoop, blood-curling laughter. Then the sound was repeated:

EEEEEGGGHHHHHHHHH

Only this time it was quickly followed by the sounds of pots and pans being struck from somewhere out in the darkness.

"Go away," I thought I heard Allen's voice shout.

I dashed out of the tent in time to see two hyenas that had slinked into our campsite disappear into the darkness as quickly as one of Houdini's magic tricks.

The hyenas are ugly little creatures with big heads and twisted backs who move close to the ground as they prowled their way through out compound.

Off in the distance they groaned at us, making a mocking laugh, then letting out a blood-curdling whine cry in the night. It was a haunting sound, like a baby in fear.

Gabriella ran out of the tent immediately behind me, a sight quickly noted by Sophie who proved equally discreet as she politely turned away saying nothing.

We were all now quite wide awake, laughing among us at the unprovoked attack. Relieved that it had been nothing more serious.

"Poachers are making us all nervous," Hughes said.

"I have the perfect remedy," Margaret said in the darkness, "Marshmallows anyone?"

How she produced them, out in the bush, I'll never know. Perhaps it was one of her husband's illusions but, whatever, Margaret suddenly had a bag of marshmallows which, at that very moment, served as an unexpected reminder of home.

Houdini got a long branch and stuck one marshmallow over the embers of the dying campfire. Mrs. Lewis quickly did the same as did Yuri.

"What they doing?" Gabriella asked.

"Didn't you ever toast marshmallows?" I asked her.

It was something Gabriella could not quite understand as I explained the unique American custom of toasting marshmallows on a stick.

"It is especially delightful during picnics," I told Gabriella, "letting them brown just a bit and then enjoying a taste of almost epicurean proportions."

Allen came over, quickly recognized what was happening, and had the guides gather sticks for everyone.

"The hyenas like the dark,"Allen said, "when they are babies they stay in the underground holes while the parents go out hunting food for them."

What an odd bush sight that must have been, our little group, in the early hours of the morning, clad in shorts and jackets, standing around a fading campfire toasting marshmallows.

"The hyenas are an odd animals "Flora said as she held her stick towards the fire.

"Excuse the expression," Allen smiled, "But the male and the lady hyena, they each have a penis."

"Homogamous," Corcoran quicky said, "I once encountered a tribe like that in the Philippines. Couldn't make love to the women because it would tickle me and I'd start to laugh."

Flora gave Corky a crack in the ribs; Mrs. Lewis turned away.

"They are the only animal whose babies often eat each other," Allen added, as he walked back towards his tent.

We watched in silence as the marshmallows toasted.

"Do you folks ever think about old 'B' movie titles?" I asked, feeling it was my time to contribute to the conversation.

"What do you mean?" Hughes asked.

"I collect old movie titles, even make some up," I answered, "Like right now, how about 'Marshmallows In the Bush?'"

"I collect old newspaper headlines,"Yuri said, "The best is one I have framed in gold and it is printed in red, white and blue. Takes up the entire front page and all it reads is 'WORLD WAR II ENDS' in giant type."

"That's the kind of thing," I answered, "Like when I flew out here at night from London and I thought a great title might be, 'Night Plane To Africa.'"

Mrs. Lewis heard a far off baboon and eagerly added, "How about 'The Call of the Wild?'"

"Halt. Stop.," Margaret said with amusement, "No points. That one has already been done. By Jack London."

"I've one for you," Corcoran said, "When I visited Mombasa before coming here we took the last plane out and it leaves every night at eleven. How about 'Last Plane from Mombasa?'"

"Sounds like a title for Bogart?"

"What is Bogart?" Gabriella asked.

"Humphrey Bogart," I grinned, "My hero. Movie tough guy. Did you ever see 'Casablanca?'"

"The film?" she answered, "Yeah, sure I know him."

"Here's looking at you, kid," I nodded, trying to mimic Bogart while blowing Gabriella a kiss.

She smiled back and for a moment I thought of her and Mombasa. Then, just as quickly, I pushed the thought far away.

The others continued to suggest movie titles as we stood over the fire toasting the marshmallows. It proved to be another warm moment of the friendship we had formed for each other during these weeks together.

Aware that we were all wide awake and to turn the evening into a small amusement, Allen and his guides started to sing Kenyan folk songs. All of their voices were out of pitch and off key, yet provided a charming moment out in the bush.

Alejandro added to the charm when he joined them, whistling "Lady Of Spain" which was upbeat and appropriate for the moment.

When they finished, Gabriella and I decided to walk to the edge of the campsite. We passed Allen's tent and Gabriella pinched my arm, nodding towards the open flap.

Inside the tent was a small framed photo of Allen's wife and children. A grinning little boy sat on Allen's lap, looking proudly up at his father. The child was wearing a hat with SIMBA written across the front.

Next to the photo a dartboard was hanging from the wooden poles but instead of a bullseye marking the center, there was an ad for some British beer torn from an old magazine. The ad showed a lion-tamer surrounded by dozens of lions and tigers in a small cage. It was obvious by the dart markings that Allen had used that target frequently.

"Good for him," Gabriella whispered.

Allen looked up and smiled.

"Remember the Ratel," he softly called to me.

I nodded my head in answer.

"What does that mean? Gabriella asked.

"Just an old African legend," I casually answered.

"I bet. Some legend," she said, playfully poking her elbows into my ribs.

We continued our small stroll and by the time we returned a few minutes later, everyone had retired to their tents. Gabriella paused for a moment when she reached my tent, hesitant to enter, thinking perhaps someone might see us.

On the other hand, we had become a bit of an open secret. We sat together at dinner and on the van and often glanced at each other knowingly as people do who share special secrets. The others knew and understood and smiled to themselves.

Gabriella was aware of all this as she paused for only a moment outside my tent, shrugged her shoulders and quietly entered.

We lay in the dark and I put my arm around Gabriella.

"We are a secret no longer," she said.

"That makes me happy. We should never be a secret."

"They worry about the poachers. We all worry."

"Allen is aware. He senses things."

We quietly whispered in the darkness afraid our voices might carry over the silent bush.

Then I felt her fingers softly touch my growth.

"Just like the elephant's trunk," she softly.

"What are you doing?"

"Trying to see if you have glands like the elephants. See if they swell up."

"Nothing swells up. Except down here. And the skin doesn't turn grey like the elephant."

"Your trunk is growing."

"Shush," I whispered, "It is the time of caressing."

"Sound like an elephant, Miki," Gabriella said.

My fingers slid along her waiting body and then I quietly sighed.

"The music of the bush," she said as she snuggled ever closer.

Then we both became silent and said nothing.


Early the next morning, before going out on safari, Allen called all of us together.

"I've been thinking about last night and I know your concern of the poachers," he said, "And I wonder if you might want to turn back, leave, maybe go to Nairobi."

"Do you think it is that dangerous?" Mrs. Lewis asked.

"Do we just give in?" Yuri said.

"It is not giving in," Allen answered, "It is just an idea for safety. This is a wide area and even if poachers are around, they could be hundreds of miles from us."

"We've come a long way just to turn around," Mrs. Lewis said.

We were standing in a small circle and each of looked at the other.

"But we should consider safety," Margaret said.

"Lets press on," Corky said, "A little adventure is good for the soul. I survived the cyclones in Madagascar and I'll be damned if some twit poacher will scare me away."

"Well, we shouldn't do anything foolish," Hughes said, kicking at the dirt as he tried to reach a decision.

"That recent report was about sightings in Tsavo," I said.

"That is correct. And it is far away," Allen nodded his head.

"You and your men are trained about poachers?" Sophie asked.

"We know about them but we are not game wardens."

"What do you suggest?" Margaret said.

"You are guests in my country," Allen answered, "I want safety first."

"Then you suggest we should turn back?"Yuri asked.

"I think we should vote," Allen said, "I just don't want to worry anyone."

"Press on," corky said.

"Yes, I agree, lets continue," Flora Zimmer said.

"I'm not sure," Hughes slowly said. He glanced out into the bush as if he expected to see something.

"I vote to stay," Mrs. Lewis said.

Gabriella tried to explain what was happening to Alejanro who nodded his head, "yes."

"I also vote accordingly," Gabriella said.

"Let's stay,"I answered, hoping we weren't making the wrong decision.

"We stay?" Allen asked once again.

Hughes looked at his wife.

"Yes, let's stay."

I studied our small group as they stood in that circle: Corky, always the blunt one. Yuri, passive. Hughes, ponderous at best. Gabriella, always alert and determined. Flora Zimmer, the oldest yet in some ways the youngest. Mrs. Lewis, filled with her own style of courage. I, too often lost in my own empty past.

We were all apprehensive but glad the decision had been made. It was unanimous.

Our small group had truly become as one.

# NAIROBI POLICE REPORT
## 22 JANUARY

Aduo leaned over and snapped a twig in anger, wishing he could crack someone's neck that easily.

"The game warden, they know about you," one of the drifters at the entrance to Amboseli had told Aduo, "Chinee Charlie reported sightings."

"They continue to stick their nose far from where it belongs," Aduo answered, thinking they might have to change plans.

Quarter said nothing. He was leaning against a tree, sipping a beer. His eyes already red and sunken even in the morning's early hour.

"Maybe if they know we should move elsewhere," Osuna said sitting in the shade, fanning himself with an old piece of cardboard. He sat worried about his little girl and his wife. Osuna felt bad about the loss of his friends bicycle and tried to put that thought out of his mind.

"Old women," Quarter mocked, "We've come too far to turn back."

"And what of the goods we already have?" Aduo said, "You forget what we have tucked away in the bush."

"There is also money out there," Quarter whispered, thinking of the visitors to his country.

"True, my friend and there are no witnesses out in the bush," Aduo said slowly, "Remember a lion can still bite if you only cut off its tail."

The men sat crouched on their haunches as they talked quietly knowing they had already stored several tusks, even a rhino horn, and that this would soon bring them much money.

"You think we just kill animals for nothing," Aduo laughed, "Like some sort of barbarians. Bullshit with leaving our goods. Bullshit."

He carried his ax and idly slashed at a nearby bush sending branches fluttering to the ground.

"We haven't even started out here," he said, "This is a big store just waiting for us to select the goods."

"I worry about the warden," Osuna repeated.

"You worry too much, old man," Aduo answered, "Let me worry."

"Don't fear the game warden," Ohel said, rubbing his thumb and forefingers together, "They just the same as us. Give them some money and they even help."

Ohel, tall and thin with a thin stubble of beard, wearing a dirty, torn

212

undershirt, had joined the group in Namanaga. He had known Aduo for years, the two often working together against the tourist on the streets of Nairobi.

"They got rid of most of the wardens who take bribes," Osuna said.

"There are always others," Quarter answered.

"How much area can they cover with their tiny jeeps?" Aduo asked contemptuously.

"The money stays with us," Quarter said, "All of the money."

"God bless the holy church," Ohel said, remembering an expression that had been taught to him by the nuns at the Catholic school. He had trouble understanding and was forced to repeat the phase over and over until he got it right. Each time he said it incorrectly Sister Nxumalo would hit his knuckles with the sharp end of a ruler.

Even now, year's later, Ohel would look down at his knuckles every time he said that and would still wince recalling the pain. "God bless the holy church," he repeated and then he would laugh, an odd, distant kind of laugh.

"It's the fucking tourist," Quarter said mockingly, "Always wanting to save the animals."

"They should be fucked," Aduo agreed, "Fucked good. Let them really learn about the bush."

"They carry good money," Quarter said, "better then ivory."

"They are truly the ones," Aduo answered, "They should pay for the slaves they took away. Our youth. They took our youth. Our strength. We should steal only from those who are already thieves."

Osuna shook his head from side to side and walked away, seeking shade from a nearby tree.

"Old women," Quarter repeated.

"I have a family," Osuna called back, "I have to think clearly."

"You have no guts," Quarter said, looking at Aduo, "You hold us back."

"I hold no one back," Osuna said.

"You can't retreat now," Aduo snapped, "You going to walk back to Nairobi?"

Osuna was quiet. He thought of the goods they had already stored away and realized they were almost through. He once again thought of the forty dollars and he smiled.

"I'm with you," he slowly answered.

"God bless the holy church," Ohel said and laughed again.

Quarter raised his beer in salute and grinned at Osuna.

There was only silence. Then a lone bird screeched from far off in the darkness.

Frank Kimba was the curator of the Kenya museum, a punctilious kind of man given to wearing suit and tie even on the hottest days and taking private delight in the fact that he never perspired. A pencil-thin mustache served as the center piece of his always somber face, a fact underlined by the glasses he wore with their steel rimmed frames and lenses as thick as the bottom of empty bottles.

Kimba had long ago become accustomed to the surrounding scent of musty books, an odor that he loved, knowing the books offered him contact to the entire world.

It was Kimba who had put together the museum's Mau Mau exhibit as a silent tribute to the children of those earlier folk heros. Kimba grew up with many of those children who now walked the streets of Nairobi.

On this day he was busy assembling a collection of ancient African artifacts, many of which were now spread all over his crowded desk.

Kimba was intently studying a jagged stone ball, holding it in his hand and turning it about, finally setting it down and writing a small label "Lava Cobble." He realized the stone dated back nearly two million years and was probably used as a hammer by some early man. The sharp flakes from the stone would easily have allowed the holder to rip open a hyena and quickly deflesh the bone.

He was absorbed in his morning's work and didn't notice when Nairobi Police Inspector Thomas Zandu gently tapped his walking stick on the curator's desk. Only then did Kimba look up and smile in friendly greeting.

"Good morning sheriff," he said, always finding amusement when he called the Inspector "sheriff," a term he had learned from watching American western movies.

"Playing with your stone balls?" Inspector Zandu joked back.

"Merely a concealed weapon," Kimba answered easily. The two had been friends since Catholic school days.

"This is official and unofficial business," the Inspector said, opening a small note pad which he always carried, "Our old school chum must be busy."

"Ohel?" Kimba knew without asking, "Is he in trouble again?"

"Another tourist beaten," the Inspector said, "and he described someone with a weird, yes that is the very word, weird, laugh."

"Ohel," Kimba sighed, knowing full well his history of violence. At

Catholic school Kimba had always admired Ohel's strength but even then worried about his friend because of the constant difficulties he had in learning the most simple teachings.

"You were the one who tried to help him at school," Inspector Zandu said, "and I know he still comes running to you when he needs assistance."

"True, of course," Kimba answered, "Only this time I haven't seen him."

"What does that mean?"

"He runs off like a jack-rabbit, wild, off into the bush."

"And he gets drunk?

"That and worse," Kimba answered, "Sometimes, once in a while, he meets some poacher friend of his. He doesn't tell me much about it. But when he comes back he has a few dollars for the next couple of days."

"Where does he usually go?"

"Amboseli is the closest," Kimba answered.

"Then I should alert the wardens out there," Inspector Zandu said.

"There is nothing to warn," Kimba answered, wanting to try to once again protect his friend who he always felt sorry for, "No one has reported anything, have they?"

"There may be poachers out there,"Inspector Zandu said, "And they know the consequence of their deeds."

"Ohel is probably down at the market place right now getting drunk," Kimba said, "You can't warn someone till something bad happens."

Inspector Zandu paused for a moment.

"That isn't so, my dear friend," he finally answered, putting his note pad away, "but I suppose I should check out more of Nairobi before I send those wardens off on some kind of wild goose chase out in the bush."

"If I see Ohel I'll call you," Kimba promised.

"Sure, after you clean him up and tell him to behave, right?" and Inspector Zandu smiled but his eyes narrowed in friendly warning.

Kimba went back to studying his ancient tools as Inspector Zandu walked out of the museum. His thoughts now were only of Ohel.

Inspector Zandu walked back into the busy streets and thought he should still make a report, alerting the wardens in Amboseli that there may be poachers in the area. On the other hand, he really had nothing to tell them and didn't want to sound foolish.

He also considered simply reporting Ohel missing but then decided that really wasn't even worth the effort.

With that concern quickly out of his mind, Inspector Zandu stopped a street vendor and ordered a can of warm Coke. Then he leaned against a building and watched the crowded traffic as he slowly sipped his drink.

Back at Amboseli, the poachers had grown tired of the day's long wait and of the uncertainty they had faced.

They had been drinking for long hours and had become loud and angry, often bitter, with each other.

The day had been spent in loud arguments, the group only finding a forced silence when they decided to stay one more night in the bush.

"I can almost smell a big elephant herd," Quarter said, taking a deep breath.

"It is the visitors on their safari that you smell," Aduo answered, still filled with his constant hatred for the foreign visitors.

Osuna continued to sit in silence far away from the others.

Ohel stood near a Thorn tree laughing over and over at some joke he kept repeating to himself.

Aduo said nothing. He thought of the warden and those on safari as he walked about continually chopping at the bush with his sharpened ax.

A baboon suddenly leaped out and Aduo threw his ax but the animal quickly moved away, darting back into the bush.

Aduo cursed again knowing that he seldom missed with his ax.

# CORKY 'N FLORA

"I live in the past," Corcoran said standing before the campfire, the small glasses that rested on the tip of his nose reflecting the fire's warm glow.

"And I live in the future," Flora Zimmer quickly added, "With my dreams. And my memories."

"Mine was but a small joke," Corky continued, "You see I am an archaeologist and I truly live in the past. I count years in the millenniums."

"That's even older then me," Flora said with twinkling eyes.

"You are forever young," Corky said, holding Flora's hand, "A rare artifact, indeed."

"And you are full of millenniums of bull droppings," Flora quickly answered.

Gabriella and I looked at each other and smiled.

"I've been all over the world," Corky continued, "New Guinea, Honduras, Madagascar, Egypt but all I've ever seen is the dirt of each country. I've crawled so close to the ground I could taste the dust."

Corky explained crawling cautiously on hands and knees, a micro inch at a time, using his hands as gentle feelers searching for the past.

"A chip, not even as big as your smallest finger, or a dried piece of bone or a sliver of pottery and for me it is like sky rockets on the fourth of July."

His studies had taken him around the world from lost Mayan temples to sealed Egyptian tombs.

"Madagascar is a dandy little island so remote it seems lost in time," Corky explained, "Some of the people still wear the bones of their dead ancestors as some sort of good luck omen. They paint their faces with yellow dots as beauty marks. Damn mysterious people."

He spoke quietly as he remembered his own past.

The cyclone broke all around Corky who was marooned in a small hotel near Hellsville at the very tip of Madagascar.

Hellsville is a small town, somewhat like Namanga, located on the very edge of Madagascar near Nosey Be.

"A damn good name for that place, Hellsville," Corky said recalling the rain and the wind swirling together in endless waves, unrelenting as they tore at the island and its people.

Corky sat drinking warm beer in a little hut called "The Saloon" and watched as nearby wooden shelters were being ripped apart by the endless wind.

"The wind packed nearly a hundred and fifty miles an hour and destroyed everything in its path," Corky quietly said, "Including over two hundred people."

The natives were resigned to the annual destruction and already were making plans to rebuild their small shelters.

Years earlier the French government had built ugly round concrete block houses for protection from the monsoon and a few native's gathered there for protection.

"It did little good," Corky continued,"A tree snapped and a little girl was mangled."

Corky looked at Flora Zimmer for a moment.

"That was when I went to that disgusting bar and sweltered away in the humid heat," Corky said, "I still can see an old whore who also sat waiting at a nearby table."

The old woman sat silently, her eyes constantly staring at Corky. She had one leg and sat with her uncovered stump facing Corky. Her face dripped wet with perspiration and the stump that had been her leg remained bloated in the heat.

"A zebu, a kind of ox but with one hump, was the only other animal in that crummy bar," Corky explained, "And it rumbled munching on weeds at my feet. Have to be polite to the little buggers because they are a sign of wealth."

When the cyclone stopped other unusual creatures in Madagascar slowly emerged. Imagine cock-roaches that are four inches long but taste like crab meat and beautiful lakes filled with man-eating crocodiles."

I noticed Hughes busy taking notes. He'd have a lot to talk about when he returned home.

"But I was there for a reason, a damn fine reason," Corky continued, "Because that little island, the furthest distance on the map from San Francisco, has ninety per cent of its animals that are not found anywhere else in the world. It's almost a lost paradise for folks like me."

Corky described the lemur, monkey-like, but which actually goes back to the dawn of time and has more "smarts then most people I know."

"Darwin could have proven his entire theory of evolution just on that one island," Corky continued, "Civilization didn't even arrive there until only two thousand years ago."

There was also beauty in Madagascar although the island remains far removed from anywhere in the world and is seldom mentioned in tourist's maps.

"You snap a branch off of a tree and they call it Elang-Elang," Corky continued, "And it is like the sweetest perfume you've never smelled. Everything smells nice. The damn citronella is all over. Wonderful."

Corky explained that Madagascar is one of the world's poorest nations adding, "You've heard of third world countries. Well this one is more like ninth world."

"One day I noted a chameleon, could hardly make the little devil out because it blended into the surrounding, it was all alone trying to come in out of the rain," Corky said, "And I thought of that old whore and how lonely I had become lost in past worlds and that it was time for me to come in out of the rain. It was at that moment when I decided to think of the future. I had always thought in terms of yesterdays and never tomorrows."


"I was in he cold tombs of Egypt searching the ruins of the Pharonic Age when it all came together," Corky said," I finally found out about the modern world."

He paused and his deep-set eyes seemed to look at all of us at once. Corky's face was now ruddy from our day's in the sun. The chalk-white look he had that first day in Namanga, the one from too many day's prowling inside ancient tombs, was gone. He looked healthy and happy.

"We are the killers of the past, my friends," he said,"Not just the looters from a thousand years ago, or the vandals who are always around, but all of us."

Working in the tombs Corky found the stale heat and the constant humidity has become destroyers of the past.

"Bacteria is created inside those tombs and slowly our past is being eroded away. Outside the tombs they sell souvenirs and the tourists take nice pictures and no one cares that our past is slipping away."

Corky paused for a moment and looked at each of us.

"I realized everything was here long before us and there would be even more after we are gone. So before my own past has disappeared and I've become history, I have decided to settle down," Corky added, "During my travels I have been seeking a peaceful place to settle. I've been everywhere from Idaho to Australia. I am a man who thinks like the past. Slowly. And I have come to a conclusion. After this safari I shall settle in Kenya."

Flora Zimmer nodded her head knowingly.

"I want to wear this old cardigan sweater, holes and all, and plant barley and potatoes and see the earth from the top and not from the bottom."

Before anyone could speak, Flora Zimmer nudged Corky aside and slowly moved before the fire.

"This man isn't the only one with Kenya plans," she quietly said.

"They called me Dynamite in school," Flora said, "Hated school and would often run off and hide from my teachers. So what am I today? A librarian helping those same teachers."

Flora had been the head librarian in San Rafael, a small California town, for over forty years.

"Once a high school math whiz, one of my better library customers, estimated that I had assisted over fifty thousand people in my time."

Yuri applauded.

"It is a good feeling to help the mind," Flora continued.

"And our minds are quite similar," Corky said, "May I tell them?"

Flora nodded "yes."

"We have both come to love Kenya."

"Corky for his hills and me for my library," Flora said, "You all saw that lovely library in downtown Nairobi."

"It looks like a small version of the New York library with the lions in front," Hughes said.

"Well, I talked to the head librarian," Flora answered, "and we have arranged an exchange program. Books. Reports. Posters. A low scale cultural exchange. Just between people. Governments need not apply."

"A people to people program," Margaret Hughes said.

"And if this librarian lady can put up with me, she will always have a place to stay at my wee retirement farm. She'll never be lonely."

"Lonely is like being hollow all of the time," Flora said.

They both knew about being lonely.

Flora and her husband had an old weathered Marin cottage near the bay and every evening would stroll the rocky beaches and watch the sunset.

"Sometimes Ed would stop and toss flat pebbles into the water and watch them skip," Flora recalled, "he would yell out the number of skips, two, three. I think his record was five."

The two would sat along the shore eating a small bag of shrimp they had purchased at China Camp, an old Chinese fishing village near San Rafael. The fishermen had huge wooden planks on the ground filled with shrimp that had just been caught and were now drying in the sun.

"The shrimp long ago disappeared from the bay and are all gone now," Flora added.

She paused remembering.

"One day Ed was gone," she quietly said, "This great huge man who took a nap one Sunday in his favorite old stuffed chair and simply never woke up."

Corky remembered much the same.

He told of his wife, Eleanor, accompanying him on his archaeological digs and how she would make herself perfectly at home no matter how remote their locations.

"This was an amazing woman," Corky said, "Had a way of getting friendly with the local folks, really friendly. They would take to her and gather around and share their local stories."

Corky told of the day when they were in Israel and Eleanor went swimming in the Dead Sea.

"I was sitting on the shore watching her swim when she suddenly rose up out of the water and lurched backwards," he quietly said.

Corky became quiet for a moment and looked off towards the bush.

"That was a shitty place to drown, like black humor, the Dead Sea."

He became silent and turned away from the fire.

Flora touched Corky lightly on the arm and the two looked at each other. Something shown in their eyes and I felt they had more to say.

Only before they could finish we all spotted something off in the distance.

A light was coming towards us out of the darkness.

# SAFARI VISITOR

We spotted just a pin-point of light from far off, weaving in and out, bouncing up and down, frequently disappearing for a moment, then growing larger as it drew closer.

As it came nearer we were able to make out the sound of an auto engine. All of us stood around our tents wondering who might be approaching in the early evening.

The car stopped a few yards away and we heard the door open and slam shut. I was startled when a voice called out of the darkness, "Hello, Allen. Hello, Michael."

Dr. Lom stepped briefly into the flickering campfire light and nodded to our group. Then he moved back into the shadows. He was still wearing the same soiled white shirt and patched jeans he had worn a few days earlier but this time he was also carrying a heavy wooden case.

He walked over to Allen and the two talked together for a moment. Then they motioned for me to join them.

"I didn't drive way out here at night for pleasure," Dr. Lom said, looking away from me, "Chinee Charlie heard more poacher talk."

"We have heard it on the radio, Allen said, "Over at Tsavo."

"Well I don't wish to alarm your visitors but they are closer to here now," Dr. Lom whispered, "The place is infected with them."

Then he turned and walked over to the camp fire.


"Greetings my friends," he softly said, "I bring you good Kenya beer. Heard you had a rough time with poachers and didn't want you to think everyone here was still the next link to savages."

He was deliberately staying off in the darkness.

"Warn your friends, Michael," he said, "Tell them I only blossom in the darkness. Like the stars, I come out at night. My face isn't as offensive by firelight."

"This is the physician who helped that young Masai child," I told the group, walking over to greet Dr.Lom.

He smiled when he saw me. At least, I think he smiled. The hole where his mouth should have been curled into a small loop. As he moved forward, I thought his features did appear to soften by the flickering light.

Dr. Lom opened the case of beer, handed a bottle to Allen and passed the others around.

The others said nothing, not certain about the stranger who had suddenly visited our camp.

"Should we all sing camp songs?" he asked.

"That was wonderful, what you did for that little boy," Flora Zimmer said.

"Thank medical science," Dr. Lom answered, "We've come a long way. Didn't even know about washing our hands before touching a patient not that many years ago."

He sat down near the fire and nodded to Sophie and Yuri.

"You're a long way out in the bush," he said, "A piss poor trail for driving at night."

"You probably drove by instinct," Margaret Hughes said.

"Ah, yes, I always trust my instincts. That is one good thing about us humans. We can send people off to walk on the moon but we can't change our base instincts."

There was silence again.

"Is it true that everything started here?" Herbert Hughes asked.

"Yes, yes, of course," Dr. Lom answered, "All us hominids, this wide, wonderful family of man. This is the cradle of the human race. Over on the eastern shore of Lake Rudolph. Be careful where you walk, you might be stepping on your own ancestors."

"Four million years ago?" Yuri asked.

"Make it more like thirty-three million years ago," Dr.Lom answered, "Once upon a time there was a small fruit eating animal called the Aegyptopithecus. Try saying that after your third beer. This aegyptopithecus weighed about nine pounds, was a wee, tiny fruit eating animal that had monkey-like limbs and ape-like teeth. That might have been my own great, great grandmother. Kind of looked like me."

Mrs. Lewis turned away, looking off into the darkness, saying nothing.

"I guess I talk too much," Dr. Lom said, "It gets lonesome out here and I miss the pleasure of company. I miss decent conversation. Sometimes I don't know how to talk nicely to visitors."

"Out here you think of the past, like Gletschergarten, the Glacier Gardens in Switzerland," Gabriella said, trying to change the subject.

"What's that?" Margaret asked.

"We found ice age fossils there, in my Switzerland, in 1872," Gabriella said. She paused for a moment and looked up at the sky, then added, "Something here makes you feel close to God. It is like he could look down and smile at us."

"God isn't a person," Dr. Lom suggested, "I renounce all that nonsense."

"Don't tell Michelangelo that," Hughes said, "He saw Him as an old man with a white beard and long flowing robes.

"What about God being a women?" Flora Zimmer asked.

"Most people believe in God, Mrs. Lewis added, "I've even seen football players praying on the sidelines."

"God doesn't give a damn about who wins a game," Dr. Lom said, "Unless he has a wager on the contest."

He punctuated his sentence with a wicked kind of laugh.

"God can't even unscramble the mess we've all managed to get ourselves into, "Dr. Lom sharply answered, "Sorry, "There isn't much time for bedside manners out here."

"I have my own theory about God," Corky said, "Got it in Madagascar when I was looking at insects."

"That's an odd equation, God and insects," Flora said.

"Ah, but it works," Corky slowly answered, "When I was a kid some of the others found great joy in stepping on bugs and listening to them squish. Even then it made me cringe because I knew we are all living creatures. Doesn't it make sense that God might not be that person in the flowing white robes but actually the smallest, most humble of all living things? Isn't that how he might behold himself?"

We were quiet as if pondering that thought.

"God can be whatever you want. He's in your heart," Yuri added, "That's my own personal philosophy. Did you see the sunset the other night? Maybe God was there."

"We have God to thank for all the beauty of Africa," Sophie said.

"Nonsense," Dr. Lom said, shaking his head,"Shakespeare had it correct when he wrote "We only owe God death. Our death."

No one spoke for a brief moment.

Before anybody answered, Gabriella, taking delight in playing Devil's advocate, turned to me, "What about you, Michael. You write. Isn't writing like playing God?"

"How do you figure that?" I answered, not expecting to suddenly being thrust in the center of the conversation.

"You create make believe people, give them feeling and passion, make them do things," she answered.

It was her own small joke between us and I knew she would find great amusement with this later when we were alone.

"The Masai say it properly," Allen added. "Elala Onv Ai," the eye of God is large."

"How about Hegel?" Dr. Lom countered, "Volksgeist, the spirit of the people."

"This is such a spiritual kind of place," Mrs. Lewis said, extending her arms, "The surroundings bring all of this out."

"So this entire conversation is but the soul searching of God," Dr. Lom countered, "For aren't we all the keepers of our own little flames?"

"Of course, God is what you want to believe," Hughes added.

"You think God smiles with equal love on all of his children?," Dr. Lom whispered.

Sophie wanted to say something but then she looked away, exactly as she did that night when she first told her story around the campfire.

"I've something to say on this particular subject," Sophie finally said, starting to slowly stand, shaking off Yuri who was trying to hold her back.

"It's personal but we're all become like family out here," Sophie quietly said, "Maybe I should get something that has bothered me for a long time off my chest. Telling you, my new family, might be like a catharsis. It's on my mind since we passed that synagogue in downtown Nairobi."

No one spoke. We looked at Sophie wondering what direction she was taking.

"Once upon a time I hurt my family," she whispered, "I renounced my religion. A religion that had guided my family, which had been their cornerstone and which dated back through all history. And I simply tossed it away."

Yuri nodded his head as if to say, "No."

Sophie looked away.

"I come from a very orthodox Jewish family and I rebelled. You know, the smart aleck kid. I resented sitting on one side of the synagogue."

Sophie, her voice hushed, told how she confronted her family, telling her father his ways were old fashioned.

"I told him the Russians were right. Religion is just opium for the people," she said, adding, "The old story of the kid who thinks they know everything."

Sophie described her father as a distinguished rabbinical scholar.

"He was such a soft, gentle man. He had a fine grey beard, always trimmed just right, and the lines on his face only underlined his dignity and wisdom. But on this day those lines on his forehead creased together and he only stared quietly at me with such deep hurt and pain on his face."

She became silent and turned away.

"It was an expression I'll never forget," she whispered, "He said nothing. I had hurt him and for the first time he was unable to formulate his thoughts."

"Your mother and I have such wonderful dreams for you," her father had answered with a voice that sounded more like a gasping wheeze.

"Religion is a crutch," Sophie continued pressing her point, not realizing how badly she was disappointing him, "It should all change. I've changed. I'm modern."

None of us had anticipated this kind of a story.

"So this modern lady went out to make her way in the world and I met Yuri, whom I love, but sometimes I still feel awful. Like when I saw that old synagogue."

Sophie paused for a moment and looked at us. Slowly her smile returned.

"My parents know and understand," she continued, "They accepted my ideals. Every time my dad hears one of my commercials he cringes. Only it is a nice cringe. You know, with pride about his daughter. We all get along fine. But I still ache when I think of the day I hurt my father. It nearly destroyed both our lives."

"Everyone does dumb things when they're kids," Mrs. Lewis said, "Aren't we supposed to benefit from our mistakes?"

"It all makes me sound so shallow, so awful. But my parents understand and we all love each other," Sophie said, "And maybe I talk too much. But sometimes it scares me. Like I turned my back on God. I think sometimes He is following me ready to point his finger of fate at me and the thought makes me shudder."

Sophie realized how serious she had become and stopped for a moment.

"Only now I feel much better," she finally added, "and I thank you for listening to my ravings."

Dr. Lom sat in the half darkness but said nothing.

Yuri looked at Sophie as the campfire glow flickered across their faces. The look of love and respect they both had for each other was reflected in the light for all to see.

"Not to worry," Dr. Lom said, "We are all locked in a similar struggle. The eternal battle between good and evil."

"The time of apocalypse?" Hughes said.

"It nears," Dr. Lom answered, "It nears."

No one spoke for a long moment and all we heard was the crackling of the fire.

There was an odd noise from out in the darkness and we all looked up.

"Whose there?" Dr. Lom called.

Allen motioned to the other guides who quietly moved off to one side. There was only silence.

Allen and the guides walked around but there was nothing to be seen.

"Probably a small animal moving about," Allen said, his eyes still looking out into the darkness.

"Africa at night makes me a bit jittery," Mrs. Lewis said.

"I believe Africa, this night, makes all of us jittery," Gabriella answered, and then, trying to relieve the tension, added, "It also makes for good conversation. We all sound so philosophical and brilliant."

"This excellent Kenyan beer also helps to loosen tongues," Hughes added.

"I told you, Michael," Dr. Lom sighed, "There are no dreams out here. Only realities. God treated me like shit."

"Reality is how you helped that little boy," I answered.

"Reality is bullshit," Dr. Lom snapped, "The only reality is that the hour grows late and I have a crappy, bumpy ride ahead of me over that excuse of a trail."

The hole that was his mouth became a circle again, his way of smiling, and then he blew all of us a kiss as he walked back into the darkness towards his car.

"Michael, damn you," he whispered to me when I walked over to his car, "Please be careful."

# VISIT TO A LODGE

All these days out in the bush were now coming to an end. We did have time for one last stop which was perhaps the most primitive of all. We visited a very elegant game lodge, smiling to one another as we entered and noticed soft lights on the nearby palm trees and an artificial water hole to attract the animals.

Those inside stared at us as much as we looked at them for we were all quite a contrast.

They were the folks who wanted to visit Africa but have all the comforts of home. They wore tailored London safari jackets and, God forbid, pith helmets.

Mrs. Lewis started to brush the dust from her jacket while Yuri rubbed his boots along his pants trying to produce even a small appearance of a long lost shine.

"Those are the one who want to see Africa but from a safe distance," Corcoran whispered, "Our scruffy little group most astound them."

Our faces were tanned, clothes grubby, we carried our supplies on our backs but we walked into that damn lodge with heads held high.

I half expected Alejandro to whistle the Colonel Bogey march but he said nothing, intimidated by all the luxury.

The people in the lodge seemed just a bit startled as we made our way through the lobby and towards the bar.

We had our tents and they had their spotlights. The lights were beamed on a small artificial watering hole at night to attract the animals near the lodge, thus assuring the guests they would see all of African wildlife, at a safe distance, while sipping wine at a fern-walled outdoor bar.

"Look over there," Corky said, pointing to a tree where meat had been carefully placed, "They hang that to attract the animals. Make sure their customers have something to write home about."

We were laughing and a bit noisy as anyone might be who has been out in the bush for any length of time and who realized it was all quickly coming to an end.

"Didn't the squalor out there bother you?" one very prim English lady, sitting alone at a table near the bar, asked me. She probably imagined I was some sort of Great White Hunter.

"We carry quite a bit of disinfectant with us," I answered, mildly ashamed, at being such a wiseguy.

"British Airway attendants actually walk up and down the aisle prior to take off and spray the entire plane," she said.

She was serious and I decided to leave it at that, so much for British humor.

"Why don't you play the piano for her?" Gabriella whispered, playfully poking her elbow gently into my side.

"Watch it, kid," I chided back realizing how well we both already knew each other.

"Did you see any poachers out there?" one man, sitting alone at the bar, asked.

"Only some lovely animals," Sophie answered.

"You don't see poachers," a crusty looking old Britisher with a long white mustache, sitting alone by the window playing Chinese checkers, snapped, "You don't see or hear them."

He turned away and looked out the window.

"But they are out there," he continued, "Probably watching us right now."

We all nervously glanced out the window but there was nothing.

I glanced at the open sky and saw the sweeping view of the endless bush and once again marveled at the many moods of Africa, moods that seem to change with the light of day. Wide views, always giving that sense of freedom, of solitude, the sense of the world before man.

The sky had turned to jade-blue, that rarefied moment between dusk and total darkness. Within a moment it was already slowly changing again, now to a soft blue. It was Lauren's favorite time of evening. The memory made me feel sad for a moment.

In the early evening twilight the small water hole took on colors of its own: the sky's soft blue; brown and greens from the bush; the red of the lowering sun. As the animals splashed about, the gentle ripples blended together into a vivid rainbow of color.

Yuri had become rather serious as he stood before us holding a glass of wine high in his hand.

"Sophie and I want to thank you all," he softly said, "for being so wonderful and allowing us to feel so at ease with you."

"To all of us," Hughes said, also raising his glass, "To all of us remarkable folks."

We truly had become as one, I thought, had shared our dreams and our hopes, even our loves.

"Should auld acquaintance be forgot, and never brought to mind," Yuri said, looking directly at each one of us, "Should auld acquaintance be forgot and days of auld lang syne."

We all stood, raising our glasses and toasted each other. The British lady looked at us as if we were all crazy.

"Auld lang syne," Alejandro repeated slowly, raising his glass.

"Auld lang syne,"Mrs. Lewis said, nodding at each one of us.

Gabriella and I just looked quietly at each other.

Auld Lang Syne.

There it was again.

Lauren had given me a music box one New Year's eve which played that sad old song.

Auld Lang Syne.

It reminded me of confetti sticking to wet pavements and lonely people dashing about, glad they had survived another year.

Auld Lang Syne.

Lauren.

Where are you, how are you, old funny face?

I looked at the others standing in that small semi-circle. No one spoke. We stood smiling proudly at one another for this had suddenly become a solemn moment for all of us.

The British woman left the bar.

"You'll have to excuse me, I really don't drink much," Mrs. Lewis said, underscoring her words with forced laughter, "This really isn't like me. But I think I'll have another glass of wine and tonight, if you like, it will be my turn to tell the story of my life."

She drank her wine quickly, too quickly for someone not really used to drinking wine, and I thought that perhaps Mrs. Lewis was suddenly just a little bit too nervous.

Before Mrs. Lewis could tell her story, however, a strange thing happened when we arrived back at camp.

We heard what sounded like thunder far off in the distance.

Allen and the other guides sprang to a quick alert and ran to the outer perimeter of the camp.

"You folks, please, stay back," Allen cautioned.

He swept the bush with his binoculars and then pointed to a spec of dust several miles away.

230

"It's zebra," he said, nodding in the direction of the sound, "It is OK. They are running in a direction opposite of us."

I spotted them in my binoculars. There were maybe twenty or thirty zebra running through the bush in a wild stampede, terrorized by something.

"But what makes them run like that?"Mrs. Lewis asked.

"Could be a lot of things. Probably a lion."

"Or our poachers," Gabriella whispered to me.

I thought of what that crusty old Britisher had said at the lodge, "They're probably out there watching us."

Allen and the other guides stood for a long time scanning the now silent bush with their binoculars but there was nothing else to see.

When the evening fire started, Mrs. Lewis decided it was time to talk.

# MRS. LEWIS

"I'm not married."

Mrs. Lewis stood in front of the campfire that night with a whimsical grin, as if letting us all share a naughty little secret.

The afternoon wine was still having its affect as her eyes roamed about our small group. We were all sitting back waiting for her story to be told, knowing this would be the last of what had become our nightly ritual.

"I hope you don't consider me a bit of a fibber," she continued, "But I travel a lot and sometimes, for a women alone, it is better to be a misses in this world of ours."

"Not to worry, Mrs. Lewis," Hughes said, "No mashers in this group."

Gabriella sat by my side and pinched my leg in the darkness.

"Oh, I'm not worried," she answered, punctuating each sentence with a nervous laugh to emphasize or conceal her thoughts, "Everyone has become such close friends and I felt just a tiny bit embarrassed. I just wanted to share my silly little secret."

"There are no secrets among friends, Mrs. Lewis,"Margaret said.

"Call me Claire," she continued, "Gosh, on our final night it would be awful to have such formalities."

I had often wondered about Mrs. Lewis, Claire, the lady with the bad foot and the keen sense of humor.

"Sing no sad songs for me," she said, flinging her arms about, "But I was the kid that no one wanted. One of those accidents that occasionally happen. And when I came out with a twisted foot, it was even worse. My dad blamed my mother, telling her God had punished her for tempting men, and my mother yelled back at him saying it was because he masturbated too much as a kid and had twisted his genes into creating a deformed creature. I am the original misbegotten."

None of us expected this, not sure if we should even be listening, thinking perhaps we were intruding in a private life. We sat in stunned silence.

"Please, not to worry," she said, reading our minds. "My life quickly got much better. Even as a youngster I developed an interest in chemistry. Besides, I could sit and work at my own pace and let my thoughts get lost in whatever project I happened to be working on at the moment."

She had been that way on the safari, always amused, never complaining, adding her thoughts, keeping up with everyone, and all because at an early age she had become a very determined woman.

"And this above all, don't worry about my being a crip," she half-joked, "When you're born like this, you don't ever know what you're missing. That's the easy part. The dumb part is kind of like Mister Hughes and his magical quest for world peace. I've also had a bit of a quest for a better world. Only through chemistry."

As a chemist she had been aware of what was happening to our planet and for years had been involved in trying to save it, long before that had become the fashionable thing to do.

"Hell, did you ever stop to think that chemistry is responsible for a woman's menopause? Just think about it. We chemists create new things for a better and a longer life. In the old days, when women died in their thirties and forties, they weren't old enough to worry about menopause."

She paused again and there was some uneasy movement around the campfire. As with any chemist, Mrs. Lewis was mixing the right ingredients to paint a vivid picture for all of us.

"I always seemed to be concentrating too much on studies, squinting into a microscope," she quietly said, "I thought coming to Africa would give me fresh air and get me way from the antiseptic laboratories I've known all my life."

Margaret nodded her head knowingly.

"Look, I'm kind of kidding about that menopause stuff but I'm dead serious about our planet. I don't have to go into that. Ozone. Rain forests. Deforestation. Carbon dioxide emissions. Pesticides. Foul air. From the greenhouse affect to the shit house. You all know that up to your eyeballs. T.S. Eliot was right, it'll end not with a bang but with a whimper."

Mrs. Lewis paused for a moment and looked at the trees surrounding our camp and then did an odd thing. She lifted her deformed foot up just above the campfire for everyone to view.

"This foot might save the world," and she laughed that nervous laugh again, "Just like President Kennedy once said. A journey of a thousand miles starts with one step. Well long ago, whenever there was those early protest marches to direct attention to the earth's problems, I'd be right there. I was always a big hit. The local television cameras would zoom into my bum foot. Tight closeup. Very dramatic, a cripple leading the way. Great shot of this little girl with the big limp, dragging her foot along the streets. It always got the point across."

"You're doing good, "Yuri said in the darkness and Mrs. Lewis nodded her head.

"I guess I just got more involved with saving the earth than with chemistry. Especially now with chemistry taking all the bad shots. Every day the headlines read of chemical spills. We are destroying ourselves through our search for better things. Buy that shiny tomato in the grocery store. Add your auto to the congestion on our streets. The biological diversity of this old planet is being destroyed and can never be replaced."

Mrs. Lewis paused for a second, collected her thoughts and then, her anger raising, added,"I drove in Los Angeles once and I choked and my eyes turned to water and I couldn't even see the City Hall two blocks away. Two blocks away."

She became quiet for a moment and no one spoke.

"The cloud, that smog, the one that hangs over L.A. really hangs over all of us," Mrs. Lewis continued,"What will those school kids in Namanga, or anywhere, inherit from us? What happens when they don't have any land to roam or air to breath?"

She hit her hands together to underline her point.

"I don't have to tell you," she added, "we are all destroying ourselves, which is why I came here, where it all started. Carbon based molecules are the most complex of all things yet are the very basis of life. And life started here. So my visit here is quite natural."

Mrs. Lewis looked about the campfire, looking directly at each of us.

"We haven't much left on this planet. The elephants can tell you that. Sounds corny but I thought maybe, somehow, I might find an answer. Or part of an answer. Just like Sherlock Holmes. Only this time, the entire world is at stake."

"You are in the front line," Gabriella said.

"When I put a glass slide under a microscope and started seeing my own life down there with all the gooey enzymes that was when I decided to come to Africa."

"The truth, the dreams, everything comes out under the glass slide," Hughes said.

"I guess I talk too much," Mrs. Lewis answered, "Here I am giving a speech. I don't believe it. The wine has made me a little bit silly. Claire, the old preacher. Talking too much. Forgive me. Sorry for this public service announcement. But that's my story and I wanted to stick in my two cents. Maybe I should just go plant a tree somewhere. Save an elephant. Plant a tree."

Corcoran started to applaud and then, slowly, we all joined in.

We were nearing the end of the safari and everyone was feeling the sadness of having to say farewell. We had become friends with whom we had shared much in a brief time. Soon be going back to our separate lives and all of us felt loose. Melancholy filled the air.

I reached out and held Gabriella's hand in the darkness, holding it tightly, not wanting to ever let go.

I glanced over at Allen who was busy on the van's radio. He again had that agitated look on his face and twice he motioned the other guides to join him.

One was checking an old rifle and I thought that seemed odd.

Yuri walked over to Allen to congratulate him on our safari and asked him to join us.

He hesitated for a moment but then said something in Swahili to the other guides and then walked over to our group.

Allen sat down and seemed at ease as he began to share other African stories with us. He spoke of the Masai and that one man could have several wives in certain tribes.

"The Masai value their wives and their cattle," Allen said.

"How do they get along with that many wives?" I asked, thinking of the failures in my own life.

"E Cuma Matanta," Allen answered in Swahili, adding with a huge grin, "No problem. One wife is like having only one arm. The women build the hut and carry the water and the wood. And have plenty of children."

"The future is with those youths," Hughes said, "May they all grow strong and lead productive lives."

"And may they all enjoy that life," Allen answered, thinking of his own chidldren, "Most important of all is life itself. The spirit of living."

There was much hugging that night knowing we would soon be off to our own scattered destinations. Everyone promised to write and we all exchanged addresses. There were tears.

"Asente Sani," everyone was saying, "Thank you very much."

Allen smiled but his eyes darted out into the darkness as if looking for something in the silent bush.

Gabriella and I stood off to one side and studied a small map of Mombasa. We had quietly made plans to stay together after the safari and fly to

Mombasa for a few additional days.

"It's a fine place for lovers," Corky, in his never delicate way, had earlier winked at us as and explained about Mombasa.

Gabriella and I had started to build a special relationship, learning about each other, longing for those few moments alone in the tent, in the darkness, sharing the sleeping bag, learning once again about feelings, about warmth, discovering one another and the place of beauty.

Allen came over to us and shook both our hands.

"Nakupenda,"he whispered, with a shy, mischievous look.

"What does that mean?" Gabriella asked.

"Another Swahili word," Allen answered with a twinkle in his eyes, "means 'I love you.'"

"Nakupenda," I repeated quietly, "It is a beautiful sounding word for love."

Allen was aware of Gabriella and me. Everyone knew and privately shared our delightful secret. They had all observed us the night of the unexpected hyena attack.

"What bothers you?" Gabriella asked when Allen walked away.

"Nothing."

"I can read it in your face," she persisted, "and your body has become like tense."

Allen had been almost correct. It had been like love with Gabriella, the same as love, only not really love, not "in love."

It was something we both understood but had not discussed.

"What Allen said. That bothers me," I finally answered, "I don't take advantage of people. It's not my way."

"Take advantage of who?"

"You."

Gabriella was silent.

"I'm not some sort of, what we call in America, player."

"I know that, no one ever said that."

"But it bothers me. We both have known hurts and if we continue like this the hurts, new hurts, will come again."

"What are you trying to say, Miki?"

"This will be over in a few days. It has to be. You know that. You have your Army. I live on the other side of the world. It's impossible for us."

Gabriella looked at me but did not answer. I knew her silent thoughts must have been the same as mine.

"You Americans. Always you Americans. You all have such guilt feelings and everything always has to be in its correct place."

Her voice had become flat and distant sounding.

"Gabby, the thought of one day parting makes me feel bad."

"I have my own life to lead," she answered, "We built our little bridge together while we were here. That is all."

"We never crossed it fully to the other side."

"We never could. In the army we always build bridges and then you know what we do with them?"

"What?"

"BANG. BOOM. We blow them up. A training exercise. Maybe you and I were but a training exercise for both of us."

She reached out and put her arms around me.

"We have had these wonderful days, our moments. Why worry. Just enjoy."

I hugged Gabriella and she placed her head on my shoulder.

"This isn't like one of your old movies," she said.

"What do you mean?"

"Like at the end when all the cast looks at the camera and laughs."

"We call that a happy ending."

"Life doesn't always give happy endings."

We both became silent for along moment. Then we heard Allen whispering.

He had returned to the radio. The guides surrounded him and seemed nervous, casting anxious looks as they continued to stare all about.

I felt a stillness in the air and thought that even the animals out in the dark bush were silent. Probably because the heat that hadn't cooled off yet.

"It's a very sultry evening," I told Gabriella when we went back to the tent.

"Your talk made it more sultry."

We felt good together, simply being with one another, sharing our special understanding.

Later that night I watched her face next to me on the pillow with the silver-grey moonlight coming through the narrow opening and Gabriella slowly drifting soundlessly off to sleep, at ease with her world. I reached over and touched her hair and felt her warmth.

Gabriella's eyes slowly opened. She looked at me but said nothing, then she rolled over, reached out and soon there was the time of love.

I felt her smoothness pressing against me, her legs curling around mine, soft hands lightly caressing my back, then came the power and the tenderness of love as it flowed between us.

Aftrerwards we lay together not talking. Gabriella's fingers gently traced my scars moving from my chest then slowly drifting down along my body.

"Your body is beautiful," she paused, "For such an old man."

"Ugly. Never use to have a scar on it."

"The scar is like a badge of honor, like a Heidelberg dueling scar," Gabriella whispered, "Makes you very distinctive."

"You should have known me before. When my skin was pink like a baby."

"You give me baloney," she answered, "Your skin hasn't been pink like a baby since dinosaurs roamed this earth. But it is still a nice body."

"For an old man."

"Even the hair on your chest is grey," she smiled, brushing her fingers along my chest, "But you're not old. You'll always be young."

Damn this woman. I had erected those boundaries against all of this, kept it all locked within myself, even thought my apparatus, that was what Lauren had jokingly called it, "my apparatus," had dried up, my love making ability had just stopped, maybe out of loss, or sadness, maybe it was all in my mind. I thought it had just dried up, like a once raging river that had slowly run its course and had finally turned to dust and once that was gone I felt as if I had become merely an observer of life. That was when the sadness came.

Only now Gabriella brought it all back to life, opened the swollen dam gates, allowed it to once again pour out, filled it with new power and energy.

No more emotional ties I had told myself. What good are they? You only end up getting kicked in the face. Gabriella had become my Josuha and she truly blew that trumpet and the walls, my walls, all came tumbling down.

Damn her. No, not damn her. Not ever damn her. Praise her. Give her my thanks. My love.

The old pains had grown more distant thanks to Gabriella and the elixir of her warmth.

"Nakupenda," I repeated softly in the darkness.

We lay together that night. Gabriella decided that it would be all right, our last night on safari. We would let the world simply disappear for a few hours and not worry about her getting up and going back to the other tent. She stayed with me and we touched each other and felt good and I knew her warmth throughout the night.

I'll never know what time it was lying half-asleep in the dark but I heard the sound of a twig crack, just a snapping sound, it came from somewhere out in the bush. I was startled for a moment but thought nothing about it as I glanced over at Gabriella, smiled and returned to my sleep.

A moment later there was another snapping sound out there in the darkness.

# ADUO AND OSUNA

All it took was the sound of those twigs snapping to change everyone's life forever.

One of the guides heard it first and started to bang a large wooden spoon along the side of a tin bucket as he ran about the camp shouting excitedly in Swahili. The sound of the clattering bucket rang out like the rolling clap of thunder echoing against the vast silence of the bush. The guide rushed towards all of our tents hitting the canvas flaps, trying desperately to wake everyone.

I rolled over on my sleeping bag and looked out the tent opening shaking myself awake, wondering if he had suddenly gone mad.

I heard another twig snap. And another.

Everyone was now up, running out of their tents, unsure of themselves until we heard the sounds of horror.

"Attack," a stricken voice shouted, "Attack."

One of the women screamed, someone coughed and suddenly there was blurred movement everywhere, people quickly rushing out of tents, running in every direction.

Men were emerging out of the bush and running towards our small compound. They carried clubs, iron pipes, sticks, one held a sword and another had an ax. All were shouting and pointing as they charged towards us.

One, a tall man with a torn tee-shirt, ran directly to me. He tightly held an ax which was raised to strike at anything. His mouth was spitting saliva.

I had already been close to death, had smelled it, tasted it, felt it and now it was here again only this time I knew about death and I wasn't frightened.

"Fuck you, baby," I shouted toward the man with the ax. My voice sounded shattering and came from deep within myself. It was a voice I had never heard before. Some sort of unexpected adrenalin was suddenly pumping through my body, "Fuck you."

Even as I called out, Gabriella was already on her feet and running out of the tent.

It had all taken split seconds but it seemed like an eternity. Everything was in wild images. People were screaming and shoving each other as they ran in scattered directions.

It was as if the entire world had suddenly gone insane and burst into an inferno of pent-up hatred, like a whirlwind from hell had suddenly torn loose and engulfed all of us.

I saw Allen moving towards one of the attackers, waving his arms. One of the other guides was already lying motionless on the ground.

The man with the ax came closer. His eyes were red and unseeing. I could smell his breath and feel his sweat as he raised the ax high making a circling motion in the air. Suddenly he started to laugh, a crazed kind of laugh, one that I recognized from before.

He was the one who had been standing outside the soccer stadium in downtown Nairobi, the one wearing the black felt hat with the red feather stuck in the band.

Funny how the mind plays tricks. It all happened within the blinding wink of a single moment. My first thought was that the African sun had created some kind of trick on my mind like a crazed optical illusion yet in that same split second I heard Gabriella's voice already shouting, sounding as though calling from deep within a well.

"ATTACK. ATTACK. ATTACK." Gabriella repeated wildly. She was instantly and fully alerted, her military training allowing her to react immediately before any of the others were even aware of what was happening.

One of the guides who had been talking to Allen was darting off towards the bush with one of the strangers chasing him, shouting in Swahili. The other guide came running towards our tents, shaking his arms, screaming at us.

"Get out, get out," he repeated in a high pitched, hysterical voice. His eyes were filled with the look of terror and death.

Mrs. Lewis, who had been washing clothes, looked up, her face and body frozen with horror. Hughes grabbed Margaret and pushed her behind him. Yuri had been inside his tent with Sophie and came running out at the unexpected sound. He stood watching the approaching men not yet realizing what was happening.

Corcoran instinctively ran over to Flora Zimmer and placed himself in front of her tent.

I saw Allen moving towards one of the attackers, waving his arms. One of the other guides was already lying motionless on the ground.

Suddenly there was a plopping kind of noise, like that of a watermelon hitting the pavement.

The sound had come from the direction where Allen was standing and when I again looked over–when I looked over–God forbid: his blood splattered head was rolling off into the bush. Just his head covered with blood.

Gabriella responded with pure instincts. Her mind was already racing ahead, considering what options we might have for any kind of a counterattack.

She grabbed my hand and was motioning me to follow her behind the tents, then she started to circle back, heading towards the empty van.

I thought her idea was to get into the van and run the intruders down.

"Allen has the only key," I shouted.

She nodded her head, "No."

Gabriella was thinking far quicker and clearer. She was immediately aware that our only possible chance was to get to the van and radio the game wardens in Namanga.

"We have to get to the radio," she called, her eyes darting towards the attackers who were scattering about the campsite, "And Allen keeps a gun in the glove compartment."

Alejandro ran out and tried to stop the man who was obviously the leader. He held his arms up, shaking them and shouting, 'ALTO! ALTO!" Alejandro made sweeping gestures towards the men as if he had finally found that bullring, facing the snorting animal, finally hearing the trumpet's call in the afternoon sun.

The man never hesitated. He raised the ax that he was holding and with a few powerful thrusts hacked into Alejandro. The savage blows cut into his neck, shoulders, tearing at his stomach and groin.

I started to run towards the intruder but was held back by Gabriella.

"They'll kill you, too," she shouted.

Someone screamed in pain and horror.

"Kill the bastards," the one they called Aduo kept shouting, "Kill the bastards."

The other poachers ran about the camp, shouting, kicking over tents, dumping supplies. One kept waving a machete high into the air.

One of the poachers, someone called him Quarter, was running like a crazed person, shouting in Swahili, laughing when he spotted Margaret Hughes standing near her tent.

"I'm going to carve someone pretty just like me," he screamed, looking at Margaret but seeing Kgase's face.

"You, hey lady, you," he screamed, suddenly turning and heading towards the frightened woman.

Quarter reached out to grab Margaret who turned and stumbled, falling on her knees.

Her lips said "please" but no sound was heard.

"Welcome to the safari," Quarter said but before he could finish he heard shouting and turned around.

"Get back, filth," one of the guides suddenly came running towards Quarter, holding a kitchen knife, "Back away."

"Fuck you, man," Quarter yelled back as he turned to battle with the guide.

Hughes quickly shoved Margaret into their tent. Corky ran over towards the dinner table looking for any kind of weapon.

The guide chased Quarter with the kitchen knife. Quarter suddenly turned and sighed, raising his own knife but it was too late. The guide's knife slipped into Quarter's stomach, tearing the flesh.

Quarter looked stunned, unable to move, once again feeling blood as it poured from his body. The knife had always been his destiny.

Quarter tried to whisper something but was unable to speak. He grabbed at the guide but his strength was already gone as he fell to the ground, choking and gagging, dying in his own blood.

Aduo continued running towards our group heading directly towards Mrs. Lewis who screamed pleading for him to stop. He paid no attention, once again starting to raise his ax. Before he could swing, Osuna grabbed the back of the ax handle.

"Stop," he shouted, "Stop. You've done enough."

Osuna had seen her limp forward, stared at her bad foot and it made him think of his own daughter with her deformed legs.

"Spare this one, she has done no harm. She is a cripple."

"You're too weak, old man," Aduo shouted, pushing Osuna backwards, swinging his ax which caught the older man on the side of the head. White specks of brain burst loose. Osuna died instantly.

"Kill them all shouted," Aduo shouted, "Send them a message. This is our country. Fuck them all. These are the ones that reported us."

One poacher had a long, bent wooden rod which made a whirring sound as he struck his way toward us.

"Stand up, stand up to the scum," Yuri was shouting, grabbing a jagged piece of heavy wood from near the fire area and swinging it madly.

"You've breathed too often in this life," Aduo screamed his rage, "stand back."

"No, we always stand back to your kind," Yuri was thinking of his parents, the Japanese prison camp, the early years of horror and now his eyes that once had glowed only with love had the look of deep hatred, "We should have stood up to your kind years ago."

Yuri was an ordinary man but one who had grown tired of seeing his people constantly being ravaged. He pulled himself together, standing tall and straight in front of his tent. Every moment of his life, his very being, came down to this second. He was driven now by a thousand voices from his past, one clearly rising above all the rest, hearing his father urging him on, "Stand up for that which you believe in."

"This abuse must end,"Yuri shouted, a man haunted by all the tragedies of the past.

"Back away, old man," Aduo repeated, his crazed eyes narrowing.

Yuri started to shout again but before he could even be heard, Aduo hit him with the side of the ax. The crunching sound was that of Yuri's jaw being broken.

"It is the time of the strong, "Aduo shouted, remembering something his father had long ago taught him.

Othel ran toward's Flora Zimmer's tent.

"I want the old one," he shouted.

"In a pig's ass," Corcoran yelled back, hitting Othel with a kitchen pan he was holding.

Sophie screamed hysterically thinking that the piercing sound might alert someone out in the bush. It was here once again, she thought, the never ending violence following wherever they go. She knew, at that moment, there would never be anywhere to hide from such senseless tragedy.

Hughes tall body suddenly crumpled and sagged as he fell to the ground in a faint.

"God bless the holy church," Othel shouted hysterically, running from tent to tent, flinging open the flaps, looking inside, then running out, always with that crazed laugh.

Even as everything blurred around me in rapid motion, I suddenly realized that was the same wild laugh I had also heard outside the soccer stadium.

All of this happened in only a few savage seconds during which time Gabriella reached the van, flung the door open, ducked inside and was already starting to shout for help into the radio.

As she did that, I cupped my hands around my mouth, recalling an old, familiar sound.

"Gobble. Gobble. Gobble."

The poachers hesitated at the unexpected noise and became distracted, stopping just long enough for me to get behind the leader. I darted forward, tackling Aduo from behind, hitting him just at the knees and making him drop. We both fell onto the ground and I reached for a rock, smashing it down on his head. I never thought I could hate another human. Hate had never been part of my conscious. Only now I hated. Aduo was stunned but was already reaching for his ax.

A blow smashed him from behind. It was Corky who had run over, carrying a broken plank from the dinner table. The thud cracked the back of Aduo's skull and he fell into the dust.

I rolled over on the ground, ready to lunge at Aduo again, wanting to hurt him as he had hurt us. I was no longer afraid to die, I had already come close to death and knew that I could look it square in the face. Only now I had found Gabriella and she showed me that which had been missing and suddenly I wanted to live forever.

I lay in the dirt frightened, exhilarated, panting for breath, seeing Aduo's unconscious body next to me.

This was all impossible, I thought, how could this be happening. Not here. Not now. There had been so much love between all of us.

So much love and so many dreams.

"Send help," Gabriella continued shouting into the van's radio, but it was over, even as she called I could see the other poachers quickly running away. Far off in the bush I could hear Othel's insane laugh.

Gabriella stood holding Allen's pistol, her body trembling. The Swiss Army had trained her well to use the gun but she thanked God she didn't have to pull the trigger.

Hughes finally appeared and surveyed the horror. His eyes constantly darted about like a wild animal and his body jerked in violent convulsions.

"My throat has gone dry," Hughes whispered. His mouth opened and he started to choke, then gag, and, shaking, he finally turned away.

Margaret walked behind her tent shaking her arms in front of her like a blind person afraid of what she might see.

Sophie was off to one side, sitting on the ground, wiping her glasses over and over, twisting her head from side to side.

Mrs. Lewis was numbed and stood motionless, staring off into the bush.

Flora Zimmer sat rigid by her tent, "I'm so very thirsty," she kept repeating.

I tied Aduo using, appropriately, the very ropes and cords that Hughes had for his magic illusions when he wanted to illustrate world peace.

I went over to Alejandro but it was too late. I heard the sound of air as if it were being squeezed from his body.

"He was only a poor kid, a Spanish fisherman who just wanted to sing," I cried within myself.

My voice had become hoarse and I breathed in heavy gasps. I thought for a moment that my chest would once again burst wide open. My hands shook and I could not stop the trembling.

"Please, God," I cried to myself,"Not now. I've come close and I won. Only not now. Not this time. Please. Don't take it away from me. Not now."

Alejandro. He was so young but somehow, in death, he looked almost like a child in sleep. A child gone off without even the warmth of a final nursery rhyme or a small hug.

Gabriella came back, stumbling as she walked. She made her way over to Allen, knelt down and reached out to him.

"No," I shouted, "Don't touch the body. Don't turn him over. Look away. There is nothing that can be done now.

Gabriella looked up at me but said nothing.


Allen dead. Alejandro dead. It had lasted less then three minutes.

Vultures already started to circle overhead in an endless flight of anticipation, the hawking sound they made was like that of fingernails being scraped against wooden planks.

There were other sounds. Choked groans and whispers, sounds of crying, all of it scattered throughout the bush.

Yuri rose, lightly touching his broken jaw, the pain searing through his body. He slowly walked over to Hughes. Blood was splattered on his torn shirt.

"What happened to your survival of the fittest?" he asked in a low, broken voice, "What happened to your world peace?"

Hughes said nothing. He was but the shell of a broken man.

Corky turned to me and nodded his head.

"He changes his colors like the chameleons in Madagascar," he quietly said.

Bodies lay tossed and strewn about like discarded clothes. One poacher lay crumbled, his right arm reaching out even in death as if clawing into the dirt.

The smell of decay already rose from the ground and filled the air.

The twisted scythe that had belonged to the poacher they called Othel was lying off near the bush and scratched on the side was written: "Jesus - or - hell."

Through the chaos and terror of battle you learn about yourself; the rites of passage were now complete.

The Army troops arrived within an hour. They were grim faced and dressed in battle fatigues. All carried machine guns ready to be used as they carefully searched throughout the entire area.

The colonel in charge was a tall, heavy man, his face set in a deep scowl. He wore a green battle beret set at a rather jaunty angle and he had narrow slits for eyes much like a gun embankment in an old world fort.

He stood off to one side carefully taking notes. When he saw Aduo the colonel brutally shoved him against the side of the army truck then shook him violently a second time for good measure.

"Your papa will be weeping in his grave for you," he cursed.

Aduo was the one who had stopped me on the street near the Thorn Tree. The Army colonel explained that his father had been a Mau Mau leader, a Kenya freedom fighter who had tried to change the course of his country's destiny by fighting for what he believed.

I remembered the museum in Nairobi and wondered which photo on the wall might have been Aduo's father.

"That fight led to his eventual death," the Colonel continued, "only before he died had taught his son well."

Aduo lay on the ground kicking at the dust.

"The first calling of a terrorist is to create terror," that is what his father constantly educated his son," the Colonel said, "Now those heroic earlier efforts had become twisted and served only an excuse for his son's consuming hatreds."

Yuri looked silently from his open tent.

Aduo and Yuri. Both of their fathers had fought for their own causes, fought with honor and dignity but now Aduo had turned that very dignity into his own twisted form of hatred.

"The only law he ever knew was survival by violence," the Colonel said, almost apologetically.

Yuri held back tears as he looked away.

Our small group sat scattered all about the destroyed campsite. No one spoke, each of us in our own private shock. All the love found on this journey now dissolved into the sadness of a tragedy that would haunt us the rest of our lives.

"There is no hope, no hope," Mrs.Lewis kept repeating, her small body trembling as she walked aimlessly back and forth in shock. Everything she had always fought for and believed ended in one blinding, shattering moment. Mrs. Lewis had shriveled up and suddenly looked like an old woman lost in her grief and pain.

"Once again the glorious call to arms is all but shit," Gabriella sat motionless, her voice hushed, almost a whisper.

Yuri and Sophie sat off to one side. Sophie was shaking uncontrollably. Her eyes were glazed and dulled.

"Y'isgadol, V'yishkadal," I heard her chanting the Jewish prayer for the dead, repeating the words over and over, her body swaying back and forth. Sophie saw me and slowly looked up. "I thought I had forgotten ," she whispered, her body numbed, "I haven't said those words for years."

Hughes and Margaret remained in their tent. Neither moved and both just stared off into space. He was tall but suddenly appeared short, sitting hunched over, his eyes darting constantly about, body trembling.

Hughes, who had lived his life for his illusions, had now become disillusioned and broken. Margaret held him tightly, trying to stop his tears, cooing to him as she would to a child. Gently she placed a blanket around him for warmth.

"Maybe I should buy a revolver when we go home," I heard him whisper, "For protection." Then Hughes turned away and sobbed, his huge body curled like that of an infant.

"This is an evil place," Margaret said, looking with eyes that were filled with shock.

The only sound was that of crying. Someone, it sounded like Yuri was mumbling to himself, repeating words that no one could understand.

Even dazed, I realized that from the moment Aduo had raised his ax for that first blow, he had also cut everything out of all our lives. Nothing would ever remain the same for any of us. We had been put to the test.

"We are all children of destiny," Hughes finally whispered. He was a man betrayed and finally self-deceived.

"Children of destiny is your usual pompous bullshit," Corcoran said, his eyes narrowing.

"What about you," Hughes continued, turning towards Flora Zimmer, "And your person to person program."

She looked Hughes directly in the eye, taking a moment before she answered.

"Bums never frightened me," she softly answered, "I shall remain in Kenya."

Corky put his arms around Flora and she clung close to him.

"You talk too much," Yuri whispered to Hughes, the light-bulbs that I thought of as Yuri's eyes during that first meeting in Nairobi now seemed dimmed, the twinkle gone, replaced by only a dull blankness.

I heard some movement and saw Hughes' old Midwestern straw hat lonely dancing about in the soundless wind of the now empty bush.

We held a quiet memorial service for our friends the next morning, just as the sun first started to rise like a shimmering red-orange globe over the bush.

The army had remained with us throughout the long night. They had already arranged canvas bags ready for the bodies and were now anxious to take them back to Nairobi. Before that could happen, however, we all felt it was only fitting that we hold this service out in the bush that both men had come to love. It enabled everyone to have a final moment of remembrance for their new friends.

Dr. Lom arrived in his battered old car, wiping the perspiration from his forehead. Chinee Charlie was with him carrying a large basket of flowers.

"Bad news travels fast," he said, "even out in this remote place."

He took one look at the bodies and shook his head. Then he quietly walked about seeing if he could help the others.

The only sound was that of weeping.

"I tried to tell you," Dr. Lom said looking at me, "Dreams are always defeated by the realities of life."

I was still in shock and could only look silently at him.

Someone behind me wheezed. Another coughed.

"It is but another abomination for mankind," Dr.Lom added, shaking his head, "Is there no limit to what we can do to each other?"

Chinee Charlie silently walked among all of us, weeping as he handed out flowers. It was the first time he had ever closed his small grocery store.

"I wanted to tell you that there are some decent people out here," he said.

No one listened to him.

"The heart is really a dark forest," Hughes said, recalling some remote line he had heard long ago.

Everything we had believed was gone, suddenly taken away. Had all of our lives been but a lie found only deep within ourselves? I walked about in a circle, too stunned to even cry.

I thought it odd but I watched as Sophie and Margaret met with some of the Masai. Though none spoke the same language all were busy nodding heads, shaking arms, even pointing with their fingers.

It finally became clear that they were trading a few items of their own for some colorful bracelets and necklaces which seemed an odd thing to suddenly be doing.

They collected two bags filled with the red beads, spiral glass bracelets even the metal bangles which the Masai wore on their arms and legs and in their elongated earlobes. Not satisfied, they gathered still more rings, beads and pendants.

Sophie and Margaret took all of it back to their tents and started to pull it all apart. Finally they began to sew everything together in a long piece of cloth.

What they were doing way a mystery until they unfurled it and quietly placed it over Alejandro. The two had put together their own version of the matador's suit of lights, a beautiful red and gold brocaded fighting jacket, the one that had eluded Alejandro all his life. They calmly draped it over his body.

"The emotional bonding," Dr. Lom said, "Thus the healing already starts."

Mrs. Lewis was crying. Margaret turned and looked away. I clung to Gabriella, fighting back tears, feeling overcome by the emotion, my body faint and drained of everything.

"We had known them only a few brief days," Hughes stood over the two graves speaking softly, his hands badly shaking, "But they had become as our own. Like brothers."

I thought of what the Africans had often told me: "We are all like brothers and sisters here."

Chinee Charlie turned away, crying for these strangers.

Hughes paused and became silent for a moment. He looked at each one of us and nodded his head. Hughes was no longer the same man I had first met in Nairobi. He was just barely able to hold himself together, a broken man whose only strength now was because Margaret stood motionless at his side.

"We had all become like a universe unto ourselves," he quietly added.

Two Masai, who had heard the sounds of battle, came over out of curiosity and now stood around in bewildered silence as we buried our dead. One was crying. The other kept saying, "Osarge, Osarge" over and over.

Dr. Lom put his hands in the pockets of the soiled white jacket he was wearing, looking at all of us, saying nothing.

"They stood out among us all as heros whose actions saved our lives," Hughes continued, again glancing around at our small group, "And we will praise these heroes through all eternity and give them our everlasting gratitude, thanks and love."

There was only silence and then Mrs. Lewis slowly walked forward.

"Cry for me a little," she said in a weak voice as she stood over the bodies, then she looked at us and added, "That's from an old Italian poem."

"We will cry," Yuri said, his voice almost unrecognizable through the bandages, "and we will all hurt. But our thoughts should also remember the good moments."

Margaret recalled an old hymn and stood before us, choked for a moment, then spoke softly.

"All things bright and beautiful,
All creatures great and small,
All things wise and wonderful,
"The Lord God made them all."

"Uhuru," Dr. Lom whispered to himself.

"What does that mean?" I asked.

"Freedom," he answered, "At last they have found their freedom."

Dr. Lom walked over to his car, opened the backdoor and pulled out what proved to be more of the unexpected from Africa.

He was holding a dusty, battered violin.

"I told you that day in my office I still had my music," he said, walking over towards the bodies.

Dr. Lom looked around, tucked the violin under his chin and started to play "Intermezzo."

He closed his eyes when he played, hutting everything else out, becoming intense as if through his music he could somehow find the beauty that was missing in his own life.

Dr. Lom must have realized my surprise for he looked at me and I saw that hole for a mouth which serves him as a smile.

"I lost my face," he called to me, "Not my hands."

I had never heard music sound as beautiful, sweeping out over the open bush. For the first time I realized there could be beauty even in hell.

One of the Masai had tears in his eyes.

No one said anything and we stood in silence for a few moments.

"Thus they enter the long night," Dr. Lom whispered.

"Everyone makes their own paradise," Chinee Charlie said.

"Or their own hell," Dr. Lom answered.

A small wind came and raised soundless dust clouds near the covered bodies. The sun was now over Kilamanjaro which looked down serenely, haughty and aloof, at our small group.

I looked at the snow-topped peak of the mountain and I knew why it appeared to remain secretive, for it had seen much during its thousands of years.

"Pee Lo; Epu Tekerio," the Masai said of Kilamanjaro, referring to the time when they came through the mountain, hundreds of years earlier. Even today revering it still as the home of their gods.

We stood motionless around the bodies listening to the words that echoed through the silence of the endless bush.

"Why? Why?," Mrs. Lewis stood crying.

"But my dear, death is merely the other side of life," Dr. Lom quietly said.

I glanced at Dr. Lom and frowned thinking this wasn't the time for his being caustic. Only I realized how gentle he really was and that he used his sarcasm and bitterness merely to hide his own lost feelings.

Yuri, his jaw now bandaged, was looking silently off into the distance.

I held Gabriella's hand and we managed to steady each other.

The safari ended with all of us going our separate ways. We would leave with our memories, hopefully someday the tragedy would diminish and we would remember only the good that had happened, the laughter we had shared, the sights we had seen.

But for now we all remained silent, feeling drained, standing by the bodies in this vast, lonely place, all of us alone, yet somehow together.

As we said our farewells, clinging together with final hugs, Gabriella and I held back, standing alone, knowing we still had one last moment to share.

# BOOK THREE

*"A long way to go to you but only four steps to death."*
Russian folk song

*"Strictly entre-nours, darling, how are things with you?*
*And how are all the little dreams that never came true?"*
"Thanks For the Memory"
Popular American song

# FLAMES OVER NAIROBI

Great puffs of white smoke billowed over Nairobi that day when Kenyan President Daniel arap Moi lit the greatest damn bonfire the world has ever known.

All the ivory that the government had confiscated was set afire in a three million dollar blaze, one glorious, spectacular, expensive protest, showing the world for all time Kenya's concern and defiance for those who trade in contraband ivory.

Gabriella and I returned to Nairobi, still dazed and numbed, filled with the tragedy of the bush. As we checked into our hotel, the clerk nodded to a man who had been seated in the lobby. He was a representative of the government who politely introduced himself as Harold Ngwa, Minister of Tourism.

"President Moi has asked particularly that you might be present at a most important public rally slated in Nairobi National park, "For you two are a symbol of precisely what the President is trying to illustrate at this rally. The tragic, senseless violence that arises from the poachers lust and greed for money."

"Mr. Ngwa," I was almost too tired to properly respond, "Look at us, we are dusty, tired, dirty and still to God-damned horrified to be part of a public exhibit."

Gabriella tugged on my arm to hold me back knowing an explosion was near.

"Oh, no, please," he answered, waving his arm in the air, "We respect that. Your time has become tragic here. We regret that."

"And you regret those who are the newly dead?" Gabriella answered, also losing her patience.

"I must apologize for what happened, "Ngwa answered, "We regret it all for we are like brothers and sisters here."

"Heard that before," Gabriella quickly said, "Someone should change your script writer."

Gabriella turned and held my hand.

"Remember that little boy at the baby elephant orphan farm," she said, "already he was only concerned about what his father had told him about the price of tusks."

"The nun caught that," I answered, "she tried to change his thinking."

"Oh, Miki, nothing changes," Gabriella answered.

We were both still in shock and I heard Gabriella's voice as if it came from a distance.

Both of us had wanted only to be alone, to find time to forget. We had planned to fly to Mombasa, on the coast, and let the waters of the Indian ocean give us those necessary moments of silence.

"The rally will be but an hour yet the entire world will know," Minister Ngwa persisted, "All of your media are here, everything is in place."

'We have no intentions of being used as pawns," I snapped, "Not after what we've been through."

"No, not pawns. Not propaganda," Ngwa quickly answered, "We want to show the world the truth. As you say in America, we are putting our money where our mouth is."

President Moi planned to destroy tons of confiscated ivory in one magnificent gesture thus letting the world know what Kenya felt as well as to shame other governments into joining the proposed international ban on even the legal sale of ivory.

"We are ashamed for what has happened to you and the others," Ngwa continued, "Nothing will return your friends or erase your memories but your presence at that rally will show the world what we mean. It is time for everyone to speak."

That is how Gabriella and I ended up sitting reluctantly in front of a small stage that had been erected at Nairobi National park for President Moi. There was already a crowd milling about the open field. Battle-clad soldiers moved through the park, weapons at the ready. Military helicopters which hovered overhead kept circling the entire area.

The weapons were necessary because standing a few yards away in a jagged pile that stretched several stories high stood the ivory that had been collected for years. Men and animals had been killed because of the greed of those trying to obtain its treasure.

"That sight makes me sick,"Gabriella whispered to me.

"This one is for Alejandro," I quietly answered.

"And for Allen," she answered, touching my hand.

The rally was held not far from downtown Nairobi. Many of those in attendance had been bussed in from the country to attend. They were standing all about talking in small groups.

Military sirens suddenly signaled the arrival of President Moi and the crowd started to applaud. He wore a dark business suit, a small flower in his lapel. Moi appeared taller than I had expected, his salt and pepper hair close-cropped, a small mustache lining his face.

He paused and smiled at a group of children in their grey school uniforms. The children were holding cardboard masks of an elephant's face and were standing near the front of the stage.

President Moi nodded at the crowd and then made his way slowly towards Gabriella and myself.

"Thank you for coming," President Moi walked over and shook both our hands, "My nation regrets what has happened. Perhaps your being here will help prevent it happening to others."

"We can only pray," Gabriella answered. She held her body rigid.

"More than just prayer," the President said, "We have started to slowly make some in-roads. American regulations are now very restrictive that if someone wanted to bring even an old Steinway piano with its ivory keys into your country, the government would now consider that as contraband."

The President paused for a moment and glanced at Gabriella.

"Kenya long ago set aside more land just for the animals then there is in all of your own Switzerland," he said.

"Nyayo," someone nearby called good naturedly and the President acknowledged the comment with a smile.

"An old expression," the President explained, "It refers to myself and Kenyatta. Means following the footsteps of the old man."

He was about to say something else but, before he could finish, a somber looking man carrying papers and a schedule suddenly appeared. He was probably the local equivalent to the public relations type because the man glanced at his watch and took President Moi by the arm, leading him towards a small battery of microphones which had been arranged at the center of the stage.

"Some say the ban is stupid," Police Inspector Thomas Zandu, seated next to Gabriella, leaned over and spoke quietly, "Like saying you should ban gold because it is worthless."

"You should know better than anyone what tragedy the ivory brings," I answered, angered at the Inspector's unexpected cynicism.

"You had your bootleggers, what did that ban stop, just made it worse," Inspector Zandu answered, "Some African countries do just the opposite, use the money from the sale of ivory to protect the animals. Zimbawe.

ALVIN T. GUTHERTZ

Botswana. Even South Africa. The animal protection gets maybe fifty million dollars a year from ivory sales."

Inspector Zandu was a realist who felt the simple burning of the ivory would really stop nothing. He was grim-faced and the complete official from the smell of the leather polished Sam Browne belt he wore strapped across his chest to the crack of the swagger stick he casually slapped into his open palm. A man who knew his business and would tolerate very little.

I observed a notepad he carried in his pocket. A quick glance and I saw that he had written many of the poacher's names in it and then had crossed them out.

"This ceremony is all but a most dramatic gesture," the Inspector whispered.

A man with thick horn-rimmed glasses sat behind us and Inspector Zandu introduced him as Frank Kimbar, curator of the Kenya Museum.

"I visited your place recently," I said.

Kimba offered a hesitant, almost shy smile.

"Yes, yes, my staff told me a foreigner had been there," he answered, "We don't always get a lot of foreigners. They would rather be out looking at the animals."

Gabriella turned to shake his hand in greeting.

"A pleasure indeed," he said, then he turned to Inspector Zandu and sighed, "I heard about Aduo. You were too late."

"It was all written in the stars,"Inspector Zandu answered.

"Forgive me,"Kimba said looking at Gabriella and myself,"At any rate, this is truly a great day for Kenya."

"It will become but another wall to fill,"Inspector Zandu said, "You already have too many pictures."

"And all important," Kimba said, already making notes as to what would have to be moved in the museum.

The crowd continued to grow as more busses arrived.

"He must worry about his pictures,"Inspector Zandu said, leaning over to Gabriella and myself, "I have to worry about even the Japanese."

"The Japanese?" Gabriella asked.

"They are famous for their precision," he answered, "While we are famous for our animals."

He was obviously enjoying the conversation for he frequenlty paused to smile and nod at friends he saw in the crowd.

"When President Moi sets his torch to our bonfire, he will also be lighting

258

flames in Tokyo," Inspector Zandu continued.

"Because of the poachers?" I asked.

"Yes, indeed. Specifically a fellow named Funada. A swanky kind of Japanese businessman," Inspector Zandu said, " At the precise moment our fire starts, Japanese police will be knocking on his door."

"That will end the Japanese connection?" Gabriella asked.

"Not all all. This Jimmie Funada," Inspector Zandu answered, stopping to snicker at the name, "He is but one small cog in the big wheel. One less spoke so to speak."

Inspector Zandu laughed at his own flair for words.

Before Gabriella or I could answer the public relations man with the President signaled to the crowd for silence, nodded towards the waiting TV cameraman and then introduced President Moi.

The President started to speak and I glanced at Gabriella. We both remained numb and now, among this crowd, only wanted our time alone.

"Wildlife conservation has been a subject of major concern not only to conservationists, but to the world community generally in the past few years," President Moi started to speak, "One hundred and two countries have agreed to ban the export of ivory. At the Swiss Convention most of the world joined in."

"There's a salute for Mrs. Lewis," Gabriella whispered, "And a nod for my country."

I recalled that first meeting with Mrs. Lewis when I worried about her limp. She turned out to be the bravest of the brave.

"Kenya is Africa's number one peace broker," the President's words echoing throughout the open space, "Regional cooperation and good neighbourliness has been the cornerstone of our foreign policy but the matter of escalating poaching of elephants and rhino is of grave concern."

Gabriella and I merely looked at each other. This wasn't the time for speeches, not for us.

"As one of the leading nations with abundance of wildlife, we have taken tangible measures to combat and eradicate the poaching menace in our country," President Moi continued, "since 1977 we have banned the hunting of wildlife and the results of that ban are now quite evident with the increase of almost all other wildlife species found in the country apart from the elephant and rhino."

"We have orders to shoot poachers on sight," Inspector Zandu said, his voice muffled, adding, "Eradicate is the correct word."

Eradicate was, indeed, the correct thought. I remembered Allen and Alejandro.

"Kenya had long appealed to the international community to ban all forms of trade in ivory, "President Moi continued, his eyes glanced toward the small hill of ivory standing opposite him, "and we could not make our appeal to the rest of the world if at the same time we are selling this same commodity."

Throughout the rally a small woman, dressed in a shiny black suit, stood alone, keeping herself slightly removed from the crowd. She stood proudly erect while three young children restlessly tugged at her skirt. The woman kept staring in our direction.

When President Moi mentioned the poachers the woman nodded her head for a second and a scowl crossed her face.

The President went on to point out that since the ban of game hunting Kenya has seen an increase in Zebra, lion, leopard, dik dik, monkeys. Only the elephant and rhino remain in danger.

"Three quarters of the black rhinos have already been killed since nineteen-eighty," President Moi said in a firm voice, "And today only thirty-five hundred remain. We have taken special measures and now have many rhinos in secure areas. And our elephants, our proud, poor elephants, half of the elephant population throughout Africa died in the nineteen-eighties. The world around us continues being destroyed for the gain of a private few."

Gabriella's hands tightened around mine. We both wanted to leave, to run but had to stay although we were starting to feel trapped.

"The price of ivory was at one hundred dollars per pound. But now the country has made many positive moves," Inspector Zandu whispered as President Moi started to walk towards the pile of ivory, "We have an anti-poaching police unit, para-military police, all trained in techniques of guerilla warfare. Thanks to Dr. Leakey and his organization, poaching has begun to show a small decline."

"Tell that to people like Allen and Alejandro," I said.

Inspector Zandu's eyes narrowed as he stared at me.

Gabriella nodded her head as if in agreement but I knew her mind was also far off, back in the blood of the bush.

The television cameramen moved closer to the President as he stood next to the pile of ivory.

The rally was brief building up to the moment when President Moi made his powerful commitment, one that was seen around the world, as he raised the flaming torch and started the fire that he hoped would burn into everyone's conscious.

I remember seeing copies of the old San Francisco newspaper banner headlines following the nineteen-six earthquake that read "Best Damn Ruins ever." I thought of the fire that was now burning, sending white clouds skyward, floating over Nairobi, perhaps the message drifting around the entire world and thought that this might well be the best damn bonfire ever.

The woman in the black suit remained silent throughout the ceremony, always a few feet away from the crowd.

It was as though she was staring only at Gabriella and myself. She never moved but continued to stare, as if trying to silently attract our attention, wanting to tell us something but always remaining hesitant, reluctant to approach.

Gabriella was the first to realize who she was and quickly leaned over to me.

"She must be Allen's wife," Gabriella whispered.

With the tragedy, and our quick farewells, no one had time to think of Allen and his personal life.

Our safari had quietly disbanded after the horror, returning to their separate ways, going back to their own dreams and now, finally, seeking their own truths.

I glanced at the women and recognized her from Allen's small photo. In all the confusion, no one had even thought of asking her to join us.

When the President left, Gabriella and I walked over to the woman who offered a shy smile in greeting.

Smoke from the nearby flames hung low and one of the children coughed and the woman bent down to help the child.

"Are you Mali?" Gabriella asked.

The woman nodded her head. She was young and might have been beautiful but working what must have been long, endless hours combined with her own private worries had made her age quickly, taking her youthful beauty away.

"Allen was a wonderful man," Gabriella said.

"You were his last safari," Mali answered, "His final friends. He always considered those he met on safari as his friends. He liked people."

"People liked him," I tried to answer but words at time like this always sound so empty and hollow, " He was a great guide and a wonderful person."

"My Daddy knows the big five animals," the little girl said. She was wearing a green sweater and had a locket around her neck, the same one

Allen had shown us in the photograph.

I fought back tears and looked away.

"I wanted my children to come today," Mali said, "Knowing this wasn't meant for Allen but, in a way, it does him honor."

"He was a good man, a peaceful man,"Gabriella said as Mali turned away, also holding back tears and not wanting her children to witness.

One of the youngsters, a small boy, looked at the bonfire and smiled.

"He was going to start a small travel business," Mali said, "That was his big dream. Now he is gone and so is our small dream."

"We all felt as if you and your family had become our friends," Gabriella answered, "He showed us his photos. He was so proud."

Inspector Zandu was standing off to one side, quietly waiting by his car.

"We had a small memorial service for your husband and the others," I said, "We also collected some funds for Allen. Not much. But it was all meant well."

"I don't expect anything,"Mali answered, "My family will continue."

"I know," I answered, "But there is an envelope for you at the hotel and I'll have someone deliver it to you."

Mali was quiet for a long moment. She finally held her hand out to Gabriella and myself.

"Thank you very much," Mali said.

We walked away and Gabriella poked me in the ribs.

"Miki, There was no such fund," she whispered.

"There would have been," I answered, "But we all got lost in our own grief and shock."

Gabriella looked at me and smiled.

"It was my last royalty check," I answered, "Not much. But something."

Neither of us spoke as we approached Inspector Zandu's car. He was waiting to usher us back to our hotel.

"Kenya is free, the people are free, you see that the animals be free," Gabriella said looking directly at Zandu, "No more blood in Africa."

"With all you tourist, the animals are worth more alive then dead," Inspector Zandu answered.

Driving back to the hotel I was too tired to think of any of this. Gabriella sat next to me, holding my hand, each of us trying to strengthen and reassure the other.

I looked at her and suddenly remembered a line I had read year's earlier.

"Mine is a love that knows no chains of time or space, only the longing

262

for you and nothing more."

Then I put my arms slowly around Gabriella thinking that at last we might be able to truly find ourselves.

We would soon have our moment together, our own small escape waiting in Mombasa.

Mombasa. Perhaps all our hurts might heal there.

# MOMBASA

"HELP, Help, Dedi, Help," Gabriella screamed into the empty darkness of night.

She lay in bed thrashing from side to side, hitting her arms against the sheets. Her face was red and covered with perspiration.

"Gabby, Gabby, you're having a nightmare," I grabbed her shoulders.

She pulled herself up and did not move for a long moment.

"Miki, oh, Miki, I'm so sorry."

"Don't be sorry. We both are the same."

"That poor kid from Spain."

My fingers gently touched her lips.

"They'll always live. Within us." I tried to reassure her. Only my voice was empty sounding and the words seemed flat and hollow.

Gabriella became quiet for a moment.

"Why did it happen?

I held her tight, unable to answer the question that had no answer.

Gabriella seemed suddenly fragile and vulnerable. I remembered the assured way she had helped me set up my tent only a few day's earlier and I held her even tighter.

I trembled as I held her. She glanced at me and I had to turn away.

"Miki," she softly said, wiping the tears that had come to my eyes.

"I'm sorry," I whispered.

"Miki. Oh, Miki."

We were both silent for a moment that seem to last an eternity.

"We were all kind of like a universe just to ourselves," Gabriella shook when she finally spoke, "Hughes was right when he said that."

"Sometimes life gives the good, sometimes the bad," I answered, "And sometimes we get only the shit."

Gabriella looked at me shaking her head.

"That's not the answer," she whispered, "We've both known enough shit in our lives."

She turned away for a moment and said nothing.

"Remember our talk about God? Allen was kind of like that," Gabriella softly said, "A symbol of God. Leading us always on. Helping everyone. Holding us together like glue. Like God."

Both of us again became silent. I put my arm around Gabriella and she leaned her head on my shoulder and then we cried together.


The warm, deep blue water of the Indian ocean were to serve as some sort of absolution, washing away much of the tragedy. That had been our plan, a gentle way to heal and to be together for a few last days.

Gabriella cried in her sleep; I cried in my heart. We both had been the same with our shattered loves and now the tragedy of the safari brought new pain. We both needed Mombasa as a time for healing, a time for stillness.


The horror of the safari combined with my having already come close to death changed the very meaning of my life. You think your course is seemingly set in one direction and then fate shakes everything up and spins it out of control. Once again I realized how fragile it all really is and how little time anyone has in this world. Each day was now something special and I lived for that day and whatever promise it might hold.

Mombasa was proving the most special of all.

I felt as though it was some sort of stage curtain, ending one act, beginning another.

Love and dreams are for the young I had kept telling myself aware that I had really concocted that idea only as a kind of protection from ever again being hurt. I felt my youth had melted away, that the old loves had nearly destroyed me and that I would never be able to share my feelings with anyone again.

Only Gabriella changed all that.

She swept away my old hurts and helped destroy that emotional barrier I had erected to protect myself.

Slowly we were leading each other back to what had been missing in our lives. Feeling. Caring. Laughter. The mending, even with all its agony, was beginning.

Mombasa held another kind of sadness for we both knew our time together was now limited. Even with that I longed for Gabriella each day, wanting only to be with her and eager to share everything.


"I am my beloved; my beloved is mine."

Those ancient biblical words echoed appropriately here, in this city that dated back thousands of years and where still today, after all the centuries, frankincense perfumes the air and the old Arab shops are still filled with spices and perfumes and silks.

I felt like a youngster again as I wandered those narrow, crooked streets, charmed by the Indian ocean, knowing this was the land of my childhood dreams. Where Sinbad once sailed. A place of pirates and flying carpets.

As if to support the memories of my youth Arab dhows still lay snug out in the calm blue bay, low, slim boats, some still with coconut matting to protect their cargo from the water, twisted, old, dirty masts rising over the boat. Their all male crews, wearing checkered Arab kaffieyhs and robes, were sitting and sipping tea in the morning sun.

"I am my beloved; my beloved is mine."

LAUREN!

Bam, just like that, it would always come like an unexpected shot, blind-siding me. Soon she would be married and gone forever.

Fuck it.

As quickly as the thought came I forced it away, pushing it back into the far distance, out of my mind. That was all part of yesterday and yesterday was gone.

Thinking of Lauren made me realize how much I had already lost and what I would never have. A cold shiver surged through me which would have made Lauren laugh. She always called that "being brushed by the devil."

For a brief moment I frowned wondering if she would ever really leave my mind. I was deep in thought when I heard Gabriella's voice.

"Look at that beautiful mosque," she quietly said.

Just as she said that a mullah began chanting an afternoon prayer and his voice echoed and vibrated through the narrow streets. His lonely wail sounded as if he was calling out to all the ghosts of the past. Even to our own ghosts.

"What a haunting sound," Gabriella added.

She became quiet for a moment and held my hand.

"Sometimes I pray for both of us," Gabriella whispered.

I glanced at Gabriella and smiled for she seemed to know and understand everything.

Mombasa. Perhaps in this two thousand year old place on the edge of the world, perhaps, just perhaps this is where we both might find our futures.


When we first arrived, we took a British styled cab from the small Mombasa airport to our hotel.

"Jambo," the cab driver greeted us, waving his hand, "Welcome to my place."

Thus began our strange odyssey through the old town of Mombasa with its narrow winding alleys and thin passages crammed together in a wild, colorful maze. We drove passed twisted streets crowded with small shops and homes with overhanging balconies that were worn with time.

The driver proudly pointed out the sights of Mombasa but we still saw only the tragedy of the bush.

"Remember what Allen said," I asked, "Animals all live here and they live together, why can't people?"

The thought of Allen made me cringe and I looked away from Gabriella.

"Only the good memories, Miki" Gabriella softly said.

I put my arm around her and I felt her shiver.

There were now long lapses following the tragedy when we would say nothing. We both knew we would never get over the horror but at least, in the time ahead, we vowed to find some escape if only for a few moments.

We found the solitude we needed at the hotel which became our shelter from the safari, from the tragedy, from life itself.

The hotel was filled with traditional African styles and decor, drums and masks lining the walls, but for us it was the beach, a long white sand-beach set against palm trees and the royal deep blue of the ocean.

The hotel porter greeted us, smiling his approval, saying something I could not quite understand. He spoke English but with a Swahili accent.

"What did you say?" I asked.

"Hallelujah, hallelujah, glory, glory, hallelujah," he grinned, "and welcome to our hotel."

We both smiled when he suddenly put his arms around me and gave an enthusiastic welcoming hug.

"Everything is okie-doakie here," he grinned.

We both tried desperately to forget the past, trying to start life, our lives, anew.

We spent long hours on the beach, running, splashing, chasing each other, trying desperately to forget. I watched her run carefree along the sand, her blonde hair backlighted in the golden morning, exactly as it might have been in a Monet painting.

Gabriella waved as she circled around and ran back down the beach.

"Nyayo," I heard her whisper a moment later and I turned to see Gabreilla standing directly behind me with both hands on her hips, "Nyayo."

That was the expression President Moi had told us, "Following in the footsteps of the old man."

We laughed together at her small joke and that was a good sign, the laughter slowly returning for both of us. I looked into her face and could see the pain had gone. At least for a few minutes.

Gabriella walked along the shore splashing her feet in the waves. She suddenly stopped, motioned for me to catch up to her. She was excited and pointing to something in the sand.

Two giant turtles, both about a hundred and sixty-five years old, were mating. The male, standing on his hunches, was able to wedge his huge shell carefully away from the female as he slowly moved back and forth.

"Another old man. You should take lessons," Gabriella said, kicking a puff of sand towards me and starting to run away.

Even as I watched her run happy in the surf I felt still another kind of sadness.

We both knew we would soon go back to our own lives and that was when the sadness came because I knew what that really meant.

"Will you write often, Miki?" she had once asked.

"Yes. We both will write often."

At first we would communicate often. There would be letters, many letters, perhaps even an occasional phone call. Cards would be sent on birthdays and at Christmas but that would all eventually dwindle down as our new lives took shape, found different interests and new friends. Soon the cards would trickle down to only special occasions with maybe just a hastily written note, for that is the way with old friends, good friends, who live world's apart. Friends who had come together and who would become alone once again. That is the way of life and it made me sad that day sitting on the beach in Mombasa.

There was also other, better times. We found quiet moments when we would lay close together on the sand, not moving, just resting snug against one another.

I would reach out to hold Gabriella's hand and she would extend only her little finger and then both our little fingers would touch and wiggle and curl together. We sat on the beach and were contented with the sheer joy of life itself as the languor of Mombasa slowly settled in and the healing began.

"Where did you ever get that "gobbel gobbel" sound?" Gabriella asked.

"Gary Cooper in "Sergeant York.""

"One of your forties movies?"

"I use to make my kid laugh every Thanksgiving with that sound."

Gabriella playfully reached over and thumped on my chest.

"See, Miki, you do have a heart," she said, "and you thought you had lost it all this time."

"I thought it died and was buried on that operating table."

"Baloney, you thought you lost it with that girl in San Francisco."

I said nothing but I noticed her accent had returned.

"Some day you should call her," Gabriella said.

"Who?" I asked but I already knew the answer.

"That lady who wrote you on the safari," she answered, " I saw your face that day in the rain. You still carry a torch for her."

Gabriella became silent for a moment lost in her own thoughts.

"She wouldn't have written if she hadn't cared about you," Gabriella slowly added, "Especially tracking you down way out in the bush. That was an effort on her part."

"She's getting married," I answered.

"Getting?" and Gabriella shrugged her shoulders, "You can go back to your true love. I can't."

"That true love is over."

"True love never dies," she softly said, "We were both vulnerable here in Africa. Don't let yourself be vulnerable ever again. Your sparks are still smoldering."

"Only smoke. Dull, grey, choking smoke."

"In Switzerland we rekindle the fire. Move the logs, just a very little bit. The smoke clears out and the old warmth returns. You can even see things a lot clearer."

"You're quite a philosopher," my voice was hushed and still.

"We are both different people now," Gabriella said, "We are becoming whole people once again."

We became silent for a moment.

"There is a saying they use in Europe," Gabriella continued, "A woman gives and forgives. A man gets and forgets."

"I never forgot for a single moment."

"And I'm sure your friend forgives."

We both paused and watched the waves. A bell was ringing far off from a dhow that was bobbing in the water.

Thus each day passed swiftly filled only with quiet conversation, casual moments and our own special solitude. At night it was all very different.

The full moon that had first greeted us at the start of the safari had now turned crescent and I thought how appropriate that it was shining over the waters that linked us to the Arabian nights.

At night the smell of frankincense drifted into our room from the ocean just outside the open window. We heard the calm, constant waves and felt the soft breeze. The waves breaking white water was the only light in the black night.

We made love. It was simple as that. Two people as one, sharing their brief moments together.

"Do you think Eden might have been like this?" Gabriella whispered.

I did not answer for the warmth of her body was answer enough as we lay together in the darkness.

"You are like Ali Babba, here in this place," Gabriella said.

"You mean like the forty thieves?"

"No," she said, curling her fingers softly around my erection, "More like open sesame."

My body did respond, quickly opening, becoming rigid, alive to her every touch and sensation.

"We are the stuff that dreams are made of," she whispered in the darkness, recalling one of our first conversations, " I love that."

"Nakusentelon," I whispered, "You are that place of great beauty."

I ran my fingers through her hair, gently down her face, along the wondrous curves of her body, exploring the paths in the darkness. I touched her hand and I grinned to myself in the darkness, remembering our walk through Namanaga.

"... Sure she's got rings on her fingers and bells on her toes,
elephants to ride upon, my little Irish rose,
Come to your nabob and on next Patrick's day,
Mombo, jombo, jitty bob jay, Oh shay..."

We lay quietly together in the darkness. Gabriella sighed as she slowly leaned over and kissed my neck.

"It's okie doakie," she whispered, then, with her mischievous way, she slowly slid down my body, saying nothing, finally, with whimsical amusement, I heard her voice as if from far off.

"Gobbel. Gobbel. Gobbel."

And then I sensed the gentle, cool, warm, soothing touch of her love as she soundlessly explored my body at the depth of my very being.

The love making, the sweet love making, wiped out all the hurts and the pain, dissolved the memories until there was nothing, there was everything, the two of us locked together as one finding the place of love, pressing together, sighing in the deep night with only the waves out there in the darkness aware, smashing their acceptance, breaking with thunder, slowly turning gently into silent small streams, trickles that hugged and caressed the ever waiting shore.

It was here, in this place, where I finally felt everything within me had finally been released. I was happy at last here in Africa with its colors, scents, sounds, the ever haunting sky, the soft winds from the Indian ocean.

I was especially happy being with Gabriella and what we shared together. Waking in the morning and seeing her face on the pillow next to me; hearing her deep, easy breathing; watching her lie silently in the soft morning light and studying her beautiful face; her relaxed body softly curled in tranquil peace.

I reached over to touch her, ever so lightly, not to wake or disturb her but just to feel her touch and the strength that it offered. Strength was the gift that we had found and given to each other, removing the clouds that had hung low over both our lives.

We clung soundlessly together in the darkness.

Finally the day came from which there was no escape.

"The bugles are calling," she said, "The Swiss Army has bugles just like the American Army."

Gabriella had warned me even back during that first talk around the campfire. Now her words, which were always understood between us, came back once again.

"I have three weeks leave," she had said that night on the safari.

Thus the moment had finally come. It was one we both had known about, each of us trying to forget, trying to tuck it away, wishing, praying by some miracle it†might never have to come. Only now it was here.

We walked the beach, holding hands, neither speaking.

"We have tonight," she said in a voice filled with what I imagined tears might sound like.

We stopped beside a cluster of palm trees and stood motionless looking at that deep blue water. Far off someone was laughing. I held Gabriella's hand tight as if in so doing I would prevent her from ever leaving.

The last day had become one of sadness. I caught myself frequently glancing at my watch trying desperately to somehow stop time from moving.

We made love that afternoon, both of us clinging together, softer, stronger, deeper, our bodies as one, never wanting to part.

Gabriella finally walked over to the window and looked aimlessly out at the ocean. She was nude and her smooth, tan body was golden, silhouetted in the sun's afternoon glare. The youthful freckles that dotted her body made me smile once again.

"Oh, Gabby," I whispered.

She looked at me, returned my smile, and then walked back and we made love again.

The next thing I knew the sun had gone down and the room was filled with the gentle rose and yellow colors of sunset.

"Remember your funny movie title game," Gabriella later said, "Well how about "Namanga, My Love?""

"A silly title," I answered.

"You and I," she answered, "And only you and I. We did have Namanaga. Namanga, my love."

I did not answer but I put my arm around Gabriella and held her close.

Then there was silence. It was growing dark outside.

Sometime later, I don't when, we decided to get dressed and have our last dinner together. A long, lovely dinner. There was candle-light and a table by an open window and we could smell the jacaranda and hear the nearby waves. We held hands and simply looked at each other.

The waiter poured our wine and Gabriella raised her glass towards me.

"Here's looking at you, kid," she grinned, remembering our campfire conversation. I reached over and held her hand.

"Big prawns direct from the ocean," the waiter said, then realized we were hearing nothing, discreetly left the dish and turned away.

"Fuck the prawns," I said.

"Fuck me," she answered.

I stood and walked over to Gabriella and kissed her forehead and then we both laughed, a silly kind of laugh. Everything from the past weeks, everything from our moments together, it all suddenly came out in this wild, uncontrolled laughter, releasing all of our pent up feelings.

The tragedy and the joy; the regret, the hope; the love and the farewells, all of it came pouring out. The emotions that had been bottled up for so long erupted in hysterical laughter for we both knew that was all that could be done.

I noticed the waiter standing off at his station looking at first bewildered and then he also started laughing.

The laughter felt good and made me realize that the time of healing was over. I could once again give of myself. I could find love and give love and be loved in returned.

Later we lay together as one.

"You brought me back to the real world," I said.

"We brought each other back," she answered, "You also returned me to finding love."

"Perhaps there really never was a past. Nor any future. Only this moment here. Now."

"Two lost souls no longer," Gabriella whispered.

Gabriella reached over and touched my shoulder.

"All that I have is now. This moment. Yesterday is gone. Tomorrow never comes," I whispered, "There is only this moment and you and nothing else."

"Now we have our own little past," she said.

She lightly ran her fingers over my chest. Her deep blue eyes now matched that of the nearby ocean.

"Everything is now," I quietly said, "It is all now."

Then our eyes talked and we both became quiet.

We walked along the beach once again, arms tightly around each other as if we never wanted to be separated, silently watching the sky and the night coming together in ink-blackness. A light, soft mist slowly filled the harbor. A single fire somewhere off in the distance could only be seen in a slight blur. Waves breaking white water was the only light in the black night.

Nearby we heard drums, probably from some local nightspot. They were the first time we had heard that during our entire trip.

"Those are the drums of return," I said dramatically.

"How do you know that?" Gabriella asked.

Then she realized I was only joking and poked me in the ribs.

"That's good, Miki, I like that," she said, her accent returning, "The drums of return."

"Like a tattoo on the muffled drum of the moon."

That was how our time together in Africa ended, slowly walking back to our room in the warm, dark night listening to those drums. They pounded like my heart beating.

We left each other at the small Mombasa airport, toasting ourselves with a glass of tomato juice. We would write each other. We would see each other again. We made the plans that every good traveler makes when they say their farewells.

Only we both knew we weren't like any tourist and what had happened to both of us in Africa would always be more then just a simple farewell. We both had found what each of us had lost. New life. New hope. Even the start of new dreams. Dr. Lom had been wrong. Dreams can be found again.

We stood on the observation deck looking out over Africa and we kissed our farewell kisses and had our final tears quietly together. Below us we could see the plane getting ready and knew it was time.

"Here's looking at you, kid," I said, hearing the plane's motors start, "You are one heck'uva dame."

"You're being Bogart again, Mr. Tough Guy," she mocked, "Only you're not. You're too sweet."

She kissed my cheek.

"My insides are crying," Gabriella said, suddenly handing me a single carnation.

I put it to my lips, unable to say anything.

"You brought me back to life, too, you know," she answered. "We were a happening. We had that great hunt we once talked about."

I looked at that lone carnation for a lingering moment and I knew, long after it would wither and die, I would always cherish it, keep it, perhaps even under glass, as a wonderful, beautiful memory of Gabriella and our moment together in time.

"Remember what we said that day out on safari," she said, "There are no happy endings."

"You said something that is all wrong," I quietly said, looking for the last time into Gabriella's clear blue eyes, "A man gets and forgets. I'll never forget. Never."

Gabriella smiled. She knew and she understood and then she raised her hand to touch my lips and I kissed her fingers.

"Tala," Gabriella used the Swahili word for "remember."

"Always, you know that," I answered adding "Tutaonana."

It was the Swahili word for "see you soon."

We both held back tears.

"We have a chocolate in Switzerland that is appropriate for us. Bittersweet."

"Take care of yourself, Gabriella. Sweet Gabriella." I wanted to say more but there was nothing left to say. It was like that day with Lauren when I felt everything had come to an end.

Gabriella walked out to the plane, looking back, pausing only to blow me a last, small farewell kiss. The plane's propeller jostled her hair in the wild and carefree way that I loved and she stopped and brushed it back and then looked at me shyly and smiled once again.

I wanted to run out, hold her one final time, but that last moment had already come and was now gone and the moment of Gabriella in my life was coming to a close.

The plane moved slowly down the tarmac and I strained to see if I could see Gabriella seated by a window but I saw nothing. Then the plane lifted off and, within seconds, disappeared into the African clouds.

# NAIROBI AIRPORT

The Nairobi airport in the early afternoon can be a most dismal place.

Everything seemed inappropriate from the American country and western music that was playing background music to the young soldiers in those damn battle fatigues strolling about, weapons always at the ready.

I thought of Gabriella and blew her an imaginary kiss of farewell. I estimated that her flight must already be halfway to Switzerland but, for the two of us, it was already an entire world apart.

Then I thought of Lauren. Gabriella had placed the thought in my mind.

"Call that girl," she had said, "she tracked you down. That was an effort on her part."

That was the clue that had been missing all this time.

Lauren had made an effort to contact me for whatever reason. It wasn't like her to tell me she was engaged as I had first thought. That wasn't her style. She knew me well enough to know writing about her engagement would only have brought out the old hurts. Lauren would never have done that. She was trying to say something else.

I sat in the Nairobi airport that hot afternoon, listening to a Willie Nelson record being played in the back ground but thinking of Lauren's letter.

Damn it, she was trying to tell me something. Something.

Gabriella was right, she had made an effort to track me down in the bush. Made an effort.

That was it, finally, I wanted to shout outloud, that was it.

I'm getting married in a month."

In a month.

Lauren didn't know Roberta and I were getting divorced but she was still sending me a last message, one final notice, a last call before the curtain went down.

One month.

Gabriella had shown that I could love again and now I knew that my love for Lauren would remain forever. I also new that it was all too late. Too much had passed between us, too much had gone wrong.

Lauren remained always in my memory. I could see her walking down Market street in the rain; heard her unexpected phone calls; remembered her riding the miniature train in the zoo. I could even still smell the grass from the empty meadows in Golden Gate park where we had once strolled.

An older British women walked passed, checking her flight tickets, carefully tucking them into her bag. She walked by a pay phone.

And that was all I needed.

All I knew was that Lauren worked for her publisher in Britain and that it would be late afternoon in London. There was a chance, a slim, outside chance.

I expected the call from Kenya would take a long time, especially having to go through British information to get the phone number but, in one of those small miracles that occasionally happens, the call went directly through.

"Dunbar Publishing," I heard a women with a clipped British accent answer.

"Lauren Milken, please," I said, politely as possible, whimsically thinking that being polite might help in getting Lauren quicker to the phone. I knew the odds were against everything, that Lauren would no doubt be away, out of the office, gone for the day, who knows what.

"Hello."

It was Lauren, as simple as that.

"Guess who?"

Her answer came with a wild, incredible, joyful shout.

My call caught Lauren off guard. Her voice was filled with surprise and she sounded excited, glad to hear from me. It was the Lauren I hadn't heard for so painfully long. The sound of her voice, filled with its enthusiasm, holding nothing back, without any hesitation, gave me a chill I never anticipated. Every emotion suddenly swept through my body. I didn't know if I should laugh or cry.

"Is he there?" I joked, recalling the way Lauren often called, "Remember me?" I use to be Michael Abrams."

My heart was thumping and my hope soaring.

"Who are you now?" Lauren immediately countered back. The sound of laughter that I had longed for underlined her every word.

It was all immediate, spontaneous and the delight in her voice was honest and sincere. It said everything.

"You silly schmuck," she screamed with delight.

We both were silent. Then we talked together.

"How was Africa?"

"I'm still there," I answered, "What was that schmucky letter you sent me. That you're getting married."

"He's a nice guy," she said, "Reminds me of you. Sweet. Even has a cute nose."

"You're getting married," I answered, "I'm getting divorced. Ironic, isn't it?"

I said that deliberately, testing her for an answer.

She was silent again. I knew she was absorbing what I had said. I could almost see the wheels cranking in her head.

"I'm sorry," she said.

"Bullshit," I answered and I heard her laugh, "I thought folks didn't get engaged anymore. They Just became, what do they call it, the significant other."

"You know me. I'm old fashioned. A nineteen forties person living in the modern world."

"I remember your old dialogue," I answered, "That makes two of us."

"Last time we talked you said dreadful things to me," Lauren added.

"You didn't do so bad, yourself," I quickly answered.

"We both said awful things. It still rings in my ears."

"I'll take back mine if you take yours back," I said.

"I took it back a long time ago," she quickly answered.

"I was wrong. I wanted to say more that day."

"So did I. But I didn't. And life goes on."

"Now you're engaged."

"Yes."

Lauren paused for a moment.

"Is the zoo in San Francisco still dirty?" she asked, trying to change the subject, "Last time I was there I couldn't stand it."

She remembered the day in the zoo and that made me feel happy.

"I haven't been there," I answered, "I was afraid to go because of the memories I would have found there."

We were both silent.

"Friends are forever. That was a line I learned from you," I said, "You and I. We were special friends."

"We'll always be special friends. You know that. But whatever you're getting at, please stop. You just call and everything is supposed to be wonderful."

I knew I had to go slowly, chose my words carefuly but I had held back so much for so long and everything just poured out.

"How is your Kandy Kangaroo character?" I asked, knowing this wasn't the time for banal conversation.

"He's hopping around," she answered, a smile in her voice.

"Funny face, old funny face, I miss you," I Said, "You always made me laugh. That's a great gift to make someone laugh. And be happy. You were the one who use to say, "You make my heart happy.""

"I miss you," she answered.

Two soldiers moved passed, paused for a second, then kept walking. One was glancing at a young African women in a short flowered dressed who was walking in front of them.

"You can't barge back into someone's life," Lauren added, "Not like this."

"This isn't the time for polite diplomacy. There isn't time any longer. I know I shouldn't be calling."

"No you shouldn't. It's not right."

"But we're old pals."

"Yes. Only I'm happy. You're not."

"How do you know?"

"I know you. I can hear it in your voice."

"Happy because you're engaged to Giles," I repeated.

"Yes. He's a wonderful man."

"You and I. We know each other well."

"Yes."

"Better then anyone else. We know each other. Everything. Our feelings. Our thoughts. We think like one."

"We haven't talked for a long time. People change."

"What we have never changes."

"Everything changes. Nothing remains the same. You can't live in the past."

"I'm trying to live in the future. Let's not make the same mistake twice in this life time."

"Whatever you're getting at is all in your mind. The past. A fantasy. Sometimes the fantasy is better than the real thing."

"Then let Giles have the fantasy and give me the real thing."

There was a moment of silence.

"Lauren, maybe your getting married and this isn't right but I'm in love," I felt as if I was shouting into the phone, "In love."

Silence. But only for a second.

"Michael, Michael you bastard," she answered.

"You're getting married," I repeated, "To Harrison Giles, famous American columnist."

"He knows about you," Lauren answered before I could finish my sentence.

"We've met. Quite a smooth character, right? Did he take you to Claridge's for tea?"

"Yes."

I smiled to myself.

"Harrison is a reporter. He observes things," Lauren continued," He read my face. Heard my voice. My gestures. It was easy for him."

"What does that mean?"

"He's known for a long time that there was someone else," Lauren answered, "But he accepted it. He said we can grow into love. He calls this an "adventure."

"An Adventure? You don't grow into love," I snapped, "It's not like buying a new pair of pants. Either you do or you don't. It's all very simple."

"It's never simple," Lauren answered, "He knows everything."

"What?"

"He knows you're sweet and laid-back. And Kind. Well, sort of sweet and laid-back and kind," she laughed, "And that you have a cute little nose. And he knows you said awful things to me the last time we spoke."

"So did you," I repeated, my voice becoming quiet, "Lauren, you're getting married. Is it too late?"

She said nothing.

"Michael, don't do this to me," Lauren finally answered, "Don't put me on the spot this way. I don't need this."

"Bullshit. You wrote to me. You sent me a signal."

"I just happened to be thinking of you," Lauren paused again, "I lie. I miss you so damn much. I miss your schmucky face."

"Lauren," I started to answer but she interrupted me.

"What the hell were you doing in Africa? Alone?"

"You already know," I said, "You know. It was a pilgrimage for you."

"Yes, I suspected that. Michael, the ever eternal romantic," she slowly answered, "That was when I decided to write my letter."

"I miss you so damn much."

There was another moment of silence knowing I was threading into areas where I really had no right to go.

"You want me to break an engagement just because some turkey suddenly has jungle fever?"

"It's not a jungle out there, it's bush."

Lauren was silent.

"I can't do that," she finally said, "It's gone to far with Harrison. It's impossible. It's not right."

"It's tragic to get yourself trapped for the rest of your life," I thought of Roberta, "Whether it is me or ten other guys. Please don't get trapped because of the moment. Think it out."

"I'm not a child," she snapped.

"I'm sorry but I've been there."

I felt I had made a dreadful error and was about to say something snappy, then politely hang up. Only I couldn't.

"The tragedy of life is that there is only one of you to go around."

"Michael, you're always so schmaltzy."

"Lauren, I'm in love," I repeated.

"I'm in love," She quickly answered, "In love. You know that. Only it's all over."

"My heart misses you," I quietly said, "I can even send you the x-rays to prove it."

"Are you taking care of yourself?"

"I walk with my head held up high only inside I crumble every day."

"Bong. Bong. Bong. That's being dramatic."

"I'm entirely new," I answered seriously,"It's my love that is old."

She said nothing for a long moment.

"We can talk about it later," she finally said, "When you come to England."

"Too late for talk," I answered, adding, "I'm sorry, kid, I misread the signals."

There was a hush, like the moment before someone is about to roll dice and waits for a long second hoping the next move will be the right one.

Everything came down to the next few seconds. Everything in my life, my love, my future. It became the time of quiet desperation.

"Confession time," Lauren said, "Harrison knows my feelings. He said he would never hold me to the marriage but it's going to hurt. He really is a nice guy. It'll hurt him. And it will hurt me."

"Why does someone always have to get hurt?" I asked, remembering my year of pain, "Lauren, I was almost killed out here."

"With your heart?" she asked.

"No, my heart is fine, except when I think about you."

"You're a writer," she answered, " Don't call half way around the world with cute comments."

"Funny face, you nut, listen," I said, "This year, between my ticker and Africa, I came close to death. Twice. I only have seven lives left and I want to spend them all with you. You and I. Life is so short and we don't have any time to waste. Not any longer."

She was soundless. Those wheels were clicking once again.

"How long does it take it get here from Nairobi?" she asked.

"Time me, funny face," I shouted, "just time me."

The public address announcement was calling my plane for boarding.

"I have a place to show you, called Namanga," I quickly added, "It's one of the world's greatest metropolises."

"Are we talking shack up or honeymoon," she snapped, " I'll have to know what to bring."

Lauren made me laugh. She always made me laugh. There was never any game playing with her, never anything false, no pretensions.

"It's better than Stratford-Upon-Avon," I said, adding, "Great place for a honeymoon. What the hell's your address."

"What?"

"My plane is leaving, schmuckette," I grinned into the phone, "your address, what's your address?"

"Three Sydney street, up three flights," she shouted back, "It's in Chelsea."

"I'm on my way," I said, delirious with joy, " It's a five hour flight."

I ran to the plane never realizing until I sat down and buckled my seat belt, hearing the sound of the jets, that I was so anxious to see Lauren I hadn't even said good-bye.

I could visualize Lauren still near the phone, aware of what I had done, and laughing her head off.

The plane started to move slowly down the tarmac and it was then, only then, that I felt my life was truly coming alive once again.

As the plane climbed, I looked out into the African night and knew Namanga was somewhere far below. I remembered Allen and Alejandro. Margaret and Houdini and Yuri and Sophie. Corky and Flora. I thought of Gabriella. Gabriella. I looked down toward Namanga and blew them all a silent kiss of farewell.

Then I sat deep back into the seat and thought only of Lauren and what tomorrow would bring.

"Uhuru," I recalled that Swahili word for freedom. "Uhuru." I knew at that moment, finally, I had at last found my love and my freedom.

*"... Rise up my love, my fair one and come away,*
*For lo, the winter is past, and the rain is gone;*
*The flowers appear on the earth; the time of*
*singing birds is come, and the voice of the turtle*
*is heard in our land..."*
Song of Solomon

Printed in the United States
46661LVS00004B/69